Ben clambered up beside her and took a look through the binoculars. The man wore a Stetson hat and a blue work shirt and jeans. He had on a coat, knee-length and heavy, the kind called "dusters" in old westerns. His jaw was powerful, and he had deep-set eyes that glinted as he lit a cigarette. He tilted his head so he could study the house.

"Nobody comes out here, Ben. Nobody." There was a sting of accusation in Patrice's voice.

He leaned so he could look her in the eye. "I didn't bring them, believe that. A kid up in Taos told me two men were around a couple of days ago looking for you."

Max jumped on the wall and started barking again. She reached to pull him down, but he leaped the other way, over the edge to the bank below. Seconds later he was streaking through the field toward the truck.

Patrice moved to stand up, to call him back. Ben held her down. "Wait. Let's see what they—"

Max tumbled, his front legs giving out, his head plowing into the ground. With a huge effort he struggled back to his feet. Stumbling sideways, he retreated toward the house.

"Jesus," Patrice breathed. She was staring through the binoculars. She shifted, and Ben took a look.

The man at the truck had seen the dog too. In the brief seconds while they had their eyes off him, he'd taken out a rifle, leveled it, and snapped off a shot. It was a vicious looking gun, pure black and large bore. There was a metal cylinder on the end, a silencer....

NO TIME TO HIDE

ROB PALMER

LEISURE BOOKS NEW YORK CITY

To Roseina, Arlene, and Marjorie,
but for TAG.

A LEISURE BOOK®

January 2006

Published by

Dorchester Publishing Co., Inc.
200 Madison Avenue
New York, NY 10016

ISBN 0-8439-5667-4

Visit us on the web at www.dorchesterpub.com.

NO TIME
TO HIDE

"Whether there were twenty warheads or twenty-one, that's not important.... Let's trust one another."

—General Anatoly Gribkov,
chief Soviet planner for the secret placement
of nuclear weapons in Cuba during the fall of 1962

PROLOGUE

Ben Tennant saw the fox when it was a quarter mile away, trotting along the edge of the country road. It didn't turn to look at the fields or the motel, didn't look at anything until it came even with Ben's car. It stopped and scratched its ear, giving him an appraising stare through the open door. Then it snapped its jaws, as if to say, *I could bite you*, and dashed into the corn. Ben shook his head. Weird. The whole night had been like that.

A storm had roared through a while ago, drumming rain and clashing thunder. It had moved on to the far side of Chesapeake Bay, only a distant twinkle of lightning now. Overhead the sky was clear, and the moon painted a silver stripe on the dead-quiet waters. In the hollows in the fields, fog lingered. Through it all, Ben sat quietly, watching.

The Bay Bluff Motel was so cheap there was a big sign in front that said, "No Credit Cards." There were three cars in the lot, nosed up by the doors. With his binoculars, Ben scanned the place, lingering on room six. A lamp was on behind the curtain. He couldn't make out more than that.

It was nearly midnight. Long ago Ben had decided the

motel was safe. No watchers in the corn, no one hiding in the cars. Still, he waited. She'd expected him an hour ago. Was she getting panicky? *She* was Patrice Callan, and every time Ben thought of her he thought of diamonds. She had a birthmark on her thigh, a perfect bronze diamond so small you had to be within six inches to see it. The first time they met, Patrice made sure Ben got a good look, just as he made sure not to touch. Maybe that was what was holding him back now. Things might get out of control if he went down there. *When* he went down there. He couldn't wait forever.

Ben jerked the binoculars up again. There was a shadow at the corner of the motel, by the office. It hadn't been there a minute ago. A man stepped out. Medium height with a muscular build, but cat-light on his feet. Patrice wouldn't hear him coming. Ben swung his legs out of the car. If there was trouble, he could be there in five seconds.

The man was carrying a plastic sack with something square inside. Just before he reached room six, he stopped, then walked back around to the office. A moment later he returned, this time wearing a straw cowboy hat. Ben smiled and relaxed.

Ben Tennant had a talent for reading people. Clothing and jewelry, twitches and frowns, shifting eyes and sighs and shrugs—he noticed it all. From those details he could piece together a story. Who is this guy? What's he up to?

The man had two drinking glasses with him, glinting in the light of the parking lot lamp. Real glass, not plastic. Most likely that made him the motel owner, or at least the desk clerk. And in the sack? Had to be a six-pack of beer. Again he made a beeline for room six. "Never visit a lady without your hat on, right Romeo?" Ben said.

The door opened almost as soon as he knocked. All Ben could see of her was her naked arm stretched across the gap. Romeo was talking, holding up the sack. Ben drummed his fingers. *Get rid of him, Patrice.* The man took off the hat as he stepped inside, and she shut the door. Ben slapped the steering wheel. "Dammit."

He tried to get comfortable. It might be a long wait, and it was so miserably hot. The last flicker of lightning from the storm was gone. The bay, the field—everything was so still it seemed painted. Ben felt a gray loneliness creeping over him, a feeling that had been coming on more and more lately. He shoved it out of his mind and stared at the yellow glow behind the curtain.

The door swung open and Romeo reappeared. Ben checked his watch and laughed. Eleven minutes—that's all it took for her to con the guy out of his beer. *And* his hat. Romeo glanced back, scratching his head. She'd already closed the door. He padded quickly around the corner.

Ben sat a while longer, collecting his thoughts. He needed to be calm, in control. It was his job. What was it about Patrice, anyway? She scared him. No, he was scaring himself. The office lights went off. All quiet now. He got out and walked down the road, across the parking lot. At her door, he hesitated. Last chance to back out. But Ben would never do that. He knocked and heard her softly call, "Come in."

She had switched the lamp off when Romeo left. It took a moment for Ben to see her, sitting under the window, the moon turning her skin silver. All that skin. She was nude, holding a magazine in front of her. A silly prop. Nobody reads a magazine by moonlight. Then she set it aside and the illusion of nakedness was gone. She had on a small white top and matching micro-short shorts. "Howdy-do," she said.

Smiling, Ben closed the door. She had to be scared to death, hiding in this little place, rumors of a price on her head. Still she made jokes. *Howdy-do.* "You want a beer?" She pointed at the nightstand.

"Still cold?"

She laughed. "You bet."

"How did you get him to leave it?"

She didn't seem surprised that Ben knew about Romeo. She picked up the hat from the bed. "The band on this is loose. Told him I'd fix it, give it back when we had dinner together tomorrow. Ladylike. And a gentleman wouldn't take his beer back."

"But you won't be here tomorrow."

She set the hat jauntily on her head, like a prize she'd won at the fair. "So the man should watch who he trusts."

She started across the room, moving slowly, letting her hips sway. Before she was around the bed, Ben's body had curved to welcome her. Then he turned, fumbling for the lamp chain. She stopped, a look of disappointment on her face.

"You shouldn't have talked to that guy," he said. "You don't want him to remember you."

"He already remembered me from when I checked in. This way, maybe he'll have a reason to forget."

"Maybe." Ben pointed at the hat. "Anyway, leave it." She set it on the nightstand with the beer. "And Patrice, that's the last con you'll ever pull."

She seemed startled, as if she had never thought of that. The last con. She nodded slowly, then opened the closet door, revealing a small suitcase. "This is all I brought." Before he could reach for it, she put her hand on his arm. She tried to make the touch right, familiar and trusting, like a sister. No con. "You'll help me, Ben? A clean start?"

"Sure. That's what I do." He sounded confident, all business. But they were so close there in the corner of the room. He grabbed the suitcase. "Let's get out of here."

ONE

"So she left you," Patrice said.

"Right," Ben said. "Went back to Toronto. Our last night together, she stood over the bed wagging her finger at me. 'Dammit, Ben, you know *everything* before I do it. "Gesundheit," you say, and two minutes later I'm sneezing!' "

He'd meant to make a joke, but he couldn't laugh. He felt a prick of sadness whenever he thought about his ex-wife, and the women since. He always could tell what they were thinking, what they were going to do next. It drove them crazy; eventually it drove them away.

Patrice chuckled, and the cloud lifted from his face. He couldn't feel down, not seeing that playful expression of hers. They were having dinner at a place called Club Monde in Georgetown, the tony neighborhood along the Potomac in northwest Washington, D.C. It had been eight weeks since the night at the Bay Bluff Motel, and they'd learned to relax with each other. They looked around the room, comfortable with a break in the conversation.

Club Monde was known more as a dance club than restaurant. Music thumped from the floor overhead. Above

5

that were two more dance floors, each with different music, different atmospheres. There was something for everybody here, from K Street legal secretaries to Embassy Row diplomats. *Something for everybody*. His gaze went back to Patrice. She'd bought a black silk blouse specially for tonight, open and cut low. She was playing with the medallion she wore around her neck, swinging it so it glittered. Ben caught himself staring, smiled, and looked down at his plate.

"I've got a bet for you," she said. She reached for her purse, a big straw bag all out of sync with her sleek outfit. "A test of your—what'll we call it?—special people skills."

Ben had never been much for parlor tricks. He didn't answer.

Patrice laid a one-hundred-dollar bill on the table. "I counted. There are forty-eight women in the room. Young, the right age group. Nobody's showing, but at least one must be pregnant. Pick her out. I'll go ask. The hundred's yours if you're right."

Ben tapped the bill. "No money. A dance instead." That was the reason he'd brought her here. It was their last night together, and he'd spent a lot of time planning it. He wanted to keep it straight, not too intimate, but something fun they could remember. A few dances. But all through the meal, each time he'd mentioned it, she'd brushed him off.

Patrice shrugged. "Come on." She shoved the money closer. "Look around. Who's on the nest?"

"A dance," Ben said again. He raised his hand, beckoning to their waitress. The woman hurried over. She was Latino, and her English was iffy. "You want I take away?" She put her hands by their plates.

To Patrice, Ben said, "Her."

Patrice was caught off guard. "She . . . what?"

"She is."

"What? Oh. Are you pregnant?" Patrice blurted.

6

The waitress's eyes glazed. She didn't understand. Patrice pointed at her belly and said slowly, "Preg-nant? Baby?"

The waitress understood now. The look on her face became furtive. After a quick nod, she scurried off. Patrice, laughing, shoved the money across the table. "How do you *do* that?"

"It's just . . . I don't know," Ben answered. He always felt uncomfortable explaining the things he noticed that other people missed. "Think about the way she stood and walked, not balanced normally. She touched her back, stretching, as if it hurt. Her feet, too. Swollen, pressing out around her shoes. It's easy to spot—" His voice faded. He was watching a quick drama across the room.

Their waitress had been heading for the kitchen, but now she turned for a door in the corner. A beefy man hustled after her. Ben had noticed him a while ago, talking to another waitress, pointing, instructing. He must be the shift manager. Just now, he'd been standing two tables away, with that couple there. Patrice had said, "Preg-nant?" The man's head snapped up. He'd heard, and now he was charging after her like an angry bull.

"Oh, hell," Ben muttered.

Patrice had her brandy glass to her lips. She coughed. "What's the matter?"

"We just got her in trouble." Ben pushed up from his chair. "I'll be right back."

The waitress and boss had gone through the door in the corner. It was still swinging when Ben got there. He could hear the man's voice, low but blistering. "You know the policy. I hire you people, OK, but after that we all gotta follow the rules." Ben slipped in behind them. It was a storage room, crowded with linens and dishes. The man stood toe-to-toe with the waitress. "Owner says nobody showin' works here. Bad for the date-night trade." He took her arm and shook her, hard. "You should'a told me."

"Hey," Ben said, grabbing him. The man whirled, glaring. Ben stared calmly back. "Our mistake, my friend's and mine." He knew the waitress's name from her shirt tag. "Marta doesn't look pregnant, does she?"

The man was too wrapped up in his own problems. "Bullshit," he said. "You shouldn't be in here. And you—" He jerked his thumb at Marta. "You're through. Clean out your stuff."

He started for the door, but Ben wouldn't take his hand off his shoulder. "Don't you think that's a little harsh?" His voice was so low that Marta, two paces away, couldn't hear. The manager did, and his eyes snapped up to meet Ben's. What he saw there made him flinch. He swallowed hard and tried to pull free.

Ben held him where he was, like a dog on a leash. "Be reasonable." He edged closer. "Be smart." The man stopped trying to get away. He knew Ben was too strong. "Now, I'll say it again. She doesn't look pregnant, does she?" Ben turned him toward Marta. "Does she?"

"Shit," the man burst out. "All right. She stays a couple weeks more, then she'll have to go."

"Six more weeks," Ben said, squeezing harder before releasing him. "I'll come back. I'll check."

The man flicked another nervous glance at him and nodded, then stomped out.

"Sorry," Ben said.

"Is OK," Marta mumbled, but she was crying.

"Come on." He held the door for her and led her across the dining room. He wanted to give her Patrice's hundred-dollar bill to make up for the trouble they'd caused. As he approached the table he stopped in his tracks. The money was gone, the purse, the coat. Patrice was gone.

Ben fumbled with his wallet and stuffed cash in Marta's hand. He swept the room for Patrice. If she had slipped away on her own, all right. He could understand. She was ready for her new life, her fresh start. That's what they'd been working on these past weeks. But if she wasn't alone, if the wrong person had spotted her and forced her to leave . . . Ben didn't want to think about that.

Marta touched his hand. "Thanks." Seeing the anxious look on his face, she added, "Good luck. The lady, I mean. She's a little too beautiful, maybe?"

He smiled at her before he turned and rushed for the front entrance. Too beautiful? Could be. But sometimes that was a real asset. Like now.

Two men were working the door, stationed there to keep out the drunks and rowdy college students. Ben described Patrice to them: five-nine, blond hair, big green eyes, short black coat, black leggings. By now they were grinning. "Nah, man," one answered. "We see somethin' like that, we'd remember."

"Uhhh-huh!" his buddy agreed.

"Is there a back way out?" Ben asked.

"Three doors. Staff only, though. Besides, got to go up the alley, come past here even if you leave that way."

"Keep an eye out for her," Ben said. He spun around, back to the restaurant, and again she wasn't there. That left only one other place. He headed for the dance floors.

On the first level, the DJ was playing a scratchy version of "Minnie the Moocher." The swing craze was long past its prime in D.C. The dancers were tired and cranky in the heat. Most stood along the sides of the polished floor, watching while six couples swooped through a Lindy Hop. Ben made a quick circuit and left, heading upstairs. Techno-pop blared on the next floor. A crush of people jiggled and stomped to music that had no beat. He didn't even go in. Patrice wouldn't be with those kids.

The top floor was unlit except for a strobe flashing green-red-violet across the ceiling. The music was Brazilian, and the dancers were as dark as the cavernous space they filled. Dark clothes. Dark hair. Dark skin. Most were women. They danced in groups, quick, sinuous motion, the charging rhythm carrying everyone at the same tempo. Ben had just pushed into the crowd when someone cupped a hand to his face. "Omar, I like the beard," she shouted over the music.

She was as tall as Ben, six feet in flat shoes. Ethiopian, he guessed, from her accent and the tiny Horn-of-Africa pin she wore. "Omar?" Ben said. "What's that?"

"Your eyes. I told my sister—" She nodded at another woman, a shorter, plumper version of herself. "This one here—sad eyes like Omar Sharif!"

"Not that sad," Ben said. She shrugged playfully, dancing in place. Her hand was still touching the heavy stubble on his cheek. He pulled it down. "I'm looking for someone, a—"

"Hoo-hoo!" the sister said. She waved. The lack of men to dance with was having an embarrassing effect.

"Someone in particular," Ben said. "A blonde with a black coat."

"Oh, *her*," both women said. The smaller one motioned, and Ben looked over the crowd. He felt a burst of relief and, on its heels, irritation. Patrice was dancing. Her partner was blond like her, a bony man a head taller than Ben. Patrice had her eyes closed, a cool, dreamy smile on her face. She always smiled that way, with her lips together. One of her front teeth was crooked, not quite perfect. She kept it hidden.

While Ben watched them, the woman pulled her hand away. He'd forgotten he was holding it. "Go ahead." She gave him a push. "Don't start a fight."

"Won't have to," Ben said. "The guy's a lawyer, can't you tell?"

He checked his watch as he eased his way over to them. He had twenty-five minutes to get Patrice away from here and make the meeting under Key Bridge.

The big blond she was with had come straight out of a mold. Thin-soled tassel loafers, Dockers, Brooks Brothers shirt with the sleeves rolled to the elbows. His dance step was a self-conscious shuffle, gangly and tight-assed. He might as well have worn a sandwich sign: *I'm an attorney* (front); *So kick me* (rear).

Ben knew all about lawyers. What person working in Washington didn't? The trick to dealing with them was to take away their only weapon: words. Say nothing, write nothing down, and a lawyer was like a tank commander without his tank.

Ben tapped Patrice on the shoulder and flashed his watch to indicate it was time to go. The lawyer said, "Help you with something?" His voice was friendly enough. Ben turned a cold eye on him. After a three-count, he stepped in front of Patrice. The man jerked back. "OK. Didn't know she was with anybody." He shuffle-danced into the crowd, cutting a path with his sharp elbows.

Ben led Patrice out to the stairs, where she stopped. "What's the hurry?"

"I thought you didn't want to dance."

"I changed my mind. You jealous or something?"

"Of Ichabod Crane, Esquire?" Ben snapped. "Dammit, Patrice, you just get up and leave like that? I didn't know what had happened."

She gave him a smile. "I'm sorry. I wanted some fun. On my own, you know? I thought you'd find me. It's sweet you were worried." She pulled him down a step and brushed her knuckles along his jaw. "I love the beard. I knew you'd look great with it."

And just that quick, his anger was gone. He knew she was only playing with him, but it didn't matter. She was enjoying herself, a big change from a few weeks ago. It was a sign he'd done his job well. Besides, she was right. She'd be on her own soon, and she needed to get used to it.

"Come on," he said. "Let's go for a walk."

Patrice threw an eager salute. "Yes, sir! You're the boss!"

"Until midnight," he said. "That's the deal."

The deal had been struck the night Ben picked her up at the Bay Bluff Motel. She was thirty-four years old; for the past fourteen she'd been a grifter. She kept a low profile, small-time hustles only. The way she saw it, it wasn't a great life, but it wasn't bad either. She was a free agent, and she was lucky. But one bleak Monday in June, the whole universe seemed to turn against her. She saw a man murdered that morning, in her own bed, a Palm Beach County commissioner who got his throat slit for voting the wrong way on a zoning waiver. Before the dust settled, Patrice had identified the killer in open court. Then the offer she'd had from the U.S. Attorney's office for relocation, witness protection, evaporated. She didn't have time to find out why. She had to disappear, and that's where Ben Tennant came in.

Years ago another con had told Patrice about Ben. " 'The Laundry Man,' folks call him. Wash you clean, give you a whole new life to start over with. *If* he thinks you can handle it. Picky sumbitch." Part of what Ben did for his clients was to make a new paper trail—IDs and bank accounts and social security numbers and work histories. The technical side wasn't his strength, though. He had a partner who managed most of that. Ben's strength was people. He could turn people sideways, upside down, inside out. Or rather, he could get them to do those things to themselves. After enough navel gazing, Ben's clients started to hate what they'd been. They couldn't wait to leave that baggage behind and get on to somewhere new. And that was where Ben really shone. He made sure they chose a life they could settle into for the long haul.

So Ben told Patrice to lie low for a day at the Bay Bluff, a blind alley for anyone who might come looking for her. From there he took her home. She ate his food, watched his television, read his books, slept in his spare bed. He kept her safe, but he didn't make life easy. Every day he hounded her with questions. High school, senior year— what was the worst thing that happened to you? Have you ever visited your mother's grave? The first man you were with—did he say he loved you? Not once?

Patrice was tough. She fired her answers back, never dissolving in tears the way most of Ben's clients did. But finally something got to her. It was after a difficult evening session, after they had mumbled a terse good night and she'd gone downstairs to her room. Ben waited a half hour, then followed. He tapped on the door, came in and knelt by the bed. For over a minute he stared at her with those dark weary eyes of his, studying every nervous shift and blink. "So Patrice," he whispered, "what's the plan? You're getting older. What are you going to do when you're not so pretty anymore?"

By morning a change had come over her. She stopped fencing with him, started answering his questions directly. She began to talk about things she liked. Sand castles—she liked to build sand castles. And draw and make pottery. Most anything to do with art. Hell, she even liked to finger paint! She hadn't thought of that in years. Soon they were working on a plan for her.

And this was their final day. At midnight, she'd be on her own. That was the deal. Still, Ben had one more lesson to teach. As they went down the stairs at Club Monde, he stole another glance at his watch. Everything was back on schedule.

The sky had been threatening when they arrived at the restaurant. Now it was snowing, a real surprise for early November. Ben led her across Wisconsin Avenue and down a flight of stairs to the old Chesapeake & Ohio Canal. "Walk here?" Patrice said. "It's too cold!"

"It'll be all right," he said, moving so he would block the wind. Smiling, she fell in step with him.

Even this late, there were usually joggers and distance walkers on the canal towpath. Not tonight though, because of the weather. The snow slanted down, a mealy mix, almost sleet. As they moved along, the light around them dimmed. The warehouses and office buildings lining the canal were dark. The snow brought a hush to the air. The only sound was the occasional *thump-thump* of car tires over an expansion gap on Francis Scott Key Bridge, a few hundred yards ahead.

Patrice's hair, lifted by the breeze, brushed his chin. It startled him. He hadn't realized they were so close. "You'll fly to Louisiana tomorrow?" he said.

"No, the train." That made sense. She had three more days until her new job started. She was going to be an assistant art teacher at a small Catholic school in New Orleans. He wasn't sure it was right for her—working with kids—but she was, and she was the one who had to live it.

"You've got a line on a backup job if the school doesn't work out?"

"Yes." He could feel her mood changing. Like him, she was sorry their time was almost up. She said, "No more questions, OK? *Tienes una cola.*"

"What?" he chuckled. It was a game they played, matching Spanish for Spanish. She knew more of it than he did. "I have a what?"

"*Nada, Guapo.*" This he understood. "Nothing, Handsome."

She turned to him. He wasn't sure who leaned forward first. The kiss was quick, uncertain. "Patrice, you could—" He broke off just in time, before he said what he'd been thinking for the past week. Those three spare days. She could stay on with him. Who could tell what might happen? He could feel the breath held in his chest, a balance tipping. Just ask her. Finish the sentence.

He couldn't. That wasn't the deal. She didn't need complications now. She needed that clean start, and he was going to make sure she got it. He took her hand and started walking again, telling her about another early season snowstorm he'd been through in D.C., talking just for the sake of talking.

It was so dark under the bridge that neither of them saw the man until he was right in front of them. He wore a black leather coat and a leather slouch hat. He stood blocking the path, his head cocked as if looking down into the canal.

"Sorry. Excuse us," Ben said.

The man's hand came from his coat pocket, holding a gun. His voice was low and growly. "There's a guy in Palm Beach thinks—"

Ben lunged at him, knocking him back into the bridge pier. As they fell Ben yelled, "*Run, Patrice! Now!*"

She hesitated, then spun and sprinted back the way they had come. A sharp thump echoed behind her. Ben shouted, "*Go!*"

She tripped and sprawled headfirst in the gravel. Before she could get up, the gun went off. "*Ben!*" she screamed.

The only answer was a furious *clap-clap-clap*, the beating wings of pigeons disturbed by the blast. Then his voice came, muffled but loud enough for her to hear. "It's OK . . . Patrice. Go. Now!"

She scrambled up and tore off toward the faint lights of Georgetown.

Ben lay still, eyes shut, listening to the fading thud of her footsteps. He had wondered what it would be like when she was gone. Now he knew. An enormous release. For eight weeks, she'd been an itch he couldn't scratch. He began to laugh. He'd seen it through, kept it professional, taught her everything she needed to know. The rest was up to her.

"Damn," the man in the black coat groaned. "You could'a broke my friggin' neck, jumpin' on me like that."

"Stop whining, Larry." Ben came to his knees, still laughing. Larry Jong was his partner, the documents man. He helped with this part, too, the final send-off.

15

Larry jumped to his feet. He was over seventy but still spry. "Yeah, someday one of those yahoos is gonna kill me, sure."

Ben stood up. "No way. They're still expecting me to take care of everything. That's why we've got to shake them up, put the fear of God—"

"Right. Mr. Fucking-Know-It-All."

Ben expected him to be edgy after his performance with the gun, but not furious. "What's the problem?"

"You want know? I tell you." Larry had come to the U.S. from Hong Kong over forty years ago. His speech still got choppy when he was angry. "That Patrice. I saw the way you walking with her. Lovey-dovey!"

"No, Lar."

"No? You telling me you kept your hands off a woman like that? All that time together?" Ben held them up—clean hands. "You got some kind'a willpower then," Larry said.

"You don't know the half of it," Ben said.

"But I'll bet you didn't collect the fee, did you?"

Ben dusted off the back of Larry's coat. "You'll get your share, like always."

"Damn tootin' I will. What you think we got here, a charity? You Mother Teresa now?"

Ben chewed his lip. He hadn't collected the fee, but that wasn't all. He'd loaned Patrice three thousand dollars, a stake to get her started. She knew where to send it after she got settled. "Speaking of charity, I need a favor."

Larry stared at him, disgusted.

"There's a waitress at Club Monde. Name's Marta. I think she's illegal. Salvadoran, probably. She's going to lose her job soon, and I had a hand in it. Find out where she lives. Help her out. Documents, job interviews, anything you can."

Larry spat in the canal. "And who's gonna pay for that?"

"I can—"

"Ben, you can't take care of the whole world."

They'd been through this argument before. Softly Ben said, "You know how it is. I help where I can."

"Just remember you're not the only one here. We got a *business* goin'." Larry heaved a sigh. "Salvadoran waitresses this time. Damn charity cases."

Ben poked him in the shoulder. "Knew I could count on you."

"Count on this, Bud," Larry said. "That other job of yours? You keep it. 401(k). Health insurance. I'm too old to pay for your retirement."

Larry started for his car, parked under the Whitehurst Freeway. As he stepped out into the falling snow, he looked up and smiled. "Isn't this somethin'? Special kind of night. You need a break after all that willpower. Go back to that club. Meet a girl. Take her home."

For a moment, Ben thought about the woman with the Horn-of-Africa pin. Pretty. Beautiful, in fact. Definitely willing. "No," he said. "I don't need—"

Larry giggled. "Yes you do!"

"Not tonight." They walked up the towpath together. When they came to the spot where the snow was scraped away, where Patrice had fallen, Ben stopped and scuffed his toe on the sharp gravel. He wished he'd been there to help her up.

TWO

The next morning, Ben crept down Georgetown Pike with the rest of the commuters. The northern Virginia roads were slick with snow. He turned on a lane lined with stands of trees giving privacy to huge brick houses. The blue-collar folks in D.C. called these places The McMansions of McLean.

He took a service road to the back of one of the estates. There was a high stone fence, and he used a key card to open the gate. On the other side, it was clear this was no ordinary house. Uniformed men with guard dogs patrolled the grounds. Security cameras were set in the trees, camouflaged from the street.

The driveway led to an underground garage. As Ben pulled into his parking space, someone yelled, "You're late!"

He forced a smile. "Morning, Lena. Busy day ahead?"

Lena Greer was the administrative assistant for the psychologists on staff here, Ben and three others. She had one speed for everything, pedal-to-the-metal bustle, and a tough-guy attitude to go with it. "You bet. Where's your damn tag? Oh, here." She grabbed the U.S. Marshals Service security badge off the dashboard and clipped it to his lapel. She reached to smooth his tie, but he caught her hand and placed it firmly back at her side.

Lena was a climber, whose only skill was organization. She was determined to file-and-memo her way to the top of the Marshals Service ranks. It was going to be hard stationed here. This was the Witness Security Safe Site and Orientation Center, the clearinghouse for people in the federal witness protection program. As far as the Marshals Service brass was concerned, WITSEC, as it was called, was a bastard child, an embarrassment to the whole federal government. The problem was the people in the program—murderers and thieves and drug dealers who turned in their friends for lighter jail sentences, or no sentences at all. They were protected and relocated, given new backgrounds and IDs and cash stipends, all at taxpayer expense. But, like everyone who worked at WITSEC, Ben and Lena didn't complain much about the customers. They just rolled up their sleeves every morning and got the job done.

A van with blackout curtains coasted into the garage. Two uniformed officers were waiting for it at the loading dock. "New family in from Houston," Lena said. "Dad and Mom. Four kids. A granny. Even a boa constrictor."

"We're relocating a snake?"

"Don't laugh. The snake's the only one without a rap sheet." They reached the door and Lena used her card on the lock. Ben said good morning to the duty guard and stopped to sign the entry log. "I already signed you in," Lena said, tugging him down the hall.

It was only a small thing, but Ben had never known her to break a rule before. "What's up?"

She glanced around. She didn't want anyone to hear. "Emile Balazs is here."

"*Balazs?*" The guard looked up and Ben lowered his voice. "Released from Mesa Unit?"

"He came in last night. You've got to talk to him."

She stepped into one of the observation rooms, where she clicked on two camera monitors and adjusted the sound level. Grainy pictures popped up, one showing a kitchenette, the other a combination bedroom/living room. Neither was occupied. "He must be on the pot," she mumbled. She passed Ben a file.

Flipping it open, he found two sheets of paper: a year-old letter from a Deputy U.S. Attorney requesting that Emile Balazs be admitted to the WITSEC program, and a Bureau of Prisons form showing his release thirteen days ago from the Mesa Unit of the Federal Correctional Institution in Phoenix. "Where's the rest of the paperwork?" Ben said. He didn't give her time to answer. "Anyway, there's no reason for me to talk to him."

"Orders, Ben."

"Orders? I did a full evaluation of Balazs. Flew to Phoenix three times. Interviews, lie detector tests. He's not fit for the program. Easy call. So I filed the rescission forms. That's all there is to it."

Ben didn't have a top rank in the Marshals Service, but his job was important. He evaluated witnesses to determine if they were suited for the WITSEC program. There was no appeal from his decisions. If Ben thought someone was too risky to relocate, would pose a danger to his new community, then that person didn't get into the program. Period.

Lena leaned on the chair at the console, not answering. He said, "If Balazs has served his time, dandy. He's out on the street, and like any other ex-con he can cover his own ass. If somebody's got to explain that to him, let his BOP caseworker do it."

"*Orders*, Ben," she said. "Main Justice. They want *you* to talk to him." By "Main Justice" she meant the Justice Department headquarters in downtown Washington.

Ben said, "Balazs is a free man now. No protection from us. What am I supposed to do, hold his hand while I walk him to the street?"

Again she didn't answer. It made him wonder what she was holding back. His decision about Balazs couldn't be overruled, but it didn't end there. The Marshals Service was like any bureaucracy. Strings could be pulled to try to get Ben to change his mind. It had happened before. And Lena would want to steer clear of that.

"Is this political?" he said. "Or maybe it's those bone-heads up the road." He pointed north, toward Langley, the Central Intelligence headquarters. Some people who came through WITSEC weren't courtroom witnesses but CIA informants who needed fresh cover.

A flushing sound came over the speakers, and Balazs appeared on one of the monitors. He was a short man with a bulky chest and thick arms. Whistling through his teeth, he stepped to a mirror, turning sideways so he could see his profile. He smoothed his jet-black hair over his ears.

"Talk to him, that's all," Lena said. "Be understanding. *Don't* make a stink."

Ben sighed. "Stink is right. Guy wears awful cologne, swims in the stuff."

Lena was already moving toward the door, smiling now that Balazs was no longer her problem. "I'm sure you'll cope. And hurry it up. We've got a staff meeting at ten."

Ben flapped his hand to say good-bye. He caught himself yawning. With the foul weather, he hadn't gotten home until two. Then he'd paced around the house. The sense of relief he'd had when Patrice left him by the canal in Georgetown hadn't lasted long. He couldn't stop thinking about her, and all the little things he was going to miss. The sound of running water when she was taking a shower. Their laundry together in the dryer. He felt as empty as the house.

Eventually he went to the room where she had stayed. His clients always left something behind, a note or a thank-you card, maybe just a pair of socks in the back of a drawer. She'd left the place spotless. Even the soap was gone from the bathroom, even the scent of it. There was nothing to do except go to bed, but he couldn't fall asleep. He kept thinking about that spick-and-span room, as if it should mean something to him. Whatever it was had eluded him.

Now, exhausted, he leaned in front of the monitors. Balazs had gone to the table in the living room and started a game of solitaire.

The arrest and prosecution papers weren't in Lena's file, but Ben knew Balazs' record well enough. He owned a fleet of transport planes that he used to run guns, drugs, stolen jewels, and art. For the right price, he'd even ferry terrorists around the world. Balazs wasn't apologetic about it either. He told Ben that he was just a simple businessman. The problem was the import/export laws. They were so complicated even his lawyers didn't understand them. That bogus nonsense wasn't why Ben had refused him entry to WIT-SEC. All cons lied about their past. What bothered Ben was Balazs' tone, the way he carried himself. Everything about him was predatory. He was a young wolf who *knew* he was going to be leader of the pack. Ben couldn't see setting him up in some small town with a spanking new background and only loose government supervision. No way.

On the screen, Balazs had been slapping cards down quickly, but now he paused, tapping the deck with his thumb. Ben whispered, "Why even play if you're going to cheat?" A second later, Balazs snuck a card from the bottom of the largest facedown pile. Then, instead of playing on, he looked directly at the camera and winked. Chuckling, Ben said, "All right you cocky bastard, let's see what's on your mind."

Balazs was in the south wing, probably the nicest suite in the Center. As Ben walked down the corridors, he thought about the cologne. It was leathery with a strong high note, something harsh and spicy, like raw sage. It had to be a personal blend. Balazs wouldn't use an over-the-counter brand. If that was so, why wear so much? To make a big splash, so people would remember him. Ben thought of the young wolf again, laying down his scent, marking his territory.

He knocked, then entered before there was a reply. "Mr. Balazs, good morning."

Smiling, he looked up from the cards. "Doctor, good morning to you."

Ben felt a jab of irritation. Some psychologists called themselves "Doctor," but not him. He'd made that clear to Balazs more than once. "So what can I do for you?" he said.

"Do for me?" Balazs glanced about the room. "Whatever it is you do here, I suppose." He had Tatar eyes, heavy-lidded, turned down at the corners. His accent was vaguely European.

"I don't have a lot of time," Ben said, "so let's not fool with each other. You know somebody with clout. You called in a favor from them, wrangled your way in here so you could talk to me." Again he caught himself yawning and stifled it. "So talk."

"Fair enough. I want you to explain this." Balazs reached into a briefcase on the floor and pulled out the rescission form Ben had signed denying him entry to WITSEC. "First, though, you're wondering, where did I get it?"

"If you know people with enough juice to get you in this place, then they could get into your file too. I told you about that form in Phoenix. The Marshals Service evaluates candidates before granting WITSEC protection. We've decided we can't take you in."

"We've decided? I thought *you* were responsible."

Ben's voice hardened. "Yes, me. I interviewed you; you didn't make the cut."

Balazs held out his hands, so reasonable. "All right, let's try again. Reconsider."

"Out of the question," Ben said. "I'm sorry if someone led you to believe otherwise. Emile, there's nothing here for you." He reached for the door.

"*Wait*. Please," Balazs said. Ben turned back to him. "Do you recognize my name? Balazs—where it comes from? It's gypsy. Very old gypsy."

"Is it your real name?" Ben asked. Cons played all kinds of games to get sympathy. This must be some new variation on the theme.

"Real enough," Balazs said. "Gypsies aren't welcome, anywhere we go. We need ways to survive." He tapped his forehead. "Some of us have the third eye. We see things in people. Weakness, maybe. You have the same talent, I'm told, but you keep it secret. The Laundry Man."

Ben was so exhausted, he hadn't seen this coming. For a moment he didn't react. Then he slipped into the kitchen. Under the counter were two buttons. He pushed them, switching off the cameras and microphone.

"Such a generous guy, this Laundry Man," Balazs continued. "Helps everybody—"

"Not everybody," Ben said, coming back into the room. "Only people who are ready to go straight, but who can't qualify for the official route. That's not you, Emile. You've got no intention of cleaning up your act. If I helped you, you'd only end up hurting people." He looked at his watch. "And I'm through wasting time here."

"Just give me a few minutes," Balazs said. He bent over the table, his hands cupped, clawlike. His eyes were shimmering. He wasn't begging, he was demanding.

Balazs gave a fleeting smile. "You're right that I have powerful friends. But this Marshals Service of yours is a strange club. Everybody tells the same story. 'Sorry, Emile, you've got to pass the psychological first. Statutory requirement. Congressional oversight. Can't help you otherwise.' It's all crap. They just want squeaky-clean records. Nothing that points to them. So I gave up on them and concentrated on you."

He leaned away from the table, revealing a new rescission form, blank. When Ben was in the kitchen, he'd taken it out. "I have a little trouble. You guessed that already. A deal didn't work out. Some people—not good people—are unhappy with me. I can set things right, but I need WITSEC protection. A few weeks is all. Take care of this for me. It's a small thing."

"I already told you, that's out of the question."

Balazs reached into his briefcase again, for a stack of papers. "Not out of the question. You see?"

Ben glanced at the papers. His eyes went wide with shock.

Balazs grinned. "Yes—your files. All your Laundry Man clients, the ones you helped to disappear." Balazs flipped through the pages. "You keep careful notes: allergies, reading habits, clothes, favorite foods, first loves, nightmares. Some of them sent you letters and Christmas cards, gave you their new addresses, phone numbers." He laughed. "Now you *are* wondering, how did I get these?"

"No." Ben tried to keep his voice level. The files had been in their hiding place at his home a week ago. Only one person could have taken them. "Patrice."

"Ah! She said you were quick! Come on, sit. We won't be long now."

Ben dropped into the chair next to him. He reached for the papers, but Balazs held them away. "Let's start with this woman." He ran his finger over the top sheet. "She turned her husband and his gang friends in to the DEA. Something about a little amphetamine factory. Now they're doing thirty to life. What do you think they'd do if they found out she was living on—" He cocked his head so he could read. "Arrowhead Road in Hermantown, Minnesota? She's got a kid, too, eleven years old. Here." He slid a photo over to Ben. Mother and son stared up at him. They were in a boat,

25

smiling and waving, ready to head out for a day of bass fishing.

Balazs gave him a moment to study the picture. "So it's simple, really. Do as I say, or they'll be dead by noon today."

Ben didn't need long to think about it. Those people had trusted him with their lives. Now they were sitting ducks. The shock he'd first felt was gone. His hands were trembling with anger as he reached for the clean form Balazs had brought, checked a few boxes, wrote "Recommend acceptance to Phase II," and signed. He then took his files back. Balazs had kept copies, certainly, and Ben was already making lists in his head. He'd have to warn them. Some would need to be moved. Which ones?

Balazs said, "Don't feel so bad. Patrice is the best at what she does. But she wasn't sure she'd ever break through with you until—" He slouched back comfortably. "She said you came to her room one night. You stared and stared at her. You didn't touch her, but you told her she was pretty. She had you then. You weren't careful anymore, let her have the run of the place. It was only a matter of time before she found the files." Grinning, he cupped his hand by Ben's face. "I just *knew* you'd look great in a beard!"

A lot of people figured that since he was a psychologist, Ben never lost his temper. They were mistaken. Lightning quick, he slapped Balazs, almost knocking him out of his chair. "Listen to me now, Emile." He slapped him again. "If any of these people are hurt, I'll come after you. Don't forget who I am, what I do. There's nowhere you can hide from me. Nowhere."

Ben left the room, slamming the door on Balazs' harsh laughter. His mind was reeling. He let his hand slide along the corridor wall, steadying him. He was already late for the ten o'clock meeting, but he didn't give a damn. He was going downstairs to the exercise room to take a shower, get rid of the stink of Balazs' cologne. He was going to shave that ridiculous beard off, too.

An hour later, Ben was in his office. He'd had a chance to go through his files, and he was feeling better. Most of the addresses were old. Only two clients might need to be moved. That was still too damn many. He needed a pen, so he banged open a drawer in his desk, then jerked back as if he'd been bitten. There was a photograph of Patrice in there. He'd forgotten she'd given it to him, one of those studio glamour shots. For a brief moment, as always, he was surprised at how beautiful she was. He reached for the pen while he studied her face, still not fully believing what she'd done to him. He thought of the trash can, then slid the drawer shut, leaving the picture where it was.

THREE

Emile Balazs stood in his bedroom, watching himself in a mirror while he buttoned his shirt. He was whistling. He enjoyed the mornings here, the soft Caribbean sunlight, the hitch and swish of the palms outside on the estate grounds.

He reached for his knife on the nightstand, but it wasn't there. "Damned Isabel," he said. His sister had taken care of the house while he was in prison and then in witness protection in Miami. That was five months ago, but she still acted as if she were in charge, cleaning and primping and moving his things around.

He checked the bathroom. "*Damn* you, Isabel." Then he saw it on the bureau, a slim jackknife in a leather case. On top of it was a bottle of One-A-Day vitamins and a note in her handwriting. "Down with one, Emby, or I'll have your arse in a sling." Grinning—"Bloody cow"—he gulped one of the pills.

His money clip was also there on the bureau. The wad was thick today. He'd had a great run at the casino last night, then lost half of it on a last spin of the roulette wheel.

What the hell, he gambled because he enjoyed the risk, not just the winning.

He turned the clip over. It was solid gold, a nice piece of work. Patrice Callan had given it to him. She was a nice piece of work, too. For a moment he wondered what she might be up to now. Back in the States, probably, running some grubby scam. He put the clip in his pocket and strode from the room, letting her slip from his mind.

On the veranda, he paused. A hundred yards below, at the foot of the ridge, lay a wide field of sugarcane. Past that was the airport. Four of Emile's planes were parked on the runway apron, each with his company's Golden Pyramid logo on the wings. Basseterre, the only town of consequence on the island, spread from the airport down to the harbor, eight miles away.

This was St. Kitts, the smallest country in the Western Hemisphere, just this island and another, smaller one: Nevis. Total population: 39,000. St. Kitts was a remote place, and poor, even by Caribbean standards. The army was tiny; the coast guard was a joke. That's why he'd come here. In St. Kitts, there was nothing to get in his way.

He caught a whiff of French toast and realized how hungry he was. He loped down the stairs but stopped again as he hit the patio. Isabel was at the table at the far end of the pool. She often dropped in for breakfast. Today she had company. "Chrisakes, Manuel," he muttered, "we'll have to start charging you rent."

The man was Manuel Herrera. He was bland and small, old enough to seem frail. Emile knew better. Herrera was a big deal up in Miami, and he was about as frail as a chain saw.

Isabel's hair was waist length, as dark as Emile's. She shook it back as she talked. "You're Cuban, Manuel, so you know. Kids need to *dance!*" A few months earlier her husband had died. She'd put on ten or fifteen pounds since then, all in her hips and chest. Her voice was high pitched for such a big woman. "Well, we—Butter? Here. Don't be stingy. Emile pays for it. So we taught the kids at Sunday school to samba. You samba, don't you? *Sheeka*-boom-*boom-boom!*" Her dress had a tight, scooped top. As she shimmied, her breasts rolled and pitched, ships on a stormy sea.

A smile crossed Manuel's face.

Emile made his entrance. "Manuel, what a surprise." The old man offered his hand without getting up. Emile bent and whispered, "Sheeka-boom. She puts on quite a show." Manuel's smile faded away.

Emile filled his plate at the buffet. Below, a cruise ship was drawing into the harbor. *"Emerald Princess,"* he said. "Eleven decks. Looks like a fucking wedding cake from up here."

"Emby, watch your mouth," Isabel clucked. She gave him a doting grin as he plopped into his chair. "Chin-chin!" She lifted her Bloody Mary.

Manuel was superstitious and never joined in toasts, but Emile did, raising the maple syrup cruet. "Yeah, bung-ho." He noticed a man hovering at the edge of the patio. Mick Laraby was vice president of Emile's transport company and his only real business associate now that Isabel's husband was dead. "S'up Mickey?"

Laraby was thin as a weasel, always smiling. He was dressed in a cream-colored linen suit and pale alligator-skin boots. "Mornin'!" he called in a cockney burr. He gave Manuel a crisp nod. "Good t'see ya, Mr. Herrera. Oh, and Isabel, naughty dress, that is. So what's the occasion? First communion today, is it?"

She scowled playfully at him.

Emile motioned at the food. "Join us."

Mick put a few things on a plate. "Boss, I hear you had quite a run at the casino last night."

"I was up and down." Emile grinned. "Mostly up."

Mick took a seat. "So what brings you out our way, Mr. Herrera?"

"Business, like usual." He looked at Isabel. The way the sun struck his glasses made his eyes seem yellow, like a bird's. "And I get to see this one here. That's always a plus."

"That's sweet, Manuel." She squeezed his wrist.

"Yeah, sweet, that's me. Some of the time anyway." Herrera stirred his coffee, clattering the spoon against the cup. All morning his movements had been tense, as if something were pent up, ready to break loose. "You know what my daughter calls you, Isabel? The 'Fruit Loop.'"

Isabel's smile sagged.

"Don't take it bad," Herrera said. "Just that you're fun. I like that. You're honest, too." He swung around to Emile. "Not like some in your family."

Emile was used to turns like this with Herrera. He stared back. "Whatever's on your mind, Manuel, we should discuss it in private. Iz, why don't you go inside."

Herrera said, "Let her stay. Maybe I'll get some straight answers for once."

Isabel touched her bracelet. It had been cut down from an old rosary. She played with it whenever she was nervous.

Emile raised his voice. "Iz, I said go inside."

She didn't like being told what to do. She glared at him. Her fingers flicked over the beads.

Herrera had taken a photograph out of his pocket. "First, have a look at this."

Laraby got a glimpse of the picture, and, quick as a hawk, he snatched it. Herrera whipped around, but Laraby was already on his way to the other side of the table. "Iz, luv, you don't want t' be here for this. Come on now, inside." Emile couldn't tell her what to do, but she'd listen to Mick. He helped her up, and she padded into the house, giving them a bewildered look over her shoulder.

When the door was shut, Emile motioned for the photo. Laraby dropped it on the table.

It was a head and shoulders shot of a dead man, laid out on a filthy concrete floor. He'd been in his sixties, good-looking with a full head of silvery hair. He'd been worked over with a knife. One ear was gone and a long patch had been removed from his cheek. But the knife wasn't what had killed him. He'd been struck on the crown of his head with something round and blunt, like the end of a baseball bat. His skull had been shattered and driven into his brain.

Seeing a dead man normally didn't bother Emile, but this made him wince. He grabbed his jackknife off his belt and began to hack up a piece of cantaloupe. "I told you to keep an eye out for him, bring him back here if you found him. *Not* cut him up like a side of beef."

Herrera said, "I put the word out on him like we agreed. Some men—friends of friends—traced him to Orlando. They wanted to impress me. Picked him up, asked him a few questions. He wasn't too polite, so this is how it ended."

Emile's jaw muscles bounced. He was ready to explode. Laraby knew the warning signs and jumped in. "Those friends of yours—what did he say to them?"

"He was a tough nut. Kept shut to the end." Manuel dabbed jam on a slice of toast. "Now Emile, you haven't said why you wanted him. You'd better fill me in."

"Terrific," Emile snapped. "You kill a man, and you don't learn a damn thing from him." He got up, muttering a curse, and strode to the far corner of the patio. From there he could see over the spine of the ridge, down to the Atlantic coast. The water was a deeper, calmer blue than on the Caribbean side. He focused on that, trying to relax.

Behind him there were footsteps, light and quick. "Jesus, Mickey," he sighed. "You believe that idiot?"

"Not hardly." Laraby leaned on the railing. "But look at it from his side. You'd still be rotting in witness protection in Miami if it weren't for Herrera. Or you'd be dead. He bailed you out of that mess, and we made a deal with him, straight up. Five months, and we haven't delivered. Some people'd say he's been damn patient."

"Patient?" Emile huffed. "Bullshit."

Mick chewed his lip, grinning. Emile knew that look and said, "What is it?"

"Was out doin' some snooping last night. I found out a thing or two."

"Well?" Emile demanded.

"Square things with the old man first. Don't piss him off."

"Piss him off?" Emile glared at Herrera. "I've had about all of him I can stomach."

"Wait, Boss." Mick put his hand out to stop him. "You seen the news out of Cuba? The last two nights there were car bombs in Old Havana. Somebody machine-gunned one of the big tourist hotels in Varadero. Sixty, seventy dead."

"You think Herrera ordered that?"

Mick shrugged. "Or friends of friends of his. Don't push him or he's liable to shove back hard. Throw him a bone. Make him feel he's part of the team."

Balazs looked at the ocean again as he thought it over. "All right. The letter in the safe—bring it down here."

Emile returned to the table. The time apart seemed to have brought a cease-fire with Manuel. They ate and talked about the food and the weather. The photo of the dead man lay between their plates, but neither of them mentioned it.

Mick came back, handing Emile an envelope, and Emile passed it to Manuel. "Open it up."

Inside was a sheet of paper with another photograph, made by a computer printer. It was the man with silver hair, when he was alive. In his hand was something that looked like a thick, gold, pocket calculator.

Emile said, "Check out what he's holding. Your keypad."

"That?" Herrera jerked the paper up for a closer look. "It's so small."

Emile said, "That's it. So, you wanted to know about him. He had the keypad. Don't ask me how, but he did." Emile tapped the back of the page, where there was a paragraph of neat handwriting. "All he wanted was a finder's fee. We could have paid him off, picked the thing up, been done with it. Except your friends killed him."

Manuel ran his fingers over the image of the keypad. His touch was gentle, reverent, and his voice was hoarse with emotion. "It must be somewhere. Someone must know. We have to find out."

"Right. Somewhere. Someone."

"We'll start looking. I'll get those people in Orlando—"

"No," Emile said sharply. "You stay out of it."

Manuel tossed the picture down and fixed Emile with his yellow bird's eyes. "If you'd told me what was going on, he wouldn't be dead. This is all on your head, Emile."

"Me? Damn you, Manuel—"

Mick jumped in again. "Mr. Herrera, we know how important the keypad is. Now this guy—" He pointed at the dead man's picture. "He was no big deal. Just a messenger. We've already got a lead up the food chain, to his boss."

Emile scowled at him. *His boss? Jesus, Mick, what are you talking about?*

"Who?" Herrera said.

"No. Please." Laraby could be very soothing when he worked at it. "Leave that to us. Go back to Miami. We'll have news about the keypad, soon."

Herrera stared into his eyes, looking for some sign of trickery. Mick gave him a steady smile. The old man stood up. He had a bad hip, so he moved slowly. "All right, for now I'll stay out of it. But you remember—nine lives is all you've got. You're starting to run short." Taking his cane, he limped across the patio to the house.

"D'you need a lift to the airport?" Mick called.

Manuel dismissed that idea with a flip of his hand.

Emile glared after him and muttered, "Manuel, you fucking moron." Soon they heard a car start and roll up the driveway. "So what's this bull about having a lead on somebody?"

Mick gave that sly grin of his. He'd taken to calling the man in the photos "Silver" because of his hair. "Been askin' everywhere about Mr. Silver. Lots of folks remember seein' him around the island, but I couldn't find out where he stayed, none of the hotels anyway. Then somebody in Basseterre said they saw him comin' out of the presbytery at the cathedral, regular like. I asked one of the maids, and she recognized him right off. Mr. Silver stayed there five nights."

"At the presbytery?" Balazs said. "How did he swing that?"

"Don't know yet, but I'll find out." Mick was still smiling, holding back.

"What else?" Emile asked, growing irritated.

"Finally got a name for him. That maid at the presbytery knew. S-a-a-r. Saar."

Emile was taking a sip of orange juice. He froze, staring over the rim of the glass. "Peter Saar?"

Mick nodded. "That's right."

Emile set the glass down with a bang. "*Christ*. Peter Saar. Patrice Callan's buddy."

"Yep. The con she used to run with," Mick said.

Emile gave a snort, half laugh, half disgust. "I should have seen it, Mickey. I should have guessed she was behind it." He banged the glass once more, almost as a salute.

Mick nodded again. "It's just her kind of deal, sending Saar down here to find the keypad, then squeeze us for a finder's fee. Patrice is a smart one. Keeps track of everything. She'll know where Saar stashed it. No worries there."

Emile was thinking, his eyes fixed on the pale blue sky over Basseterre.

"So do you have any idea where she is?" Mick asked.

"What?" Emile murmured. "Oh. No. No idea."

Mick said, "Patrice and Isabel used to talk. She might have said something, mentioned a place she went. I'll ask Iz—"

Emile snapped back into focus. "No! You leave Isabel to me."

"Sure," Mick said. Isabel was always a touchy subject. "So what next? We call out the bloodhounds to look for Patrice?"

"Not yet. We'll try something easier. I think there's somebody who can point us right at her."

Emile pulled out his money clip and rolled it over in his palm, watching it flash in the sunlight. He seemed to have gone into a trance. Smiling faintly, he lifted his hand to his cheek, where Ben Tennant had slapped him five months ago. Then he rose to make a telephone call.

FOUR

Ben sat on the porch of his home, sipping his first cup of coffee of the day. A deer was grazing on the tulips across the yard. "Mooo!" Ben called resignedly. The buck blinked, then ambled off into a thicket of oaks.

The sky was clearing after a hard rain. It would be a fine April morning, the best kind of weather in Northern Virginia. That was good because Ben was going to be stuck here all day, waiting for a workman to fix a leak in the roof. Ben didn't take care of the place the way he should. It wasn't much of a house anyway, an old split-level with cramped dark rooms. He lived there because of the land, six densely wooded acres at the end of a tiny road. There wasn't a neighbor in sight. Ben's partner, Larry, called it "Laundry Man Forest." Larry didn't like to visit. It was too much country for him.

Usually, Ben didn't notice the isolation. It was part of the price he paid for his clients, a place for them to hide out while he worked with them. But sometimes it got to be too much. Then he'd take a trip to New York or San Francisco, some big city. He'd go to the clubs and bars, where he'd watch the people, meet a woman, or two, or three. But those encounters never got serious. He wasn't around long enough. On the second night out, his senses would start to overload. All those people—so much for him to take in. A man grinning, oblivious, while his wife made eyes at a pretty woman across the floor. A drunk at the end of the bar, unemployed, staring through tears at his last paycheck. A woman in six-inch heels, feet wobbly with pain but dancing on, hunting for the perfect partner. After a few days Ben would come home, ready for another stretch on his own.

But today he wouldn't be alone. There was the roofer, and another man was coming, too. That other visitor had Ben feeling nervous. His mind skipped along, early morning free association. Clients. Fee. Income. Death and taxes. Ben heard a car on the dirt driveway as he finished the free-association string: IRS.

The car drew to a halt and the driver heaved himself out. His name was Arne Guttersen; he was an Examining Agent from the IRS District Office in Richmond. They'd only talked on the phone, but Ben had a strong mental image, and he wasn't far off the mark. Guttersen had a pear-shaped body, his belly hard as iron. He wore a blue suit and white shirt, just as Ben expected. The only surprise was the suspenders. They were brand new, fire-engine red, with straps two inches wide.

Guttersen tossed down a half-smoked cigar and ground it into the mud. "You must be Tennant." He lifted his nose and sniffed, like a hound on the scent.

"Yes," Ben said. "And you must be a pain in the ass," he added under his breath.

As Guttersen trooped up the yard, a plane flew low overhead, bound for Dulles Airport. He hesitated, cocked his ear to listen, and gave a fleeting smile. Ben didn't have time to figure that out because Guttersen was already past him, opening the front door without offering to shake hands.

Inside, Guttersen said he wanted to be shown around. Ben glanced at his muddy shoes, but decided not to ask him to take them off. He might take offense. When they'd talked on the phone, Ben had gotten a taste of Guttersen's temper. He was a walking minefield, the kind of man who'd blow up over a trifle. So they tracked through the kitchen, dining, and living rooms, then down the half-flight of stairs to the family room, which Ben had converted to a spare bedroom for his clients.

Guttersen was here because of the home office deduction. Ben took depreciation on a portion of the house and deducted part of the utilities. He was entitled. He conducted business here and reported every penny he earned on his tax return.

Guttersen stood over the bed. "So you train actors here? Give 'em like, what, acting lessons?"

That was Ben's cover story. He couldn't tell Guttersen the truth about his clients, so he told him he moonlighted as a coach for Hollywood types who needed to polish up a particular character before working on a movie or TV show. He had to keep their names confidential. If it got out that they needed coaching, it might hurt their careers. Guttersen hadn't been very understanding about the need for secrecy, but he and Ben seemed to have reached a truce on the issue.

"We work on mannerisms, voice inflections, things like that," Ben said.

"Hmmmm." The tax man didn't sound like he believed him. He looked at the bed pillows. "Actors *and* actresses?"

"Sure."

Guttersen pushed on the mattress, testing the springs. "You ever use this room for personal purposes? Like, you and one of those actresses ever—?"

"Nope, not once," Ben put in.

Guttersen gave a snort of laughter. He turned, glancing

around the room, and Ben got a look at those suspenders. The clasps were tiny airplane propellers. That explained the do-si-do in the yard. Guttersen had heard the engine, IDed that plane without looking at it, and gave a smile when he glanced up and saw he was right. Something else came to Ben's mind. He'd seen a headline in the morning paper, something to do with airplanes.

They finished the tour and Ben led him back to the dining room. "We can spread out here. I'll get coffee. Instant's okay, I hope?" He closed the door to the kitchen so he could have some privacy. While the water heated, he shuffled through the newspaper, finding the article on the front page of the Metro section: "Air Show Today at Dulles." Largest show of its kind in the country, it said. Prototype planes. Racing pilots. Autographs.

Ben had known all along there was something odd about this meeting. Guttersen was the one who'd set it up. Why here? Why not tell Ben he had to come down to Richmond? Airplanes, that's why. Guttersen wanted a shot at that air show, without having to take the day off work. Shows like that were clubby things. He'd bought a new pair of suspenders to show off to his friends.

Ben scanned the article. Admission: $9; gates open at 11:00. Arrive early; big crowds expected. Perfect. Go slow, Ben decided. Play dumb. Rope-a-dope until 10:30, and then Guttersen would want to leave. "Arne?" he called. "Cream and sugar?" To himself he said, "Of course not."

"Nah. Black."

Ben returned with the two mugs. Guttersen was across the hall in the living room, studying some pictures on the wall. One was of a dog Ben had owned, a nervous German shepherd named Barney Fife. Next to it was a photo of a football team. Guttersen whistled as he read the inscription. "State champions, huh? What position'd you play?"

"Quarterback."

Arne snorted and tapped his chest with his thumb. "Tackle, both ways."

He moved to a second group of pictures. One was of Ben in a parachute ready to jump out of a plane; another of Ben rock climbing; Ben kayaking on an azure-colored river through a jungle backdrop. In each picture there was a woman with him, all different, all attractive in a four-hours-a-day-at-the-health-club sort of way.

Guttersen broke into a grin. "You're divorced!"

"What?" Ben said, taken aback. "Oh. Yes."

"You used to file joint returns. Saw that in your records." He tapped the photo of Ben skydiving. "This was right after you split with her, right?"

Ben nodded. There had been a lot of women in those days. At first they loved the fun and special intimacy with Ben, but eventually they all needed some private space. One by one they drifted away.

"Same thing happened to me after my wife left." Guttersen jabbed himself with his thumb again. "I got into drag racing."

"Did you like it?" Ben asked.

"Well enough. Until I got in a wreck and broke my ass bone." He rocked his hips and winced, as if it hurt. "You know what it'll do to your love life to have a broken ass bone?"

Ben laughed. "Nope. I've got no idea."

Arne was laughing, too, but he broke off suddenly. He stomped back to the dining room. "Enough fun and games. Let's get to work."

They'd just gotten seated when they heard a vehicle approaching on the drive. "That's a workman, Arne, for my roof. Be just a minute."

He was already out the door before he realized it wasn't the roofer's van but a Chevy sedan. Two men got out, then a woman. Ben recognized her just from the color of her hair, a deep, coppery red. He stopped, struck by the odd coincidence. He'd just been looking at pictures of women he'd known during that rowdy year after his divorce, and here was one of them. Rand Mosby. She worked for the Marshals Service.

He waited at the top step, feeling a ripple of uneasiness. What was she doing here? Not a social call, not with those two men tagging along. She seemed nervous, too, hanging back instead of coming to him. Then Ben smiled. He'd always had a special feeling for Rand. She had the best laugh he'd ever heard—sexy and full-bore, bursting unexpectedly from such a small woman. Whatever she wanted, he was glad to see her.

It started for them five years ago, at a weekend conference in San Diego. They met at the hotel registration desk. It was a white-hot couple of days. Mosby was great company, in bed and out. But she had a secret. Sunday morning, Ben went out to get a newspaper and discovered he'd left his wallet behind. Returning to the room, he bumped into her coming out of the closet. She spun away, but he'd already seen her face. Her nose was streaming; there was a tiny white fleck on one nostril. Cocaine. He sat on the bed and pulled her down next to him, where he could hold her. They stayed like that for three hours, talking. Rand had laid off the junk all weekend, but when she thought about going back to Chicago, the stress of work and the loneliness, she couldn't hold it together any longer.

She did go to Chicago that afternoon, but she and Ben stayed in touch by phone, three or four times a day. He helped her off the coke and back on her feet. He wanted to come to Chicago to see her, but she said no. And after a couple of months she stopped calling, and stopped returning his calls. He realized what the problem was. He knew too much, all her fears, all the dirt in the corners that could never be cleaned away. He could be her confessor but not her lover.

Rand had made a lot of changes since he'd last talked to her. She was now a big gun in the Marshals Service, Southeast Regional Director for WITSEC. She looked good, too, trim and clear-eyed.

She glanced at the two men before she stepped away from the car. One was young and tall, with chiseled features, a body like a Greek statue. The second was so nondescript and pale he seemed ghostlike, a real Casper. They waited while she approached. "Ben, how are you?"

She held out a business card. He thought that was strange, but he took it anyway. "Fine, Rand. You?"

"Great!" she said with a little too much enthusiasm. "Sorry to bother you at home. We need to talk."

Ben glanced through the window. "It's not so convenient right now."

"This isn't his," the Greek statue said. He was looking at the license plate on Guttersen's car. "Must be somebody inside." He bounded past Mosby to the door.

"Whoa, friend." Ben reached out to stop him. "First, let's get the players straight. Rand, who are these people?"

She smiled vaguely. "He's Ken."

"Nice to meet you Ken. How about a last name?"

"Not just yet," Ken said. He yanked the door open, but, before he could go in, Guttersen stepped out.

The tax man studied the newcomers. "Clients of yours, Tennant?"

"Not by a long shot," Ben said.

Mosby handed another business card to Guttersen. "And you are . . . ?" she asked. He fumbled his IRS identification out of his pocket and explained why he was there. She said, "Something's come up, and we need Ben's help. It may take a while. Why don't you head back to Richmond? Give him a call in a day or two to set up another appointment."

During this exchange, Ken had gone inside. He returned with Guttersen's briefcase, which he shoved into the IRS man's hands. Guttersen's jaw rocked forward. "What are you, some kind of Miss Manners retard? You don't touch my things."

Ken tossed his head, flipping back his wavy brown hair. "She showed you her card. U.S. Marshals Service. That's all you need—"

"I don't care if she's the damn Kaiser of New Jersey," Guttersen growled. "You *don't* touch my things."

Ben stepped between them. "Arne, come here." He indicated the far end of the porch. "Down here. We'll work something out."

Ken pulled them apart. "No. He leaves now."

It was his smirk that got to Ben, the whole preppie attitude he had. "Ken, buddy, tell me the truth. What's Barbie really like in bed?"

Ken's brow wrinkled. He was very ugly when he was angry. He made a show of tugging back his coat, exposing his gun in its holster. "Go *now,* Mr. Guttersen."

"Like hell I will," Guttersen said, starting for the door. Ken gave him a shove, and he went stutter-stepping down the stairs. He tripped and fell seat-first in the mud.

"Jesus, Rand," Ben said, "call off this clown." She did nothing, just stared into the woods.

Guttersen was trying to get to his feet. Ben scrambled to help, but the tax man shook him off and stamped to his car. He pointed, sweeping them all in. "You work with these people, Tennant. I'm holding you responsible."

Guttersen gunned the engine and roared down the driveway, throwing a spatter of red dirt. "Goddammit, Rand." Ben kicked a stone across the yard. "I don't need that kind of crap. You damn well better call him, apologize—"

Ken had come off the porch, behind him. The gun was in his hand. "Shut up."

"Rand," Ben bellowed, "what in the name of hell—"

"Get in the house," Ken snarled.

Ben glared over his shoulder. "Sorry about that Barbie

44

crack, Ken. Forgot your little problem. The not-anatomically-correct thing."

Ken snapped out his fist. Ben lurched and the punch clipped him low behind the ear. "Rand—?" he wheezed, dropping to his knees.

Mosby did nothing. Someone else spoke. "That's enough, Kenneth. Bring him along," said Casper the Ghost.

FIVE

Ken jerked a pair of disposable handcuffs around Ben's wrists and dragged him into the living room. Ben was too woozy to struggle. After tossing him down, Ken dropped a photograph on the floor. "Take a look." Ben shook his head, trying to get the world to stop spinning. "You twerp, *look,*" Ken snapped, pulling back to hit him again.

The pale man intervened, calmly stepping on Ken's toe with his heel. "*Enough,* Kenneth." Ken hopped away in agony.

The pale man stood over Ben, holding a meat cleaver in his hand. He'd slipped into Ben's kitchen to get it.

He picked up the photo. "You asked, so I'll tell you. My name is Aaron Joquand." He nodded at his partner. "Barbie's better half is Kenneth Van Allen." He dropped his voice to a stage whisper. "Don't take him personally. He hates all psychologists. Says 'dey screw wit yer mind.' He should write copy for Merriam-Webster, don't you think?"

He lifted the cleaver. "You should sharpen more. This is the only thing you've got with an edge." He bent and sliced off the handcuffs. "I don't think we'll need those."

"Now, next question," Joquand said. "Who are we? We're

just a couple of government stiffs. Special Assistants. And friends of Ms. Mosby."

Ben shook his head again, getting rid of the ringing in his ears. *Pay attention. Focus.* He looked Joquand up and down. Cheerless gray eyes. Limp hair. Milky complexion. Shiny blue suit. The Langley Look. He said, "CIA. You're Special Assistants with CIA."

Joquand nodded and smiled, saluting his deduction.

That took care of them, but what about Mosby? Ben said, "What's your story, Rand? Your business card has a Washington address. L Street. That's not Main Justice, and that's certainly not Miami, where you were last I heard. I doubt you've had a promotion, not working with this circus act."

Mosby cleared her throat. "No promotion. Temporary assignment."

"Doing what?" He waited while she stared out the window. Her face was slack; her eyes never moved. Ben knew what that meant. She was separating herself in her mind. "Come on, Rand, you're with them, but they don't own you."

She said, "We're with a task force. Four agencies."

Ben didn't believe her. Her voice was a drone. She was only reciting what they had told her. "Four agencies," he said. "That must be something. So who runs this task force? What are you after?"

"Orders from the top, the Attorney General," Mosby droned on. "We're—"

"That's very good, Rand," Joquand cut in. "We're after information, Mr. Tennant. First, this man. Do you know him?" He held the photograph in front of Ben's eyes.

A man with silvery hair. Skull crushed so badly his face was distorted, flattened. A missing ear. Jagged tears in the skin.

It was a sickening sight. Ben turned away. "I've never seen him before. Who is he?"

"Look again," Joquand demanded. "The face is basically intact."

Ben shook his head. "I don't know him." He looked at Jo-quand's hand, at the meat cleaver. The man in the photo had obviously been tortured. As if reading his mind, Jo-quand breezed into the kitchen and put it away.

"Who did that to him?" Ben asked.

"Yes, who?" Joquand murmured. He strolled about the living room, touching things, snooping. He studied the photo of the dog—"Aw, an animal lover!"—then the team picture. He began to hum "You've Gotta Be a Football Hero."

They were quiet after that. It was a standard interview technique. Let the clock tick; let the subject begin to panic. Ben wasn't so easily manipulated. He'd once been caught in an uprising at a prison in Michigan. He'd gone there to interview a WITSEC candidate. With the guards down and the security cameras out, one of the inmates, a huge man with the unlikely name of Cleo, picked him out as a special plaything. He prodded Ben with a shiv, telling him exactly what he was going to do with his body after he killed him. Ben kept his cool by concentrating on Cleo, reading his ha-tred and fear. Eventually Ben got the opening he was wait-ing for. And later he helped carry Cleo to the prison hospital, where they set his two broken arms.

Van Allen picked up the picture of the dead man and went back to massaging his toe. Joquand poked through the front closet. Mosby had been standing nearby, but, when he came close, she moved away. The two men made her nervous. More than nervous, afraid.

She broke the silence, her voice still flat, reciting. "We've known for a long time about your business here, Ben. The Laundry Man." Ben didn't react, not even a blink. He was surprised, but not shocked. He worked with cons, and cons could never be trusted. Some Marshals Service bigwig was bound to get wind of his operation eventually. Still, some-thing wasn't right. If they wanted to come down on him about his private clients, this wasn't the way. They'd have him hauled into Main Justice. Interviews, polygraphs. Instead, here was Mosby making an early morning house call, flashing a new business card and a guilty attitude. Not to mention the two CIA goofballs. This visit was unofficial, way outside normal channels. It could be just Joquand and Van Allen on a lark of their own, dragging Mosby along. Or it could be a lot bigger. Ben would have to feel his way through, see how much they'd give him.

Mosby continued, "It wasn't a problem for us, though. The Marshals Service has no grudge against people who aren't accepted into WITSEC. We just don't want responsibility for them. You helped there. You gave the rejects a place to go, turned a lot of them into upstanding Joes and Janes."

"Bravo, Mr. Tennant," Joquand intoned. He slouched over to a bookcase and began checking the collection.

"OK, Rand," Ben said, "but you didn't come here to tell me something we both already know. What do you really want?"

"We need to find one of your clients. We have reason to believe someone is trying to kill her."

Ben shrugged. "Somebody wants to kill most of those people. That's why they come to me in the first place."

Van Allen got up and took a second photo from his pocket.

"That's her," Mosby said. "The dead man in the other picture was a con, like her. They used to run together. Turns out he was her father. He was found four days ago in Orlando. There were no . . ."

Ben didn't catch the rest. Just before he saw the photo— when it sunk in that Mosby had said kill *her*— the thought flashed through his mind. *Patrice*. The photo was an old mug shot in black and white. Even there she looked beautiful. He fought to keep his expression blank. Since last November he'd often thought about Patrice. He wondered if he'd ever see her again. It happened with some of his clients. He'd run across them in the most unlikely places. More than once, he'd thought of trying to track her down so he could talk things out with her. Now, looking at her picture, he forgot about Mosby and the others. A strange feeling came over him, the feeling that comes at an amusement park watching a thrill ride, deciding whether to buy a ticket. Excitement mixed with vague dread.

Mosby was still talking: local coroner, Cuban mafia, no leads.

Ben shoved the picture aside. "It's got something to do with Emile Balazs."

Mosby hadn't expected this. Before she could think, she nodded. Finally, a little truth.

Joquand broke in, "Mr. Balazs isn't important. All we care about is Patrice Callan. We have to get to her, warn her." He squatted so he and Ben were level with each other. "Please. If you know, tell us where she is."

"What's Balazs up to?" Ben asked.

Joquand looked at him, earnest as an altar boy. "If you don't know where she is, help us find her. You can save her life, Ben."

The atmosphere had changed in the room. No one was moving. Van Allen's fingers had stopped in the middle of re-tying his shoe. Idiots. They'd practiced this part. The Big Lie.

"Sorry," Ben said with a sigh. "Patrice is a smart, smart lady. I wouldn't have a clue where to start looking for her."

Joquand didn't waste time asking again. "Kenneth—with me," he ordered. They went onto the porch, and soon Ben heard Joquand mumbling into a mobile phone.

"Rand," Ben whispered. "What's this all about? Those two jerk-offs have got you so scared you're liable to stain your panty hose."

Her lips moved, hinting at a smile. She had a pretty smile.

Ben was surprised they'd left him alone with her, but then they probably didn't know how close he'd once been to Rand. "Tell me," he said.

"This is Joquand's show," she said. "They only need me for cover. They won't work out in the open, so they hide behind my badge." She shook her head, as if shaking off a bad dream. "Joquand got a call from Balazs yesterday, asked him to come here, find out if you know where Callan is."

Ben frowned. "Why would somebody from the CIA do favors for Balazs?"

"Not just somebody—Joquand." She bit her lip, deciding how much to tell him. Tears welled up in her eyes. She owed Ben so much, her life maybe. "Balazs is after something, and Callan's put herself in the middle of it. Joquand's got some interest in the deal, too. *Personal* interest. I don't know what they're after, but it's way above my pay grade. Big enough to get armies moving, Joquand said."

"All right. But we can still work it out—you and me."

"No," she said sharply. "You can't help me on this. You know those bumper stickers that say 'No Rules'? That's Joquand. *No Rules.*"

They both sensed the silence outside. Joquand had switched off the phone. He and Van Allen turned for the door. Mosby looked at Ben. "Just do what they want, whatever it is."

The two men came back inside, and Joquand went to the bookcase. "Everything here in order. Sports. Biographies. Travel books. Poetry. You like things organized." He waved his hand through the air. "Small house. Won't take long to search."

Ben was in no position to complain. "Be my guest."

Joquand stared at him. He never seemed to blink. He tossed another pair of plastic handcuffs to Van Allen. "Take Mr. Tennant to the basement, Kenneth, and see to it he's not comfortable." He beckoned to Mosby. "We'll start in the bedrooms." The last Ben saw of them, Mosby had stopped at the bottom of the stairs, forcing Joquand to go first. She turned aside long enough to glance at Ben, speaking to him with her eyes. *Please just go along.* Then her face took on that dead look.

Ben didn't want those handcuffs on again. He shuffled down the steps with his head bowed, the picture of meek surrender. Upstairs he could hear Joquand and Mosby tossing things around in the rear bedroom. There wasn't anything to find in there. Next they'd move to the smaller room he used as a den. There they'd find the safe, and they'd come to the basement to get the combination from him.

Van Allen was fumbling for the light switch. "It's here," Ben said helpfully. A couple of dingy fluorescents flickered on. The room was narrow, with a low ceiling. At the far end was a door leading to another room. Boxes were stacked against the long wall, together with fishing gear and camping equipment.

"Wow! An outdoorsman!" Van Allen mocked. Ben wandered down to the other door and peeked inside. "What's that?" Van Allen asked. When Ben didn't answer, he moved up and shoved him roughly out of the way. Ben had controlled his temper so far, but now he felt it flare. The second room was well lit. There were mirrors on three walls, a treadmill, a stack of free weights and two lifting benches, a stationary bike. Van Allen's eyes sparkled, like a child seeing new toys. "Work out a little, huh?"

"A little," Ben said. He willed him. *Take a look, you SOB.*

Van Allen went straight for the weights. He didn't notice the speed bag in one corner, the body bag in another. A bar was set on the incline bench, ready for lifting. He counted the weight and sneered, "Two-ninety? Bullshit."

Ben slipped up behind and waited for him to turn around. "No, Ken. No bullshit." Then Ben hit him, a single crossing punch that rocked him on his heels and made his eyes go out of focus. He hit him twice more, left-right hooks, both cheeks. Ben pulled every punch. He knew how hard his anger was driving him. He didn't want to kill anyone. Still, Van Allen reeled back, unconscious before he hit the floor.

Ben left the room and was back ten seconds later with a roll of duct tape and a big knapsack he kept hidden with the camping gear. He bound Van Allen's hands and feet and put a wrap around his mouth for a gag. He went through his pockets to see if there was anything useful. He left the gun. He didn't want the kind of trouble that could bring. Then Ben checked the knapsack. A change of clothes. Money. Credit cards. Driver's license and insurance card. Fishing license. Everything was in the name of Murray Lawrence of Gaithersburg, Maryland.

He heard a crash upstairs, and Joquand cursed. Ben scooped the things back into the knapsack and went to the outer room. Behind the furnace was an access panel. He removed it and slipped outside, through a yew hedge. He followed the hedge to the woods, and from there he cut to the abandoned road that ran along the rear of his property. He was heading for Great Falls Village. He could call for a cab from there.

When he reached the old road, he slapped the knapsack on his back and took off at a hard jog. His face was grim; his body was wound up tight. He was mad at the whole damn world. He needed to channel his anger, figure out what to do next. He tried to remember everything Mosby Joquand, and Van Allen had said. It was a jumble. Four days ago in Orlando. Cuban mafia. Armies moving.

A mile flew by. Out of the tangle of thoughts, his mind began to focus. A single word. *Patrice.*

SIX

That afternoon was sunny and muggy. Ben sweated it out in the shade of a tombstone in Congressional Cemetery in southeast Washington, a few miles from the U.S. Capitol. Weeds had grown high around the grave. South of him, down the hill, was the Anacostia River. It gave off a rank smell of mud and dead fish.

He was keeping an eye on a shabby row house on Seventeenth Street. On the lower floor was a convenience store. The sign in front was cracked and too faded to read. People straggled in and made their quick purchases—a loaf of bread, a six-pack of beer.

Ben leaned back, trying to get comfortable against the hard marble. In a bush next to the tombstone, a spider was patiently devouring the head of a moth. It was a weird place to wait, especially for Ben. For him, every cemetery had real ghosts.

The year he was thirteen, he'd gone with his parents to visit his uncle in New York. It was the Fourth of July and blistering hot. Ben's father had to work the next day, so they headed back to Virginia right after the fireworks. No air conditioning in the car, the windows rolled down and the wind roaring in. Ben remembered the noise and the smells, the songs on the radio, everything his parents talked about that night.

It was too long a trip to make in one stretch, so they pulled off at a rest stop in central Pennsylvania. That late, the place was deserted. Next to it was a big cemetery.

As soon as they got out of the car, Ben said he wanted to go for a walk over there. It would be fun, reading the gravestones in the moonlight. His mother didn't think the cemetery was a good idea, but Ben's dad said OK. He was like that—easygoing, always willing to bend for somebody else. Eventually the three of them climbed the low fence and started to walk the rows of tombstones.

They were on their way back when a car rolled into the rest stop. The driver, a woman, got out, and Ben immediately could tell something was wrong. She was old and overweight, and in too much of a hurry, slamming the door, running for the pay phone. She never made it. Two more cars pulled in; one of them cut her off. Six men got out, dark suits in the gloomy parking lot. She tried to fight, but it was like a house cat fighting lions. They grabbed her and dragged her to one of the cars.

Ben stood frozen, his mother beside him. This couldn't be happening. In a city maybe, but not a place like this. Then he felt his father's hand on his shoulder, and he and his mother were both pushed down behind one of the gravestones, and Ben knew it was real. Ben had never seen his father do anything forceful like that. It *hurt*. But he wasn't even looking at them. "Stay here," he whispered, and he started toward the parking lot, toward their own car. It wasn't till he reached it that he shouted, "Hey! What's going on over there?"

Instantly the men fanned out. The dark suits. Ben's father—a man who worked for the health department inspecting nursing homes, a volunteer referee for Pop Warner

football, a quiet guy who called men he didn't know "Sir"—
fought. He put three of them down before one got behind
him and hit him so hard that Ben and his mother, fifty yards
away, heard the *crack*. She had both hands over Ben's
mouth, keeping him still. If he was surprised at how strong
his father was, he was even more surprised at her. He
couldn't move an inch. She was praying. He'd never heard
her pray before.

The men carried Ben's father across the parking lot,
shoved him in the car with the woman, and drove off. Ben
had played it so many times through his head that he knew
exactly how long it had taken. Forty seconds from "Stay
here" to the last glimmer of their taillights on the highway.

The woman, they learned later, was the head teller at a
bank in Philadelphia. The bank was used by a New Jersey
drug ring to launder money. She'd been giving evidence to
the police, and her boss found out. Making a run for it, she
got as far as that rest stop. The police weren't too sympa-
thetic about Ben's father. Wrong time, wrong place, they
said. Too bad.

The two bodies were never found, but Ben sometimes
imagined them. He wondered if his father had woken up
and talked to that woman. He would have called her
"Ma'am," and he wouldn't have blamed her for anything.

Ben tried to talk about it with his mother, but she quietly
told him no. She wanted to turn the page and forget that
night. Maybe she should have listened to him, not kept it
all inside. A few years later, the month Ben entered college, she died, only forty-nine, her stomach eaten away by
cancer.

Those forty seconds continued to haunt Ben—the riddle
of his life. He'd been able to bring back every detail, down
to the shape of the woman's eyeglasses, the color of her
shoes. That was how he learned about the talent he had for
seeing and remembering. And one thing he remembered

didn't make sense. His father stepped over the cemetery fence and walked to their car. He put the key in the lock and opened the door, then: "Hey! What's going on over there?" Why the car? Why open the door? It came to Ben suddenly one evening, as he was falling asleep. Because those men in the dark suits weren't going to leave any witnesses. By opening the door, Ben's father showed the car was his. There was no one else in sight. The men naturally figured he was the only one around. He went out there and showed himself to protect his family as much as to try to save that woman.

Figuring that out made Ben understand some things about himself. That's what he told the recruiter from the Marshals Service when he interviewed for his job. He was fresh out of school and naive enough to think he ought to tell the whole truth. He wanted to help people, the same as his father. It was a way to repay the debt. The recruiter shifted nervously in her seat. This was only a job interview. She hadn't expected a story like that. "Ben, we do a job. Nobody who works for WITSEC can be obsessed with it. You can cope with that?" Ben assured her he could, and not long after that he started work. It was only a year later that he took on his first private client, a woman, a middle-aged, overweight accountant who'd been pressed into running tax dodges for a crime family in Atlanta. She came up with the new name, The Laundry Man.

A siren cut the still air of Congressional Cemetery. Ben jerked up, looking around the gravestone. OK, OK. Only a police cruiser, headed for the D.C. jail a few blocks north. He settled back. A fly was buzzing in the weeds next to him. He watched as it came closer and closer to the spider's web. When it was too close, one leg already stuck, Ben reached over and freed it. Obsession? Maybe. But he coped.

About six o'clock Ben stood to stretch his legs. He spotted a man getting out of a rust-bucket Buick on H Street. It was his partner, Larry Jong. Larry went in the side door of the convenience store. He owned the store and lived in the converted carriage house in the rear. Ben waited a while longer, until dusk, watching for signs that the police were keeping tabs on the area. He saw nothing, so he walked casually around the block, then ducked inside.

He expected to see Mrs. Liu at the cash register. She'd worked there since before Larry took over the place. Instead there was a younger woman. Ben didn't know her, but she had the same stick-thin build as Mrs. Liu and the same tired smile. "How's your mother?" he said politely.

"Doctor say four weeks in traction, then better. Able to walk again, sure."

"Oh?" Ben said. This was news to him. He'd ask Mrs. Liu's husband about it. Evenings he worked in the storeroom in the back, sorting stock. Mr. Liu wasn't there, though, and the room was a mess.

The carriage house was on the other side of the rear courtyard. The lower level was dark, and Larry's cat was snoozing in the doorway. Upstairs, Ben could see the blue flicker of a TV set. He picked up the cat. "Frosty, boy, how ya been?" At the top of the steps he tapped on the door, and it swung open. Larry was on a high stool, bent over a work table. "Hey, what happened—" Startled, Larry spun around, and the stool tipped sideways. He barely caught himself, and hurt his hand doing it.

"Sorry," Ben said. "Didn't she ring?" He meant Mrs. Liu's daughter. She should have rung the warning bell to let Larry know a visitor was on the way out.

"Nah, that kid don't know nothin'," Larry said. "Don't you knock anyway?"

Ben set the cat on the sofa. "Thought I did."

Larry went into the kitchen and came back with a couple of beers. "What happened to Mrs. Liu?" Ben asked.

"The old lady?" Larry applied his beer to his hand, rolling the can gently around the sore spot. "She got mugged down there in the store, two nights ago. Some ass-hole from that new crack lot by the river. Needed a few extra bucks for a deal, so he brought a lug wrench up here and went over her good."

"That's why her husband isn't here," Ben put in, "and why you're so jumpy." Larry nodded. "Did they catch the guy?"

"You betcha. Yuppie from Bethesda. Works for the Bureau of National Affairs. Drove down here in his wife's station wagon. Baby seats in the back. Man, what's the world comin' to?"

Ben couldn't answer that.

Larry opened his beer. Automatically, they toasted. Larry said, "You didn't call to say you were comin', and you look jumpy yourself. You got a problem, I think."

"I do," Ben said. "Well, we do." He pulled a chair in from the kitchen and sat down. He told him everything about the visit from Joquand and Van Allen and Mosby.

Halfway through the story Larry picked up the remote and clicked off the television. He listened to the rest staring at the blank screen. "Patrice Callan?" he muttered. "Damn. No more files, right?" He was stroking the cat, nose to tail, over and over. "You got rid of the files?"

"They're in storage," Ben said. "Lar, you're hurting him." He reached over and set the cat on the floor. "Just calm down, OK? Nobody's going to find the files. But that's not the problem. I didn't call right away because I don't have my phones."

The phone companies kept records of all calls made. Hardwired phones would have tied Ben and Larry together. If one of them got in trouble, the other would be in for it, too. So they always used mobile phones, bought and paid for under false names.

"You didn't!" Larry shouted. "You gave them your phones?"

"Not gave them. They were in the safe in the den. They couldn't miss the safe, and by now they've got it open."

Larry threw the remote, not right at Ben, but close enough to make him duck. "Oh, this just jim-dandy. Pretty soon it'll be rainin' around here—plop, plop, plop—U.S. Marshals and CIA spooks. They'll go through all my shit. I don't keep clean taxes like you, Ben. I'll do time over this." He closed his eyes and pinched the bridge of his nose, and then he exploded, "*Goddamn,* I told you she's trouble! That Patrice, first time I saw her picture, I told you she's gonna be a problem."

Ben retrieved the remote and set it on the television. "Nope. You said she was a cupcake, that's all. 'Wow, man, this one's a cupcake.'"

"Yeah, cupcake, I remember. So what? You screwed up Ben. It's your job to spot the fakers, not mine. You blew it."

"I did, Lar. It's my fault. I'm sorry."

"Then you make it right. You help that Joquand and Mosby and whoever. Send 'em off after Patrice, leave us alone."

With all the shouting, the cat had gone into hiding under the sofa. It came out now and streaked into the kitchen. Ben stood and looked at the table where Larry had been working. There was a New York driver's license with the lamination peeled back, a new photo ready to be inserted. "I need two full ID packs, one for her, one for me. Licenses, credit cards, the usual. And passports, good ones." He laid a wad of money on the table.

"You *help* this Joquand guy," Larry pleaded. "Get him off our backs."

"No. Patrice was a client. I won't roll over on her like that."

"Client?" Larry spat out. "She got us in this mess. Her and that Balazs. She stole your damn files, remember?"

"I remember. But have you wondered why? Those people in Palm Beach were for real. She was on the run. Why would she mess with me when I was helping her? Somebody had a lever on her. Balazs."

"You don't see it, do you?" Larry said. "That night by the canal in Georgetown. The two of you. Lovey-dovey, I said, and I meant it. She had you wrapped around her finger. You can't think straight about her." He sighed. "Look, it's not our problem, right? We'll go away, take a vacation. Let Joquand find her on his own."

"No. I can't leave it like that." Ben sat next to him on the sofa. "I spent eight weeks working with her. She lied to me, sure, but I got through to her." Larry started to argue again, and Ben held up his hand to stop him. "She changed. I have to believe that, Larry." They were quiet for a moment. The cat watched them from the kitchen. "Now she's in trouble. She may not even know it, but she needs help. I won't turn my back on her. You understand, as much as anybody."

Slowly Larry looked away. It was something he and Ben never talked about. A few years back, Larry's wife—married twenty-one years—died of an aneurysm. It was just as they were getting out of bed in the morning. She only had time to grab his hand before it was over. Larry loved her and needed her more than he realized. He went into a tailspin, depression growing so deep he eventually wouldn't leave his apartment except in the middle of the night, then wouldn't go out at all. Ben pitched in to help him, visiting every morning before work, and every evening. He tried talking him around, and, when that didn't work, he bought Frosty for him. Larry liked the cat, but it wasn't enough to spark him back to life. So Ben convinced him to buy the store. It didn't take much—in those days Larry could be pushed into doing just about anything. The store gave him a routine to help him through his days, and, before long, Mr. and Mrs. Liu had become his new family. It was exactly the right prescription, the life Larry needed. Up to that point, Larry had never thought much about what Ben did for his clients. It was all mumbo jumbo to him. But now he knew. He was living proof.

"So what are you going to do?" Larry asked quietly.

"Think about the big picture," Ben said. "Joquand and Van Allen—those CIA boys aren't on any task force. They're freelancing. And Balazs—I don't know what deal he's working on, but you can bet it's real trouble." He pointed at the money on the table. "I'll find Patrice. She'll know what's going on. Then I can try to work it out from that end. With luck, we'll all come out clean."

"With luck," Larry murmured. He stared at the floor for a long while before he reached for the cash. "Since Mrs. Liu, you know, the way she looked after she got beat up—I'm feelin' old these days." He glanced at Ben. "Where am I gonna go?"

"California. Go see your nephew in Fresno, the new doctor."

"That twerp? What kind of person becomes a proctologist by choice?" Larry scuffed his foot on the linoleum. "OK, sure. What the hell. Fresno will be all right."

As soon as Larry said it, he turned away, embarrassed. He'd lied, and Ben could always tell when he was lying. It put a wall between them, just as it did between Ben and everyone else. He didn't want to pry, but he couldn't help doing it. And about Fresno, he didn't care. It didn't make any difference where Larry went, as long as he got out of town.

Larry went into the kitchen and took a Cheerios box from the cupboard. He pulled out a Ziploc bag, then a second. "Patrice is blond, right? These should do. Say, what happened to the package I gave you before—Lawrence Murray?"

"It's Murray Lawrence, and it's already blown. It's the name I used for the phones."

Ben checked the things in the bags, the photo IDs (not bad, close enough), the expiration dates on the credit cards, the old visa stamps in the passports.

"How you gonna find her?" Larry said. "She was goin' south. New Orleans. She could be anywhere by now— South America, who knows?"

Ben was distracted, holding the two driver's licenses up to the light, looking for slit marks and excess glue. *"Tienes una cola,"* he answered after a moment.

"What's that mean?" Larry asked.

"Something she said that last night down by the canal." Ben closed the bags and put them in his knapsack. "She wouldn't have stuck with her original plan, not after she took those files. So where'd she go? There were a few clues, things she did and said, but one thing stuck out—*Tienes una cola.*" He nodded. "She's in New Mexico."

Larry gave a laugh and lifted his beer can in salute. "No use arguin' with that kind of logic." Then he held up the money. "Forty-five hundred here. Too much. Three grand's the charge for two full packages. You know that."

Ben zipped the knapsack shut. "Keep the rest on account. I may need to ask for help. How can I reach you?"

Larry took a piece of paper and wrote a phone number on it. "Ask for Chin. He'll know where to find me." His hand was shaking as he passed it over.

Ben wanted to give him a hug—crazy old man who'd been his friend for so long—but that wasn't their way. All he could do was mumble, "Sorry," again. He hitched his head toward the other room. "I'll help you pack. We can go to the airport together."

Ben took the bedroom, where he started tossing shirts and pants and underwear into a suitcase. He had just made his fourth trip into the closet when he noticed lights dancing in the trees out on Seventeenth Street. Red and blue—police bubbles. They were right in front of the store, two or three cars.

Ben had never been on the run in his life. He'd heard stories, from his clients, from Larry too. In the 1950s, Larry had spent three years dodging Mao's blanket-coated troops around Guangdong Province before he made it across the border to Hong Kong. He spent six months in a hospital recuperating. A tremble of fear still came into his voice when he talked about it. He always summed it up the same way. It wasn't running *away* that was the problem, it was having no place to run *to,* no sanctuary. That wore you down to dust.

The police out there might have nothing to do with Ben. They might be after some crackhead, or kids spray painting graves in the cemetery. It didn't matter. Once he'd slugged Van Allen and run, Ben's world had turned upside down. There were people he trusted—some he'd known for years—but he never let them get too close. The Laundry Man was that kind of secret. Larry was the only one he could count on now.

"Lar?" he called. "Better look out front."

"Damn!" Larry appeared in the doorway. He pointed at the clothes and suitcase. "Forget that garbage. We gotta go now."

They went to the kitchen. Larry took down three more cereal boxes and dumped the stacks of forms and certificates inside into the flight bag he'd been packing. He jerked open the window. A few feet below was the tin roof of the neighbor's garage. On the far side of that was an alleyway that let out on the back end of the block.

"You wait till I'm down. That roof's not so good." Larry tossed his bag out, then looked back at Ben. "You watch out for Callan. Maybe she changed, maybe not. Either way, she got under your skin."

He was halfway out when he heard a soft *yow.* Frosty was on the kitchen table, watching him with round green eyes. Larry hesitated, debating in his mind. "You're one damn good cat." He twisted through the opening and disappeared into the darkness.

As soon as Larry was out of sight, Frosty headed after him. Ben scooped him up. The cat spit and sank his claws into his arm, but Ben held tight, stroking him between the ears. "It's all right." There was no way Ben could just leave him. He'd spotted a pet carrier in Larry's closet, and, seconds later, he was ducking out the window, juggling the carrier and his knapsack.

The roof was slippery, but he made it across and swung down to the crumpled blacktop below. He looked around. "Larry? Larry, come on, take your damn cat!"

Larry was gone.

Ben took off up the alley. The cat was scared, crouched in a ball in a corner of the cage. He let out a long howl that ended in a choking cough, almost a sob. To Ben, it was the loneliest sound in the world.

SEVEN

Emile Balazs was home in St. Kitts, waiting for a phone call.
He heard laughter and looked out the long row of windows
fronting his office. Mick Laraby was on the veranda, playing rummy with Morena Herrera. Morena was Manuel's
daughter. She had a high forehead and perfectly propor-
tioned eyes and mouth. Her auburn hair fell straight and
sleek to her shoulders. As always, she sat in the shade. She
said it was for cancer protection, but Emile knew better.
For some Cubans, especially Miami Cubans, skin color was
a badge of rank. Morena kept herself pale enough to be
Cubano royalty.

She glanced up, and, catching his eye, blew him a kiss.
He smiled back. *Emile's girl*. That's what she called herself,
his *girl*, though she was forty-two years old. They'd had a
thing going for a few months. Her father didn't know about
it. Emile had started the affair figuring Morena could help
keep Manuel in line. But she was a tough one to figure, a
real hard case at times. Today would be a test for her. The
Herreras had come here expecting to meet a man from

Cuba, someone crucial to their plans. The meeting had fallen through, and Emile would soon break the bad news. Manuel was going to blow a fuse. Then Emile would see whose side Morena was on.

But that was for later. He pressed a button on the wall. A motor hummed; the blinds dropped over the windows. He put his feet up and watched the clock on his desk. The instant it clicked to 3:30, the phone rang. Before he picked up, he switched on a tape recorder. It was an expensive machine, undetectable by even the best technology. "Yeah?" he said.

"Emile, hello." Aaron Joquand's voice was flat and empty as a pane of glass. Did they teach him that at CIA school?

"Have you got anything for me?"

"Tennant seems to know what he's doing. We haven't found any sign of him yet. But it's early—"

"Early? It's been four days since you lost him."

"I lost him," Joquand admitted without any embarrassment.

Emile ground his teeth, holding back a curse. The two men had known each other since Joquand was assigned to the Caribbean beat by the CIA. Over the years they'd swapped a lot of information, traded favors. But they certainly weren't friends. They used each other, at times badly. More than once they'd come close to open war.

"What are you going to do next?" Emile asked.

"Keep looking for him," Joquand said, still with that silky-calm tone.

"Keep looking," Emile mimicked. He got up and paced behind the desk. "You'd better come up with something, Aaron. You started this whole landslide."

Joquand gave a quiet chuckle. "It was awkward, Emile, yes. But the keypad was important. Getting it out of Russia was important."

The keypad. Emile wished he'd never heard of it. The day he was being processed out of prison in Phoenix, Joquand had come to him with a proposition: go to Russia; pick up this small electronics item, a keypad. He offered a healthy fee. Joquand wanted Emile to do the job himself, not pass it off to someone else. They always did business one on one. Emile agreed, and the next day he left.

He got a room near Sheremetyevo, the Moscow airport, and spent his time hanging around the hotel coffee shop, waiting for a man named Yogi. Yogi, like the Indian wise men, like the Jellystone Bear. After two days Yogi showed up, a jumpy kid with a New Wave haircut and a cell phone on his belt that wouldn't stop ringing. Emile handed over the sealed courier bag Joquand had given him. Yogi gave him the keypad in a felt-lined case, together with a bundle of papers, Russian blueprints. So simple. Yogi didn't even open the courier bag, just gave it a shake—something inside rattled—and waved good-bye.

Emile went to the airport after the exchange. On the way, he looked over the blueprints and just about choked when he realized what the keypad was. He took it straight to a courier company and shipped it to the U.S. He damn well wasn't going to carry something like that through customs. Before long, his plane was taking off for Paris. Emile figured he'd lay over for the weekend, get some rest, maybe roll out to Longchamp and play the horses. Monday, he'd head back to the States.

It was in Paris that the wheels started to come off. Emile caught a nap when he got in. He was on his way to a late breakfast when he spotted two men following him. Tough looking, but old, well past their prime. One was carrying a flight bag. In the restaurant, Emile had just gotten settled in a booth when the men pushed in across from him. The one with the flight bag set it on the table and unzipped it. Yogi's head was inside. His hair was still perfect, moussed in place, but all his earrings had been ripped from his ears. He'd been alive when they'd done that, still able to bleed.

The man left the bag open. His Russian accent was so thick he spit when he talked, trying to get the English out. They'd been cheated, he said. He slammed a white stone on the table. Supposed to be rough diamonds, straight out of Sierra Leone. Six and a half million dollars' worth. Instead, quartz. He shook the stone in Emile's face. Worthless fucking quartz. Yogi swore that was all Emile had delivered. The man jerked the flight bag. The head lolled inside. So where are the diamonds? Where?

It didn't take five seconds for Emile to figure out what had happened. Joquand had stiffed them. No use wondering why. All that mattered was Emile didn't have anything to offer those two Russian mastodons. Not the keypad. Certainly not the diamonds. They glowered, waiting for an answer.

Emile had been in spots like this before. His way out was to gamble, betting on surprise. Smiling calmly, he reached as if to get something from his coat pocket; then he slapped the flight bag. Yogi's head bounced down in the aisle, where a waitress stopped it with a neat soccer-style toe trap, while balancing a tray of crêpes on her shoulder. She thought it was a joke, a mannequin's head, until she felt the dead flesh give under her shoe. The scream she let out brought people to a halt a block away.

And that's how Emile's bet paid off. Both Russians had turned their heads, just enough for him to rear back and slam the table into them. He was at the door before they had their guns out, and, with all the customers scrambling around, he made it to a cab before the Russians got outside. Seventy minutes later, he was on the train for London. There he caught a plane to Montreal, then hopped another one for home.

He picked up the keypad from the shipping company and phoned Joquand to tell him he had it. Emile asked for a hefty sweetener to their deal. That keypad was worth six and a half million. He ought to have a piece of that for all the risk he'd taken. But Joquand just chuckled, that purr of his, like a kitten. He never intended to pay for the keypad, not millions anyway. Maybe he could scrape together fifty grand for Emile. Fickle bastard. Always with his side bets and angle plays. He had more phases than the moon.

The Russians didn't want the keypad back, either. They knew who Emile was, and they let him know they were going to get paid, or he was going to end up with *his* head in a bag—or worse. That's what drove Emile into witness protection, and drove him eventually to ask Manuel Herrera for help.

Herrera came up with the six and a half million for the diamonds, and the Russians went home happy. That would have been the end of it, except, before Emile delivered the keypad to Herrera, it vanished, right out of Emile's office safe. Now he had it, now he didn't. And that put him where he'd been for the last five months, trying to find that damn keypad so he could close his account with Herrera and end this nightmare. Seemed like that was the story of Emile's life, jumping from one fucking hot spot to another, hoping someday, *someday*, he'd end up on the jackpot.

On the telephone there was silence. Joquand had been waiting patiently all the time Emile was thinking. "You know Aaron, you're a grade-A prick, hanging me out to dry like that."

Joquand laughed. "The game never changes. I keep today's promises today. Tomorrow, we start over again."

It was one of Joquand's favorite sayings. How do you deal with a man like that, a man who *tells* you he's not going to be honest?

Joquand said, "I'll keep an eye out for Tennant. He'll turn up. And there's one other thing. I was looking into Patrice Callan's background. Did you know when she was a kid, she spent some time in New Mexico? Somewhere north of Albuquerque."

Emile did know this, and Mick Laraby had come up with another lead pointing to that part of the country. Mick had hired a couple of men—bounty hunters, a nasty pair, real leeches—and sent them to New Mexico to see what they could turn up on Tennant or Callan. Emile wasn't going to share that with Joquand, though. "New Mexico? Could be useful. Thanks."

"Sure. I'll call tomorrow, same time."

Emile gave a cold laugh. "That a promise?" After he hung up, he clicked off the recorder and checked the clock. The call had taken only eight minutes, and put him in the worst possible mood. He felt like throwing something, hitting somebody. He went to the bar in the back of the office and poured a shot of 180-proof rum. He downed it in a gulp, and mixed three rum and Cokes. These he took out to the veranda.

When Morena saw him, she glanced around to make sure no one was watching, then gave him a lusty kiss. She had two temperatures, volcanic and icy. Seemed like it was going to be a hot night, if he could just get through this pissing afternoon.

"Boss, you don't look so good," Mick said. "Bet I know who you were talkin' to." He ran his hand through the air and hissed through his teeth. *Shsssss*. That's the way Mick always referred to Aaron Joquand. The Rogue Wave.

"What? Yeah." Emile had been distracted by a flash in the jungle below the house. He decided it was nothing and sat down.

Mick was smirking. "I know what'll cheer you up. Strip poker. Whatcha say, Morena? I've been wonderin' all day what color your panties are." Then he hitched to attention in his chair. "Mr. Herrera, ya get everything fixed up with your pilot?"

Morena's father was coming up the steps. With his cane, he moved sideways, crablike, but quickly. Behind him was one of Emile's guards. The guards usually wore gray uniforms, but this one had on a flowered shirt, thinking he'd be less conspicuous. It wasn't working. "Quit following me, you jackal," Manuel snapped.

Morena scrambled up. "Papa, come, sit." She kissed his cheek. With a grunt, he brushed her aside.

Manuel jabbed his cane at the swimming pool below. "Sister's got a new boyfriend, eh, Emile?"

Balazs came to stand beside him. He hadn't known Isabel was here. She'd been staying at her own house in town the last few days. When he saw her, his jaw muscles tensed with anger. She was lying facedown on a chaise with her bikini top undone. A short, dark-skinned man with broad shoulders and a wasp waist was slathering sunscreen on her back while he whispered in her ear.

"Looks like she's been watchin' too many *Gidget* movies," Mick said. "If that joker gets any closer, they'll be wearin' the same bathing suit."

"Who is he?" Emile said.

"Nobody, Boss. A tourist. Iz met him down the market yesterday."

"Isabel!" Emile called. She didn't respond. The wind was too strong. He was going to have to yell to be heard, and that would be a further humiliation in front of Herrera. Isabel had brought one of her house servants with her. The woman glanced up at the veranda, then spoke a quiet warning. Isabel quickly slid over and resnapped her top. Chuckling, the man unsnapped it again.

Balazs gave up. He'd deal with Isabel later. Just one more ball to juggle.

He led Manuel to the table. As they sat, the old man shoved the chair next to him away. This was another of his superstitions: bad luck sitting beside an empty chair.

Emile made a show of stretching out, getting comfortable. "Mick told me you had lunch in town. O'Malley's. Nice place."

Mick grinned. "Except ya gotta watch out for the roti. Use their own special meat. Woof-woof."

Emile gave him a sharp look. Lay off the jokes, already. But Manuel seemed to enjoy it. He cackled. "Thought I recognized the taste."

As the laughter died, a bird landed on the table. The finches here were tame as puppies. Manuel flipped one of the cards at it, and the bird fluttered away. "Sunday afternoon, Emile," he said. "We been sittin' on our asses all weekend, and I still don't see any Air Force officers. You hiding him somewhere?"

He was talking about Luis Roque, the man he and Morena had come here to meet. Roque was a colonel in the Cuban Air Force.

Mick answered. Balazs had told him to, figuring that might take some of the sting out of it. There was no joking in his voice now. "There's a problem in Cuba. Somebody tried to blow up a coast guard boat the other night at Mariel Port. Castro's got the red arse over it, big time. Colonel Roque's in lockdown on his base at Holguín. Same thing for the whole damn Cuban military—"

"*Jesus, Mick!*" Balazs exploded. "Why the fuck didn't you tell us?"

"Yeah, sorry." Mick hurried to explain. "I was still hopin' Roque would make it off the island. But you gotta understand, those Secret Police of Castro's are everywhere. If Roque does a runner today, he never gets back in. Then where would we be?"

Manuel had picked up another card. He was holding it so tight his hand was trembling. "Emile, you made me come down here for one reason: to meet Roque." His voice dropped to a teeth-clenched whisper. "But instead what I get is a lecture from this whore about Castro's Secret Police. You think I don't know about those bastards?"

Mick was scared, but he wouldn't back down. "Cuba's a

powder keg right now. Your people fuck around there—shoot up a hotel, blow up a boat—and Castro just clamps down tighter. Last time you were here, I thought we had an agreement. You stay out of it, let us do our job."

Manuel's face was pink with rage. "I'm not gonna wait forever while you two jerk yourselves off."

"Dammit," Mick snapped, "we need Roque. Do you want him safe and sound? Or do you want to blow his cover, just so he can come here and kiss your ring?"

"Mick, that's enough," Balazs cut in. "When *can* you get Roque out?"

Mick's face was as flushed as Manuel's. He drank half his rum and Coke to calm down. "Not tomorrow, for sure. Tuesday'd be my guess, but—"

Balazs broke in again. "Tuesday then. Manuel, why don't you go back to Miami? I'll bring Colonel Roque there. We can meet at the Biltmore, have a long talk."

Mick said, "No good, Boss. Roque shouldn't be in the U.S., him bein' a Cuban citizen, military and all. If anybody found out—"

Balazs shook his finger like a club. "Enough bullshit, Mickey. Fix it."

"I hear ya," Mick muttered. Then he turned to Herrera. "All these fireworks you've got goin' in Cuba—if you aren't careful, Castro's gonna start giving tit for tat, blow up something in Miami. You prepared for that?"

Herrera stared at him but wouldn't answer. He pushed up from his chair. "Emile, you finally said something right. Our deal's broke. You *fix it*. One week. You get Colonel Roque out of Cuba and bring him to me. And you get that keypad. *One week*." He hobbled down the stairs.

Morena followed him, not saying a word to Emile. So much for helping to keep her father in line.

The two men toyed with their drinks and looked into the haze. "That went well," Emile said sourly.

Laraby breathed out a sigh, getting rid of his own tension. "Let it go. Herrera's a tough-ass. Gets off on stirring things up. Just play him along like always."

Emile thought a while before he answered. "You're right. I'll show him the blueprints before he leaves, the ones from Moscow. That ought to make him feel better. What do you make of that 'one week' nonsense? Herrera's never talked about any kind of deadline before."

"I dunno. Maybe he got it from his tarot cards, the loony bugger."

Emile gave a dry laugh. "When can you get Roque to Florida, really?"

"Not for a while. Thursday, earliest."

"Damn," Emile groaned. "Never do business with Cubans, Mickey, that's lesson number one."

"Way I remember, we didn't have much choice. It was Manuel's six and a half million or nobody's. And if we come through for him, he said—"

"I know. A big payday. You and me'll be rich gents living on the Riviera."

"At least we know what Herrera wants," Mick said. "What about your CIA pal? Why's he bein' so helpful?"

"Joquand's still after the keypad. He couldn't pay six and a half million for the damn thing. He's on his own in this, no help from the Agency. He's just hoping that keypad will fall in his lap."

Mick finished his drink. "He's too unpredictable. I say we drop him."

"No," Balazs said. "We need to string him along. Why do you think I've been getting Joquand on tape? If this deal goes sour, we're in deep trouble. Joquand's got a lot of reach, can help us a lot of ways. He's the best hole card we've got, and we can squeeze him with those tapes. He won't want that stuff to leak back to his CIA buddies. They'd kick him out on his ass." Mick could see it now. He grinned. Balazs went on, "That little jerk is like the monkey under the coconut tree. Shake the tree and see what falls out. Doesn't care who gets hit. This time, maybe Joquand's going to be the one who has to duck."

Balazs stood up. "When I'm through with Herrera, I want to talk to Isabel. Make sure she sticks around."

"Will do," Mick said.

Emile turned slowly to him. His eyes were hard as bullets. "And call your bounty hunter friends in New Mexico. See if they've got a bead on Tennant or Callan." He tapped Mick hard on the chest. "You hired them, Boy-o. They damn well better come through for us."

"They will, Boss. Don't worry."

As Emile walked off, Mick reached behind his shirt collar, wiping away the sudden sweat on the back of his neck.

EIGHT

Ben left the photograph next to the cash register and walked to the shop window, humming casually. The photo had spooked the boy, and Ben wanted to give him some space, let him settle down.

It was Sunday, midday, in Taos, New Mexico. A raw north wind rattled the flags and pennants along the storefronts. For a few seconds the sun broke through the clouds, turning the adobe buildings glacial white. The cold didn't deter the shoppers. They scurried in and out of the art galleries and stores around the plaza like ants in search of prize crumbs. High Road Souvenirs was an exception. Ben and the boy were the only ones there. The merchandise—gaudy kites and pinwheels, cheap T-shirts, turquoise jewelry made in Taiwan—wasn't upscale enough for the tourists of Taos.

For the past four days, Ben had been making his way north from Santa Fe. He stopped at gas stations and curio shops and front porch art galleries and at all the Indian casinos, showing the mug shot of Patrice he'd taken from

Ken Van Allen. "You know this woman? Take a good look. The picture's old." He got a lot of raised eyebrows and a few lewd comments, but the boy was the first one who seemed to recognize her. And so far, he wasn't talking.

"My name's Ben."

After a moment the kid mumbled, "I'm Denny." His eyes darted around, out the window, under the counter.

"It's nice to meet you, Denny." Ben moved farther away, to the far side of the store. There were some airbrushed paintings on the wall, tawny high-desert scenes. The signature at the bottom of each was big and childish. "Did you make these?"

Denny answered slowly, as if he didn't want to admit it. "Yeah."

"I like this one," Ben said, pointing at a howling wolf.

Denny's face softened. He almost smiled. "Yeah?"

"You got the shadows just right, pale from the moonlight."

Ben turned and looked at him. He couldn't have been more than fifteen. Red ridges of acne covered his cheeks. He had a way of dipping his head to try to hide it. Ben came back across the room and tapped the picture. "She's pretty, isn't she? Most guys would notice." Denny's face turned a darker shade of red. "And her eyes. Bright green. Hard to forget eyes like that." Denny shot a glance up at him, then looked away again.

Behind the counter was a doorway closed off with a beaded curtain. Another door back there opened and banged shut. Someone sighed loudly. Denny half turned in his chair.

"Maybe your boss knows something about her," Ben said, loudly enough so his voice would carry.

The curtain parted, and a gray-haired woman hobbled through. She had a walking cast on one foot and used a single crutch to help her balance. She fumbled with the zipper on her parka. "Knows something about what?"

Ben pushed the photograph forward. "Ever seen her before?"

"No." She was too quick about it, barely giving the picture a glance.

"You sure?"

She shoved the mug shot back at him. "I said so, didn't I?" She sounded blustery, short on patience, but it didn't cover her fear. She looked under the counter, just as the boy had done. What did they have under there? An alarm? A gun?

Now that Denny wasn't alone, he seemed to relax a little. He leaned forward, studying the photograph. The woman laid her hand on his shoulder. "Sorry, mister. We can't help you."

Ben clicked the edge of the picture. All those days coming up empty, and now this. The two of them so scared, so fast. Why? Patrice wouldn't make anybody feel that way.

He set the mug shot back on the counter and crossed his arms. He wasn't going anywhere until he got some answers. "Her name's Patrice." He stared into the boy's face. "What do you know about her?"

The woman stiffened. He was as much as calling her a liar. "Goddammit then," she said, bending under the cash register. She came up with a canister, half the size of a shaving cream can. Before she had it leveled, Ben vaulted the counter. He grabbed the can, and grabbed her so she wouldn't trip over her crutch.

"Grizz," it said on the can's label, over a picture of a bear. Pepper spray.

"For God's sake, settle down," he said. "I'm not going to hurt you."

The woman glared at him, quivering, anger and fear flitting through her. She had to crane her head far back, he was so much taller. It made Ben feel suddenly foolish. He went back around the counter. "This can's brand new, not a speck of dust. You don't even know how to use it." He yanked out the safety pin and, after a moment, tossed the can to the boy. "What are you two so scared of?"

The woman pursed her lips. She looked mad enough to chew glass.

The boy eased off his stool. "It's okay. He wasn't one of them."

She blinked but didn't take her eyes off Ben.

"What do you mean, one of them?" Ben said.

The boy rolled the can from one hand to the other. It gave him comfort, a feeling of confidence. That's what Ben had expected. "Two men were here yesterday looking for that woman. Had the same picture. I let on maybe I'd seen her around."

"What men?"

"I don't know. Big, that's about all I can remember. Dressed like cowboys. And mean. I've never seen guys as mean as that. As soon as I said I might know her they started shoving me around. Real threatening, you know?"

"So what happened?" Ben said.

"Aunt Luce"—Denny nodded at the woman—"heard from upstairs and called the cops. They came with the siren on, and those two jerks lit out. We haven't seen them since." He shivered slightly, chilled by the memory of it. "Why are you looking for her?"

Ben shrugged. "That's sort of complicated." It wasn't good enough for the boy. He set his jaw, as if maybe he wouldn't talk anymore. "She's headed for trouble," Ben said. "Sounds like you caught some of it yesterday." He fingered the mug shot, still on the counter. "I want to warn her."

Denny slumped back onto his stool, thinking it over. "She liked my paintings. We talked about them a long time—the paper I used, cutting the masking, mixing the paints, all that. It was fun."

"When was that?" Ben asked.

"She only came in once, in January. We've got that 'Help Wanted' sign in the window. Been there over a year, but I'm cheaper than anybody else Aunt Luce would hire." The woman sputtered a curse, and Denny grinned. "When she found out there was no job, she stayed on, maybe half an hour, talking. She was nice. I liked her."

Of course you did, Ben thought. She's got that knack. "Do you know how I could find her?"

"Not really. She said she lived south of town. That was all."

"It's a start. Thanks."

"None of our damn business," Aunt Luce mumbled. She threw one last glare at Ben and hitched back through the curtain.

Ben pocketed the mug shot. "Why'd you decide to trust me?"

Denny said, "That picture's black and white. You said her eyes were green. You must know her." He seemed proud of his deduction. "I figure that makes you better than those other two assholes."

"You figured right. Did you tell them what you told me—she lives south of town?"

Denny gave his biggest grin yet. "Fuck, no. I sent them north, toward Costilla and the border."

"Good for you," Ben said.

Denny looked around at the curtain and lowered his voice. "You'd better go. She's probably calling the cops again."

Ben reached to shake his hand. "Keep up with the painting. I'd like to come back someday, see one of those galleries out there with your name on it." Denny blushed the color of a plum.

Ben had parked his rental car a couple of blocks away. For ten minutes he sat behind the wheel, poring over the map of Taos he'd bought that morning. Roads spidered out of town to the south. He'd just come from that direction and hadn't found anyone who knew Patrice. That meant she was really lying low. That was good. As long as she stayed hidden, she stayed safe. That wouldn't last forever, though.

He took out the mug shot and ran his finger slowly over her face. It was all he'd had of her the last few days—that cold black-and-white picture. More than ever, he wanted to see her in the flesh.

NINE

It was late afternoon in St. Kitts, and the heat of the day lingered. Emile Balazs stood in front of his office, looking down at the pool. His sister still lay on a chaise, snuggling with the man with the wasp waist. Her house servant had moved to the corner of the patio to give them some privacy. Isabel's laughter carried up to the veranda, making Emile smile. He liked having her around. Lately he'd been feeling slow and heavy, boxed in. She buoyed him up. She could shine a light on the gloomiest of his days. Still, he wasn't looking forward to the conversation he was going to have with her. It was business, and he didn't like getting her involved.

"You wanted to see me, Mr. Balazs?" The guard with the flowered shirt was on his way up the stairs.

"Yeah, Layton, come here," Emile said. He pointed past the patio, to the trees down the slope. "There's something out there in the jungle. Flashing, bright, like a mirror. Seen it a couple of times. Go down to the lower path and check it out."

83

"Sure."

"And change that shirt. You look like fucking Don Ho."

"Yes, sir." He took off at a trot. Emile followed a few seconds later.

Isabel's house servant was named Mary, and Emile didn't care for her much. She didn't act like a servant, but rather like a nanny. She cooked Isabel's meals and picked out her clothes, did her nails and trimmed her hair. And she was too protective when it came to Emile. When she saw him padding down the steps, she hurried across the patio. "Isabel, you better be gettin' up from there. Your brother don't want to see you makin' no man like that."

Isabel flopped off the chaise. The man stood up, duck-walking around the bulge in the front of his bathing suit. Mary choked down a laugh. "Af'noon, sir," she called to Balazs.

Balazs didn't even glance at her. "Isabel, I need to speak to you." To the man he added, "You can wait inside." Then he changed his mind and stepped closer, giving him a hard stare. "Or better yet, head back to your hotel."

The man shuffled nervously. The lump in his trunks shriveled. "Sure. I'll catch you later, Isabel."

"Bye," she called, without much emotion. She'd had enough attention for today.

Emile waited until he heard the man's car leaving. "Haven't seen you around lately, Iz."

"The other day you were mean to me, you and that awful Manuel. I'm not a Fruit Loop."

"Old news. Get over it."

Isabel settled on the chaise, stretching from head to toe. Her breast almost slipped out of her suit top. She left it that way, hoping to nettle him. "I've been around. I was here last night . . . with Davey."

"Davey? That your friend, is it? You smug twit."

She hated to be called names, since they were kids. She punched at him, only half in jest. Laughing, he dodged her.

84

Balazs turned to Mary. He didn't speak, but nodded at the far side of the pool, indicating she should leave them alone. When she was gone, he said, "It's been a tough day, Iz. Don't make it worse. I've got some questions for you. Important."

"For me?" She tried to keep it light, but it was hard. Emile's tone was crisp, metallic, like a machine stamping out the syllables.

He tapped her finger, where she used to wear her wedding ring. "You've been a busy girl since Finney died. How do you think he'd feel about all the men in your life?"

Under the best of circumstances, Isabel didn't like to talk about her dead husband. "Finney . . . he always wanted me to have fun."

Emile eyed her steadily. "Let's talk about one man in particular. Peter Saar. Pretty silver hair. Stayed down at the presbytery with the priests."

Surprise came onto her face. "How'd you know about him?"

"Found out yesterday. Your gardener remembered seeing him. Said Saar visited you a couple of times. What'd you two talk about?"

Isabel wasn't sure where this was leading, but she sensed it was dangerous ground. She covered her hesitation by coughing and tucking her breast back into her top.

Emile said, "Let's start with where he came from: New Mexico. Saar had a letter of introduction from an Archbishop out there, in a town called Gallup. That's how he came to be at the presbytery. Did he mention that to you?"

Isabel stood up and he grabbed her wrist. "Look," she said, "I spent some time with Peter. He's a friend. So what?" She tried to pull away but he held firm. Exasperated, she said, "I'll answer your bloody questions, Emby, but I'm cold. I'm going to put on a shirt." She kissed her finger and laid it on the end of his nose. After a moment, he let her go.

Emile wandered over to the edge of the patio. To the west, in the cane field on Monkey Hill, someone had started a fire. Smoke swirled up, lacing the air with the scent of char and molasses.

Behind him, a car started. Now who's that? he wondered lazily. He turned and saw Isabel's Toyota lurch up the driveway. *"Bitch,"* he snarled. An instant later he was sprinting down the steps to the lawn.

The gravel road curved up to the ridge and back around. There was a shortcut to it through the jungle, and that's where he headed. He was so filled with rage he was spewing curses and didn't know it. Around a bend, one of his guards appeared, walking the other way. He was carrying a machine pistol in one hand. Emile grabbed the gun, shouting orders. He didn't know the man's name. "Stop the car. Isabel. *Come on!*"

Balazs was first to reach the road. He was in his bare feet and his soles shrieked with pain, skidding on the sharp stones. The car was already twenty yards below and gaining speed. He bellowed for her to stop. She didn't. He clicked off the safety and leveled the gun.

No, he couldn't shoot. His eyes locked on hers in the car mirror. Isabel's hand slipped out the window. She waved brightly, and then, as an afterthought, she flipped him the finger.

The guard had stopped at the edge of the road. Emile flung the gun to him. Stomping up the path, he barked, "Bring her back!"

TEN

In the jungle below Emile Balazs' mansion, a man named Oscar Alarcon crouched in a blind of palm fronds. It was suffocatingly hot, and he was so dehydrated he felt dizzy. He shifted his weight, trying to ease the knotted muscles in his legs. Despite the pain he chuckled, recalling a fable he'd heard his father tell. The thirsty elephant and the river snake. Then his eyes filled with tears. Papa was dead, only ten months, and remembering him still stung.

Oscar was an emotional man. He cried at weddings and retirement parties. He cried at high school soccer matches. Oscar Alarcon was a spy for the Cuban government. All that crying was odd for a man in his line of work, but his masters in Havana saw a benefit in it. No one would ever suspect a tender fish like Oscar was a spy. So, as soon as he completed his training, they sent him north to Miami. His job was to keep an eye on the Cuban-Americans in South Florida.

Oscar ran a high-class insurance business in Coral Gables. Life insurance was his specialty. Of course he cried at all the funerals. Behind their backs he called his clients *"Gusanos."* Worms. He went to their cocktail parties and country club dinners. He picked up all the gossip. And that's just what the honchos in Havana wanted. Oscar was a success, the perfect man for the job.

But recently, he'd dropped out of the social scene. His masters in Cuba thought something big was in the wind, and Manuel Herrera was in the thick of it. For over a month, Oscar had been tailing Herrera and reporting back on everything he did.

Oscar adjusted the fronds in the blind. He couldn't hold out much longer. He'd already started to make mistakes. Twice in the last hour he'd leaned out to take a photo, and the lens of the camera had caught the sun. Might as well send up a signal flare: Here I am! Stupid pictures. All they needed in Havana was the voice recording. They could screen out the background noise, break down every word.

He studied the mansion with his binoculars. Emile Balazs was on the upper veranda with one of the guards. In his earphone Oscar heard: "Yeah, Layton, come here." The rest was muffled. He tweaked the parabolic microphone, trying for a better angle. Damn cheap equipment. He'd bought it in Miami Beach, a store called The Spyhop Shop. It was pure crap compared with the equipment he'd trained on in Moscow. So long ago. Russia had fangs, America had that chump Ronald Reagan, and Oscar still had his hair.

He grinned and stroked his bald head, then his beard. He was vain about the beard. He trimmed it to a point, which highlighted the white streak in the middle. In bed, his wife called him Pepé, after Pepé Le Pew, the cartoon skunk. He didn't mind. She was only twenty-four, and she was beautiful. Fidel Castro had sent her to Oscar as a gift. She helped write his reports to Cuba, and she was a salve to his loneliness.

Balazs finished with the guard and jogged down the steps to the pool. Oscar continued to adjust the sound equipment. The voices faded in and out, then suddenly came through clearly. ". . . you and that awful Manuel. I'm not a Fruit Loop."

Oscar jerked out the earphone. He'd heard something new, off in the trees.

Sheeew, shew. Sneezing.

Before he set up the blind that morning, he'd sprinkled a big bottle of hot pepper over a stretch of bushes crisscrossing the path upslope of him. The path was rarely used, but someone might come down that way, and they'd have to climb through those bushes. The pepper was an early warning system. *Sheceew.* Maybe not early enough. The intruder was a hundred meters away and closing.

Oscar slapped the blind apart and stuffed his equipment into his two duffel bags.

Already the intruder had cut the distance in half. Worse, Oscar had caught a new sound, a faint *clink-clink*. It was metal, probably a shoulder strap for a shotgun or machine pistol.

Oscar didn't have any science-fiction spy gadgets to protect himself. Cuba was too poor for that. He had to get along with what was on hand. All through these hills there were marijuana patches planted by Rastafarian growers. They couldn't guard the crops day and night, so they left booby traps. Nothing too dangerous, just warnings. On his way in that morning, Oscar had found a pot garden. It was surrounded by concealed strips of lath spiked with nails. He'd picked up a few and brought them along.

He scurried forward, setting out three of the strips. After dropping a palm frond over each, he backed off, using another frond to brush away his footprints. Then he ducked behind a big cycad, where he could watch. From one of the duffels, he took out a knife, a delicate looking thing, but big enough to be deadly.

The guard was twenty meters away, crashing through the undergrowth, cursing each time he sneezed. If he stayed on the path, he'd go right past. His eyes and nose were streaming, and he stopped to wipe them on the tail of his flowered shirt. Looking up, he spotted something. A red bandanna. Oscar's. He must have dropped it.

The guard stepped down the slope, bringing his shotgun to port arms. His foot missed the first lath strip. The second. From the look on his face, he wasn't worried, just curious. Oscar crouched, ready to jump out. He had killed before, without hesitation. And afterward, he had not cried.

Another step. The man leaped in the air and crashed to his knees. *"Bloody whore!"* A nail had gone deep into his heel. Yanking it free, he glanced around at the way the fronds were arranged. "Fucking Rasta bastards." He shouldered his gun and limped up the path in the direction he'd come. The pepper got him again, bringing another round of sneezing. "Jesus, love me," he muttered.

Oscar waited for the man to get well away before he took off downhill. The slope was clotted with weeds and palms and scruffy banana trees. The duffels weighted him down, slapping at his sides.

After twenty minutes, the land leveled out. Here the sugarcane began. His bags snagged on the tall plants, and he had to bull his way through. It was even hotter here than in the jungle. His head spun, and he grew short of breath. Then without warning, he broke free, falling facedown on a narrow sandy lane. The cane trucks used this track during the harvest. Somewhere along here, he'd left his car.

Oscar took a bearing with his compass and stumbled off to the west. Soon he came to the car, parked in a cleft in the cane. He popped open the trunk and grabbed the extra canteen he'd left behind. He poured water down his throat. Better. Better.

He was in no hurry now. He couldn't leave until dark, when no one would spot him. He took another long drink. The rustle of the cane in the breeze was gentle, lulling. It reminded him of where he grew up, the little sugarcane town of Aguacate. He sat down in the shade of the car. Before a minute was up, he was asleep.

Oscar awoke in the dusk. He heard a droning sound, and it took a moment for his thoughts to clear enough for him to recognize it. He stood and watched as a twin-engine plane nosed into the sky above the cane. The Basseterre airport was right over there. Enough light remained for him to make out the ID number on the tail. It was Manuel Herrera's plane. He was heading back to Florida. Oscar smiled. His work here was done. Tomorrow, he'd be with his wife again, in his own bed.

He opened the car trunk and took out a satchel holding a satellite telephone and scrambler. The phone was one of his most prized possessions, not off-the-shelf junk, but high-quality electronics, sent to him from Havana just a few weeks ago. He connected the wires and antenna and dialed. On the first ring a woman answered, and Oscar said, "This is Orchid. twenty-two, nine, twenty-two, four." The numbers were today's access code.

He waited through the interminable clicks and buzzes as the call was transferred. Someone coughed delicately and said, "Orchid, how are you today?"

The voice was distorted by the scrambler, but Oscar thought he recognized it. He imagined Fidel Castro seated at a simple desk, the phone cradled to his ear. "I am well, sir. I am in St. Kitts." Oscar was standing tall, at attention. "I have news of Manuel Herrera."

"Good! Listen, Orchid, a colleague is here. Give your report to him." The great man coughed again, and murmured something as he passed the phone over.

"Orchid, good day."

Even with the scrambler, Oscar knew that breathy, unctuous tone. Carlos Sarabia was Interior Minister of Cuba, in charge of the Secret Police. Lately he'd grown closer to Castro than his own shadow. "Good day, sir," Oscar said.

"Manuel Herrera just left St. Kitts. He spent the weekend with Emile Balazs."

"And did you find out anything interesting?" He sounded distant and lazy, a cat just roused from a nap.

"I'm not sure. They mentioned a Colonel Roque from our air base at Holguín."

"Roque? Yes?" Sarabia's voice picked up. "What did they say about him?"

"Herrera came here to meet him, but one of Balazs' men told him Roque was in lockdown at Holguín and would not be able to leave. Herrera was furious."

"Colonel Roque is in lockdown," Sarabia said, "and he'll stay there a few more days. You are married, Orchid. You know. On the wedding night, the bride keeps the groom waiting. She seems all the more beautiful when finally she comes to him."

"I see your point." But Oscar didn't see the point at all. He had no idea who this Colonel Roque was or how he fit in. That was nothing new. Oscar's job was to be eyes and ears, not brain.

He said, "They talked about the attacks in Cuba, the Coast Guard boat at Mariel. They are worried we will retaliate, in Miami maybe."

"Good," Sarabia chuckled. "Let them worry."

Oscar had no comment on that. He said, "I'll send the audio tapes and photos to you by the regular courier." Then he hesitated. "There was one other thing."

"Yes?" Sarabia said, impatient now.

"Balazs is trying to find some people for Herrera. In New Mexico. A—" Oscar closed his eyes to help him think. "Patrice Callan and Ben Tennant."

"Mmmmm," Sarabia murmured. He chuckled again. "New Mexico. Very good. Callan and Tennant. We'll look into it."

Sarabia started to sign off, then said, "Wait." Oscar heard the phone being handed over.

"Orchid, you still there?"

Oscar stood at attention again. "Yes, *Señor Presidente.*"

"Don't fool yourself about Herrera. He is old, but not so old, and he has many friends. Congressmen, judges—all the ones in Washington lick his boots. Be careful, but stay close. Stay with Herrera. With you, we keep one step ahead." He coughed again, a painful hack. Was he really ill? There were so many rumors. But the voice came back strong. "Orchid, of all my flowers, you are my favorite. Good luck."

Oscar slowly put down his phone. He looked around at the sugarcane. The wind sighed through the leaves. It made him think again of the fields of Aguacate, and of his father. Homesick, exhausted, he sat down in the sand and wept.

ELEVEN

Tienes una cola . . . you have a tail. The words were like song lyrics that Ben couldn't get out of his head. It was Monday morning, the fifth day since he left Washington. The harsh New Mexico sun beat through the windshield of his rented Ford. He glanced away at the pastureland beside the road. That was stretching it some, calling the track he was on a road. Spring runoff had turned the red dirt into soupy mud. The rear wheels of the car spun toward the ditch and back. It was like a dance, sway to the right, sway to the left. *Tienes una cola* . . . you have a tail.

He had stayed the night in a chain motel on the outskirts of Taos. That was after spending the afternoon and evening showing Patrice's picture around the south side of town. Except for the boy at the plaza, nobody remembered seeing her. Still, Ben felt he was close now. That's why he'd had trouble falling asleep. When he found her, what then? How should he handle her? He tried to plan it out, but his mind wandered. He thought about the way she had left her room at his house, clean as a hospital operating room. She'd fleeced him and washed her hands of him, that easily. He remembered her that last night in Georgetown when she was dancing, her eyes closed, a distant, bewitched smile on her face. What was behind that smile? Something? Nothing? It all made him feel edgy—that old itch coming back.

At dawn he got up, grabbed a cup of coffee at a gas station, and headed out of town. His first few stops hadn't panned out, but luck struck just after nine o'clock. He was in the hamlet of Truchas, eight thousand feet up in the Sangre de Cristo Mountains.

Truchas was so small it had only one street, angling off the back road from Taos to Española. Sometimes locals came out to the intersection, just to watch the traffic pass. Today it was an old man named Ernesto Vigil. He was drinking Mountain Dew and eating a peanut-butter-and-jelly sandwich. As Ben pulled over, Vigil scowled and hunched in his coat. He didn't like having his breakfast interrupted. Then, when he saw the picture, he had a moment of surprise. "Hey," he sputtered, "that's Sweetheart!"

"You know her?"

"Sure. She's diff'rnt, you know? But yeah, that's her, by golly." He kissed the air. "Sweetheart!"

So Vigil drew Ben a map. Back end of Truchas, turn right on the dirt farm road. Follow across the big promontory to the south. Last house on the road.

Vigil graciously accepted the ten dollars Ben offered and waved an impish good-bye with his sandwich. Now, struggling to keep moving, almost up to his axles in mud, Ben wondered if sending him out here was the old guy's idea of a joke.

There was still snow in the low spots in the fields. The mountains were blanketed with it, and plumes of spindrift wafted off the summits. Spring was coming, though. There were wildflowers, millions of tiny yellow and lavender dots speckled across the meadows. It was forty degrees now; by afternoon it would be sixty-five. Then the ditch would overflow and the road would be truly impassable.

Houses were sprinkled along the road, some big ranch homes, others little more than shacks. The track began to peter out as it ran down the back of the promontory. Ben studied the ruts in the mud ahead. They were old. No one had been out that way in the last day or two—including the two cowboys looking for Patrice.

He went a half mile further without seeing a building. He wondered if he'd taken a wrong turn. Then there it was, exactly as Ernesto Vigil had described it.

The house was an odd rounded design, built of cinder blocks. The roof was flat and the walls rose up in a parapet. On the side Ben approached, the building was dug into a slope, nearly buried. The road ended in a rocky parking area beside the house. Here the promontory fell away at a head-spinning sixty degrees into a deep slot canyon.

Ben killed the engine and got out. A rusted pickup truck was parked near the house door. Past the truck was a court-yard filled with a heap of firewood. There was no smoke coming from the chimney, but the crisp smell of burnt pinyon hung in the air. Except for the sigh of the wind, everything was quiet.

"Hello!" Ben called. The curtains didn't move; the door didn't open. He did hear a faint scratching. "Hello!" The scratching grew louder. By turning his head and listening, he pinpointed it, on the roof.

A ladder was leaning against the side of the house. He started up. "Anybody home?" As he came level with the parapet, he jerked back, almost falling. He was staring straight into the mouth of a Rottweiler. What he'd heard was the dog's toenails scrabbling on the cinder blocks. Its ears were laid back and its lips lifted in a snarl. Ben expected it to growl, but it was hellishly silent. Its teeth were inches from his nose.

"So?" someone said.

That one word was enough for him to know it was Patrice. He kept his eyes on the dog, but he could see her at the edge of his vision. She was on a plastic-and-aluminum deck chair, bent over, working on some small object in her hand. She was dressed in a velour robe, a silly thing, tie-dyed and much too big, and black knee socks. She kept her head down, refusing to look at him. Some welcome, after he'd come two thousand miles.

"Could you call off the dog?"

"Max, get down." The dog didn't budge. "Sorry. Guess he doesn't listen. So how'd you find me?" Her voice was calm, not surprised. She'd watched Ben coming up the road.

"*Tienes una cola,*" Ben answered. "Our last night together you said that. There was a lot of stress then, for both of us. Had to be important to you." He walked his fingers along the wall until he found a spot where the mortar was loose. He began to pry at it. "So I looked it up. It's a funny phrase, Spanish, but it comes from the Tiwa language, Indian. Tiwa's only spoken two places, Taos and Picuris Pueblos, both just north of here." The mortar broke and crumbled to dust. He inched his hand farther down and tried again. The dog ducked forward, licking its chops. "You have a tail. A Tiwa storyteller says that when he finishes his story. The next person picks up with another story. Sort of like saying, 'your turn.' You were sick of lying to me; you wanted to stop. That's why you said it."

"That's all you needed to drive right up to my door?"

"No. Had to show your picture around. That took some time. An old guy down in the village, Ernesto Vigil—"

Patrice groaned. "I should have known, the creep. Every time I see him he points at his crotch and does a grouper." She opened her mouth and sucked air like a dying fish.

Ben gave a shallow chuckle. He had the mortar almost free. There. That football photo in his living room in Virginia was for real. He'd played high school quarterback for a state championship team. He had a strong arm, deadly accurate. "Ernesto drew me a map, and here I am."

Patrice was still bent over her work. "If this is about the money you loaned me, I—"

Ben feinted with his left hand, for a split second distracting the dog. He heaved the chunk of mortar. It went where he aimed, clanging off the leg of the chair. Patrice screeched with surprise, and the dog wheeled to look, just what Ben had hoped for. He snatched the collar, pulling the dog over the wall.

The weight was more than he expected, almost jerking him off the ladder. He made a wild grab for the top with his other hand. By then, the dog was snapping, trying to turn and get at his side. Ben could have just dropped him, but, from that height, the dog might have been killed. He was only doing what he'd been trained to do, protecting Patrice. Ben twisted away from the teeth and staggered down a half-dozen rungs before he let go. Max landed in a heap and came up snarling. By then Ben was scrambling onto the roof.

"Damn you!" Patrice came at him. "Look what you did!" Whatever she'd been working on had shattered in her hand. She threw it, just missing his head, and he grabbed her arms and pulled her back to the chair. Her robe came open. She didn't care; she kept fighting. She was so strong there was a moment when he thought she might be too much for him. Finally, she gave in and sat down.

They glared at each other. "What do you want?" she said.

He didn't answer, but looked around instead. The view was stunning, white peaks in the east, ochre-red valleys undulating away to the west. Nearer in, the pastures gleamed emerald in the dazzling sunlight. Despite the sun, it was freezing up there on the rooftop, the wind much stronger than on the ground.

"What do you *want?*" she repeated.

He stayed quiet, biding his time. Next to the chair was a rough-built table. On it stood a pair of binoculars on a short tripod. They were aimed so she could watch anyone coming down the road. On the other side of the table a dozen clay figurines were laid out. That's what she'd been working on. He bent to study them and laughed. They were replicas from the *Kama Sutra,* each labeled. Position 31. Position 104.

"Georgia O'Keeffe," he said.

Patrice pushed herself upright in the chair. "What's that mean?"

"She used to live around here, Abiquiu. You know that. When you were at my place, you read her biography." He saw a flicker of surprise in her eyes. "I watched you. All part of my job. What television programs you liked, what food you snuck out of the kitchen at night—raw carrots and cold soup. I know the kind of makeup you used, and hair spray. And Georgia O'Keeffe. You read that book twice in eight weeks. Something about her fascinated you. So what do you do with the little statues?"

"Sell them," she huffed. She was still angry about the one that had broken. "A shop in Albuquerque. I've got to make a living, you know."

"An artist's life, just like Mother O'Keeffe." The wind rose, moaning over the parapet. "It's not as glamorous as you thought, is it? All those hours alone, working to scratch out a few dollars."

She turned away. "If you're here for your measly three thousand, I'll write you a check. Then you can just go."

He put an arm on the back of the chair and leaned over her. "What about the files you stole? *My* files? Those clients of mine who never did a thing to you. Are you going to write checks to them?"

She pulled her knees to her chest, hiding from him. He let her be, and gradually the tension went out of her. "What are you here for? Just . . . tell me, okay?"

Ben hadn't come up with any easy way to explain it. One point was at the heart, and it was going to hurt. He reached for his jacket pocket, for the photo of the murdered man with silver hair. "It's bad news, all of it. First, your father—"

"My father?" She looked at him curiously. "What are you talking about?"

"Patrice, I'm sorry. He's dead, last week in Florida."

"Who told you that?" she said.

"Some people. One from the Marshals Service."

She laughed. "He's dead, all right. Twenty-one years ago in Pocatello. Car accident, but they still had an open casket."

"But—okay." All he could do was show her the picture. Before he had it out, he heard a noise and turned. Max was clawing his way over the roof wall. That was the north side of the house. The dirt was high enough there for the dog to make the top with a strong leap. Ben cursed his stupidity. How had Max gotten up there in the first place?

He backed away while Max heaved up the last few inches and cartwheeled down to the roof. He was on his feet in a heartbeat. Gone was the cold reserve he'd shown earlier. The dog was in a rage, streaking forward, roaring like a lion.

"Max, no," Ben called. He felt the wall behind him. The dog jumped, snapping, but, thank God, the teeth stopped just short.

Patrice was up, clapping her hands wildly. "That's it, Maxie. Go!"

In the corner of his mind, Ben knew what was making her so giddy. She'd been penned up here for months, always watching, scared of every shadow. The dog was one of a hundred precautions. Now, in the first real test, she'd scored a smashing victory.

Max latched onto Ben's jacket and reared back, almost pulling him down. That's the way it would end, when Ben lost his feet. Then the dog would tear him to pieces.

"Picture—*my pocket!*" he yelled. "You'll see. Your father." The dog was still jerking on his coat. Ben indicated the other side. He held his arms up to give her a clear path. Keeping as far away as possible, she snaked her hand into the pocket.

"Oh, great." She was looking at her own mug shot.

"The other one," Ben hollered. Max let go of the coat and

jumped for his face. Ben swung his elbow, just in time to block him.

Patrice had turned to the second picture. As soon as she did, she stopped moving. The mug shot fell from her hand. Her body convulsed. She made a horrible choking sound.

The dog danced on his front paws, searching for a way in at Ben. "Quit it," Patrice mumbled. Her eyes were frozen on the photo. Max, paying no heed, darted low, grabbing Ben's pant cuff.

Patrice came out of her trance in a fury. "I said stop it, you jerk!" Max only barked and tried for the other pant leg. Patrice collected herself. *"Hier,"* she said. *"Sitzen, Max."*

The dog blinked at her and sat, panting from exertion, grinning as if expecting a doggie treat.

Ben edged forward. "Who is it? Your father?"

"No . . . a friend." She had her back to him, so he pulled her around. Tears were streaming down her cheeks. She was crying so hard she was having trouble breathing.

She tried to say something. Ben shook his head, not understanding. Her robe had come open again. He pulled her close, put his arms around her. He could feel her inside the fabric, pressing against him.

"Emile." She broke into another round of sobbing. "I'll kill him," she whimpered. "I'll kill him."

TWELVE

"Sorry," Patrice said as she handed over a glass of flat ginger ale. "It's all I've got. There's water, but that's from the well. It'll give you the runs if you're not used to it."

Ben took a sip to be polite and set it aside. They were in Patrice's living room, a big space filled with harsh sunlight from the wall of glass facing south over the canyon. There was a lot of clutter: stacks of books and maps, an old potter's wheel, boxes of tools. Ristras were piled in one corner, strings of dried green and red chiles that people usually hung on their doors.

Patrice sat on the floor, leaving Ben the only piece of furniture, a ratty denim sofa. Max was curled up by the door. "You ol' wiener dog," she crooned, "eat up." She tossed him a hot dog from a package she'd brought in from the kitchen. *Clomp,* he caught it in midair. "*Guter Hund.* He only speaks German. I mean, the people who owned him only spoke German. I got him at the pound. He wouldn't have hurt you. He's scary, but he's all bark." She tossed another. *Clomp.* "You're staring at me, Ben. Is it that bad?"

"Bad? No." He wished she would look at him, but she kept her eyes on the dog. "Just . . . your hair, different things. Changes."

When she had gone into the kitchen, she'd locked the connecting door. She came out wearing a baggy pair of bib overalls and a flannel shirt. She was limping, too, something Ben had noticed on the roof. It reminded him of a TV show he'd seen in reruns, *The Real McCoys*. Walter Brennan played an old farmer who dressed the same way and limped. Five months ago it would have been ridiculous, thinking of Patrice like that. But that's what five months of hard living could do to a person.

Her hands were calloused, rough, the nails chipped nubs. Her skin was grainy, and she wore no makeup, only an oily skim of sunblock. She'd lost ten pounds, maybe more. What was left had been toughened by hard work. It showed in the angularity of her face and the ripple of muscles on her forearms. Her hair was the biggest change. The cascade of gold was gone. Now it was dun-brown, cut short and combed over like a teenage boy's.

"What happened to your leg?" he asked.

"I twisted it. No big deal."

As she spoke, she hitched her head toward the windows, as if to indicate the scene of the accident. Not likely. The house was built into the side of the promontory. All that was out there was the near-cliff down to the canyon.

He waited. After the scene on the roof she needed time to decompress. He'd have to be patient, gain her trust. It might take two hours, or two days. "Who gave you the picture?" she said.

"Two men from the CIA. They were with a woman I know from the Marshals Service. They said they were part of a special task force, but that was just a cover. They were pretty rough. Too rough."

Patrice was looking down, rubbing a scar on her palm. The scar was old, but he hadn't noticed it before. When she realized he was watching, she curled her hand away.

He said, "I don't know much more about your friend than I've already told you. They said he was killed last week in Orlando. Who was he?"

"He was a con," she said, "one of the best. Peter Saar. His real name was Peter Kiefer, but that never sounded honest enough to him." She laughed softly. "Sometimes he told people he was Carl Jung, for fun, to see if they got the joke. Or Martin Luther. He'd been a priest when he was young—"

Surprised, Ben broke in, "A priest?"

She hugged her knees and began to rock. "One of those mistaken career paths, you know? He always kept up with the church, though. Funny that way. I met him when I first started scamming, on the Gulf Coast, St. Petersburg. He was nice, old world, a gentleman. He introduced me around, showed me the ropes. Peter was the one who told me about you. The Laundry Man. Said you gave people new lives. He called you a 'picky sumbitch.'" Ben smiled, but she shook her head. Tears streaked down from her eyes.

"How did he know Emile Balazs?" he said.

Patrice stood and looked out the window so he couldn't see her cry. "Peter was careful, always a background player. He's the kind of person Emile wouldn't notice."

"But Emile did notice him, somehow."

She cried harder. "I'm sorry, Ben. It's just . . . he was good to me. Really good to me."

"But now he's dead," Ben said quietly. "What did you have to do with it?"

She snapped around. "Right, he's dead. My loss. Enough, okay?"

"Okay," he said after a moment. "Then tell me about you and Emile and my client files. How did that happen?"

She pulled a tissue from her pocket and blew her nose. Her expression was still belligerent. "It's not much of a story. He wanted the files, and I got them for him. If you want an apology, get in line."

She turned back to the window, and she grew restless, tapping her fingers against her sides. What she'd seen in that photograph had sunk in. It was scaring her. "The people who came to see you, the woman and two men, what did they say about me?"

He told her, and she listened without comment, chewing her cuticles. He ended, saying, "Joquand wanted me to think they were there to protect you, but Mosby told me the real story later. They're trying to find you for Balazs, doing a favor for him."

Patrice stopped fidgeting, and she sighed. "I can't stay here." It was as much a question as a statement. She wanted Ben's advice.

"No. I found you. They will, too. We'll have to go. But Patrice, if we're going to sort this out, you'll have to tell me what's going on. How you got tangled up with Balazs. What happened to Saar. Everything." He was beginning to see what came next. They'd drive down to Santa Fe together. In the car, he'd get her to talk. Once she leveled with him, they could come up with a plan.

She turned and looked at him. No tears this time. "You could have told them where I was, saved yourself all this hassle. What are you after, Ben? Why help me?"

He could have made a joke, said he was still hoping for that dance she'd denied him at Club Monde. Or he could have gotten closer to it by telling her about the picture of her he kept in his desk at WITSEC, and how often he looked at it. What he did say was as much of the truth as he'd been able to figure out. "Because I think you're worth it."

Her shoulders drooped, as if she'd just felt a weight on them. "Give me fifteen minutes to pack some things." She headed into the kitchen. Her bedroom was somewhere beyond that. In the doorway she paused. "My friend Peter could read people. Not as well as you. Anyway, he was a cynic. It's nice the way you see good things in people." She picked at the flaking paint around the doorknob. "Even if it's your imagination."

Before he could reply, she swung the door closed and clicked the lock.

He waited for her footfalls to move away before he got up. He wanted to check the place over, see what he could find out about her. It might help him draw her out later.

Ben knew his clients had a hard road to travel once they left him—money problems, isolation, all the lies they had to tell. And they were constantly afraid. That odd phone call in the middle of the night. Someone staring at them the wrong way in the grocery store. A lot of people would say: who cares? They made their own troubles. Ben couldn't do that. He saw too many sad details—the threadbare clothing, the cough medicine they drank to calm their nerves— and he could only feel sorry for them. Larry Jong had once told Ben, "You save 'em from hell, leave 'em in purgatory."

He circled the room, inspecting the stacks and boxes of things, trying to piece together Patrice's life here. He'd made it most of the way around when he spotted her purse behind the pile of ristras. It was the same frumpy straw bag she'd had last November. Bending for it, he saw something under the sofa, an intricate paper cutout of Santa Claus, colored with crayons. In his mind's eye, he imagined the scene: some neighbor's kid come to wish Patrice a happy Christmas; Patrice offering flat ginger ale and stale cookies in return. It must have been a lonely holiday for her. Then he thought of his own Christmas at home. Larry had backed out on his invitation at the last minute, and Ben spent the day watching dreary rain fall outside and listening to the disembodied cheering of football crowds on TV. But Ben was used to being alone. He was surprised Patrice had lasted as long as she had here.

As Ben sat down to go through the purse, Max started to whine. "Quiet, boy," Ben whispered. He pulled out her wallet. Patrice was still using the driver's license he'd given her last fall, but she had a new library card and a grocery club card. He smiled. Those were good signs. She really had tried to settle in here.

Max's whine deepened to a growl. "Quiet," Ben said. The dog began to pace. Ben tried German. "*Sitzen, Max.*" Max sat but continued to shuffle his paws. Then all at once he bounded against the door, barking wildly.

Ben heard Patrice's footsteps, and he just had time to stuff the purse under the sofa. She rushed into the room. "Max, what?" She shot a look at Ben. "What the hell's the problem with him?"

"I don't know, he started—"

She swung the door open and Max burst outside. Patrice and Ben followed. In the courtyard everything seemed normal. Max had gone to the far side of the house, still barking but not as loudly. There was a scramble and the barking moved to the roof.

"Come on," Patrice said. She climbed the ladder, calling, "We're coming, idiot dog." At the top she stopped so abruptly that Ben ran into her from below. She was looking at something, up by the crest of the promontory, from the way she held her head. "Dammit," she muttered, and she dropped over the parapet. Ben pulled himself up a couple more rungs. A green sport utility truck sat in the road a quarter mile away. The windows were tinted so he couldn't see inside. A trace of exhaust wafted up from the back.

Patrice crawled on hands and knees to the binoculars. About then the passenger-side door opened and a man got out. She adjusted the focus. "I don't know him."

Ben clambered up beside her and took a look through the glasses. The man wore a Stetson hat and a blue work shirt and jeans. He had on a coat, knee-length and heavy, the kind called "dusters" in old Westerns. His jaw was powerful, and he had deep-set eyes that glinted as he lit a cigarette. He tilted his head so he could study the house.

"Nobody comes out here, Ben. Nobody." There was a sting of accusation in her voice.

He leaned so he could look her in the eye. "I didn't bring them, believe that. A kid up in Taos told me two men were around a couple of days ago looking for you. He thought they were headed north."

Max jumped on the wall and started barking again. She reached to pull him down, but he leaped the other way, over the edge to the bank below. Seconds later he was streaking through the field toward the truck.

Patrice moved to stand up, to call him back. Ben held her down. "Wait. Let's see what they—"

Max tumbled, his front legs giving out, his head plowing into the ground. With a huge effort he struggled back to his feet. Stumbling sideways, he retreated toward the house.

"Jesus," Patrice breathed. She was staring through the binoculars. She shifted, and Ben took a look.

The man at the truck had seen the dog, too. In the brief seconds while they had their eyes off him, he'd taken out a rifle, leveled it, and snapped off a shot. It was a vicious looking gun, pure black and large bore. There was a metal cylinder on the end, a silencer.

Ben worked to keep his voice calm. "Is there another way out of here?"

Patrice didn't answer. She was staring at the dog, hobbling painfully across the field. She turned to Ben, and he saw terror in her eyes. She scuttled back from him.

He took hold of her shoulder. "I didn't have anything to do with this. We'll be all right, but we've got to get out of here. Is there another way? Patrice?"

A light seemed to go on in the depths of her eyes. "I . . . yes." She pointed behind her. "The tractor path. That field. My truck can make it."

He craned to see. It looked more like a goat path. "You're sure?"

"Yes." Her voice was stronger, quite steady. "I've used it when the ditch overflows. It'll take us back to the main road near town."

She was first down the ladder. Ben followed and paused at the top long enough to check on the man in the Stetson. He was in plain view, walking beside the truck as it slogged through the mud toward the house. The man had removed his coat and had the rifle balanced across his forearm. He looked comfortable, carefree, someone out to plink a few tin cans, maybe kill a few varmints.

Once down, Ben found Patrice standing in the doorway. "I'll get my keys and bag," she said. She ducked away, closing the door.

A second later, Ben heard noises coming from the side of the house. They were here already? He looked around for something to fight with and grabbed a stick of firewood.

But the noise was coming from Max, not the shooter. The dog was down on his belly, pulling himself along with his front paws. Blood pulsed from his shoulder and dripped from his gaping mouth. He hitched past Ben, not noticing him.

Ben knelt, patting the dog's side, looking for some way to help. There wasn't anything to do. Nothing could stop all that bleeding.

He left Max and went to his car to get his knapsack. It was filled with clothes and maps and other things he'd picked up since arriving in New Mexico.

He ran back to the shelter of the house. Max had reached the door and started scratching. Every move brought a howl of pain.

No need for him to suffer out here. "Maybe there's some water in there, huh, boy?" Ben murmured.

He pushed on the door, but it didn't move. It was locked.

"Hey, Patrice, come on!" The silence stretched on. Out on the road, he heard the first faint rumble of the truck as it rolled toward the house. He rattled the door. "*Patrice! Get out here!*" She didn't answer.

Ben was stunned. What he was thinking was impossible—with the cliff, the way the house was built—but he was certain it was true. Something about the way she'd looked at him when she shut the door. A good-bye look. Patrice was gone. He bent over the dog, stroking his ear. "Well Max, any suggestions?"

Max didn't hear. Max was dead.

THIRTEEN

Ben had only two options and about fifteen seconds to decide. He could make a run for the clump of junipers in the field, then hunker down, wait out the rifleman. Or he could break the door in and try to follow Patrice, however she'd done her disappearing act. The truck sounded so close. He scanned the field. First the fence, then thirty yards to the trees. Too far. He reared back, kicked the door, and the jamb snapped inward. He jumped over Max's body and wrenched the door shut behind him.

He noticed the ristras first, scattered on the floor. Patrice had been looking for her purse. He reached under the sofa for it and slung it over his shoulder with his knapsack. He stole deeper into the house, the kitchen, and closed the door there. This was the room where she really lived. Art prints on the walls, a calico tablecloth, even a nice overstuffed chair. There was another door leading outside, but it was blocked by a stack of newspapers. She hadn't gone that way, not without some serious magic to get the stack back in place. The only window was plateglass. She couldn't have gone through that either.

In the corner was a set of stairs, heading down. That's where the bedrooms were. The steps creaked as he took them. At the bottom he stopped and listened for sounds overhead. All quiet. He was sure she wasn't here, but he called anyway. "Patrice, come on!" There was no answer.

In the hall, the doors were closed. He opened the closest, into a large room. It was spartan: a bed, a chair, a pine bureau. This was Patrice's room. Her half-packed suitcase lay on the floor. He checked the closet, then the window.

Thirty feet below was the face of the canyon slope. Most of it was too steep for vegetation, just gravel and bedrock. The trees began a hundred yards down, near the canyon floor. *Where did she go?*

He tracked back up the incline with his eyes. There was a broken window screen and a couple of old plastic bottles. Then he noticed the depressions in the gravel. If the sun had been higher he wouldn't have seen them, but this early the light slanted, throwing shadows. They were regular, broad scoops at huge steplike intervals, twenty or thirty feet apart. . . . To hell with it. No time to figure it out.

He moved into the hall, to the next room. Something was different here. The light under the door was warm and red, like a photographic darkroom. He stepped in, to the foot of a single bed. It was dressed in a pink chenille spread. The shag carpet was pink, the walls covered with pink-striped wallpaper. On the nightstand a dozen stuffed animals were piled. He opened the closet and stood gawking. Little girl's dresses. Little girl's shoes. He looked in the chest of drawers. Little girl's underpants and T-shirts.

His mind churned. Toys. Clothes. That Santa Claus cutout in the living room. A kid? *Patrice with a kid?* In spite of everything, he had to laugh. How wrong he was about her, time and again. Then he wondered, had the girl been here all along, hiding? Patrice had locked the kitchen door so he couldn't follow her to this part of the house. He looked around again. No. A girl used this room, but not recently. It had a stale feel, too much dust on the woodwork, a dry musty smell in the air.

His head snapped up. He could hear the truck, a faint rumble coming through the ceiling. His time was about up.

He started for the hallway, but a riffle of movement caught his eye. The window was open; the curtain shifted on the breeze. He looked out. The screen was there down the slope. Directly below was the first of those depressions in the gravel, and another and another down to the shelter of the trees.

"I'll be damned," he whispered.

It all fit. Last fall when they were working together, Ben had told Patrice, pounded it into her. *Always have an escape route. Memorize it. Always.* She'd told him she'd twisted her leg. That was from practicing—the long jump and out-of-control tear down the hill. She hated heights, too. He shook his head, marveling at how much guts it had taken for her to do this. Well, if she could do it, so could he. It was that or wait around for his own personal bullet to arrive.

But first he needed to get something, if there was time. He raced to the bottom of the stairs and stood listening. The truck engine was shut down. He heard the ladder rattle and a man's voice. "Nope, nobody up there. You think that dog's dead?"

He was answered by a metallic *thup.* "He is now," a second man said.

The first one laughed. "Wha'd'ya call that, the Death Enema?"

Ben bounded up the steps. On the refrigerator was a sheet of paper with a calendar grid, a school menu. He'd only half noticed it when he was here before. He stuffed it in Patrice's purse. The front door opened. He could tell because the kitchen door swung a few inches on the draft. As quietly as he could, he ducked back down the stairs.

In the girl's room, he checked the depressions on the hill again, then stood, waiting. If he went now, he'd be in plain view from the windows above. The shooter had needed only one bullet to stop Max, and Max had been two hundred yards away, low in the grass, running flat out. The man would have a much easier time picking Ben off the bare hillside.

He jammed Patrice's purse in his knapsack, straining to catch what was going on above. Footsteps in the living room. The kitchen. The living room again. With every moment that passed, Ben felt like a clock spring wound tighter and tighter. *Come on. Come on.*

His eye fell on the pile of stuffed animals. One was separate from the others, a bright green frog in a shoe box with a tissue-paper bed and a cardboard sign that said, "Future Prince." The frog was badly worn from being played with so much. A precious thing. He could imagine the tears when the girl found out it had been left behind. On a whim, he shoved it in his pack with the purse. He heard the stairs creak. The men were on their way down. Time to go.

He slipped out the window. Underneath was a ledge of concrete, just wide enough to stand on. Good. He wanted to close up the room before he jumped, so they'd have no reason to suspect anyone had gone that way. The window was a slider and he had to pull hard to get it to move. Then it skipped, and *wham*, it was shut, and he lost his balance, all in the span of a heartbeat.

The fall seemed impossibly long. His mind screamed, *FEET DOWN, FEET DOWN!* If he turned over in the air, he'd bounce off the slope like a rock in an avalanche. He'd be dead before he reached the canyon bottom.

Uff, his foot hit. The gravel was deep, pillowing the fall enough so his leg didn't break.

Then he was in the air again, flying downhill for the next depression. His trajectory seemed perfect. He even had time for a funny thought. *Neil Armstrong on the moon. One giant leap . . .*

Uff. Something was wrong. He'd missed the mark and was heading for a rock, not the soft gravel. He took the jolt and felt something in his ankle pop. No time to worry about it. Through some miracle, he kept his balance. *Uff. Uff.* He was rocketing now. Steps so fast he couldn't count. He ripped past the first tree, ten yards on the left. Almost down. Just veer—Damn, more trees. No room to stop or even duck. A three-inch-thick limb loomed in front of him. He blew through with his chest, shattering it like a cannon shot.

The ground was leveling out. The trees were thinning. A few more yards and he'd begin to slow. Oh shit—a rock wall, dead ahead. No way around. He turned and took the blow on his shoulder, protecting his head. He fell flat on his back and lay stunned, blinking through the trees at the sky.

Several minutes passed before he could sit up. He was in one piece, more or less, and still had his knapsack. Far above he could see the glare of the sun on the house windows. He wiped the sweat off his face and gave a thin laugh. He'd never again assume he could do everything Patrice could.

Getting to his feet was a struggle. His ankle made an awful crackling sound and the pain made him dizzy. There seemed to be only one way to go—down. After hobbling twenty yards, he came to a stop, leaning against a big ponderosa pine. Down the defile he could see a piece of cloth waving on the sharp end of a broken sapling. It was from Patrice's flannel shirt. Even from that distance he could see it was bloody. She hadn't been any luckier coming down the hillside than he had.

Ben could only guess where he was. The canyon headed generally west, which eventually would take him back to the Española-Taos road. How far? Maybe three miles, maybe six or seven. Depended on how much snaking around he had to do, following it down.

The bottom of the canyon was a wide V cut in the rock, the only place level enough to walk. It was wet underfoot from the runoff above. The big pines soon gave way to willows, scrubby bush-like trees that clawed at his clothes. The wetness changed to a spring and the spring to a full-fledged stream. He tried to stay on the bank, but the undergrowth forced him back in the water. It was just as well. It was slow going, but the flow was ice cold, and that numbed his ankle and kept it from swelling.

After a while the stream opened up. The willows grew tall, interlaced overhead, so he was sloshing down a dim tunnel. It was hypnotic, the noise of the water, the occasional flit of a songbird. He might have continued for hours in the creek if not for the spiders' webs.

So far he'd seen masses of webs above him in the top branches. Suddenly he was batting them off his cheeks and wiping them off his lips. He paused, thinking. Patrice had come down the creek before him; she'd broken through all the webs up to head height. Why were there webs here? Because she'd left the creek, somewhere above.

He pushed back upstream to the spot where he'd first noticed the change. Sure enough, on the bank there was a gap in the willows. He fought through, cursing as the whip-like branches tortured his face and arms. Then he was standing in the broad sunlight on what looked like a road, a jeep trail anyway. He dropped to one knee. There was a boot print in the sand, very fresh and the right size to be Patrice's.

He had visions of catching her now. He was a good runner, and she couldn't be far ahead. Ten steps later he changed his mind. His ankle was in no shape to run. He adjusted his knapsack and limped on.

He spent an hour and a half on that lonely track. Often he spotted Patrice's footprints. They were widely spaced, tracking evenly. She was making good time in spite of her own injured leg. His ankle hurt like blazes and kept him at half speed. Still, in the race to catch her, he had one advantage. He had money; she didn't. If he could get to a town, he could rent a car or take a cab. The question was, where was she going? He had an educated guess, no more than that. But that was Ben's stock in trade, making educated guesses about people. He was confident.

Finally, just when he'd reached his limit and was looking for a shady place to rest, he heard the whine of car tires on a real road. He scrambled up a bank to the edge of the blacktop. Just as he'd expected, it was the back road from Taos, somewhere above Cordova. There were no houses in sight and no cars at the moment. Patrice was nowhere around, either. She must already have hitched a ride—south, if his guess was right. He'd have to do the same thing.

Over the next twenty minutes, half a dozen cars passed, one with its horn screaming and the driver bellowing, "*Buy a bicycle, asshole!*" Then a truck came around the bend, poking along below the speed limit. Ben collected himself: expression cheerful, both hands in view, now . . . thumb out. The sun was glinting off the chrome and glass, so he didn't catch the details of the truck until it was already slowing. It was a green sport utility with tinted windows.

It came to a halt, and the passenger window began to drop. A gray Stetson appeared. Ben pulled back, ready to dive down the bank behind him. Then he could see the face, the flat cheekbones, dark almond-shaped eyes, chestnut-brown skin. An Indian's face. Not the man with the rifle. Ben let out a gasp of held breath.

"Where to?" the driver said.

"South."

That didn't satisfy the man. He leaned back, pursing his lips. "South? Lotta country there."

Another sport utility was rounding the bend in the road. Ben couldn't tell the color yet. "Albuquerque," he said, struggling with his knapsack. He pulled out Patrice's purse and, from it, the school menu he'd taken off her refrigerator. There was an address at the top. "Sacred Heart Girls Academy, San Pedro Drive, Southeast."

"Girls Academy, huh?" the man drawled.

"That's right," Ben said. He could see the second SUV clearly now. It was also green with tinted widows. There was mud on the undercarriage.

"OK," the man said. He reached across but stopped with his hand on the door. "That your purse?" When Ben didn't reply right away, he said, "Take your time. It's a tough question."

"It's a friend's. I'm taking it to her."

The man chuckled. "Good answer. I wouldn't have thought of that." He popped open the door. Ben climbed in as the other truck shot by in a swirl of sandy wind. The driver eased out behind it. "Looks like somebody's in a hurry."

Ben nodded. "Yes, somebody."

FOURTEEN

With dusk, a storm came slashing down on Basseterre. Emile Balazs stood on the porch of his sister's home, watching as curtains of rain swept over the cemetery and government house, and up to the island's massive central peak, Mt. Misery. Isabel lived in a good neighborhood by St. Kitts standards, a street of cement block bungalows, two-beds-and-a-bath each, with close-clipped lawns and riotous gardens.

Even in nice neighborhoods in the Caribbean there are mosquitos. One landed on the back of Emile's hand. He let it stick him and watched, expressionless, as it drank its fill. Then he swatted it, spraying his own blood across his knuckles.

A car splashed around the corner at the end of the street. Emile recognized it by the running lights as Mick Laraby's BMW. It rolled to a stop across from the house. In the front seat were two of Emile's guards. Mick sat in the back with Isabel.

As Mick helped her out, the rain increased to a roar. They were sopping wet when they reached the porch. Her dress was ankle-length, simple white cotton. It clung to her like paint. Emile could see the outlines of her nipples and the dark triangle of her pubic hair. On her cheek was a nasty bruise. "Hey, Sis," he said. "Missed ya."

"Like hell you did," she hissed.

She had eluded Emile's men for over twenty-four hours. He wanted an explanation. "Where?" he said gruffly.

Laraby was wringing water out of his necktie. "Jack Tar Village. One of the dealers at the casino let her stay in his room."

"And this dealer . . . ?"

"We suggested he find work elsewhere."

"You *broke* his hands," Isabel bleated.

"So we did, luv." Mick gently brushed her hair back from her face and pushed the front door open for her. She stomped past him, but jerked to a halt on the threshold.

Emile's men had spent the day at the house. The carpet was pulled up, the furniture sliced open, even the wallboard was ripped down and piled in a heap in the hall. Mary was there, Isabel's housekeeper. She buzzed from spot to spot, trying to clean up. Everything she picked up she put right down again. Where to start with a mess like this? She noticed Isabel and the two women stared at each other and around at the room, too shocked to speak.

Balazs guided Isabel to the kitchen, where he had a chair waiting. "Everybody out, Mick. Just Isabel and me left."

Laraby didn't like the looks of this. There was an electric cord on the floor with the end snipped off and the insulation peeled back. Next to it was Emile's jackknife. The long blade was already out. He'd seen Emile use these things before, persuaders. Get a person to cooperate, quickly. Mick spoke softly so no one else would hear. "It's Iz, Boss. Remember that. You don't want t' hurt her. Scare her, yeah, but—"

"*Out!*" Balazs barked.

The men were still working on the sun porch and in the guest bedroom. Laraby herded them out the back door. In the rush he forgot about Mary. She stood in the hall, considering what to do. As if to give her an answer, Balazs turned his back, pacing around the kitchen. Mary slipped into a closet, to a dark hiding place behind the water heater.

"Now, Iz," Emile said, "we can have that talk. No interruptions."

Her initial shock had been replaced by boiling rage. She pointed around at the wreckage. "Why did you do this?"

"You ran out on me yesterday. Made me a little suspicious of you."

"Suspicious of what?"

He hunched over her. "Something of mine's gone missing. I thought maybe you had it."

"I've got nothing of yours. Now you're going to clean up every—"

He clamped his hand on her jaw. "It's not the time to be giving me orders, Sis." He released her but stayed close. "We'll have our talk. If I like your answers, I'll see about straightening up."

He moved his hand as if he might grab her again, and she flinched. That made him smile. "Good, let's start with this." There was a leather bag on the counter, and from it he took a wood box with Russian lettering, the box he'd picked up five months ago in Moscow with the keypad. "You know what this is?"

She curled her lip. "A present? For me?"

"Not a chance. You don't recognize it?"

"No, I don't."

Emile stared at her, his eyes hard and shimmery. "Look here then." From the leather bag he took out a bundle of papers, which he spread on the floor at her feet. Blueprints, in Russian. There were no walls or floors: they weren't for a building. "It's a wiring diagram," Emile said. "Have you seen it before?"

Isabel couldn't make head nor tail of it, except something she figured was a date in one corner, 6-4-1962. She shook her head. "No, never. What's it got to do with me?"

Emile went back to pacing. "Peter Saar—that's what. The man from down at the presbytery."

Isabel was wearing her bracelet of rosary beads, and she started toying with them. "I told you, Peter's a friend. So what? I don't understand any of this."

Emile watched her fingering the beads. She'd been angry until he mentioned Saar. Now she was nervous. "Why did he come to see you?"

"There was nothing to it. We went out to the Lemon Inn for a drink. I made him dinner here. We talked—gossip mostly, island chatter. Ask Mary. She knows. He's good company, that's all."

"Good company? Your friend Saar was a fucking thief."

"You're crazy."

"No, Iz, not nearly crazy. This box and the blueprints came from Russia together. There was something with them, a piece of electronics. This keypad." He drew a circle on the blueprints with his finger, around a squarish thing with buttons and two dozen wire leads. It might as well have been Sanskrit as far as Isabel was concerned. He said, "Saar got his grubby hands on them. Sent me the box and blueprints, along with a letter. Taunting. Wanted money. A finder's fee for the keypad. Now I've *got* to have that thing, Iz, but the bastard's dead—" He saw the abrupt change in her face. "You didn't know, did you? Saar's dead, murdered up in Florida."

"I don't believe any of that."

She tried to stand, but he grabbed her by the wrists and forced her down. "I don't care what you believe, all right? What did Saar say about me?"

122

"We didn't talk about you. Emby, you're hurting me."

"There had to be a reason Saar came to you. Did he mention Golden Pyramid? Anything about my business? Maybe something about the Herreras?"

"The Herreras? *No!* Emile, *stop* this." She wrenched her arms, trying to get away. He squeezed harder. The string of her bracelet snapped and the beads cascaded to the floor. "*You bloody jackass!*" she screamed. "Those were Mum's!" Then she burst into tears. "*You're hurting me!*"

From her spot in the closet, Mary heard everything. She couldn't just sit there. Maybe a small interruption, something to give Emile a chance to cool off. She thumped the hot water tank with her fist. *Tap . . . TAP.*

He twisted to see what it was. For a moment, his neck was exposed. Isabel yanked her arm free and raked her fingernails from his ear to his breastbone.

Emile didn't make a sound, but his face went white. He was so angry he forgot about the cord and knife on the floor, forgot why he'd even come there. He lunged for the counter, for a big framing hammer one of his men had left. He smashed the coffee maker, the microwave, the oven door. "Goddamn *bitch!* You think this is some kind of game?" He turned, wheeling the hammer at her shoulder. Something blocked his swing.

Mary was there, babbling, "No, no, Mr. Balazs. You don't want t' be hurtin' Isabel. She sorry for scratchin'. Sorry."

Emile glared at her, then down at the hammer. The claw had raked the length of Mary's forearm. That's how she stopped the blow. It was a sickening sight, the rusty metal, the blood and gouged flesh. Her face was twisted with pain. Her voice shook but was still soothing. "You two's like a coupl'a pups, fightin' for no reason."

Emile shoved her into the hall, then rounded on Isabel.

Through the years of living with him, Isabel had developed a knack for blanking out violence. She'd seen what had happened to Mary, but in her mind it didn't register. She focused on Emile, eyes smoldering. He was six years younger, and she still had some of her older-sibling authority. One corner of her mouth turned in a "what'cha gonna do now, little boy" smirk. She even lifted her chin, offering him a target.

Slowly he lowered the hammer. His face was frozen. Only now did he realize how out of control he'd been. Isabel let him off easy. With a huff, she smoothed the wrinkles in her dress. "Wanker," she muttered.

It was from their childhood name-calling matches. Emile gave a wan smile. "Cow."

They both looked away, slipping at light speed back from the brink. His forehead was glistening with sweat, and he wiped it off. He remembered what Mick had said. *Don't hurt her . . . just scare her.* Good man, Mick, always a steady hand.

Emile thought it over. Isabel had been scared, but she stuck to her story. He was sure she'd never seen the box and blueprints before. So what had Peter Saar been after? Maybe he'd only been playing with her. Or maybe he'd used her for something, and Isabel hadn't realized it.

Outside, with the storm, it was pitch dark. Emile could see his reflection in the sunporch door, and, behind him, Isabel's back. She was stiffly erect in the chair, shaking her hair proudly over her shoulders. If she did know anything, she wasn't likely to tell him now, unless he really did hurt her.

He remembered a time right after their mother died when the two of them had fought. He didn't recall what set it off, but he ended up throwing Iz on her bed and holding his knife against her throat, hissing in her ear that he was going to kill her. He came to his senses in time then, too. The next day he bought her a whole gallon of mint chocolate ice cream, her favorite. At first she refused it, but he wheedled and begged until she forgave him.

He took a last look at the hammer and tossed it down.

Emile bent and put the blueprints and the Russian box back in the leather bag, then put his jackknife away. Isabel waited for him to finish. "What are those diagrams?" she asked.

He stared down the hall where Mary was huddled on the floor, cradling her arm. "It's history, Sis." He rubbed the smooth leather. "A blast from the past."

Emile stepped onto the porch. He felt strange, outside himself. His heart was still beating hard. "Close one tonight, Iz." He drew a deep breath and pushed on into the rain. "We'll talk again, soon."

When he was out of sight, Isabel stood up. She kicked some of the clutter with her toe. She still didn't realize Mary was hurt. "We'll have to get someone to help with all this."

Mary's voice was leaden. "My brothers can come. Uncle Winston over from Nevis, too. He bring his tools."

Outside, they heard Emile drive away. Isabel went into the bathroom. The medicine cabinet had been ripped off the wall. Mary watched as Isabel used a toothbrush to pry up the lower two-by-four brace in the opening where the cabinet had been. She stuck her hand far down into the wall cavity. It was undisturbed, protected by the vanity and sink. She pulled out a bulging manilla envelope.

After settling on the floor next to Mary, she dumped out the contents, a pile of mementos: ticket stubs from a Miami Dolphins game; a certificate her husband had won for coaching a girl's netball team; Isabel's diploma from a home decorator's college in Saint Thomas; pictures, hundreds of pictures.

"Those Mr. Finney's things," Mary said. Isabel's husband had kept them in the bedroom closet. Mary hadn't seen them since before he died.

"That's right," Isabel said. "He made that hiding place in the wall." She picked through the pile and found a stubby key with a thickened, flat head, the kind used in bus station lockers and safety-deposit boxes. Her eyes twinkled slyly as she turned it around.

"What am I gonna do with you, woman?" Mary said. "It's dumb hidin' things from your brother. He's goin' through changes, actin' like a wild man lately. You've seen it. If all he wants is this trash, why don't ya just give it to him?"

"Because—" One of the beads from Isabel's bracelet had rolled into the hall. She picked it up and squeezed it tight with the key. "Whatever's going on is Emile's business, and I don't care. But I *won't* let him treat me the way he has been. That's all there is to it."

"*Not* all there is. You're not kids anymore. Someday, he's gonna break your neck for you, sure."

Isabel reached to take her hand. She noticed Mary's arm then, and made a little in-suck of breath. Tears sprang into her eyes. She picked up a towel from the floor and dabbed at the blood. "It'll be all right," Isabel whispered. "Be all right." She cuddled her and kissed her on the temple, like a child soothing a broken doll.

FIFTEEN

It was a fine, sunny day in Albuquerque, but Ben's taxi driver was complaining about the weather. That was after he'd complained about gas prices and the traffic and how much he paid in alimony. Ben tuned him out and pulled off his shoe to give his ankle the once-over. The man who'd given him a ride on the Taos road (his name was Harold) was a retired safety patrol officer from Angel Fire ski resort. When he noticed Ben rubbing his leg, he asked what was the matter. Soon they were parked by the roadside, and Harold was applying a wrap of medical tape from his first-aid kit. "Pretty bad sprain," he said. "Ought to have a cast, but you won't. I can tell. Keep it immobile like this—crisscross—and take these." He handed Ben a bottle of aspirin and the roll of tape.

Harold was good company, but he wasn't any speed demon. The one-hundred-mile trip from Cordova took two and a half hours. Ben kept checking his watch and wondering how far ahead Patrice was getting. Finally, Harold dropped him at a hotel in downtown Albuquerque. The hotel was where Ben picked up the cab driver, and, after twenty minutes with him, he was an inch shy of telling the man to shut the hell up. "You take the Kennedys. You think it's a coincidence those boobs all ended up in politics? Nossir. Everything's organized, and us serfs don't get told spit." The cab slowed. "So here ya are, Sacred Heart Academy."

Ben's head shot up; then he slouched over. "Don't stop in front!" The muddy green SUV was parked on a side street, catty-corner to the entrance of the school.

"Go around the block," Ben said, keeping low. "Behind the park." The truck didn't move, and no one got out, so odds were they hadn't spotted him.

The fact that the truck was there told him a lot. The two men had the same hunch he did, that Patrice was going to show up at the school. They'd come straight from Truchas. It would have taken a pile of luck for her to get here first. So she was probably still on the road. And if they'd all guessed wrong, and she wasn't on her way here? This was where Ben needed to be anyway. After Patrice, those men were his only lead. If worse came to worst, he could try to get one of them alone, scare the bejeezus out of him, find out who hired them and why.

Ben tossed the fare to the taxi driver and got out, surveying the park. It was a flat space covering three city blocks. Most of it was an expanse of ball fields along San Pedro Drive. Across the drive was the school, an aging desert-brown structure taking up another whole block. Except for a couple of girls playing hopscotch by the entrance, it was quiet over there. School had already let out for the day.

Ben chose a spot under a spruce tree to wait. The branches hung low, hiding him, but he could see through the gaps. The lowering sun cast a yellow glow through the smoked windows of the truck, so he could see the men inside. The driver used a mobile phone a couple of times. The passenger seemed to be dozing. On the street, traffic was picking up. It was nearing rush hour. A pack of teenage boys arrived and started a game of football. They were good kids, laughing and running and tumbling after each other.

Ben watched the street. Ten minutes later a SunTran bus pulled to the curb on San Pedro. The doors opened and Patrice stepped off. A man in a sloppy, wide-striped suit got off behind her. He said something to her out of the corner of his mouth while patting his hip pocket where his wallet was. With a hard look, she sent him packing, back on the bus. It roared away, leaving her alone. "Look around, Patrice!" Ben whispered. "The truck!"

She only looked at the approaching traffic. When she saw a break, she darted through, angling for the school.

The shooter opened the door and stepped out, pulling on his duster. Then he reached back for a nickel-plated pistol, a real heavyweight. He checked it over before he stuck it behind him in his belt.

The second man was out of the SUV now, too. They moved quickly across the playing fields, through the fringes of the ball game, straight for the school entrance. Ben watched with growing alarm. Lights were on everywhere over there. Dozens of people must still be inside, some of them kids.

He scrambled from under the tree, ready to take off after them. Just short of the street they stopped. A few words passed between them, and then they were quiet. They didn't try to hide or blend in. They were like carrion birds, silently roosting, waiting for their meal.

Ben glanced up and down the street. There was no chance he could reach the school. They'd see him and cut him down before he got near it. If he could get closer, though, he might be able to warn Patrice when she came out. Get closer how? There was no cover, no trees, no parked cars—only the boys playing football. The team on his side of the field was huddling up for a new play. He jogged toward them, doing his best to ignore his sore ankle.

The boys were built for football. A number of them were three or four inches taller than Ben and outweighed him by thirty pounds. But the shortest one was in charge. "Yeah?" he said as Ben approached. There was an edge in his voice. Crazy people hung out in this park, strung-out dopeheads, winos with the DTs.

"Mind if I play?" Ben kept half an eye on the men. They hadn't moved.

The boy looked him over, uncertain. "I don't know. Maybe later, okay?"

He was wearing a New Mexico Lobos baseball cap, turned backward. Grinning, Ben grabbed it and put it on, pulling the brim low over his eyes. "Come on, Hoss. Let an old man have some fun. I'll stay in and block." There were chuckles and murmurs of assent. Nobody wanted to block. They wanted to be out in the pass patterns, looking for downfield glory. The boy shrugged. "Just don't get in the way. All right, on three." The huddle broke.

They ran a couple of plays, both incomplete passes. The small boy—Joey, the others called him—was lightning quick, but he couldn't throw for beans. That was fine with Ben. He was where he wanted to be. He picked out a chubby kid on the other team and bumped forearms with him, steering clear of the swirl of bodies at midfield. That way he could watch the two by the street. They stayed as still as if they were planted in the ground, not even looking back when one of Joey's passes bounced close to their feet.

The door to the school opened, and a nun came out on the steps. She was talking to someone and pulled up when she realized they hadn't come with her. Then a girl appeared, seven or eight years old, lugging a plaid suitcase. She was dressed in a baggy school uniform and a lime-green knit watch cap. Patrice stepped out behind her, grabbing at the hat, but the girl had her free hand on it and wouldn't let go.

130

Ben watched all this from the huddle. Joey called another play, and the boys lined up on the ball. Ben stayed back. He didn't want to get in a scramble now, knocked down. The shooter and his partner were glued on Patrice, leaning forward, antsy, but not yet moving. Ben could yell, but there was so much traffic noise Patrice probably wouldn't hear.

Joey shouted the cadence and the ball was snapped. Boys fanned out over the grass. The men had their arms crossed, no weapons in sight. Ben made his decision. He swooped forward and snatched the ball from Joey's hands. "Man, what are you doin'?" the kid bawled.

Ben took two steps to gain momentum and whipped a pass, right at the shooter. It went a little high, skipping off the top of his head. Still, from that short distance, it hit like a brick. The man went down in a heap on top of his partner.

Ben was on them before they could move. He grabbed the duster and yanked it up. Where was the damn gun? The shooter launched an elbow at him, trying to turn over. Ben swatted him. *There.* He pawed the gun free and dropped with his knee in the middle of the man's back. "Stay down!" He stuck the barrel against the man's cheek.

Seeing the gun, the boys scattered like doves, except Joey. He ran in the other direction, coming to see what was happening. He stopped in his tracks. Ben sailed his Lobos cap to him. "It's all right. You'd better clear out."

Joey had a dazed look in his eyes. "What . . . what are you, man?"

Ben raised his voice. "Get the hell out of here!" Joey turned and bolted. Within seconds, Ben was alone on the field with the two men.

He looked across the street. The school entrance was empty. Then he caught sight of the girl's green hat half a block away, bobbing along behind a hedge. Patrice was in front, dragging her by the hand. She'd seen what was going on in the park. She glanced back and met Ben's eyes and hurried faster.

At that moment, the shooter's partner reared up on his hands and knees, charging forward. Too slow. Ben clubbed him backhanded with the pistol, and he went down and didn't move again. Ben turned the gun on the shooter. "Who sent you?"

The man had the brass to actually laugh. "You're gonna lose her, Bub, you waste time with us."

"Bub? You don't know who I am?" Ben said.

"I don't *care* who you are."

"Let's see if this changes your mind." Ben put the gun against the man's rump. "The Death Enema—that's what your pal called it. How'd it look when you were through with the dog? Real mess, I'll bet."

The man went limp underneath him. "Mister, come on now—"

"Who sent you?"

"Our boss in Phoenix got a call, that's all. We don't know who from. Don't ever want to know that kind of thing."

Ben leaned on him with the gun. "Were you supposed to kill her?"

"No! Just bring her to Miami. Don't get paid a penny if she's not alive."

"*Where* in Miami?"

"Gonna find that out later, after we had her."

Ben glanced up San Pedro again. Patrice and the girl had disappeared. With his left hand, he scrounged in the driver's pockets for his keys. He shifted his weight off the shooter but kept the gun where it was. "*Please, mister,*" the man whined.

So far Ben had kept his temper in check, but now he let go. "This is for Max, and for my damned ankle." He threw a punch at the man's head, so hard he cursed from the pain in his hand as he connected. They'd both be out for a long, long time. Ben sprinted for the truck, grabbing his knapsack as he ran by.

Three blocks down San Pedro was a major crosstown road. That meant more traffic, more chances for Patrice to catch a bus or flag down a car. Ben hopped behind the wheel and gunned the engine, squealing around the corner. He glanced around the truck. It was a rental, clean inside except for a leftover bag from McDonald's and the rifle the shooter had used at Patrice's house. A telephone book was in the map compartment on the passenger's door.

Ben swept the street ahead and saw them—the girl's hat was like a beacon—in front of a Circle K store.

Patrice recognized the truck as it came into the parking lot. She'd been talking to someone in a convertible. She turned and yanked the girl around the corner of the store. It was the wrong way to go. The lot was bordered by a high stockade fence. Ben angled the truck in, trapping them. He rolled down the window. "Patrice, come on."

"Get away from us." She pulled the girl behind her. Her eyes flicked wildly from side to side, searching for a way to escape.

Ben shut off the engine and started to get out. "We can figure this out. Just—"

Patrice lunged, banging the door into him, snapping his head into the roof. By the time he recovered, she was waving a short-bladed knife in his face. She was as quick as a bee with it.

"Get in the truck, Cherry," she said. The girl stayed put, her eyes narrow and angry. "*I said, get in the truck!*"

Cherry marched stiffly around and climbed in the passenger's seat. Patrice checked to make sure the keys were in the ignition. "I don't want to hurt you, Ben. Just get out of the way."

For a brief second he thought of making a grab for her hand, then let the idea drop. He didn't want anyone hurt either. He moved, and she edged by him.

"Patrice, I swear, I only came here to help you."

"By bringing those goons to my house?"

The girl cut in. "You shouldn't leave Max alone. You're always doing that."

"Be quiet," Patrice said. Her voice was fluttery. She was near the breaking point.

She held the knife out the window on Ben as she turned the key. The motor jumped to life. "Wait," he pleaded. "There's something in there. Gallup. Gallup, New Mexico."

Patrice already had the truck in reverse and was checking the mirror. She swung back on him. "What?"

"There's a phone book from Gallup, on the door. They must have been there or made calls." She stared at the book, surprised. "What's it mean, Patrice?"

She didn't answer but her arm sagged. Ben could have easily knocked the knife away. Instead he stepped forward, letting the point touch his breastbone, putting his life back in her hands. "I didn't bring them, believe me."

She wouldn't look at him, but he could see her eyes. They were brimming with tears as she fought with herself. Trust him, or not?

The girl was the one who decided. She saw Ben's half-open knapsack. "He brought Smoochy!" It was the toy frog-prince he'd taken from the pink room in Patrice's house. The girl cuddled it to her cheek. The green fleece was the same color as her hat. "Here Mama, kiss him. Good luck!" She held out the little frog.

Smiling weakly, Patrice gave it a peck. She wiped her eyes and glanced at Ben. "Get in."

SIXTEEN

Patrice only drove a block before she pulled over. "You can't sit there."

The girl's mouth turned down at the corners. "I *like* to sit here."

"Not in front. If we get in an accident, that air bag will put a *permanent* pout on your face. Switch with Mr. Tennant." Patrice leaned over to open the door. "Go on."

Ben helped her get settled, then climbed in the front. "Your name's Cherry?"

Patrice cut in. "Curl up with Moochy. Take a nap."

"He's Smoochy, not Moochy," the girl corrected. Then she turned away and clamped her eyes shut.

Patrice pulled onto Gibson Boulevard. Traffic crept along, held up by poorly timed stoplights. Every few seconds she checked the mirrors. She was worried someone was after them.

There was a bloodstain on her shirt from a scratch from the sapling she'd run into on the hillside by her house. Her eyes were red-rimmed and she had quite a sunburn. Her cuticles were ragged where she'd been chewing them.

She sensed Ben's eyes on her. "You don't need to feel sorry for me."

"No, but maybe you're the one who could use a nap."

At the mention of napping, Patrice motioned to the backseat. The girl was already sleeping. "I taught her that, falling asleep anytime. I couldn't have a little girl hanging around, listening in when there's a scam in the works." Her voice was tight with sarcasm—and guilt.

"Yes," she said, in response to his earlier question, "her name's Cherry. It was my aunt's name. Not really my aunt, but I called her that. She and her husband took me in after my father died."

"That was here in New Mexico?" Ben said.

Patrice nodded. "They were Picuris Indians. That's where I learned some of the language. They're both dead now, too, but the mountains, that whole place up near Taos—I knew my way around. That's why I came back."

Cherry stirred and Ben looked at her. Her face had the same strong angles as Patrice's, but she had almost-black eyes. The hair peeking from under her cap was thick and dark. He wondered who her father was. An Indian maybe? Was he the real reason Patrice had come back?

Patrice guessed what he was thinking. "No, he's not from around here, Ben. And he's the last person I'd go to for help." She signaled and changed lanes. "How did you find out about Sacred Heart?"

He pulled out the menu sheet.

"Hell," Patrice said. "I tried to keep the house clean, nothing that could lead somebody to her, but things creep in." She snapped her finger. "Cherry won a spelling bee last month at school. She brought the certificate home and left it in her nightstand. I'll bet that's how those two with the guns figured it out."

Ben nodded. "How long have you been hiding her?"

"Hiding? I suppose that's right—away from me anyway. Cons get in trouble; their kids are taken by social services.

That's the way it goes. I've kept her in different schools. It wasn't until I got picked up in Palm Beach last year and had to testify that I really made a point of keeping her secret. That wasn't easy either. Couldn't see her, couldn't even talk to her. Cherry started to hate me for being away so much."

They were nearing the interchange with I-25. "Go south here," he said.

"To the airport?"

"No. That's the first thing they'll check, the flights out of here this afternoon. We'll have to drive."

She agreed, but she wasn't happy about it. They rounded up the on-ramp and eased into the heavy flow of cars. Ben was glad she was driving. It gave her the feeling of being in control, and that would make the truth come easier. Still, he'd have to be careful, open doors with his questions, invite her to talk, not push her.

"How long have you known Balazs?" he said.

"Years—from back when we both were working the Gold Coast. He was just another green banana from Miami then, no focus, waiting for the perfect score to fall in his lap." She lowered her voice, embarrassed to admit it. "We had a thing going for a while."

This wasn't big news to Ben. He knew the kind of life she'd led. Still, he felt a stab of something. Jealousy, maybe.

She said, "That didn't have anything to do with your client files. I felt terrible about that. But I just couldn't—"

"Tell me about Cherry," he put in. He smiled at her surprised expression. "I've been wondering for months what made you turn on me. Money? Not a chance. You wanted a clean start too much to risk it for that. As soon as I saw Cherry's clothes at your house, I knew. You'd steal those files to protect your daughter. How did it happen?"

"I'd been staying at your place about a month," she said. "One afternoon while you were at your office, the phone rang. I didn't answer, but I listened as the message came in on the machine. It was Emile. Straight off he said, 'Pick up,

Patrice. I have someone to talk to you.' Next thing I knew, Cherry was on the line. I had her in a school in Montana—Billings. One of his men just walked in and snatched her off the playground. Emile wanted your files, so I took them. I had no choice. That's all there was to it."

She was nodding her head, not to Ben, but to herself. After five months she was still trying to convince herself she'd done the right thing, hanging him and his clients out to dry so she could save Cherry.

"Most mothers would have done the same," he said softly.

After a moment, she mumbled, "Thanks." Her guard was coming down. He could see it in the way she settled her shoulders into the seat and relaxed her grip on the wheel. She felt it too and gave a husky laugh. "Damn, I'll bet you're good at picking up women in bars." Ben shrugged and smiled.

"Do you know how Balazs found out you were staying with me?" he asked.

"One night in Palm Beach, after I testified, I needed a place to stay. I'd heard Emile was in jail, but one of his sidekicks was in town. Roddy Finney. He took me in. I told him I was trying to look you up. The Laundry Man. He must have told Emile."

That explained the files, but that was only the beginning. "What happened after you left Washington?" Ben said.

"After I gave Emile the files, I didn't have anywhere to go. The plans I'd made with you were shot. So—" She drew a deep breath. "I went with Emile, first to Miami, then to an island in the Caribbean. I know, it sounds stupid."

"No," Ben said, "not stupid at all. You were planning to con him."

Patrice looked at him and back at the road and at him again. "It's creepy, you know, this mind reading stuff."

"Mind reading? I'd have better luck reading Smoochy's mind than yours." He reached in his knapsack for her purse. "I grabbed this before I left your house. After I caught a ride on the Taos road, I had a chance to go through it."

He held up her checkbook. "According to the register in here, these past months you've been living on almost nothing. Deposits of sixty dollars, a hundred. Payments for groceries, rent, electric. Then two weeks ago, a single deposit of thirty thousand dollars, and no note where it came from. With your history, I'd say that was a scam paying off. And now Emile Balazs wants to find you, so I figure that's where the money was from. What did you do, decide to get even with him for taking Cherry?"

"Yeah. Something like that, I guess."

"Okay." Ben leaned over to look at the instrument panel. "We've got a full tank of gas and a long road ahead. Tell me about it."

"That thirty thousand was supposed to be onesies—like jacks, the game, an easy pickup. I wish it had worked out that way." She talked in bursts, winding up, letting loose, winding up again. Ben let her go at her own pace. He could get her to fill in the blank spots later.

She said she got the idea of running a con on Balazs even before she turned Ben's files over to him. She wanted enough cash to get a jump on a new life, and then she'd be out of the game for good.

After Balazs was admitted to WITSEC (on Ben's say-so), he went to Miami. Patrice followed a couple of days later. She kept out of sight, still worried that the people from Palm Beach were looking for her. Emile was caught up in a big deal, and things weren't going well. He must have worked it out because one night he showed up at her hotel driving a new Jaguar, beaming from ear to ear. "Time to pa-a-arty!"

And party they did. A long weekend in New Orleans, an overnighter in Las Vegas. Then he took her to his new house in the Caribbean, an island called St. Kitts. "You ever heard of it?" Patrice asked.

Ben gave a curt shake of his head. He was used to other people's dirty linen. The stories he'd heard at WITSEC could fill books on deviant psychology. Somehow, it was different coming from Patrice. He felt like a voyeur, peeking at something he shouldn't.

She noticed the look on his face. "It's a job, Ben. Nobody said I had to enjoy it."

He just nodded for her to go on with the story.

Maybe she didn't enjoy being with Balazs, but she kept her mind on her goal: getting enough money so she could live in peace for a while with Cherry. And Cherry was another problem. Balazs had insisted that Patrice bring her to St. Kitts. That made everything she did doubly complicated, and doubly dangerous.

Patrice never intended to go after Balazs directly. He was too unpredictable, raging one minute, charming the next. He scared the hell out of her sometimes. She had somebody else in mind as her mark.

Roddy Finney was married to Balazs' sister, Isabel. Finney worked as Balazs' accountant, and he ran the air-freight business. He knew all about the pilots, the planes, the hidden airstrips. He was a brilliant manager. Finney loved Isabel, but he kept her at a distance, never telling her what was really going on in his life. He was lonely, always working, always under pressure. He was a perfect target for someone like Patrice. Especially Patrice. He'd always had a crush on her, even years ago, when she and Emile were first together.

Reeling Finney in didn't take much effort. The night Patrice arrived in St. Kitts, she took him on a starlit walk in the jungle. She played footsie with him at breakfast the next day. She gave him a present, a little pot-'o-gold paperweight. He fell for her like a schoolboy, mindless, careless.

Her plan was to get Finney to skim a stack of cash for her, maybe a hundred thousand if he could swing it. Then she'd run away—from him, from Balazs, from everyone. He could cook the books, cover it up. Finney would go back to Isabel, and life in St. Kitts would roll merrily on.

Everything was falling into place, too, until Finney started to have trouble with Balazs. Being with Patrice made Finney rethink a lot of things, and it brought out a streak of conscience he'd buried a long time ago. The deal that had gone bad in Miami was back in a new incarnation, and Finney didn't like the smell of it. He didn't give Patrice many details, but he said it started with a trip Balazs had taken to Russia. He'd picked up something there and now had to resell it. The whole thing was too hot, way past dangerous.

Finney was so worried, he stopped sleeping. He was a wreck. Rule number one in running a scam is that if you've lost control of the mark, you've lost, period. Patrice was ready to give up, grab Cherry and make a run for it on a cruise ship or fishing boat, anything that floated. That's when Finney disappeared.

He was gone for two days. Patrice spent every minute she could down at the harbor, looking for a way off the island. Then, the second evening, while she and Cherry were walking through Basseterre, the main town, Finney pulled up beside them in a car. He looked like seven kinds of death. He wouldn't answer any questions but drove them straight to the airport. There was a plane waiting, a Carib Aviation charter, already warming up.

Ben broke in. "Got a problem?" He pointed at the rearview mirror. Patrice had been glancing there as she talked.

"Just a car behind us." She checked again. "No problem, I guess. So back to Finney. At the airport, Cherry got on the plane and Finney hugged me. I knew he was in trouble, but I didn't have any idea how bad it was until then. He kissed me; even his lips were trembling. I asked him what he'd

141

done, and he pulled this awful sad grin and said, 'Something good, I hope.' That's when he gave me this."

Patrice lifted a thin gold necklace from under her collar. Dangling from it was a key. "What's that?" Ben said.

She tucked it away. "It goes to a safety-deposit box. Finney said there wasn't time to explain, but he gave me a note to read on the plane. *Shit!*"

Patrice accelerated and swerved into the fast lane. Ben glanced around. The traffic had thinned to a trickle. On either side of the highway there were farms. A line of trees rose ahead, intersecting the road. Patrice pumped up the speed, to seventy-five or eighty. "What's the matter?"

"Behind us. That car." Her eyes jumped to the mirror.

It was the same car she'd been watching before. It was fifty yards back and closing, right on the center stripe. Ahead, the shoulders of the highway pinched in. The trees were cottonwoods along the banks of the Rio Grande. The bridge over the river was low and narrow. The car would catch them there, where there was no place to get out of the way. "Damn," Patrice said, ducking down. "He's got a gun!"

Ben could see the pistol silhouetted in the car's rear window. There was someone in the backseat. The car wobbled, sliding back and forth over the center line.

Smiling, Ben turned back around. "Pull over. Let him pass."

"What? Like hell, I will."

"Forget the gun. Look at the driver, his face. That guy's got problems of his own, not with us."

She studied the mirror. "What's wrong with him?"

"Just slow down."

They were on the bridge now. The river was murky brown, roiling along a few yards below the decking. She moved to the right and the other car rolled by. The driver was furious, shouting and swatting the air around his head. In the back was a young boy, holding a water pistol. Every few seconds he fired a stream into his father's ear.

"There's a kid who's going to have trouble sitting down later," Patrice said.

Ben laughed. "A good lesson for you, too. Not everybody is out to get you, Patrice."

She glanced at him. Her face was serious. "Maybe. I'll think about that."

They traveled a half mile in silence, through the green swath of the Isleta Indian Reservation. "What did Roddy Finney's letter say?" Ben asked.

Patrice checked to make sure Cherry was still sleeping before she answered. "About Emile's Russian deal, not much, only that Finney had put an end to it. I don't know how." She looked away and her voice quavered. "Finney expected Emile to find out and kill him, that was clear.

"The rest of the letter was about Isabel—where they met, their first date, why they never had children—personal stuff like that. Finney was afraid of what would happen to her if he wasn't around, so he wanted me to look out for her. Me, of all people, take care of his wife, get to be her *friend*. He had it all planned for us, a new place to live away from Emile. L.A., or maybe even Europe. That kind of life was going to cost money, and that's where this key came in." She touched the necklace.

"Finney's letter didn't say how much money was in the safety-deposit box, only that it would keep us safe and comfortable. He didn't trust me enough just to give it to me. He said that flat out. So he had the bank make a special box, with two keys. He gave me one; Isabel got the other. Needed both to get in."

"Where is the bank?" Ben asked.

"The letter didn't say, but Isabel was supposed to know. That was Finney's plan. I had to go to Isabel before I could get the money, tell her what had happened between him and me. That conscience of his—he wanted a clean slate, even after he was gone."

Ben had noticed the tension in her voice. She was coming to a part of the story she didn't like. "How did Peter Saar get involved?" he asked.

"My friend Peter," she sighed. "He put Cherry and me up for a while after we got back, until I found the house in Truchas. I told him about everything—Emile and Finney, Isabel, the money. Things had changed for me. In St. Kitts I was scared nearly out of my mind. I put Cherry in school in Albuquerque and started making my little statues to sell. I figured six months of that and things would cool off. Cherry and I could go somewhere, be together, be *normal*. One way or the other, I was done scamming."

She grew quiet, so Ben prompted her. "But Roddy Finney's money was still out there, and you still had your key."

"Yes," she said. "Peter had been thinking about that. Rich single women were his specialty. He came to me, laid it out. He could cozy up to Isabel, get her key, go to the bank, walk away with a bagful of cash. Onesies. I didn't want anything to do with it. I argued with him, told him it was too dangerous. I should have argued harder."

She was squeezing the wheel, really angry with herself, and Ben understood why. She hadn't asked for part of the take, but she hadn't turned it down either. Thirty thousand in dirty money, bought with Saar's life. Ben slid his hand across the seat, not touching her, but close enough to comfort her.

She said, "I told you Peter had been a priest and that he kept up with the church. That's how the phone book from Gallup ties in. Peter lived there, near a friend of his, another priest, Monsignor Blaize. He's the secretary for the archbishop. Blaize was always fixing things for Peter, for me too. He got Cherry into Sacred Heart tuition-free. Before Peter went to St. Kitts, Monsignor Blaize wrote him a letter of introduction. That gave him a perfect cover."

"Cover?" Ben said. "As what?"

"A priest." He seemed so surprised that she laughed.

"There's no magic to it. If you know the talk—the gospels and liturgies and all the rest—if you say you're a priest, you are one as far as the rest of the world is concerned. Nobody's going to ask for ID."

She laughed again, because Ben still had that uncertain look on his face. "Peter was going to stay at the presbytery in Basseterre, say he was on a retreat after working too hard with the Indians, something like that. What he really wanted was to get to Isabel and from there to the money."

"That explains how Rand Mosby and her CIA friends got mixed up about who he was. Your father—Father Saar." For a moment Ben was quiet, thinking. "And now you've got your key back."

"Peter sent it to me from St. Kitts, in a package with a cashier's check for the thirty thousand. There was a note, typical Peter. 'Payday! I'm staying on for a week or so. I'll bring you a present.'"

"Why would he stay on if he already had the money?" Ben said.

"That's what he meant by the rest of the message. It was a code we used. He had another scam going. When it was over he'd come home and bring me a present."

"What kind of scam?" Ben asked.

She shook her head. "I don't know."

Ben stared across the desert, watching the sun edge down behind a low butte. Peter Saar had gone to St. Kitts quietly acting the part of a priest. In the beginning things went according to plan. He got the second safety-deposit key from Isabel, and that led him to the money Roddy Finney had stashed away. But that wasn't enough for Saar. He'd gotten tied up in another scam, and he'd gotten himself killed.

"It isn't the thirty thousand Balazs wants," Ben said. "He probably doesn't know about that. Saar stole something from Balazs, didn't he?" Patrice didn't answer. "The shooter, back there in the park, told me he hadn't come to hurt you but to bring you to Miami. Balazs must think you've got whatever Saar took. That's why he's after you."

He waited, but again she didn't answer.

What did Balazs want? Armed kidnappers in broad daylight on the wide open streets of Albuquerque—there weren't many things worth that kind of risk. And what about Patrice? Parts of her story didn't hang together. Like what she'd said about Cherry. Something not quite right there. But it could wait. She'd told him enough for now.

Patrice was caught up in her own thoughts, and Ben could read nothing in her face. It gave him a nervous feeling, drawing a blank like that. He thought over everything she'd told him. So many twists and turns trying to leave her old life, always getting sucked back in. Quicksand.

He continued to watch her, letting his mind drift with the hum of the tires. Back, months ago. The Bay Bluff Motel. She crossed the room to him. A gentle touch on his arm. *You'll help me, Ben? A clean start?—Sure. That's what I do.* Such simple words, but nothing was simple with her.

Patrice looked at him, her face still empty. Then she smiled and laid her hand on the exact spot on his arm he'd just been thinking about. The touch was enough to send a shock right through his body. He wanted to pull away, but instead he took her hand and held it.

SEVENTEEN

Patrice turned off the highway in the central New Mexico town of Belen. It was a dusty place with a big Wal-Mart on the northside and a string of fast food joints along the main drag. Trains hooted in the rail yard by the river. They picked a quiet motel and got a pair of thirty-dollar-a-night rooms, paying cash. Inside, Cherry made a beeline for the TV. "No HBO," she grumbled.

Ben was feeling sluggish from all the time on the road, so, when he got to his own room, he pulled off his shirt and started a set of calisthenics. He kept it simple—decline push-ups with his feet on the bed, one-legged squats, crunches. He was heading into the bathroom for a shower when a knock came at the door. Before he opened it, he heard arguing. Patrice stood, hands on her hips, frowning at Cherry. "You had better shape up, little lady."

The girl glared back. "Grace Kelly says you're a whore."

"Don't you mention that name to me!" Patrice herded her past Ben into the room. "I've got to go out. Buy us some clothes, for one thing. Can you watch her?"

Ben had given Patrice her purse, and she'd taken some time to put on makeup. The change was dramatic. She'd loaded on the base to cover her sunburn, then added an extra-heavy tinge of eye shadow and mascara. He could smell perfume, too. "Well?" she demanded.

"Sure, I'll watch her. You might . . ." He made a fingering motion over her chest. She had two undone buttons.

"Oh, I forgot." She fastened them up.

"Remember," he said, "no credit cards, especially if you make any phone calls."

"Right, right," she answered, turning to go.

Cherry was already seated on the bed, watching a cartoon show on television. She still had that green hat on and had Smoochy cradled in her arm. "I'm going to take a shower. Will you be okay?" he asked.

"Of course," she said with a world-weary tone.

Ben put the chain on the door and went into the bathroom. When he was finished showering, he called out, "Who's Grace Kelly?"

Cherry took a while to answer. "A girl at school. She's thirteen, the oldest girl there. That's for the boarding kids. There's older ones with the day-schoolers. _I'm_ her best friend."

"And her name's really Grace Kelly?"

"Grace Kelly Martino."

"Ah. She called your mom a whore?"

"Grace Kelly says anybody who wears makeup is a whore."

Ben stepped out of the bathroom and went to the mirror to comb his hair. "I'll bet she makes you call her 'Princess Grace.' "

Cherry looked at him, frowning. "How'd you know that?"

"Just a guess." He sat beside her on the bed. She'd brought a few sheets of motel stationery with her. Some quick outlines were sketched on them. "What's this?"

148

Cherry glanced over. "That's our dog, see? Maxie. His legs here. The rest of him. Mom made it before she left. I can fill it in, pencil or crayons."

Like the Santa Claus cutout Ben had seen at Patrice's place in Truchas, a beautiful little thing. "You do this a lot with her?"

Cherry's expression became wary. This was private. Maybe she shouldn't be talking about it. "Yeah. Mom's always making them for me. It's kind of fun."

She turned back to the television. The cartoon was an old *Beavis and Butt-Head*. Ben knew about cartoons from the children he worked with at WITSEC. To a lot of those kids, the shows were their lives: "My dad is so like Wile E. Coyote, you know?" Whether they followed cartoons or not, Ben could always read kids, and there was a danger in that. It was too easy to drive a wedge between them and their parents, to use them. Ben was careful not to. The children he saw were damaged enough. They didn't need another adult messing with their heads.

Beavis laughed; Cherry laughed. When Ben joined in she clammed up and gave him a cold look, as if he'd intentionally spoiled her fun. He said, "You don't like grown-ups much, do you?" She huffed and aimed her nose in the air. "At least you don't like your mom very much."

"What's to like?" she said. Her voice was suddenly small.

He nudged the paper with the outline of Max. "She's teaching you to draw. You're good at it, too, I'll bet."

Cherry picked at the ragged threads on the bedspread. "She probably won't come back. She does that, just leaves me places."

For a fraction of a second Ben wondered if she could be right, then dismissed it. "Don't worry. She won't be gone long." He leaned back on his elbows. "I meant to ask you, who cuts your hair?"

"My hair?" She touched the cap, making sure it was still there. "Sister Marguerite. Why?"

"You tell her how to cut it?"

She frowned at the TV. "Of course, dummy."

He slipped the hat off her head. "So that's why it's like your mom's." It *was* the same style as Patrice's, but lopsided and far too short around the ears. Sister Marguerite had done a terrible job.

"Gimme that back," Cherry bawled, lunging for the cap.

"Sure. No problem." Ben tugged it down on her head. He traced a stain on the nightstand with his finger. "Your mom's really pretty. That's nice. But you know what I like about her?"

Once more, Cherry tried the world-weary tone. "I couldn't begin to guess."

"She can chew nails up and spit them out."

"She can *not* do that."

"It's only an expression. Anyway, I expect she chews your butt quite a bit."

That brought a smile, and a giggle. "That's gross."

"Only if you take it literally." He slapped his hands on his knees and stood up. "Tell you what. Let's go bowling. I saw a place right up the street." He grabbed one of the pieces of paper she'd brought and started to write a note on the back for Patrice, letting her know where they were going.

"I don't know how to go bowling. I want to watch TV."

Ben finished the note and slid across the floor, aiming an imaginary ball. "Come on. We'll bowl a few lines, drink some soda pop, have a great time."

She giggled again and started to stir off the bed. "Do you always act this weird?"

He slipped on his shoes and opened the door. "Nope. Sometimes I'm worse."

Ben really had no interest in bowling. He wanted to use a pay phone, and he figured the bowling alley would have one. It was called the Serial Bowl. Inside the door was a wall of posters from the old movie serials: Buck Rogers and Zorro and Roy, Dale, and Trigger. He rented shoes and got a score sheet from a woman with coke-bottle glasses and a beehive haircut. She smiled at Cherry. "Your daddy gonna teach you the fine points, honey?" Cherry hid behind Ben's legs.

The six lanes on the left were taken up with league play. The other six were empty except for one family, a mother and four kids. They were chattering in Spanish, rolling frames in no particular order. Ben set up next to them. While he was getting Cherry a ball, he looked at the coffee shop in the corner of the building. At the end of the counter was a pay phone and, sitting a couple of stools away, a deputy sheriff.

By the time Ben returned with the ball, Cherry had made friends with a girl from the next lane. "Mimi said I could share her ball," she proudly announced. Mimi was shorter than Cherry but a few years older. Earnestly, she was demonstrating the slide and delivery.

Her mother, smiling at Ben, said in unaccented English, "She wants to be everybody's mama."

He let the two girls have their fun while he waited for the deputy to move. Ben didn't want to get too close to him. For all he knew, there might be a nationwide all points bulletin out on him and Patrice. Aaron Joquand would have no trouble arranging a thing like that, and that was why Ben wanted to use the phone. If he could get through to Rand Mosby, she might be able to tell him what Joquand was up to.

After half an hour, the coffee took its toll. The deputy plodded into the rest room, and Ben headed for the phone. He paid with a phone card and dialed his own number at WITSEC, adding the code to get the voice mail menu. Sure enough, the fourth message in the queue was from Mosby.

"Ben," she said, "we need to talk." He listened carefully. She sounded tired, but not too stressed. "Things have changed. Call me, and hurry." She gave three numbers: work, home, cell phone. "We can have this all cleared up in a day or two."

Ben tried the home number first, then her office. A secretary answered and put him right through. "You're working late," he said when Mosby picked up.

"Where are you, Ben?"

He laughed. "I'm in trouble, that's where."

"Nah, you're fine." Almost joking. Definitely more relaxed than she'd been the last time he saw her. "Nobody's got a beef with you. Except Ken Van Allen. That Barbie crack really ticked him off. Ben, I'm sorry about all this. You're the last person I want to hurt." Her voice became slow and buttery. "I've thought a lot about you."

He let that pass.

"So where's Callan?" she asked.

"She's safe, barely."

"She's with you then? What's that noise in the background? Sounds like bowling."

"You're as subtle as a jackhammer, you know that Rand?"

She made a noise in the back of her throat, like a purr. "The way I remember, you don't like it subtle."

"I give as good as I get," he said, laughing. Okay, enough foreplay. "You sound pretty sassy. What's up? Your message said things had changed."

Mosby was all business now. "And how. There's a warrant out on Balazs. Just came in this morning. Racketeering and conspiracy. But he's got dual citizenship, and that complicates it. The arrest has to be on U.S. soil. Can Callan get him to come here? Anywhere in the country will do."

The front door opened and Patrice came in. She had a big plastic sack with her and a smaller paper one. She spotted him first, then Cherry. She went to the girl.

"What's in it for Patrice?"

"Balazs gets put away. She's out from under. Everything's hunky-dory."

"What about benefits?" Ben said. "Health insurance, retirement plan."

Mosby gave an angry sigh. "Look, Callan's every guy's dream girl. That scores some points with you, but not me. That tramp's not getting a penny."

"All right, but she may not buy it," Ben said. "Where's Joquand in this?"

"Out of it. As soon as he found out about the warrant, he backed off. I checked with some people at Langley. Joquand's in deep shit for being too close to Balazs. That gives me a free hand—for now anyway."

"All right. How about if I run this by Patrice and call you back?"

"Sure, but don't take too long," Mosby said. "I'll be leaving here in a few minutes. You can get me at home later."

"Rand," Ben said before she could hang up, "I'm counting on you to be straight with me."

She didn't hesitate. "It's no skin off my knuckles, Ben, and I owe you. Consider it partial payment. Just tell me the place and the time, and I'll take care of the rest."

"Okay. I'll get back to you." He put the phone down and stood for a moment, thinking it over. He'd spent a lot of hours on the phone with Rand. It was a long time ago, but he remembered the quirks of her voice. He figured she was telling the truth. Still, he was going to check out the warrant on Balazs. If that was on the level, then this could be a real patch of blue sky.

The deputy was coming out of the bathroom, but he didn't seem to notice Ben as they passed each other. From the stiffness of Patrice's neck he could tell she was angry. He dropped into the seat beside her. "You bring me something to eat?" he said, picking up the paper bag she'd carried in. She grabbed at it, but he already had it open. There was a snub-nosed pistol inside. "Uh-oh, Mommy's been shopping at Wal-Mart again."

"I got clothes at Wal-Mart. *That* I got from a guy in a bar."

153

"Just some guy in a bar?"

"Yeah. Why'd you think I put on my makeup with a fire hose? You want to attract some bees, you got to put on some honey."

"I wonder what Grace Kelly would say about that," Ben replied.

Patrice's eyes flared. "Dammit, Ben, I leave you alone with Cherry for five minutes and you bring her here. Bowling, for God's sake!"

He laughed. "Count yourself lucky. I could have taken her to the American Legion. I saw an ad over there by the phone. They've got line dancing tonight." She gave him a sour look. "So what do you want a gun for? We've got two out in the truck."

"Cannons. I need something small I can handle." She took the bag from him.

Cherry had been sitting with her new friends, and she got up to take her turn. The ball rolled true, her first strike. She and Mimi huddled by the scoring table, bouncing on their toes while Mimi's mother toted the pins. "All right," Ben said, "she's having fun with me instead of you. Ease up a little. Give yourself a chance."

Patrice looked down, slowly shaking her head. "Maybe that's the problem. I've had too many chances. I can't seem to get it right with her."

"You get scared, Patrice, put in a corner, and you make bad choices. Join the crowd. Perfect parents don't exist."

"I had a plan," she said. "I wasn't going to leave her in that awful school. With the money Peter sent, we were going to move away. I'm supposed to be in Denver the day after tomorrow for a job interview, receptionist at an art gallery. Now that's ruined."

"Maybe," Ben said. "But there are other jobs."

Patrice didn't seem to hear him. "I've got to get to Miami. Tonight."

"Oh? You've been busy."

"I called Emile in St. Kitts. He was out, but I talked to his buddy, Mick Laraby. Mick wouldn't say what they wanted me for. Better leave that for the boss. I meet him tomorrow at one-thirty, in Miami. That's it." Patrice kneaded her palm, that old scar. She was nervous. Tomorrow afternoon wasn't far off.

Ben could have told her about his conversation with Mosby, that this was exactly what they wanted, to get Balazs in the U.S. so they could arrest him. Something made him stop. He glanced at the paper bag, the bulge of the gun in there. He didn't like the way Patrice was pulling back from him, the way she'd said, "*I've* got to get to Miami."

"I know a travel agent, super-discreet," he said. "So discreet I don't even know where her office is. She can get us plane reservations."

She looked at him. "You don't have to go with me, Ben."

He held her gaze, smiling. "Sure I do."

All the air seemed to go out of her at once. She leaned her head on his shoulder. "Thanks . . . Really, thanks."

"Where are you going to meet him?"

"Mick wanted me to go to the Biltmore. That's where Emile always stays in Miami. No chance, I told him. Co-coWalk instead, that's—"

"I know," Ben said. "I've been there. I'll make my call, and we can get started."

As he headed for the phone, he heard Patrice say to Cherry, "We've got to go now. Finish up."

"I'm not *through!*" the girl replied.

The sheriff's deputy had taken a stool at the far end of the counter, so Ben had all the privacy he needed. As always, his travel agent was in. He sometimes imagined her as a survivalist freak, hiding in a high-tech bunker in Montana. She tsk-tsked when he told her what he needed. He said he wouldn't fly out of Albuquerque. This late, there probably weren't any flights from Las Cruces or the other small airports nearby. After a minute she murmured, "ain't we the lucky duck." There was a 1:00 A.M. flight from El Paso, connecting through Dallas. Get him into Miami by 8:00 in the morning.

"Good," Ben said. "Go ahead—" He stopped because he heard loud voices behind him. Cherry had squared off with Patrice. The girl didn't want to leave, and she was letting everyone in the place know. Patrice tugged her into a chair and knelt in front of her, speaking sternly. "Book three seats," Ben said into the phone. He had a squeaky-clean credit card number already on file, an account Larry Jong had set up for their Laundry Man clients. That took care of the bill. She clicked her computer keys and hummed a tune and in a moment the transaction was complete.

After the travel agent hung up, Ben stood with the phone at his ear, watching Patrice and Cherry. The girl had her hands clenched on the bottom of the chair. She was snapping her legs the way an angry cat snaps its tail. Patrice was trying to reason with her, but she was getting nowhere and quickly losing what was left of her temper.

A woman came in the front door, young, pretty. Half the people in the place turned and waved or called hello. A quiet town like this—that's what Patrice needed. That, and time to get to know Cherry. But she was going to Miami. To Balazs. And who knew where that would lead. The middle of a damn firestorm, probably.

It was time to end this, grab for that patch of blue sky. Rand Mosby wouldn't be home yet, so he dialed her cell phone number.

As it rang, Patrice put her hand on Cherry's arm and tried to pull her off the chair. "Get away!" the girl shouted. "Quit hurting me!" Patrice wasn't hurting her, but that didn't matter. The league bowlers gawked; the deputy scowled over his shoulder.

Mosby answered the phone. "Yeah?" Thank God, the connection was clear.

"Rand, it's Ben. We've got it set up. Balazs will be in Miami tomorrow."

"Damn, that was quick! Here, let me get something to write with." She fumbled away from the phone for a moment. "Okay, where?"

"CocoWalk Mall. One-thirty."

"Got it. You know, this might even be fun."

"Maybe," he said. "After it's over we can work on Joquand—whatever he's got on you."

Mosby laughed. "You never give up, do you?"

Then all hell broke loose across the way. Cherry was yelling again, and she tried to kick Patrice in the shin. She hit the paper bag instead. It split wide open. The pistol went spinning down the alley into the gutter.

Ben said, "Rand, I've got to go. See you tomorrow."

He hung up and took off at a sprint. "Whoa, honey." He gave Patrice a strained grin. "Next time buy her a doll. These toy guns excite her too much." He scooped it up and slipped it back in the torn sack. The crowd had formed into a ragged semicircle. The deputy was ambling up to the back of the group.

"Come on, sweetie," Ben said to Cherry. "Gotta go!"

She gripped the chair tighter. Her face was purple. She was holding her breath out of spite.

"Okay, Cherry. Don't say I didn't warn you." Ben reached out.

"Hey, don't hit her," the deputy said.

Ben grabbed her hat and headed for the cash register. *"Give me that back!"* she shrieked. *"Here, give it!"* She shot out of the chair, chasing him.

Ben tossed a twenty at the woman with the coke-bottle glasses and coasted out the door. Cherry was beside him, hopping and howling, trying to reach the cap. He shoved it in her hands, while Patrice came running up from behind. "You're a real pair of peaches," Ben said. "Could you keep a lid on it? In public at least?"

"It's her fault," Cherry grumbled.

"Forget it," Ben said. "We've got to get on the road."

EIGHTEEN

The lobby of Miami's Biltmore Hotel was dark and cool as a cave. Ben had taken up a post on one of the old-style settees, where he had a view through the main door. He yawned and stretched. He'd gotten only two hours of sleep the night before, on the plane from Dallas. The rest of the trip had been one long bickering match between Cherry and Patrice. They were doing better this morning. He'd heard Cherry say, "Thanks, Muzzy," when Patrice gave her a new shirt to wear. Patrice bent and kissed the peak of the girl's hat. "Sure, Yodel." Nicknames were always a good sign. Besides, now that they weren't around, Ben missed them, even the arguing.

He'd left them an hour ago in a hotel out by Miami International. His first stop was a pay phone, to call the morning Duty Officer at WITSEC. Bert was chatty, as usual, giving no sign he knew anything about Ben's troubles. Ben asked him to check for a warrant on Emile Balazs. The WITSEC computers could access the Justice Department main database. After a few minutes Bert said, "Yep. Balazs, Emile.

Arrest warrant issued yesterday. Judge Tays, Northern District of Virginia."

Ben then phoned Mosby's office. Her secretary said she was out. "I'm supposed to meet her in Miami today," Ben said. "Do you know when her plane gets in?"

"No," the woman said. "She made her own reservations."

Mosby didn't answer her cell phone either. That put her in the air, on her way south. He checked his watch. Plenty of time for her to get there and get set up at CocoWalk.

With that done, he'd come to the Biltmore. Maybe someone could tell him what Emile Balazs was up to in Miami. With luck, Ben might even get to see him. Just watching for a few minutes, he could learn a lot. Balazs was headed for jail, but he'd still have a long reach from inside. The more Ben knew, the safer he could make things for Patrice.

He started with the hotel grounds crew, but they spoke no English, and Ben's Spanish wasn't good enough to hold a real conversation. He moved on to the doorman, who was out on the lawn, sneaking a smoke. He was tall and lean and had the manner of a church deacon. When Ben described Balazs and asked if he was staying there, the man sniffed, "We don't give out information about guests, sir." Then he made a point of looking at the tennis courts. There was Balazs, whacking balls back and forth with one of the hotel instructors. Actually, he seemed to be hitting balls *at* the instructor.

It was too open there for Ben to stay and watch, so he went inside. He'd wait for Balazs to finish his practice session, and then he'd follow him, picking up what he could.

Ben's eyes and ears were always working, absorbing information. If he concentrated, he could magnify his skills, tuning in on the tiniest details. He did that now, focusing around him. The shade of the big orchid on the table; the French-Canadian accent of the man at the check-in desk; the elegant six-stone engagement ring worn by the woman getting off the elevator.

After a few minutes a man and woman came in, a father-daughter pair. Ben noticed on the way up to the door that the woman looked at the tennis courts. Her face lit up with a smile. Balazs? Ben wondered. Was he the one she was looking at? The old man used a cane, but it didn't slow him down much. The woman wore sunglasses. The smallish oval lenses were a perfect fit for her narrow, haughty face.

The man picked a place to sit on the far side of the lobby. In the middle of the floor were two massive cages filled with songbirds. He waved his cane overhead. Startled, the birds fluttered about, a whirlwind of bright color. It made him chuckle, but soon he was sour-faced again. He began to lecture his daughter about something. She nodded, making sure he knew she agreed.

Ben leaned forward, listening. It was Spanish but he might catch something. Next thing, he was pulling back behind the orchid. Balazs had come through the door.

Even from that distance Ben caught a whiff of his cologne. He seemed bigger, more exaggerated than Ben remembered—his buoyant stride, his perfect suntan, his grin, especially his grin. "Manuel, Morena, hello!" His voice boomed so loudly that the songbirds flew into a frenzy. Balazs gave a look of annoyance. He didn't like being upstaged. "I'm starved," he said to the two visitors. "Let's go downstairs."

Ben knew from the lobby signs that there was a cafe on the lower level. While they took the elevator, he slipped down the stairs. He stopped a few steps short of the bottom. Ahead, the members of the restaurant staff were lined up, saying hello to the old man, the one Balazs had called Manuel. They fawned over him, shaking his hand, patting his arm. "Good morning, sir. Wonderful to see you." Balazs and Morena stood a discreet distance away. The head-waiter showed up and led them to a table.

"May I help you?" another waiter said to Ben. His tone was a little condescending. Ben was dressed in jeans and running shoes and a cheap sport coat he'd bought at the airport gift shop. There was a bulge in his coat pocket, from Patrice's pistol. He wasn't going to leave it with her, not with the mood she was in.

Ben scanned the restaurant. There were two sections, an ornate outside courtyard and a smaller inside dining room, divided from each other by a two-story wall of glass. Balazs' party was outside, seated by a large fountain. Ben would have to be right next to them to hear what they said. He decided to stay inside and watch through the windows. With the sun angling down, they wouldn't be able to see him. He pointed back by the kitchen. "That booth there."

The waiter raised his eyebrows but didn't argue. "As you wish, sir."

The busboy in that section had been first in line to greet the old man. He'd done more bowing and scraping than anyone. Ben wanted a chance to talk to him. But first he turned his attention to the three in the courtyard.

One thing was obvious. Balazs and Manuel didn't get along. They sat across from each other but made little eye contact. Morena, in the middle, was trying to get a conversation started. When neither man took up the thread, she tittered nervously.

Then she did something that made Ben sit forward and stare. She reached down and took Balazs' wrist. Smiling, she pressed his fingers to her belly. Balazs seemed confused by this, but he didn't pull away. The old man saw nothing because their hands were hidden under the tablecloth.

Upstairs, Ben had noted the way the woman walked and sat and he'd thought maybe she was pregnant. He wasn't sure since she was wearing a loose pantsuit, and he was too far away to see the other things that would have clued him in. Now he was certain. And whom did a pregnant woman want to touch her belly? The father, only the father. He wondered if Balazs even knew. The way he reacted, probably not. Ben shook his head. Damn. Satan's spawn.

"Somethin' funny, sir?" It was the busboy—Abel, accord-

ing to his name tag. "You were laughing." He had a flashy
grin and a blunt Spanish accent.

"Not really. Something I saw." Ben moved his water glass
so Abel could fill it.

"Do you know anything about that man?" He indicated
Balazs. "I was going to ask him for a game of tennis."

Abel's expression became uneasy. "Nice day for tennis."
Ben remembered what the doorman had said, that they
didn't give out information about guests. Abel arranged a
few things on the table. "You want me to bring you some orange juice, sir?"

"Sure," Ben said. He watched him walk away. He needed
new shoes, and his shirt cuffs were frayed. So he wasn't a
clothes hound, but he did like to spend money. He had a
gold chain on each wrist and wore three gold rings.

Ben pulled a ten and a twenty from his wallet. He hid the
twenty under his napkin and put the other bill on the corner of the table.

Abel returned with the juice and a pot of coffee. His eyes
locked on the money.

Ben nudged it. "That man . . . ?"

Abel was a quick study. Stashing the ten in his pocket, he
nodded toward Balazs. "Once a month, maybe, he comes
here. Always takes the Capone Suite."

"Capone?" Ben said.

"Yeah. Al Capone. Stayed here in the old days." He
pointed upward with his thumb. "Suite at the top of the
tower. That man there, not much of a tipper, you know?
Likes to bet on his tennis matches though. And he cheats,
so I heard."

Ben laughed. "I'll remember that. Who's that with him?
He called him Manuel."

"That's *Mister* Herrera. His daughter, too, Morena. You
don't know him?" Ben shook his head. "You're not from
around here then."

"He's pretty important?"

163

"You know it. Look around, you see his trucks all over the highway. Herrera Construction. He built half the buildings in Miami, I think."

"They don't seem to like each other much, Herrera and the other guy."

Abel studied them for a moment. He could see it, too. "You're right. Not such a happy thing for the other one, to have Mr. Herrera mad at him."

"Why's that?"

Abel got a crafty look in his eye. "You're a pretty curious guy, know that?"

"I am," Ben admitted. "So why isn't it good to have Mr. Herrera mad at you?" He slipped his napkin aside, revealing the twenty-dollar bill.

Abel's face instantly brightened. "Mr. Herrera's a real story around here. Not just a businessman, see. Notice how he limps? Bay of Pigs. He was one of the pilots, flew cover for our boys out of Nicaragua. CIA trained 'em all. He got shot down by one of Castro's planes. Hit in the hip. Was ten hours in the water with that bullet in him. Then four days in the swamps before the Commie bastards caught him. For people here, *Cubanos,* Mr. Herrera's a hero. Somebody makes him really mad, they're gonna live to regret it."

"Bay of Pigs—that had to be a long time before you were born. You know all about that?"

Abel shrugged. "Some people, it's the stock market. My family, what else we gonna talk about at the dinner table?" He bent and gave Ben a tap on the shoulder. "Manuel Herrera's a real man, I say." He must have thought Ben didn't believe him, because he went on in a rush. "You talk to people around here. They tell you. That Lee Harvey Oswald? It's bullshit. Was Mr. Herrera who got that prick Kennedy killed. Set it up, paid the freight, everything. Like I said, a real damn hero!"

Ben let him have the money, and stared after him as he

strode into the kitchen. The Kennedy story was weird enough by itself, but he was thinking back to when Rand Mosby had visited his house. She mentioned the Cuban mafia. And the CIA—they definitely had a finger in what was going on with Balazs. Either it was a very small world, or there were angles working here that Ben couldn't begin to figure.

He watched the three outside again. Balazs and Manuel were finally speaking to each other, but it wasn't going well. They seemed to be exchanging debating points, one sentence each. Morena broke in, starting quietly but finishing with force, chopping the air with her hand, then pointing her finger at Balazs' chest. She must have taken her father's side because he wore a satisfied smirk. Balazs was shocked into silence. He looked down at his plate, as if to concede the argument. The Herreras couldn't see his face, but Ben could. It was filled with contempt.

The waiter approached to take Ben's order. Ben told the man he would get his food from the buffet and sent him away.

Outside, there was a flurry of activity among the staff. Six men in Navy dress whites were led to the table beside Balazs'. They were pale and bleary-eyed, their movements sluggish. That's all Ben needed to guess their story. They'd had a party-till-dawn blowout last night. They weren't just buddies on shore leave, not at the Biltmore, not at three hundred dollars a night. They must be here for some special function.

Ben wouldn't have cared about that, except for what was going on at the other table. Morena was talking to Balazs, trying to coax him out of his sulk. Manuel's attention was on the Navy men. His face was rigid, his eyes narrowed to slits. Just the presence of those men made him angry. They were loud, getting a little rowdy. Was that the problem?

Ben rattled the ice in his glass, getting Abel's attention.

Grinning, he hustled over with his water pitcher. For thirty dollars, Ben had bought a friend for life. "Tell me about the woman, Morena. Is she married? Got a boyfriend?"

Abel chuckled. "You know how to pick 'em. She's married though, to her papa's business. Mr. Herrera's got no sons. Too bad, huh? He stays most of the time now down in the Keys. Big place. Beautiful. She runs the company, day-to-day stuff. Got no time for men."

Ben thought about Balazs' hand on her belly. She had time for one man.

Abel turned away, but Ben grabbed his arm. "Did you see that?"

"What?" Abel said.

"Herrera. He took some juice— There, he's doing it again." Manuel dipped a drinking straw in his orange juice, then capped the end with his finger. It was an elementary-school trick. He lifted the straw and up came a tubeful of juice. Casting around to make sure no one would see him, he flicked his hand, spattering the pant leg of the nearest Navy man.

"That's really rank," Abel laughed.

"Do you know who he is?" Ben asked.

"Those Navy fly-guys, here for a wedding in about an hour. That one there is the groom. He looks like a dog peed on him."

Herrera slouched sideways, grinning. He didn't share the joke with his daughter or Balazs.

"Why would he do that?" Ben asked.

Abel gave a shrug. "Bay of Pigs. See, the Navy guys were there. Big aircraft carrier. Could have fished Mr. Herrera out, but they didn't. Left him to rot." Abel moved on, laughing. "Study your history, man!"

Perhaps someday Ben would do that. Now, though, he turned back to Balazs and Manuel Herrera. They were speaking again, small talk, Ben guessed, from the way they gestured. Balazs pulled a case from his sweat suit pocket and extracted two cigars. He slid one across to Herrera, a peace offering.

Balazs launched into a monologue. Ben couldn't read lips, but Balazs' hands and body spoke their own language. Head tilted, shoulders slumped. *You can trust me. I respect you.* Hand cupped to his chest, then held out. *I give you everything I have.* Hands crossed one over the other, the safe sign in baseball. *Let's cut through this foolishness.* Finger circle, tap his wristwatch. *Just a little more time.* Hand patting downward, like petting a cat. *It's okay. Everything is okay.*

Then Balazs made a mistake, saying something he shouldn't. He stopped abruptly.

Herrera was livid. He struggled to his feet, dumping his napkin and cane on the floor. Morena scooped them up. The old man's voice was loud enough for Ben to hear through the window. "You say this to me? ¡No te preocupes! Oh, you've got worries, Emile. Big worries."

Herrera grabbed his cane and pegged toward the door. On his heels came Morena. She shot a sad glance at Balazs, but that was all, no good-bye kiss or even a pat on the hand.

Awkward silence lingered in the courtyard, and then the jabber of conversation picked up. Balazs sat comfortably, unconcerned with it all. His eyes swept along the windows until he was staring directly at Ben. Ben stared back, nowhere to go. Involuntarily, his hand went to his pocket, the gun. Then he realized Balazs was only looking at his own reflection in the glass. For a long moment Ben fingered the gun, letting his mind range on the possibilities. He let it drop. With Mosby's help, he'd see Balazs back in prison. That would be enough.

Ben stayed until Balazs left, watching with the same cold fascination he felt when he watched a snake at the zoo.

Nineteen

CocoWalk Mall sweltered in hazy afternoon sunshine. Ben had been there forty-five minutes, long enough for his shirt to be soaked with perspiration. He rubbed a glass of ice water across his forehead for a little relief.

The unenclosed mall was two stories tall, shaped in a U. At the mouth of the U was a smaller building facing Grand Avenue. That was where Ben was now, on the upper floor in a combo bar/restaurant called Big Mouths. The place was open-air, with a half-wall railing all around, giving him a view of everything below.

Out on the avenue people clotted the sidewalk, gawking in the shop windows. It was easy to tell the locals from the visitors. The locals were tanned and fit and gorgeous in their slinky dresses and silk suits. The tourists, the Belgians and Germans and Iowans, were fish-skinned, lugging backpacks, and sweating, always sweating.

Ben followed the railing around to the back, where he could see into the mall's lower court. Down there were several rows of umbrella-covered tables. A trio of women in halter tops and short-shorts chatted over salads. The other tables were empty. That was where Patrice planned to meet Balazs. Ben was to wait upstairs in the bar, keeping an eye out for trouble.

Trouble. He was in for a load of it when Patrice found out about the deal he'd cut with Rand Mosby. He felt guilty for not telling her, but that was how it had to be. Patrice might have skipped out. The feds had turned on her before; why should she trust them now? Later, Ben would make it up to her. Pacing around Big Mouths in the stifling heat, he thought about that. He'd buy three first-class tickets back to D.C. Then they'd have a special dinner to celebrate, Le Rayon de Lune, the little French place he knew. And later, after Cherry was asleep—

Ben caught himself. What the hell was he thinking? The same things a hundred other men had thought after spending some time with Patrice. How did she do it—get so deep inside his head? He shrugged it off. Stay focused and everything would be all right.

He checked his watch as he headed back to the avenue side. One thirty-five. Patrice was late; Balazs was late. It was a power game. Neither wanted to be first to show up.

A few blocks south, a knot of people stood on the curb, holding placards. The signs were too far away for him to read, but he knew what the demonstration was about. The Cuban-American Freedom Foundation in Key West had burned to the ground the night before. Apparently it was arson. Talk radio was full of it. Everybody blamed Castro. The people waved and shouted, and drivers passing by honked encouragement.

Ben kept moving, watching the crowd closer to the mall. He wondered where Cherry was now. He'd asked Patrice what she was going to do with her while they were both at CocoWalk. Patrice had given him a *what vegetable patch did you grow up in?* look and said, "The concierge." He wasn't sure what that meant, but he had visions of her leaving Cherry in the hotel luggage closet with a claim check on her finger.

Ben reached the back of the bar again, and stopped. Balazs was at a table opposite the three women with salads. He'd cleaned up since Ben last saw him, putting on a pale green shirt and charcoal-colored linen trousers. He seemed cool and at ease, one of the beautiful people, the home team.

Another man was sitting a few tables away. Because of the angle of the umbrella, Ben could only see the lower part of his body, the mid-blue pants and Hush Puppy shoes. Ben remembered a name Patrice had mentioned: Mick Laraby. Guarding the boss's back.

Now they'd wait for Patrice. Ben circled back to watch the avenue. The minutes ticked away. He looked for signs of the police and came up empty. He'd expected that. Mosby was a professional. She'd keep her people out of sight until the time was right. She wouldn't want any rough stuff now, with the crowds all around. She'd wait until she had Balazs in a corner, somewhere on his way out.

Ben spotted the taxi as it nosed to the curb a block up the street. Patrice got out and paid the driver through the window. Ben had phoned their hotel room twice in the last couple of hours and no one had answered. Now he understood why. Patrice had been shopping, and to the stylist, and the makeup counter. She wore a black minidress with spangly silver thread stranded through it. Her shoes were black too, pointy-toed flats. Her hair was blond again, showing red highlights. The effect she had, coming up the street, was something to see. Men stepped aside, as if afraid of her, and then they turned to get a look from behind. A shark cruising up the sidewalk wouldn't have caused such a stir.

Ben was staring too, and that was a big stroke of luck. If he'd looked away, he wouldn't have seen Ken Van Allen pulling up in a car behind Patrice's cab. He had a sweater tied loosely over his shoulders, the perfect accessory for a Ken doll.

It took a moment for Ben's mind to click into gear. What was Van Allen doing here? Worse yet, what was he doing following Patrice? Ben hadn't told anyone where they'd be in Miami, except here, CocoWalk. He looked again for Mosby, for the police. Nowhere. Van Allen was out of the car, closing on Patrice, his eyes locked on the middle of her back the way a linebacker zeroes in before a tackle.

Ben waved his arms. *"Patrice, behind you!"* She kept coming, shading her eyes to see him better. *"Watch out!"* Van Allen had spotted him. He dodged through the crowd, picking up speed. Ben's hand went to his coat pocket, to the gun.

For an instant, everything was crystal clear: Patrice looking his way, a curious, startled expression on her face; Van Allen ten paces back, pushing between two women; a man walking a poodle and staring down at Patrice's legs as he passed her.

Ben aimed high and fired, only a warning shot. The bullet tore through the roof. A puff of dust from the rafters settled on his shoulders.

People on the street reacted first, scattering, diving. The screaming started a split second later. Inside Big Mouths there was sluggish silence, and then a woman bellowed, *"That's a gun!"* Tables crashed over. People darted for the escalator.

Van Allen was caught in the swirl on the sidewalk. He got tangled in the dog's leash and went down, slamming into a parked car. Patrice froze, then came running toward Ben, just what he didn't want. Balazs was here, and Laraby, and maybe others. *"No! The other way!"* he yelled. With all the noise, she couldn't hear. He had to get downstairs.

Patrons scuttled out of his way. Somewhere a baby was wailing. He shoved a little boy aside. Top of the escalator—

171

there. Oh, goddammit to hell. Up escalator. No time to find the down. He hopped on the handrail and slid, the way a child would go down a bannister. Toward the bottom his feet clipped an old man going up. Ben flipped around and crashed headfirst into a table.

He'd lost the gun. There it was, climbing the escalator. Just before it passed out of reach, he grabbed it. He knelt beside the overturned table. This is where Laraby had been sitting. He was gone now. Across the courtyard, Ben saw Balazs. He was heading for an exit that led to a side street. Ben leveled the gun, hesitated, and pulled it down. There were too many people in the way.

Reaching the door, Balazs turned. His eyes went straight to Ben. The son of a bitch was grinning, as if everything were going as planned. He tapped his brow, an impudent salute, then stepped out of sight.

Ben wheeled the other way, toward the street. People were still running, helter-skelter. One of them collided with him, spinning him around. That's when he saw Patrice.

Under Big Mouths was an alley, with a couple of boutiques and a door leading down to the underground parking lot. Patrice was at the far end. A man stood behind her, his hand locked on the back of her neck. Blue suit, Hush Puppies—the man Ben had seen guarding Balazs' back, the one he'd thought was Laraby. It was Aaron Joquand. In his free hand was a pistol, aimed at the down escalator. Patrice was a wildcat, kicking at him, flailing with her elbows, but she couldn't get away.

Ben surged up the alley. A woman in one of the boutiques screamed. She hadn't seen his gun, only the expression on his face. "Looking for me, asshole?" As Joquand turned, Ben hammered the pistol barrel into his ear like a ramrod. Joquand fell, howling. Blood streamed down his cheek.

Ben kicked him in the ribs and hauled back to kick him again. "Jesus, don't kill him," Patrice said. With a curse, Ben stepped away. She scooped up Joquand's gun.

Ben dragged him down the parking lot stairs. "You set this up?" Joquand didn't answer. Ben threw him down on the concrete landing and stood over him.

"We wanted to keep you busy," Joquand panted. "Distracted until we had Callan."

"Where's Mosby?" Again, no answer. Ben jammed the gun in Joquand's good ear.

"Delayed." Joquand gave a tight laugh. "The warrant on Balazs was fake, planted in the Justice Department computer. I started the rumor she heard—that I was in trouble at Langley over Balazs. I'm sure Rand's worried about you."

Ben dug the pistol into the hard cartilage of the lobe. The ear is an exquisitely sensitive place. Tears ran down Joquand's face. "What are you after?" Ben said.

Patrice had stayed at the top of the stairs, keeping a lookout. Joquand whispered so she couldn't hear. "Callan stole something." He took a long breath. "A lot more important than she can understand." Another breath. He was buying time, hoping Van Allen would get there with the cavalry.

Ben probed his ear again.

"God, *stop* that!" Joquand whined. "Look, it's over. She's finished. You can pack up and go. No hard feelings."

"What do you mean, she's finished?"

Joquand glanced at Patrice, the pistol in her hand. He was afraid of that gun, of what she might do with it. "She's got to give it up now. No choice. Go back home, Tennant. Forget you ever knew her."

Upstairs there was a clatter of feet and the squawk of a handheld radio. Patrice scrambled down to the landing. "Police."

Ben pointed down the steps to the parking lot. "This way."

"Wait," Patrice said. She grabbed Joquand's necktie and pulled him to the handrail. She made a knot and yanked it tight. He was left hanging, barely able to breathe. He wouldn't be calling for help.

They took off down the steps, Patrice clutching Ben's arm. She was charged with nervous energy. At the bottom she pulled him around and kissed him. "Thanks."

"Let's go," was all he said. She wouldn't be thanking him later, after she figured out what he already knew, about Balazs, and about Cherry.

TWENTY

They made it out of the parking garage without any trouble. Ben was driving, powering north through a sleepy residential neighborhood. A police car with lights flashing came at them from the other end of the street. "Better slow down," Patrice said.

"They only care about the gunshots at the mall," Ben said, hoping he was right.

The cruiser ripped past, the two cops inside not giving them a sideways glance. Ben squealed around the corner onto Bird Road. Patrice bounced off the door. "Dammit, ease up!" He didn't, and she said, "What's wrong?"

"The man in the stairwell wasn't one of Balazs's. He's CIA, Aaron Joquand, the one who was at my house last week."

"How the hell did he get here?"

"I called Mosby last night from New Mexico and told her you'd be at CocoWalk with Balazs. I thought they were going to arrest him. Game over. We could go home."

She glared at him. "Why couldn't you just let me take care of it? Damn you! What did he want?"

"You. Something you stole, he said."

175

"I didn't steal anything!" She rubbed her forehead, trying to ease the tension. "Last fall, when I was with Emile here in Miami, he hooked up with somebody with a lot of juice. He was a scared rat when we started off, then next thing I knew he seemed to have an army backing him. Maybe it was the feds, he'd cut a deal with them, the CIA, somebody." She slapped the dashboard. "Why don't they leave me alone? And *slow down!*"

Ben didn't slow down. "Back at CocoWalk, there was somebody behind you when you got out of the cab. He's CIA, too. He—"

"Another one? Jesus, Ben—"

"Listen to me. He was behind you, in a car, following your cab."

"How?" In her mind's eye she raced back through the day: the hairdresser, the store where she'd bought her dress, the hotel with Cherry. Her voice pitched up. "Following me from where?"

The Dixie Highway loomed ahead. The light was red. Ben shot through without slowing, and someone pounded a horn in protest. "He must have picked you up at the hotel," he said. "We flew in so early, they missed us at the airport. But they could trace us from there. Call around to the hotels, ask for a man and a woman who checked in with a little girl this morning."

He looked at her. "Joquand told me you were finished, that you had no choice now. It's Cherry. They've gone after her."

She stared in disbelief. As it sunk in, she turned away. "I left her with a babysitter. The concierge had a list. She seemed nice. Haitian, I think. A tiny thing, mousy. She wouldn't even fight if they came." A tear rolled down her cheek. She was picking at the calluses on her fingers, ripping at the flesh.

Ben pulled her hands apart. He would have said anything, done anything if it would have helped her.

She leaned forward. "Hurry. Come on, hurry."

Their hotel was the Airport River Plaza. The only people in the lobby were the desk clerk and two women dusting the leaves of the ficus trees by the door. All three stared as Ben and Patrice rushed past into the elevator. Patrice punched the button for the fifth floor and kept punching until the doors closed. When they opened at the top, she sprinted into the corridor. Ben was only a step behind.

Halfway down the hall he noticed the smell: Balazs' cologne, thick and cloying in the tight space. Patrice was too frenzied to notice. She already had her key card out. "Wait," he said. "If they're in there—"

She snapped the card in the lock and heaved the door open.

It was dark inside. The air conditioner hummed quietly. Ben clicked on the light. The place was immaculate, bed made, towels put away, everything as it should be. Then he glanced in the open closet behind the door. Cherry's clothes were gone.

Patrice stood at the foot of the bed. Her eyes darted around as if she expected Cherry suddenly to pop up from under the covers.

They both heard the faint sobbing at the same moment. Ben stepped over and ran back the curtains. The baby-sitter was curled up in the corner of the balcony. Her hands were tied to the railing, and a piece of white medical tape covered her mouth. When she saw Ben, her eyes flew wide and she screamed. The sound was muffled by the gag. Her face on one side had been battered until it looked like raw beef. Mousy or not, she'd put up a hell of a fight.

Ben knew why she was afraid. He was big and white and a man, like the ones who'd beaten her. He waved for Patrice. "Help her. Talk to her. I'll stay out of the way." He slid the door open. A moment later he heard the *zzzip* as Patrice pulled off the tape. The two women talked at once. *What happened? Sorry, God, I'm so sorry. How long ago? I couldn't stop it. Believe me. How many of them? Three, four, I don't know. Poor little one. Sorry. Please. I'm sorry.*

Ben circled the room, checking the nightstand and under the bed pillows. He flipped through the message pad by the phone. Balazs must have left a note, something to say what he wanted. Everything was tidy. Then Ben spotted a sheet of paper on the floor, and he grabbed it. It was the drawing of Max. Cherry had filled it in with colored pencils. Max grinned; his eyes glinted. Cherry didn't know Max was dead. Ben dropped the picture on the bed.

He checked the bathroom next. Cherry's hat was on the counter. Behind it, against the mirror, was a sheet of stationery.

Balazs had used a fountain pen, and some of the ink had bled through the paper. His handwriting was angry, bold scratches and sharp angles.

Patrice:
  She's grown! Spitting image of you. So, we trade. My property for Cherry. Simple. I'll be back in St. Kitts tomorrow.

Emile

  PS: Hats off to Tennant for the performance at CocoWalk. You tell him, from here on he minds his own business, or you'll be the one who regrets it.

Ben looked at the cap. *Hats off.* He picked it up and lurched back.

The inside of the headband was soaked with blood, and there was a pool of it on the counter. A Swiss Army knife lay inside the pool, blood glistening on the open blade. On the knife was another square of paper. Balazs had scratched a second note.

Just a nick this time. Don't play with me, Patrice.

178

In the other room, the door slid open. He heard Patrice's voice. He didn't want her to see this. He swung the bathroom door around.

Ben stared at the hat, the blood. He should clean it up. Under the sink. Into the toilet. Just save the first note. Patrice didn't need to know the rest. He stopped before he made a move. He'd interfered enough already.

The women's voices passed into the outer hall. Ben dropped the hat on the counter.

Patrice returned. "Sela's gone. She was afraid we'd call the police, and they'd send Immigration after her. Mick Laraby showed up an hour ago. Said he was hotel management, so she let him—"

Ben swung the door open. As she took it in—the notes, the blood—she started to tremble. "No. *God no!*"

He pulled her out to the bed and sat down beside her. He spoke quickly, trying to sound calm. "We'll get her back, then you can go somewhere. Just you two. Nobody will bother you again."

Patrice thrashed, trying to get away. He wouldn't let go. "She's a smart kid. Tough. You taught her that."

She shuddered and grew still. She didn't seem to know he was there. The picture of Max had fallen to the floor. Seeing it, she started crying.

Ben stroked her back and her hair. "She'll be okay. I promise."

Her lips were moving. Was she praying? Was she cursing him?

All he'd wanted was to keep her safe, and Cherry. Ben thought about what Cherry must be going through. He remembered Balazs' sneering salute at CocoWalk. He felt a surge go through his body, the energy lift of his own rage. Ben had once warned Balazs—there's nowhere you can hide from me. Now he'd have to prove it. He'd get Cherry back, and then he'd turn his full attention on Emile Balazs.

Ben lifted the necklace from under Patrice's collar, letting the safety-deposit key dangle free. "Whatever Peter Saar took, we have to get it. We'll start with this key, see where it takes us."

Her eyes swam into focus. "Two keys. Emile's sister has the other one." Her voice was bouncing, barely in control.

"Then we'll go to her. Get her key." He turned Patrice's face to him. "We play by our own rules now. We get what Balazs wants, then we use it to go after him."

"Go after him," she repeated. But she didn't understand. She was too far away, spiraling down in her own world of fear and guilt.

TWENTY-ONE

Ben went out to the balcony to do some thinking. Getting to St. Kitts wasn't going to be easy. They couldn't take a regular flight. Balazs would have men watching the Basseterre airport. Ben could arrange some other way in, but it would take him too long, days maybe. He was going to have to call in his favor from Larry Jong.

Inside, he heard Patrice cleaning up the blood in the bathroom. She was sniffing away her tears. Ben went to the phone and dialed the number Larry had given him. It was a Baltimore area code. The man named Chin answered. "Yeah, Tennant. Larry said you'd call. What's up?" Ben explained that he needed transportation to St. Kitts, *quiet* transportation. Chin was a man of few words. "Gimme your number. Call you back."

He rang twenty minutes later. "Can set something up," Chin said. "You gotta get to Key West, the airport."

"Then what?" Ben asked.

"Wait, that's all."

Ben heard a low cackle, which he recognized. "Larry? Let

181

me talk to Larry." Chin hung up. "Damn clown," Ben grumbled.

A few hours later Ben and Patrice were crossing the bridge from Stock Island to Key West. After they'd changed clothes, they'd decided to drive down from Miami instead of catching one of the commuter flights. On the road, they couldn't be traced.

Key West was buzzing with people. There was only one space left in the small airport parking lot. They climbed out, stiff from the long ride and dazed from all the sun. While he drove, Ben had tried to get Patrice to talk, but she huddled in her seat, lost in her own thoughts.

The terminal was a low building, not very large. Inside, people were milling around like sheep in a pen. Everyone was speaking Spanish. The baggage area was less crowded, and that's where they went. "I'll look around," he said. "Maybe there's somebody with a courtesy sign for us, a charter pilot."

He hadn't gone far when he heard someone call his name. Larry Jong was pushing through the crowd. "Hey, par'ner! Saw you comin' across the parking lot."

"What are you doing here?" Ben asked.

Larry burped. "Drinkin'. Stayin' warm. It's cold up north. I hopped a plane right after you called." He was on his tiptoes, looking for Patrice. He grinned. "Oooh. She's still pretty. Lost some weight though. Don't look like a cupcake anymore. More like a Twinkie." He glanced at Ben. "So what'd you do with Frosty?"

"Took him to the pound." Larry looked so shocked that Ben quickly relented. "He's at a kennel—Cat's Cradle out in Arlington."

"That place?" Larry groaned. "They feed him those ice cream treats. Spoil the hell out of him."

"He's your cat, Lar. You could have taken him anywhere you wanted."

By then Patrice was on her way over. "I'm Larry," he said, stepping forward. "Ben and I work—"

Patrice said, "I remember. By the canal in Georgetown. You had a gun."

"It was just a little joke."

"I'm still not laughing," she said. "Forget it. Can you get us out of here?"

"Maybe," Larry answered. He wasn't pleased with her attitude. He'd flown all the way down here to help, and now this.

Ben said, "We've got real trouble and not much time."

Larry tossed his hands up, as if to say *everybody's* got troubles. "I need another drink." He plowed into the mass of people, heading for the far end of the terminal.

The bar was called the Flying Conch. It was as crowded as the rest of the building. A Spanish-language news program was blaring from the television. Larry led the way to an empty space at the rail, where two bottles of beer were waiting. Looking around he said, "Where'd that flaky SOB go?"

"We meeting somebody?" Patrice asked.

"Yeah, and you be on your best behavior, or you aren't goin' anywhere."

For a moment he and Patrice tried to stare each other down. Then he took a swig from one of the beers. "Ben, you don't have good luck with the ladies, do you?"

"What do you mean by that?" Patrice asked.

"Lar, drop it," Ben said.

Larry took another sip. "Unh-uh. You haven't done either of us any good, Patrice. I'd like to be home with my cat, all cozy. *Jeopardy*'d be on soon. Instead I'm runnin' around the country, hidin' my ass from the damn CIA."

Ben took the bottle from Larry and put it back on the bar. "How many of these have you had? Anyway, blame me for your problems, not her."

"Damn right I blame you." He turned to Patrice again. "Did he tell you about that Mosby chick? Bad luck with the ladies." Patrice frowned, not understanding, and Larry laughed. "Ben and Mosby were real buddies once. Ol' girlfriend."

Patrice shot a cool glance at Ben. He shrugged. Now

wasn't the time to explain about Mosby. "Enough whining, Lar," he said. "You're here. Beautiful Key West. Go to the beach when we leave, or try some fishing."

"Yeah, right," Larry mumbled.

Around them, the people grew quiet. They were watching the TV. Fidel Castro appeared, giving an interview. A buzz ran through the crowd, like the sound of a hundred angry bees.

"You see the news?" Larry asked. "Big building got fire-bombed here last night. Some Cuban-American deal."

"I heard about that," Ben said. "Anybody hurt?"

"Nah. Place was being renovated. Folks still pissed about it, though." Larry waved around at the people. "This crowd's down from Miami. They want Castro's head for it. Gonna have a rally. More like a riot, maybe." He giggled. "Be fun to watch."

Larry reached for his beer while he motioned at the other side of the room. "Here comes our boy." He wagged his finger at Patrice. "Mind your manners. Remember that."

The man approaching didn't look like somebody who'd care much about manners. He was a short stack of muscle in tight jeans and a sleeveless T-shirt. His head was shaved, and he had gang brands on both biceps. Ben knew where men got brands like that: in prison.

"Deke, this is Patrice and—" Larry began.

Deke shut him down with a cold glance. He bent close to Patrice and wrinkled his nose as if he didn't like her smell. "St. Kitts, huh? What for?"

Patrice wasn't going to answer that. "Can you take us?" she asked.

"Part way," Larry said. "Puerto Rico. I've got something else set up from there."

Deke ran his eyes over Ben. "I don't like outlaws."

"Good for you. A man with your background can't be too careful," Ben said. "I'm Ben Tennant." He put out his hand and left it there for ten seconds until Deke took it.

"You fly in my plane, you follow my rules," Deke said. "No guns, drugs, contraband. Nothing illegal. I take you to San Juan and that's it."

"Jesus, you're touchy," Patrice said.

Ben leaned over and sniffed, and caught a whiff of stale gunpowder from the pistol in Patrice's bag. "We'll get rid of it."

Deke's mouth quivered. Maybe it was a smile. "Smart man. I'll finish my beer, and we can be on our way."

Patrice argued, but Deke held firm. No gun. *No,* he didn't give a damn what kind of trouble they were in. So she marched off to the ladies room to dump it in the trash. Deke leaned on the bar and guzzled his beer. "You want to go with us Larry? Quick run. Be back by tomorrow noon."

Larry had his eye on a corner table, where some men were playing poker. "I think I'll stay here, watch the good times roll."

"Suit yourself," Deke said. Patrice was coming back, and he put down his bottle. "Plane's ready. Let's move."

Larry said to Ben, "It's all set. Guy's gonna meet you in San Juan. Just go along." He reached to shake his hand. "Take care, okay?"

Ben nodded. "Thanks Lar, for everything." He followed Deke and Patrice out.

By the ticket counters it was even more crowded than before. Deke inched ahead. "Excuse us. Excuse us please." Back in the bar, the TV interview ended. Someone started a chant. It swept the building like a wave, everyone joining in until the air reverberated with the rhythmic Spanish. *¡Cuba sí! ¡Castro no! ¡Cuba sí! ¡Castro no!*

Ben hurried Patrice and Deke toward the exit. He wanted to get to the plane and into the air before the lid blew off this place.

TWENTY-TWO

Ben's first view of St. Kitts came from the passenger's seat of an aging twenty-six-foot speedboat named *Sinkin' Feelin'*. It was two hours before dawn, and they were plowing southeast through a nasty chop. "Is that it?" he called, pointing at a dark velvet triangle cut in the glittery backdrop of stars.

"*Sí*, Mt. Misery," answered the pilot, Alex. He throttled down and stood on tiptoe so he could search ahead for shoals. "Five minute, you on de beach." Then he cursed in Spanish and whipped the wheel to the right and a second later headed back bow-on to the waves. Patrice was going through their knapsacks, checking the things they had brought.

As planned, Deke flew them to Puerto Rico. From there they caught a chartered Twin Otter to the tiny Dutch island of St. Eustatius. The second pilot didn't care if they were outlaws, or space aliens, or cadavers. He was so high his pupils were pinpricks, and he spent the whole flight humming along to sitar music on a Walkman.

Alex had met them at the St. Eustatius airfield and took them down to the harbor to his boat. The eight-mile cross-

186

ing to St. Kitts took less than an hour. Ahead they could see the pale curl of breakers and hear the *swoosh* of the surf. Ben wanted to know more about Alex. They were putting a lot of trust in him. "Where are you from, Alex?"

"Havana, then, ninetee'-eighty, the Mariel boats to Miami." He tapped the steering wheel proudly. "Now, anawhere you need me."

What Alex lacked in English he made up for in seafaring skills. He gunned the twin outboards, catching a wave that carried them over a low spot in the reef. They settled into the calmer water beyond.

A dozen chunky wooden fishing boats rolled at anchor forty yards out from shore. Alex cut the engines and grabbed one of the anchor lines, bringing his own stern around. The moon hung on the horizon, three-quarters full. Above the beach they could make out the tops of a few houses and, further inland, a string of lights along a road.

Ben already had his shoes and socks off and his pants rolled to his knees. As he swung over the side, a school of flying fish broke from the tops of the waves, flashing quicksilver in the moonlight. The tidal current was so strong he had trouble keeping his footing on the sandy bottom.

He took the knapsacks from Patrice. "You'll stay here?" he said to Alex.

The pilot glanced along the shoreline. "Not this place, no."

"How will we find you?"

Alex said something that sounded like "Assakeeds."

"What?"

"Keeds. You know—" He made motions with his hands, indicating a child. "Play 'long de beach. Ass 'em where I'm at. Can't hide nothin' from keeds."

Ben helped Patrice out of the boat and they slogged to shore. On the hardpack at the edge of the water they sat to put on their shoes. The trade wind riffled the palms behind them. Alex started the motors and angled off to the north. He didn't wave good-bye.

Ben led the way up the beach, toward the lights on the road. Sea grapes snagged their ankles; they stumbled on windfall coconuts. They reached a dirt lane and the going was easier. On each side were small stucco-clad houses, two rooms, three at most, with dirt yards and tin roofs that creaked in the breeze. All the windows were dark.

The name of this place was Dieppe. It was on the opposite end of the island from Basseterre. They had offered Alex more money to run them down there, but he refused. "Basseterre got Customs men," he muttered. "Find de boat. Take de boat."

Somewhere nearby a dog barked. Ben stood still as stone. They wanted to get out of Dieppe quietly. In Basseterre, they could blend in with the tourists. Out here in the country people would remember them, and word might get back to Balazs. The dog settled down. Ben tugged Patrice's arm, and they scuttled on.

Patrice knew her way around St. Kitts from her previous trip. The main ring road was just two narrow lanes of blacktop. They figured on catching one of the small bus-vans that circled the island, beginning at sunup. The vans were always crowded, so there was a good chance they'd get through unnoticed. They waited, sitting on a low stone wall off the verge of the road, talking about what they would do when they reached Basseterre. Find Isabel. Find the other safety-deposit key. Then decide where to go from there. Their voices dwindled and died.

Ben knew it didn't do any good, but he couldn't stop worrying about Cherry. He'd never felt so guilty about anything. Patrice hadn't said a word to blame him. He almost wished she would—really unload on him. It might make him feel better. He looked over at her. She was exhausted, her face pale and drained. And how many hours would it be before they could get some sleep?

They hadn't seen any cars on the road, but one came along now, trolling over a hill to the west. Ben spotted the lights on top before Patrice did. "Police," he whispered. He didn't want any brushes with the cops. He didn't know what the penalty was for entering St. Kitts illegally. Most likely a spell in jail followed by a bum's rush back to the States. Definitely something they couldn't afford. He pulled Patrice off the wall and hurried her across the road. There was a spindly hedge between the nearest house and the lane. They could hide there.

Patrice didn't see the box-shaped contraption of chicken wire until she tripped over it. She went down with a crash, then lay still. The police car rolled by, close enough for Ben to see the driver. He was half-asleep, his head back and his eyes locked far down the road.

Ben turned to help Patrice, but she was already getting up, cursing a streak. Ben started chuckling, but stopped as if the laughter had been yanked out of his throat.

"Don' look like no fish," someone said, very near.

"What?" Ben said, wheeling.

The voice had been a man's. Now a woman spoke, quickly, tensely, from inside the house. "Who 'e be, 'e be?"

"Dunno," the man said. "Standin' in dat busted fish pot, but ain't no fish."

A light snapped on, and Ben stumbled back. The man sat in a metal chair not three feet from him, in what had been the darkest part of the yard. He had a machete in his hand, held upright on his lap, like an obscene prop for the Marquis de Sade. "So what you be, nephew? A tief mebbe? Gon' steal some our goodies?"

"No. . . . We were just out walking."

The man was at least seventy, with crinkly gray hair. He wore whisper-thin Bermuda shorts and a shirt buttoned up only to his navel. In the low light his skin gleamed a dull ebony. "Walkin' you say?" He twirled the knife so the blade glinted.

"Who he *be?*" the woman inside persisted. She was too far away to hear what was being said.

The old man seemed to notice Patrice for the first time. He ran his eyes up and down and smiled. "Look like Henny Penny . . . and Randy Rooster."

The woman shoved open a shutter and stared out. She was very short. Her eyes, round and chestnut brown, barely reached the windowsill. "What they want this time a' night?"

Patrice stepped boldly forward. "We need a ride to Basseterre. Is that your truck back there?" She pointed behind the house.

The old man got to his feet. He was serious now, not smiling. "Yeah, our truck. You in a hurry, then? Petrol cost money, you know."

They started to haggle. Twenty dollars; no, twenty-five. Eastern Caribbean dollars; no, U.S. It was settled before Ben could say a word. The old man put the machete down and offered his hand to shake. "I'm St. Clair. St. Clair Saddler. You go on, get in. I'll get the keys, tell Violet what we're up to."

Ben watched him walk away. St. Clair must have seen them ducking that police car, but he hadn't said anything about it. Maybe Patrice had bought off his curiosity with the twenty-five dollars. Still, he was going to remember them, just what Ben had hoped to avoid. He could see now that St. Kitts was too small a place for them to slip around unnoticed. Everything they did would be out in the open; every step would be a risk.

Patrice was already waiting at the truck so he hurried to join her. It was a small Japanese pickup, a tight fit for three adults. It was spotlessly clean, with a picture of Jesus taped to the glove compartment.

St. Clair returned, still dressed in his scruffy shorts and shirt, and he'd added a pair of flip-flop sandals. He brought the machete, which he propped on the seat as he started the engine. Staring at it, Patrice slid away, into Ben. "Jus' an ol' cane knife," St. Clair said. "Won' hurt nobody." But he pulled it closer, where he could get his hand on it quickly if he needed it.

The truck was right-hand drive, though that didn't make much difference to St. Clair. He went right down the middle of the road. It wound on hairpin turns in and out of tiny hamlets and along oceanside cliffs. He was proud of his island, happy to show the sights. Not that they could see much because it was still dark. They did get a good look at the prime minister's house, a low bungalow like many of the others around, except it had a wrought-iron fence and a fresh coat of white paint.

Forty-five minutes later they rolled into Basseterre. The town was still asleep. The only person they saw was an old man sweeping the sidewalk on one of the main streets. St. Clair honked his horn and waved.

Patrice had to think for a moment when St. Clair asked where they wanted to be dropped off. "Center of town," she decided. "By the Catholic church."

All three of them were yawning as they piled out of the truck by the cathedral on Independence Square. Ben handed St. Clair his twenty-five dollars. "We're going to need transportation. Is there anywhere we can rent a car around here?"

St. Clair motioned with his head. "Avis right ov' dere. Opens about ten o'clock."

"Anything earlier?" Ben said.

The old man scratched his thin hair. "Well . . . mebbe. You wait. I'll be back."

He drove off, and they found a bench to sit on in the square. It was a small bench, and, however they arranged themselves, their legs or hips or shoulders touched. Ben seemed to notice more than she did. The sky in the east turned pink, then yellow. In front of the cathedral a rooster was scratching in the dirt. It stopped and gave a half-hearted *cock-a-doodle-doo*. People began to trickle up and down the streets.

They were both feeling drowsy in the growing heat. The first rays of the sun peeked over the hills. "That's his place up there," Patrice said.

"Hmmm?"

"Emile's. That's his. Canada House he calls it."

Ben sat forward, staring. The house was a behemoth, set on the crest of the ridge. Its size wasn't what made it impressive, though. On top was a high pyramid, the faces angled to catch the sun. It was aflame with light, splendorous, the color of pure gold. Ben whistled. "Half the people on the island must be able to see that."

"More than that," Patrice said. "See it from Nevis too, and Montserrat, and even from Antigua if the weather's right, sixty miles."

"Why Canada House?" he asked.

"The name of those hills, I think. It's weird, isn't it—the feeling it gives?"

Ben had a hard time taking his eyes off it. A prickle of unease ran up his back. He thought back five months to that morning at WITSEC, the brash way Emile Balazs tapped the middle of his forehead, the third-eye spot. "It's like somebody's watching from up there. Like the Greeks and Mount Olympus."

They heard a horn beep. It was St. Clair. He had a man with him, and in the rear of the truck was something covered with a dirty tarpaulin. Both men acted hangdog as they got out. "This here's Justin," St. Clair mumbled. "He gotta car, but it's not runnin' so good. Thought you'd take this mebbe." He used his cane knife to cut the cord that held the tarp, and flopped it back. It was a Peugeot motorbike with a bent muffler and, from the looks of the stains on the block, a major oil leak.

Ben didn't laugh right out, but he did grin. "I knew they wouldn't want it," Justin said. He gave the curb a thump with his toe.

"Hold on," Ben said. "It's not pretty. Does it run?"

Justin and St. Clair both replied. "Sure. Good."

"We'll take it then." Ben didn't want to get tangled up with a rental agency if he could avoid it, with the forms and credit cards and electronic records.

They settled on a price and Ben paid for three days. Justin handed ten dollars of it over to St. Clair. Both men were smiling ear to ear as they hauled the motorbike to the ground and showed how to work the clutch and shifter, where the gas valve was and the ignition. They shook hands all around.

Ben said, "Before you go—there's a house we need to find, here in Basseterre." He pointed at Patrice. "She's been there before but can't remember the street."

Justin threw his arms out. "Whose house, where?" He was merry as a cricket now.

"Isabel Balazs. Or maybe she uses Isabel Finney. She—" Ben didn't have to finish. They knew who he was talking about. Justin's smile was gone. St. Clair's eyes seemed to have pulled back a thousand miles.

St. Clair did the talking. "Sure. Mrs. Finney lives up on Flambouyant Drive." He indicated the direction. "Yella' house on the corner there." He and Justin climbed into the truck.

"I say something wrong?" Ben asked.

Justin didn't move, only looked at his lap as if in some kind of trance. St. Clair stared ahead, over the roofs to the blazing pyramid on the ridge.

Ben laughed, trying to make a joke. "The gods are watching, huh?"

St. Clair cranked the engine. He still wouldn't look at them. "Ev'ybody 'round here likes Mrs. Finney, but—" He shook his head, deciding not to finish what he'd started. "But you jes take it careful." He eased away from the curb and was gone.

Twenty-three

Patrice toyed with the food on her plate, then set her fork aside. It was too early to visit Isabel Finney, so they'd decided to have breakfast in a cafe off Independence Square. All she'd eaten was a few bites of toast. "Are you all right?" Ben said.

She shrugged and looked away, not happy that he was watching her so closely. He tried another tack. Anything to get her to stop worrying. "Tell me about Isabel. What's she like?"

"She's—I don't know—like a big kid." Patrice sighed, frustrated with him, and with herself for not being able to keep up the conversation.

Gently he said, "Just try to eat something, okay?"

He turned back to his own plate. He hadn't eaten since yesterday morning, so he was famished. When every scrap was finished, he checked his watch. "It's late enough. Let's go." He led her out to the motorbike.

A cruise ship had anchored in the harbor at sunrise, and the town was jumping with activity. Taxi-vans roared down the streets, horns crying to warn the pedestrians out of the way. Twice Ben had to ask for directions to Flambouyant Drive. Patrice sat behind, silent and stiff. By the time they found the place, though, her mood seemed to be improving. "There," she said. "That house, next corner." He pulled to the curb.

Isabel would recognize Patrice, which would complicate things, so they'd agreed Ben would go alone to talk to her. As he got off the motorbike, Patrice looked at him with a curious, almost shy, expression. "Tell her she looks like Cher. She likes that."

"I'll try to fit it in," he said with a laugh. He gave her hand a squeeze. She didn't pull away, but she didn't respond either.

Ben walked off, taking in the surroundings. The neighborhood was only a half mile from the harbor, but there were no crowds up here. The homes were tidy and the gardens well cared for. Two boys went zipping downhill on a pair of roller skates, like a three-legged race on wheels. They giggled when Ben called good morning.

A woman was coming out of Isabel Finney's house. She had a load of wet linens in her arms, which she began hanging on the clothesline. She must be the housekeeper. Patrice had told Ben about Mary, how protective she was, acting like Isabel's castle guard.

He stopped next to the hedge. The bright, waxy croton plants nodded in the humid breeze. Inside the house he could hear hammering, and then a man laughed softly. Ben coughed to let Mary know he was there. "I see you," she said. Her tone was none too friendly.

"Is Mrs. Finney home?"

"Who be you?"

"Dale Blodgett." It was the name on the passport Larry Jong had given him. "I'm a friend of hers." When that didn't bring her around, he rephrased. "A friend of a friend, actually. I was on the island and thought I'd look her up."

"Just what Isabel needs," she muttered, "'nother man lookin' her up." There wasn't room on the line for all the sheets. She bundled up the extras, then turned a cold stare on him. "You off the boat?"

"No, I'm here for a few days." A jet rumbled in toward the airport. Mary frowned up at it. The plane was already out of sight by the time Ben turned. He did see the heap of broken wallboard on the porch. "You remodeling?"

"Fixin' a few things." Down the street an engine coughed, *rnn . . . rnnnggth*. For such a quiet neighborhood, there were suddenly a lot of distractions. Mary was ready to go inside. Wincing, she lifted the sheets. There was a bandage under her sleeve. Ben had noticed that; he'd noticed her hands, too.

"Who does your nails?" he said. They were long and decorated with four or five colors in intricate patterns.

"Why'd'ya ask?"

"They're pretty. The red matches . . ." He made a motion by his head. Her hair had been straightened, and she'd added a chestnut streak in front. "You don't do them yourself, do you?"

Mary broke into a grin. "Well now, Isabel's sure to like you, I say."

"Is she here?"

"Church. Helpin' w' some fund-raisin' thing." She thought a moment. "Maybe I'll tell her to give you a call. Where you stayin'?"

This caught Ben off guard. Hotels, hotels. St. Clair had mentioned a place where all the business visitors stayed. That engine cranked over again and caught. *Rnng . . . rnnnnngngngng.* It was the motorbike. "OTI, that's it," he said to Mary. "Ocean Terrace Inn. Have her call. Dale Blodgett. I'd really like to see her." The engine sound moved, heading down the hill. He backed away. "Sorry, I forgot I'm late for something. Remember, OTI!"

He cut across the property and dodged out in the street. Patrice had the motorbike all the way down to the next corner, where she had to wait for a dump truck to turn out of her way. Ben sprinted and caught her, hopping on behind as she got started. "What are you doing?"

"That plane—Emile's private jet." She shot him a glance. "He'll have Cherry with him."

"Stick with Isabel. Stay away from Emile. That's what we decided."

"We can *see* her! See if she's all right!"

She went left up a steep street, heading away from the center of town. Soon they were on a country road between sugarcane fields, the plants waving high over their heads. "Where to?" he asked.

Patrice pointed into the wind with her chin, up the ridge to Canada House. "There's a lookout at the crest, hidden from the house. We can wait there, watch when they take her inside."

Ben gave a curse. Balazs' note in Miami said he'd be getting back to St. Kitts today. Patrice probably knew the flight schedule he kept. That's why she'd been so quiet at breakfast. She'd been planning something like this. "Turn around," he pleaded. "We can't do any good up there." He was only wasting his breath.

They drove through a settlement on Monkey Hill, a few wood homes bordered by more cane. Above that the jungle began. The road turned to gravel, pitching up at an awful angle. The little motorbike started to labor. Within a hundred yards they had slowed to a jogging pace.

They rounded a bend and Ben saw a flash of light on the section of road they had just passed. At the next opening in the trees, he looked back. Three big white cars, BMWs, were flying upward in tight formation. "Behind us," he yelled. Patrice got a glimpse of the motorcade. She cranked the throttle, but she already had it nearly to full. Ahead, the road was even steeper, with nowhere to turn off. Palms and massed weeds crowded to the edge of the gravel, making a wall of green.

In a matter of seconds they could hear the cars, engines roaring, rocks clattering on the undercarriages. "You go on," Ben shouted. He leaped off the bike before she could answer. Without his weight, it shot forward. He used his momentum to plow into the foliage. Wiggling, tearing at the plants, he flung himself flat to the ground. The BMWs roared by, so fast they were a blur of white. As soon as they were around the next bend, he jumped up and sprinted after them.

He almost missed Patrice. She had found a turnoff, a footpath at the top of the ridge, and dumped the motorbike in the weeds. She was twenty yards down the trail, kneeling on a ledge of rock. He hurried up beside her. "What the hell were you thinking, coming up here? No place to get off the road—"

She pounded his shoulder with her fist. *"Shhhh!"*

They were at the same level as the estate grounds. An alley of trees, bristling with copper-colored seedpods, angled down out of the jungle. The BMWs were already parked in the circular drive in front of the house. From the first car stepped a thin man in a seersucker suit. "Laraby," Patrice whispered. He held the rear door open and Balazs climbed out. He hadn't shaved yet, and his clothes were badly rumpled. He was nervous and tired, slouching from one foot to the other. His eyes roved over the yard and around the rim of jungle.

Ben felt an uptick, a quickening in his heart rate. It was good that they'd come here. They needed to know what they were up against. Balazs was dangerous, but he wasn't invincible. Find the weak spots. Exploit them. Just like dealing with any other thug.

Balazs and Laraby moved to the second car. A woman got out, old enough to have gray hair, which she tied in a bun. Her face was set in a look of stoic patience. She beckoned through the open door, but no one came out. Laraby reached in, first his arm, then the whole upper half of his body. "Aie!" he squealed. "Bite me, would ya, ya little blighter!" He dragged Cherry onto the lawn, holding her away from him by the shoulders. Still she managed to kick him in the knee.

Ben was relieved to see she was all right—better than all right, full of vinegar. He was stunned when Patrice jumped up and raced toward the house.

She had a fifteen yard lead by the time he started after her. She went straight on, tearing through the underbrush. He kept to the path, dodging low, running hard. *What the hell is she doing?* Her shirt snagged on a thorn bush, slowing her down. It was enough. He caught her just short of the jungle's edge and hauled her to the ground. He pinned her shoulders with his elbows. Her eyes were frantic, rolling in her head like a wild animal's.

"I know," he said. "Her hand."

He'd figured it out as he tackled her. For the past eighteen hours, she'd had only one thing in her mind—the blood in their Miami hotel. Was it really Cherry's? Or Emile's idea of a sick joke? Now she knew. Cherry's hand was swaddled in bloody gauze. While Ben saw how lively she was, Patrice only saw her hand. All the desperation she'd been holding in had boiled over.

Ben kept whispering, talking her down. "She's okay. She was fighting with that hand. The cut can't be that bad." Patrice went on struggling. "You can't do anything for her now. Later, when we've got something to trade; but not now."

Patrice relaxed all in a split second. The frenzy left her eyes. "We've got to get away from here," Ben said. "We can get some rest, decide what to do next."

He helped her to her feet and up the path. She was so weak he almost had to carry her. At the rock ledge they knelt and looked back at the house. The cars were still there but everyone had gone inside. The only sound was the eerie jingling of the copper-colored seedpods.

Ben was pulling her up again when he spotted the guard. Dressed in faded gray, the man was nearly invisible against the dim jungle backdrop. He stood sideways to them, urinating on a leaf of a huge elephant ear plant. A shotgun was slung over his shoulder. As he finished what he was doing and tucked himself away, he tipped his head and scratched his jaw with the gun barrel.

Patrice was watching too, but she wasn't tense like Ben. Her face was chalk white. If the guard turned and saw them, she wouldn't run. She'd just take what came. Ben drew her close, waiting.

Luck was with them. The man swung the other way, spitting at his feet before he trudged up the hill.

Ben drove the motorbike back to town. He didn't start the engine right away, but held the clutch in and let it coast. Patrice sat behind with her arms looped around his waist. "You were right." Her voice was calm again, but thin and weary. All the stiffness was gone from her body, the hidden strings and pulleys that kept her wound so tight.

"How's that?"

"I should have stayed away. I should have listened to you."

He laughed. "You? Listen to me?"

"No joke, Ben. Thanks." She nestled closer, her cheek pressed against the back of his neck. Maybe he only imagined it, but he thought she kissed him then.

TWENTY-FOUR

The quiet ride down Monkey Hill was good for Ben, settling his mind. For a while at least, Cherry would be all right. Balazs had no reason to hurt her now. In the meantime, he and Patrice had to get some sleep. They were both dead on their feet, and people that tired became reckless. They couldn't afford another mistake like the one they'd just made, going up to Canada House.

During her first trip to the island, Patrice had had dinner with Emile at the Ocean Terrace Inn. She recalled vaguely where it was, on a hillside overlooking the western reach of the Basseterre harbor. They found it with no trouble, and Ben went in to register them. The main part of the inn was full, the desk clerk explained, but they did have space in the cottages across the street. Might be a little cramped for two, but they were clean. Ben shrugged. "Okay, fine." At that point he'd have taken a tent and a pit toilet. He passed over his Dale Blodgett credit card and soon was on his way out, key in hand.

It was hot in the room. The air-conditioning had been off for days. Ben switched it on and they both collapsed on the bed, too worn out to be shy. The mattress was narrow and squeaked when they moved, so they lay motionless, flat on their backs, touching from shoulder to knee. Maybe they were too tired, or maybe it was all that touching, but they couldn't fall asleep.

"Ben?"

"Hmmm."

She traced a line on his knuckle with her finger. "Mind if I ask a question?"

"Hmmm."

"We never talked about why I wasn't admitted to WIT-SEC. The U.S. Attorney I testified for in Florida wouldn't tell me. I was going to ask you that first night we were together at your house, after you picked me up at the Bay Bluff, but you seemed—I don't know—so cold to me. I felt like a bug in a jar." She paused while Ben tried to guess what brought this on. "It's no big deal, but if you're not fit for witness protection, it makes you wonder what's wrong with you." She touched his hand again. "You saw my file, didn't you?" He was quiet for so long she said, "Still awake?"

"Yes." Another half minute passed before he said, "It was the psych evaluation."

She pulled her hand away. "But you were the one who did that."

"Yes." He sat up. "I came down to Florida to interview you, remember? Twice."

"Sure. That cheesy hotel in West Palm Beach."

"It's my job at WITSEC to figure things out about people, what kind of life they'll lead if they're granted relocation." He dipped his head, then looked at her. "That second time in West Palm, the way you dressed and moved around the room, you didn't leave much guessing to it. You were going to sleep with me to get a clean evaluation."

Her body went rigid. "I knew it! They told me it was the psych test but wouldn't let me look at the write-up. I remember thinking, what the hell's the problem?" She grabbed her pillow and batted him on the arm. "Oh-oh, maybe Benjy doesn't like fast girls."

"Or maybe I don't like girls—people—who won't change, who are headed right down the same road they came in on."

She slammed her fist into the mattress. "Did you ever think I was sick of the routine there? Sick of the goon-squad FBI agents? That I just wanted some fun with you?"

"Nope. Never crossed my mind."

"Nope. Never crossed my mind," she mocked. "Bastard!" She smacked him with the pillow again, this time in the back and much harder. It split open and goose down cascaded around them.

Ben brushed off his shoulders and arms. "Well, that's been bothering you for a while. Feel better now?"

"Yes. No! This is all your fault. If you'd given me a pass, everything would have been all right. I'd be . . . Oh dammit, never mind."

She rolled away from him. Her body began to shake.

Ben didn't want to see her cry. He laid his hand on her side. "Listen, maybe you're right. I could have seen things differently in West Palm."

She turned to him, laughing, not crying. A two-inch feather was stuck in his hair, another behind his ear. He was so intent on making her feel better, he hadn't noticed. She plucked them out. "*You* are something else," she murmured.

He looked into her eyes, wanting to kiss her but holding back. Seeing his indecision, she laughed again, a soft trill. They were so close he whispered. "You surprise me, do you know that?"

"What?" she said.

"I never know what to expect. I watch you, like I do with other people, but I'm always guessing. You surprise me."

"Ben, hel-*lo!* I'm a con."

He put his finger to her lips, hushing her. "Were a con. *Were*. . . ."

She kissed his finger and settled on her back again. They were both smiling as they fell asleep a few minutes later.

Ben awoke slowly, sounds filtering through. The air-conditioner hum, low bird calls from outside. He was lying tight behind Patrice, their bodies contoured together. Her shoulder rose and fell with her breathing. Her smell was there, subtle but unmistakable, shampoo and day-old perfume and a faint musk of sweat. Her skin was flawless except for a tiny mole on the back of her neck. Normally her hair was just long enough to cover it. It reminded him of the other things—her crooked tooth, the scar on her hand, little things she kept hidden. Little mysteries.

Again, he wanted to kiss her. She moved, wiggling her backside against him. *"Tienucol,"* she slurred.

He did kiss her then, on the curve of her neck below her ear. "What'd you say?"

She reached back between her legs, caressing him. "You have a tail."

They both laughed as she rolled into him. Their first kiss on the mouth was dry and quick, and then they were fumbling with the buttons on each other's shirts. The shirts landed in a heap and they knelt, facing each other, nuzzling. Ben knew this was only a rebound from all they'd been through the last three days. He knew it was dangerous, childish. That didn't change things. He wanted her—all of her.

He unbuttoned her pants and she pulled them off, along with what was underneath. She lolled on her side, while he ran his eyes up along her body, not studying, just enjoying. He stopped midway. Her birthmark. The bronze diamond on her thigh. It was gone. Not just gone, but no scar, no mark at all. Another surprise. Another mystery.

Laughing, he kissed her again, but softly, trying to slow them both down. She pushed him up, tugging playfully at the waistband on his pants. "These have to go."

He must have sensed a vibration then, through the floor from the porch, because he looked at the door. A second later someone knocked.

As he stumbled to his feet, she lunged off the bed and into the bathroom. Her clothes lay scattered across the floor, underwear, pants, shirt, shoes. The knock came a second time. Ben checked to make sure his jeans were still fastened, calling, "Yes, coming." He cracked open the door.

A lone figure was silhouetted against the glaring sunlight. "Mr. Dale Blodgett?"

Ben hesitated. His mind was a tangle of loose threads. "I . . . right. Blodgett."

The man held up some sort of ID, but Ben's eyes hadn't adjusted to the light. "I'm with the Basseterre police. Could I come in, sir?"

Ben shuffled back. As the man moved over the threshold, the room seemed to get smaller. He was half a head taller than Ben and solidly muscled, especially through the chest and shoulders. Handing Ben the ID, he looked slowly around. Vance Audain, Inspector, the card said under an out-of-focus photograph. Ben passed it back and saw where Audain was staring. "Oh, those feathers." He gave a tight laugh. "Pillow fight . . . we just . . ." He kicked her underwear out of sight. "What can I do for you?"

Patrice poked her head out of the bathroom. The inspector nodded but said nothing in greeting. He had one of those Caribbean faces that seem carved from exotic dark wood, burnished and ageless and close to indestructible. "Could I see your identification please?"

Ben's head was beginning to clear, enough for him to wonder how the hell the police had found them. "Is there a problem?"

Again Audain said nothing. He had a stick in his hand, a long, stiff, riding crop, and he used it to swing the door closed. With that small movement he set the ground rules. He was in control here; they were not.

Ben pulled one of their knapsacks onto the bed and unzipped it. Clothing and papers and maps tumbled out. He considered turning over their driver's licenses. All the man had asked for was identification. No, that would only prolong the inevitable. He held out the two phony passports.

Audain opened one and flipped past the frontispiece, with the photograph and other information. He went slowly after that, no doubt checking for a St. Kitts entry stamp. While he was concentrating, Ben looked him over. His uniform had been dry cleaned and pressed with razor-sharp creases. The sunglasses in his shirt pocket were Ray-Bans, the pen a Montblanc. His belt buckle was gold, as was his watchband. The stick he carried had a sterling-silver handle. All that on an inspector's salary? Ben wondered.

"You don't travel much, Ms. Royden," he said, loudly enough to reach the bathroom.

"Riordan," Patrice corrected pleasantly. "No, not much." She swished into view, wearing only a towel, and gathered up her clothes. Before she returned to the bathroom, she gave Ben a steady stare followed by a wink. She'd been in this situation dozens of times, slow-dancing with the police. Easy does it, keep it short and breezy.

Audain had finished with the second passport by then. "How long in St. Kitts?" he said to Ben.

It was a masterful question, a sly little trap. Did he mean how long have you been here? Or how long till you leave? While Ben was considering an answer, Patrice called, "Not long enough. Beautiful island. Just beautiful."

The inspector thought over her reply, and, while he did, he leaned back on the wicker chest of drawers, a casual gesture that made him seem even more at home. When he spoke his voice had changed, with more of the island banter in it. "Dis morning you come wanderin' up de beach on the north end. Got a ride t' Basseterre from an old Dieppetown man. Then you rent a piece-a-junk motorbike from

Justin Nisbett. A few hours ago, you seen up at Monkey Hill, goin' up, comin' down again." By now the accent had turned angry. "You're a coupl'a busy folks, first day 'round."

Ben began stuffing their things back in the knapsack. "You seem to know a lot about us."

Audain stared hard at him. "Seem to, yeah." Then he smiled. He'd made his point: You can take my good side, or you can take my bad. He slouched lower against the bureau. "Small island, lots of gossip. I hear things. Got 'specially lucky with you two. St. Clair Saddler's my uncle, mother's brother, one of seven."

"That's funny," Ben said. "My uncle, too. He called me nephew anyway."

"Ah!" Audain's eyes sparkled. When he wanted, he could be quite cheery. "That's our way. Welcome everybody right into the family." He glanced at the top of his shoes and slipped on his Ray-Bans. It was as if the sun had suddenly set on his face. "Uncle said you were askin' after Isabel Finney. What would that be about?"

Ben started to reply, but Patrice cut in on him. "She's an old friend of mine. You know her too?"

"Everybody knows Mrs. Finney. Nice lady. So, you folks here on business?"

"Just a holiday," Ben said.

"You sure 'bout that?"

Patrice came into the room, combing her hair out with her fingers. "Sun and fun, that's all!" She kissed Ben on the cheek.

Audain studied them from behind the sunglasses.

Ben was tired of sparring. He wanted to know if this was about more than the entry stamps on the passports. "What's your interest in Isabel Finney, Inspector?"

Patrice threw Ben a warning glance: just drop it; get him out of here. If Audain noticed he didn't show it. He replied, "Like I say, nice lady, sort of simple though. Naive. People take advantage. If I can, I like to look out for her."

Ben used his eyes like a pointer, staring at the expensive pen then the gold watch. "That's good. We wouldn't want people to take advantage."

Audain found this amusing. He smiled and rubbed the watch with his palm. "I think I've taken enough of your time." He sauntered out the door.

Ben stepped after him, holding out his hand. "Our passports?"

Audain kept moving. The walkway was lined with potted hibiscus plants. He rapped each pot with his stick as he passed. "You want to talk to Isabel, she's down the market."

"Down the market? Where's that?"

"Public market, Bay Road, by the harbor. Can't miss it . . . or her." He reached his vehicle, a maroon Suzuki Samurai with POLICE stenciled on the hood. A woman in uniform was sitting behind the wheel, and he exchanged a few quiet words with her.

"Our passports?" Ben repeated.

Audain glanced at his hand as if he'd forgotten they were there. He tucked them into his shirt pocket. Without looking back at the cottage, he called, "G'day, sir." The woman was smirking as she drove off, but there was no expression at all on the inspector's face.

TWENTY-FIVE

Ben quickly showered and shaved. He tossed on his only spare clothes, along with the sport coat he'd bought in Miami. Then he and Patrice rolled down to the harbor on the motorbike.

Bay Road ran in a long arc at the foot of town. On one side was the seawall and a narrow strip of sand leading to the water. On the other was a line of old houses, white-washed, shuttered, battered around the edges by countless storms. Halfway down this line was the public market, a faded turquoise building open on all four sides. People were milling around out in front.

Far enough away so the market goers wouldn't notice them, Ben pulled the Peugeot to the curb. He handed Patrice the keys as he got off. "How do I look?"

She straightened his collar. "You'll knock her dead." Her smile was warm and open. "Back there, when we woke up—" She blushed slightly. "Sorry we were interrupted."

"Me, too." He brushed his hand along her arm. "You'll wait at the room?" She hesitated. "Patrice, promise you won't do anything."

She slipped the key in the ignition. "Okay. I promise." He touched her again and strode into the crowd.

He had to take a step down into the market, as if the town were growing up around it, leaving the old place behind. Inside were long tables, divided and numbered so each vendor had an assigned spot. But the piles of produce were too big, running together in motley profusion: peppers and pumpkins and finger-sized bananas and breadfruit and coconuts. There were a dozen kinds of tubers. In one pile was the biggest sweet potato Ben had ever seen. The people were a tangle, too. He couldn't tell the shoppers from the sellers, nor begin to understand them. They spoke with a quick patois, laughing, teasing each other.

He made nearly a full circuit of the market before he found Isabel Finney. She and four or five others had taken over some spare tables in the corner of the building, under a sign that said, "Help the Immaculate Conception." It was a miniature version of an old-fashioned English fête. There was a place to buy raffle tickets, another for guava jelly. A peptic-looking priest was prepared to guess weights and ages. At Isabel's table the poster said, "Palms Read, Fortunes Told."

The first impression Ben had of her was how alone she seemed, even with all the hubbub. People passed by and nodded hello but moved on before she could draw them into conversation. Even her own group had abandoned her, fiddling with their wares or chatting with customers. People liked her, yes, but her presence made them uneasy. Through all this, Isabel smiled serenely, not noticing the way she was treated.

Ben approached slowly, making sure she saw him before he reached the table. "Does it need help?"

"What?" Isabel said.

"The Conception."

She looked where he was pointing at the sign. After a quick laugh, she whispered, "Let's find the Madonna and ask!" She brushed her long hair back on her shoulders. "It's for our church, Cathedral of the Immaculate Conception. Want a reading?"

"Two," he replied, sitting opposite her. "You do mine; I'll do yours."

She beamed. "Oh, great fun!"

Ben passed her a double fee, ten dollars U.S., and she took the bill to a cash box kept by the dour priest. He wouldn't touch the money. Palm reading was against his principles. Isabel nodded happily at him just the same. All around, men followed her with their eyes but looked away when she started back. They wanted to ogle but not to catch her attention. She was wearing a vivid green wrap skirt, slung low and tight, slit up the sides to mid-thigh. Her orange tube top was only four inches wide, made of a skimpy material that didn't seem quite up to the job at hand. She felt the stares. Her shoulders went back; her stride became more confident. "Who's first?" she said as she sat down again.

Ben held out his palm. "The lady, of course."

Her grip was firm. Her nails were painted the same way as Mary's, her housekeeper. "Good life line," she said. "Excellent love line." She twitched her hair back from her face again. "You have recently completed a great journey." That was a safe guess on this island. "You travel by ship." Ben made a slight frown. She got the message. "Um, not by ship." She closed her eyes, concentrating. "You traveled over water and saw ships. You . . ." She touched her fingertips to the center of her forehead. For an instant Ben had a startling image of Emile doing the same thing, the third-eye spot. She had her brother's cheekbones and jawline. Then she moved her hand away and smiled, and the illusion was gone. "This is your first day here. You're planning to go to the casino. You'll have wonderful luck."

Ben made his eyes round with delight. "How did you know—my first day here?"

"You haven't changed money yet. And that sport coat, you'll get rid of it by tomorrow. Too hot."

Ben applauded her effort while she gave a bow. She offered her palm. "Your turn?"

Ben glanced around. In Basseterre, Isabel was a major curiosity. He'd been with her a while already, and people were beginning to notice. If he was going to talk to her, he'd have to get her away from here. He locked eyes with her as he took her hand, and he thought: *taking candy from a baby*.

"You live here, of course," he began. She nodded, wanting to encourage him. "Very active in church. Your car is . . . a Toyota, I think."

"How'd you guess?" she said. He smiled modestly and didn't answer. Her keys lay on the table in plain view.

"You broke a bracelet recently." There was a mark on her wrist where she had worn it. She nodded again, but not so quickly. This was something she didn't want to get into.

Ben's eyes flicked down to her chest. She wore an amethyst pendant, nestled in her cleavage, and amethyst earrings. The head of her key chain was a plastic "I," the same shade as her jewelry. "Your favorite color is purple."

"Yes!" she said. "Great!"

"And . . ." He noticed the smooth, muscled contour of her shoulders and the tan lines around her neck. "You swim for exercise."

She clapped her hand to her mouth in surprise. "You're wonderful!"

"I'm not," he insisted, smiling at her. "I'll tell you what I am, though. Starved. No lunch yet. Would you like—?"

She steamrolled over his invitation. "I'd love to. I know a great place."

Isabel took a moment to explain to the priest that she was leaving. She wasn't getting much business anyway. She and Ben gathered her things and headed for her car, which, she explained, was parked only a block away. As they walked, the first bit of awkwardness passed between them. For Isabel, what had started as a chance encounter had now turned into a date. She was nervous and tongue-tied. Ben was distracted, too, thinking about how he could turn the conversation to a visitor named Saar and a safety-deposit key.

He went to the driver's side of the car and held the door for her after she unlocked it. Behind him, he heard the scratching of feet on pavement. When he looked, he saw only an empty alley, but he had the feeling someone had been watching. Patrice? he wondered. Isabel had the car started so he hurried to climb in beside her.

The place she chose for lunch was the Jumbi Cafe. It was in the center of town, on the second floor of a building overlooking a traffic rotary called the Circus, like London's Piccadilly, only miniature scale. Taxi-vans were lined up here, the drivers lounging on the front fenders. As Ben and Isabel came up the sidewalk after parking, several of the men nodded and called, "Af'noon, Miz Finney." She gave them a cheerful wave.

The Jumbi was meant for tourists and expats. The furniture was blond veneer; the music on the sound system was easy-listening American rock. The waitresses wore neat uniforms, conservative cornrows, and bored smiles. The one who led them to their table offered paper menus, but Isabel pushed hers away. "May I order?" she asked Ben.

"Yes. Please."

"Okay." She put her fingers to her forehead again. "A bottle of that merlot I like and start with the pumpkin soup, and the appetizer plate, too, and for the main course make one of those sharing plates, okay dear? Jerk chicken and mahimahi, and plantain chips, and dip for that, and somebody stop me before I order a whole cow."

"Yes, stop!" Ben said, laughing with her.

They were seated on the balcony, which overlooked the Circus. As they talked, they watched the cars roll through and the tourists meander in and out of the shops. The cafe was quiet, with only one American family still having lunch, so Ben was quick to notice when two men came in and took places at the bar in the far corner. He couldn't see much of them back in the gloom, but they were large men, dressed in dark clothes. They ordered drinks and sat brooding over them.

Ben tried to get Isabel to talk about her recent life on the island, but he didn't make much progress. She had a mind like a grasshopper. If he asked a question, she'd spend a sentence or two answering, then hop off to a new subject. He had to slow her down, get her attention. They were nearly through with the chicken and fish when he decided to bring out the heavy guns. With the next lull in the conversation, he smiled at her. "I've been trying to think. You remind me of someone. Isabel, you know, you look just like Cher?"

She started blushing low on her cheeks. The pink spread over her face and down her throat, all the way to her breasts. "Cher? Really?"

"Really," he assured her.

She put her fork down and didn't pick it up again. She was through eating. She took a long sip of wine, keeping her eyes on Ben. "Tell you what," he said. "Want to play a little game? Helps people get to know each other."

"Sure!" About then, she would have agreed to chop sugarcane with him, as a fun way to spend the rest of the afternoon together.

"It's called 'Mystery.' We'll try to figure out some mystery about each other. I'll go first, ask you a question. Anything I want. You answer, then it's your turn to ask."

"Mysteries? Me?" Her eyes danced.

Now, with patience, he could move the conversation where he wanted. "Why do you live here?" he said.

"Business, I guess. But not only for that. We've built a great new house. We've always moved around a lot, Barbados and Grand Cayman and Miami." She brought herself up short. A guilty look crossed her face. "I meant my brother when I said 'we.' I'm not married, not now. Finney, my husband—his given name was Roddy but everybody called him Finney—died last year. I would have told you, but it just didn't fit in, you know?"

Again, a few sentences on topic, then off on a ramble. "I'm sorry about your husband. And you're right, it didn't fit in. So you live with your brother?"

"That's *two* questions," Isabel said with a laugh.

"Caught me," Ben said. "Your turn."

While she thought about what to ask, he looked at the two men at the bar. They slouched on their stools, silent and immobile. They hadn't touched their drinks. One of them looked his way and stiffened when he noticed he was being watched.

Ben had glanced away too long. "What?" Isabel said. She saw the men. "Oh, sugar!"

Ben reached for her. "Wait—"

Isabel was already on her feet. She stormed across the restaurant. "How dare you follow me around! Parasites! You go tell Emile to leave me be! *Go!*" The men looked at each other and slid off of their stools. They jogged down the stairs without a backward glance. She stood with her fists on her hips, puffed up with victory. Then she grinned at Ben. "Little girl's room," she mouthed, tipping her head toward a nearby door. "Be right back."

Too late, Ben returned the smile. He looked where the men had been sitting. Balazs' men, obviously. Did they know about him and Patrice? Were they on the lookout for them? Or were they there for Isabel's sake, low-profile bodyguards? No way to know. Still, he couldn't waste any more time. Those men might come back, with new orders. Every minute he spent here pushed up the risk of that.

He heard the door across the way squeak and looked over. His heart stumbled.

In the rest room, Isabel had rearranged her skirt, wrapping it so tight she could only take mincing steps. Her bottom hung suspended like two melons in a sack. She'd pulled her tube top down so that a sliver of nipple showed on each breast. Before Ben could speak, before she was fully in her chair, she said, "Do you like to dance?"

"Yes, sure I do. Isabel I—"

"I just learned to samba. We could—" She fanned herself with her hand, as if she were suddenly too warm. "A friend of mine has this super house by Frigate Bay. Terrific sound system. She's home in Texas, but I've got a key. Let's go. Let's go right now. We can play Mystery in the car." The fanning got faster. "There's a hot tub. We could skinny-dip." She leaned forward. Her nipples winked at him.

Taking candy from a baby.

Ben looked down at the tabletop. Skinny-dip—people did that kind of thing all the time. Nobody died from it. But they could get hurt, especially people like Isabel.

He reached for her hand. By then, her expression had started to turn brittle. He said, "I think I know your mystery."

"What?"

"You're in trouble," he said. She began to deny it, but he went on, "Those were pretty scary men you just sent away. Who are they?"

"They work for my brother. It's nothing. Forget it." She smiled. She was still hoping for a trip to her friend's house by Frigate Bay.

"Why were they here?" He felt her hand tense, the first sign of wariness. He turned it over, palm up, and ran his finger across the mark on her wrist. "I noticed this at the market, remember? A bruise. Look at it. Not one bruise, but little ones in a pattern all the way around. There's only one way I can think of to get that. A bracelet of beads—someone with big hands, squeezing." He wrapped his thumb and forefinger around her wrist. "Like this. Whoever he was, he must have really wanted to hurt you."

She looked away. "Like I said, it's nothing."

He cupped his hand to her face, turning her back around to him. "He hurt you here, too. This cheek. The bruise is gone, but not all of the swelling."

Isabel blinked at him, mesmerized. How did he know all this? She started to speak, but stopped.

In the end, trust usually has to be bought with trust. "I'll let you in on something," Ben said. "You would have found out anyway. I didn't just run into you at the market today. I've been looking for you. I stopped by your place this morning and talked to your housekeeper. Later, it was a police officer—Inspector Audain—who told me where to find you."

As soon as he said Audain's name, she brightened. "You know Vance?"

"We've met." He took both of her hands. "Isabel, tell me. Are you in trouble?"

Once she decided to talk, it came in a burst. "It's Emile—my brother. He can be so *irritating*. He thinks I've got something of his, but I don't. He sent those men to watch me. They're not around all the time, just enough to be a nuisance."

Over her shoulder he could see the far curve of the Circus. Balazs' men were there, staring up at the balcony where he and Isabel sat.

Ben touched her cheek. "Is Emile the one who hurt you?"

She shrugged. "He's not normally like that, but there's a lot of stress now. Business." Then she shook her head violently. Why should she make excuses for him? "Emile hurt my wrist. One of his men slapped me. I don't understand. I haven't done anything wrong."

"No, I'm sure you haven't," Ben said.

She was glad he agreed so quickly, but, a moment later, her smile changed to a frown. "You said you were looking for me. Why?"

"Because I need your help."

She continued to frown, waiting for him to explain.

He'd known this time would come. He wished he'd had more of a chance to prepare her. Behind her, one of Balazs' men was talking on a mobile phone. The other had disappeared. Ben looked into her eyes. "A man came to see you a few weeks ago. A priest."

Her hand tensed again. He stroked it. "You just asked me to go skinny-dipping. If you trust me for that, you can trust me with this. A priest came to see you. You talked about a safety-deposit key."

"How did you—" She broke off, lifting her wineglass, but she didn't drink. In her face there was confusion, and a little fear. "Did Emile send you?" she said.

"No."

She stared, not knowing whether to believe him.

It was time to turn the conversation. A plunge, a chance. Something to show they were on the same side. "How did your husband die?" Ben said.

"Finney? He was drowned. Lost off a boat."

Ben could tell from her tone it was just a story. She didn't believe it. "No. Is that what he told you?"

"Who?"

He stroked her bruised wrist. "Your brother."

"Yes, he was the one who told me," she whispered. She had that mesmerized look again. "Who are you?"

"Somebody in trouble, just like you."

The waitress was coming with the bill. She told Ben to pay the cashier. It was good timing. He didn't want to push Isabel any further. She needed a chance to calm down and think.

Taking the bill, he stood up. "I'll be just a minute."

From the cashier's station, Ben watched her. Her face changed from moment to moment, frowns and head shakes and nods. She was having a conversation with herself. Serious talk. Patrice had been wrong about Isabel. She wasn't a big kid; she just put on a big act. And from the look of those bruises, she was in real trouble with Emile. Ben wondered—if he could get Isabel away from St. Kitts, where would she go? He smiled to himself. That was for another day, a chance to introduce her to the Laundry Man.

The cashier handed him his change. Time to get out of there. The friend's house by Frigate Bay was out of the question. Ben didn't want that kind of complication. He'd walk Isabel to her car, then ask her to take him for a ride, tour the island. They'd have time to talk, and they could lose the two watchers on the trip.

Back at the table, she was passive, letting him help her up, mumbling thanks for the meal. As they passed the bar, he pointed at the spot where Emile's men had sat. One of the stools was bent. "Does your brother pay for his gargoyles by the pound?"

Isabel broke into a grin. "They're still no match for me."

They went down the stairs to the lobby. Through the wide entry doors, Ben could see across the Circus. The gargoyles weren't there. He caught sight of them rounding the street, heading back toward the café. One had something in his hand. Silver, glinting. Dammit—a camera. They sure as hell weren't out sightseeing. If they got a picture of him, it would go straight to Balazs.

He jerked back, pulling Isabel with him. Off the lobby, there were three or four shops. One of them—a jewelry store—had an exit onto the adjoining street, a clean escape. But what to do with Isabel? There was no time to make a game of it. If he dragged her along, running from those two thugs, he'd scare the living hell out of her. Then she'd never open up to him.

He could hear footsteps approaching. "I have to go—take care of something," he said.

She nodded slowly. She seemed to be expecting this, being left on her own.

Ben knew the risk he was taking. She might make a mess of everything. Go to the police, or Emile. He gave her a kiss on the cheek. "I'll need to see you again."

"Sure." She seemed so vulnerable. She still hadn't pulled up her tube top.

The footsteps were just outside. He gave her hand one last squeeze and headed into the jewelry store and out the back door.

Turn left, turn right—it didn't matter. Just get away from the Circus. The street was quiet in the midafternoon heat. A block away, a taxi-van was parked. The driver spotted him and called, "Taxi, sir?" Ben tried not to walk too quickly.

The driver hopped out and opened the door. "Welcome, sir! Where to today?"

Ben glanced over his shoulder. The two gargoyles were coming out of the jewelry store. Ben jogged the last few steps and ducked behind the van, watching through the window. He didn't think they'd spotted him, but the man with the camera started his way. The other one called him back. They strode around the corner, gone.

By then, the taxi driver's expression had changed. He'd seen the whole thing, and he knew who those men worked for. He slammed the van door. "Sorry, sir. Just going off duty." He jumped behind the wheel and drove quickly away.

TWENTY-SIX

Ben spent twenty minutes trying to find Isabel, but he came up empty, so he caught another taxi back to the Ocean Terrace Inn. He tried to sort out what to do next, but his mind spun in circles. What had happened was plain bad luck, but that didn't make it any easier to take.

The cab driver pulled over across from the cottage. Through the gate they could see into the back angle of the garden. Patrice had brought a chair out in the shade of a frangipani tree. She was asleep, her lips pointed in a Mona Lisa smile. The driver whistled. "Dat's something to come home to, yeah mon?"

"Pretty as can be," Ben sighed.

He waited for the man to drive away before he went through the gate. Patrice woke as he knelt next to her. "Hi."

In her lap was a sheet of paper. She'd sketched an outline of a girl running on a beach. "For Cherry?" Ben said.

She nodded. "Something to pass the time." As she touched the picture, her fingers trembled. "I keep seeing her—her hand, the way she was cut. She loves to draw more than anything." She rubbed the scar on her own palm. Someday, Ben promised himself, he'd get her to tell him about that scar.

He said, "Try to think ahead. You'll be with her, away from all this." He tugged her shirtsleeve. "That's my job, remember? To find a safe place for you."

She managed to smile. "Sounds great." Sitting up, she said, "What about Isabel?"

Ben leaned against the block wall that surrounded the garden. The ferry to Nevis was about to leave from the main Basseterre dock, and the captain gave two blasts on the horn. As the echo died, Ben began to tell her.

He kept it brief, saying nothing about how Isabel was dressed, nothing about hot tubs or dancing the samba. Patrice joined him by the wall. "You're sure the two men were Emile's?" she said.

"Yes."

"Then we have to find Isabel again, right now."

She started for the gate, and Ben grabbed her hand. "Patrice, don't—"

"We need that second key," she said, "and we need to find out where the bank is. If Isabel doesn't want to help us, then we'll make her."

He said, "I saw the way she took care of those goons of Emile's. You won't be able to scare her."

"Just watch me." She twisted free, as a car horn beeped behind them. They turned, and an old Mazda sedan rolled to the curb. Inspector Audain was at the wheel. He got out but left the motor running. "First the pillows, now this. You two always fightin'." It could have been a joke, but his voice was hard, ringing like a hammer. "Need to talk to you. Get in."

Alarms went off in Ben's head. Audain had changed from his uniform into civvies, and he wasn't driving a police car. He was wearing a Windbreaker, intended to hide the gun on his hip. Earlier, when he was on duty, he didn't have it.

"No," Ben said. "We talk here."

Audain moved around the front of the car. His hand went to the gun. "Don't forget where you are. I shoot you down right here, and everybody in town will say it's suicide, if I tell 'em to." Ben didn't move, and Audain yanked open the rear door. *"In!"*

Patrice was calculating the angles here, too. "All right, all right." She took Ben's hand. "Come on. Let's just get it over with, whatever the hell he wants." She pulled him after her, through the gate and into the backseat.

The car was Audain's. The Lord's Prayer was stuck to the dashboard and dozens of copies of *Sail* magazine were stacked on the floor. "You own a boat?" Patrice asked after they got started.

"Sellin' one." Audain's tone made it clear he wanted them to keep quiet.

He took the ring road out of town, going up the west side of the island. He drove with cool fury, flying down the straightaways, attacking the corners. On a hairpin in a small village, he nearly hit a dog. This dog was a slow learner. It had only three legs. Audain honked his horn, and it hobbled out of the way.

After twenty minutes he turned off on a side road by a sign that said "Brimstone Hill." They made a long pull uphill to a gatehouse with another sign: "Entry, E.C. $10." Audain glared at the woman in the booth, and she nervously waved him on without collecting the fee. The road rose steeply and the turns became tighter. In the cramped backseat, Ben and Patrice were tossed around as if they were on a roller coaster. Suddenly they broke free of the trees and had a stunning view, six hundred feet below, of the blue-green ocean waters. They passed through an arch in a rock wall, and Audain slammed on the brakes, kicking up a cloud of dust. "Out," he ordered.

Ben caught a whiff of sulfur in the air. That had to be the source of the name, Brimstone Hill. It was an old fort. A grassy promenade led to a five-sided stone bastion topped by cutouts for cannons. Audain, riding crop in hand, directed them across the grass and onto the stone courtyard. They went to the farthest point of the battlement, a spot perched on a sheer cliff with a two-hundred-seventy-degree view of the Caribbean. Out here the wind was nearly gale force. Ben usually didn't mind heights, but this was unnerving, all that wind and sea and sky, and only a spit of stone to hold them up. Patrice's reaction was worse than his. She crouched against the low wall, her eyes fixed on solid ground. Her face was as white as milk.

Audain twirled his stick and snapped his words out angrily. "Brimstone Hill Fortress—construction started 1690. Occupied mostly by the British, but the French had it one year, 1782. From here, with good weather, you can see five islands." He pointed at spots in the haze. "Nevis, St. Eustatius, Saba, St. Martin, St. Barts."

Ben glanced over the cliff. Far below, a sailboat was heeled over, winging through the water. He tried to inch away from the precipice, drawing Patrice with him. Audain blocked their way. "So," the policeman snapped, "you've seen Dieppe and Basseterre and the harbor. You've been to the market and had lunch at our wonderful Jumbi Cafe. Now you've seen our fort. Most efficient. Not much else to offer you here. You should make the best of your trip. Try another island, I think."

Ben's temper flared. He took a blatant step forward. "You know about the Jumbi Cafe. You must have talked to Isabel."

Audain gave the nearest cannon a rap with his stick. It rang a low hollow note. "She came to see me straight from the restaurant. Said you'd implied her brother was involved in her husband's death, some such nonsense."

"Emile killed Finney," Patrice said. She was shaky on her feet, but her voice was steady. "You're a cop here; you've got to know that."

Audain stared at her, and a glimmer of amusement came over his face. "You're right. *I've* got to know that, but Isabel doesn't. At least she didn't until you two came along."

Ben said, "That's what you do to look after her? Keep her from finding out the kind of man her brother is?"

"What's the point of her knowin'?" Audain said harshly, his island accent coming through strong. "Listen now. Back in the big hurricane last year, lotta rich folks, holiday people, write a check for a hundred dollars t' the relief fund, mebbe give some canned goods and blankets. Isabel? She opens up her house. Let folks stay there three, four months while they get back on their feet. Whole families in that little place a hers. I worked with her up Christ Church Parish. A whole day, she's luggin' cement block to rebuild a house for somebody she don't even know. She's special, one of God's people, we say. Don't need to be dirtied up with her brother's doin's."

"How about you?" Ben cut in. "Gold watch, fancy belt, a boat to sell. Are you dirtied up in Emile's business?"

Audain snapped his gun out and jabbed it in Ben's chest. His face was twisted with rage. "You doin' a lotta lippin' for a man in your position."

The wind rose to a howl. Audain, despite his size and muscle, was driven back against the cannon. Ben went lurching into the courtyard. Patrice kept low, hunkered behind the wall. When the gust died, she rose and stepped in front of Audain, right up to the gun. "We need Isabel's help. When we get it, we'll leave. If you don't like that, then go fuck yourself."

Audain chuckled bitterly. "We give people thirty days for cursin' here. You wouldn't like our jail. Not at all." He continued to stare at her while he slowly holstered the gun.

Ben pulled Patrice back beside him. Audain tapped his thigh with his stick, a slow rhythm to calm himself. "This wristwatch, that boat, were my brother's. Selvyn had a job with Emile Balazs unloadin' planes at the airport. Good job, all us in the family thought. Then one day, 'stead of Selvyn coming home from work, it was that little prince of Balazs', Mick Laraby. Laraby says Selvyn's dead. Got in a car accident way off in Mexico, doin' some work for the company. He gives my mother ten thousand dollars in cash and tips his hat and walks away. Funny thing, though. Coupl'a weeks later a man's cuttin' cane up Cayon. What's he find? Shallow grave with Selvyn's body in it. That boy's an angel, I tell Mama. Flew all the way home from Mexico. So we had the funeral. Mama banked the ten thousand. I got his jewelry to wear and his boat to sell."

"What do you think happened to him?" Ben said.

"Balazs. Everybody knows it."

"Why don't you do something about him?"

The inspector hit the cannon again with his stick. "Sure, sure." There was more fury than ever in his voice. "You people from outside all de same. To you, we're just happy island folk livin' in paradise. Look there. Over by my car. That's a mongoose. See it? Know how dey got here? White planters brought 'em in, turn 'em loose t' kill the rats. Thing is, the rats come out durin' the night, and the mongoose hunts by day. They still got t' eat, so the mongoose kills chickens instead and kittens and anything else that's weak."

He pushed off the cannon, toward them. He stopped so close they could see the tiny red veins in his eyes and the throb of blood at his temples. "Emile Balazs is just like that mongoose. We can't get rid a them, and we can't get rid a him."

Ben said, "If you need help, you could ask. There are people in Washington—"

"*Washington!*" Audain thundered. "Coupl'a months ago somebody from the Justice Department up there decided it'd be a good idea t' extradite Emile Balazs, put him on trial for somethin'. They filed the papers with our magistrate, all official. Next thing we hear, they change their minds. Don't want him back in the States, want him left here, safe 'n sound."

"Somebody's protecting him up there. Who?" Ben said.

"Mebbe the army, or Drug Enforcement, or the President, or mebbe God Almighty. I don't care. I can't do a thing about Emile Balazs." Audain's voice dropped to a mutter. "He's our plague on this island, just like the mongoose."

The inspector paced, riding his anger. "Back to the point of comin' up here. I don't know what you want with Balazs. I don't think I want to know. But I've lived here all my life, and I see things clear. Somethin' bad's comin'. People bound to get hurt."

He looked up at the sky, then wheeled and strode to his car. They didn't follow right away, but did when he got in and started the engine.

He was glaring ahead over the steering wheel. "Isabel's a grown lady, makes her own decisions. She should be at her house now. Wants to talk to you." He reached into his shirt pocket and pulled out the two passports he'd taken from them earlier. He tossed them on the ground. "I'm no taxi driver. You get your own ride back to town."

Ben bent to pick them up while Audain put the car in gear. He raced the engine but kept the clutch in. "Like I say, people gonna get hurt. It better not be Isabel. Somethin' happens to her, I'll be out huntin' you. I'll give you up to Emile myself." He roared through the stone arch while they leaped aside, away from the blistering jet of stones cast up by his wheels.

TWENTY-SEVEN

Emile stared at the nameplate on the desk. The brass had begun to dull. Roddy Finney's name was hard to make out. This used to be Finney's home base, the communications room behind Emile's office at Canada House. Emile kept the nameplate as a reminder: trust can be a damn dangerous thing.

One of the phones rang, and Emile picked up. "Yeah, go ahead." With Finney no longer around, Mick Laraby kept the books and managed the planes and pilots. When Mick was away, Emile had to take care of things himself.

The man on the other end was surprised to hear his voice. "Um, sure, sir. This is Royal Seven. Package delivered. Wire transfer to the Caymans confirmed."

Royal Seven—one of the pilots, Bud Roulan. The package was five computer engineers from Sri Lanka, delivered to one of the big Seattle high-tech companies. The company needed on-site code writers and couldn't wait for the immigration red tape to clear. Emile pulled a few strings and paid a few bribes and Roulan made a quiet run under the radar.

Emile looked at the ledger Mick kept. "Mexico City's up next. Check—"

A shriek cut the air, faintly, coming from the basement of the house. That damn little girl. The cry stopped as abruptly as it started.

Scowling, Emile went back to the phone. "Check in when you get there."

"Sure thing, sir," Roulan said. "Be airborne in an hour." He hung up.

After paying off Roulan and the upkeep on the plane, Emile's profit on the Seattle deal would be ninety thousand dollars. When Finney ran things, that kind of job was the bread and butter of the business. These days, all Emile cared about was Manuel Herrera. If he could pull that together, Manuel would owe him more than he'd make in five years humping dodgy cargo. Then he and Mick would be off to the Riviera for that vacation. Saint-Tropez or Nice. Maybe they'd stay on there, away from Cuba and Herrera and the whole fucking mess in the Caribbean.

Thinking of Manuel reminded Emile of Morena. She was supposed to phone him half an hour ago. He'd have to wait around or catch a bushel of complaints from her later. He slumped back, twirling Finney's nameplate on the desk.

A *squeak-squeak* came from the outer office, from one of the captain's chairs at the bar. "Who's out there?"

A blocky head with short, spiky dreadlocks poked into view. "Edmund, Mr. Balazs." He touched his forelock, like a page boy meeting the squire. "I'm Edmund."

"I know who you are. What do you want?"

"I heard ya talkin' and didn't wanna interrupt." He wore black clothes, and his huge frame seemed to blot out all the light from the doorway. "Dese pictures." He held up an envelope from a photo shop in Basseterre. "Mr. Laraby asked for someone t' follow your sister, see who she meets up with. She had lunch with a man t'day. Jumbi Cafe. Got pictures of him here." Edmund lowered his eyes. "Not so good, though. From way across the Circus." He looked up again. "I'd give 'em t' Mr. Laraby, but he's not around."

Balazs said, "Jesus, another one of Isabel's horndogs. All right, I'll take them." Edmund dropped the folder on the desk and retreated, but he didn't leave. "What else?" Emile snapped.

"My cousin Glenroy, sir, he works for you too, uh . . . Do you know Glenroy?"

Balazs only stared at him.

"Glenroy's with dat girl, Cherry, and he's got into some problems."

Emile's stare turned deadly. "What problems?"

Edmund whined, "I'd tell Mr. Laraby, but he isn't—"

The phone rang again. Reaching for it, Emile motioned Edmund out the door.

The call was from Morena. She was late, she said, because she'd been at the doctor's. "What's wrong?" Emile asked.

"Nothing," she said.

Emile stifled a curse. He knew that flirty tone. She wanted to play twenty questions. How could he win at that? *Let's see: tummy tuck? skin peel?* Screw it. Instead, he asked how the trip home from St. Kitts had gone the other day. She was sulky that he didn't want to talk about the doctor, but that passed. The trip had been a nightmare, she said. They hit a storm, and the plane's radio went out. They had to land at her father's place in the Keys. That plane was an old junker anyway. She wanted a new jet, like Emile's, but Manuel said it would be a waste of money.

Emile mumbled, "Uh-huh, uh-huh." He was thinking about Cherry, what kind of trouble that freak Glenroy could have gotten into with her.

When Morena was finally through, he said, "How's your father? Not mad at me anymore?"

There was a pause. "Papa's not happy. Twice you've let him down, promising he could meet Colonel Roque—"

"The secret police in Cuba wouldn't let Roque out. That's as much your father's fault as anybody's, screwing around down there with his bandito friends and their homemade bombs." They both fell silent for a moment. "Anyway, it's taken care of. Mick's in Santo Domingo now, picking Roque up. They'll be landing in the States in a few hours. I'm coming later, around midnight."

"Good. Be at the racetrack tomorrow morning, seven o'clock."

Dammit! She was giving him orders now? He couldn't get through to her, no matter how much mewing and swooning he did. Mention her father, and she became a different person: protective, rigid, downright vicious. Emile figured everybody had a weak spot, but maybe not Morena.

He struggled to keep the anger out of his voice. "What your father said about giving us only seven more days—he didn't mean that, did he?"

"He meant exactly what he said. There's been a change—" She hesitated. She was worried about the line being tapped. Balazs had warned her on this. "A change with the target."

"We've got that paced," he said. "No worries there."

She sighed and said, "We'll discuss it tomorrow." Then her tone brightened. "If you can spare a few hours after the racetrack, you can take me shopping. I need some new clothes."

"Love to," he said. But he was thinking, *Wonderful, a new wardrobe for Jekyll and Hyde.*

They said good-bye, and Balazs sat in festering silence. He rubbed his jaw. It always hurt after he talked to her, from grinding his teeth. The *squeak-squeak* came again from the outer office. "Edmund?"

The giant shuffled through the door. Emile picked up the package of photos and snapped open the flap. "So what's the problem?"

"Dat li'l girl, Mr. Balazs. You know the lady Mr. Laraby hired to take care of her run off after she got bit." Balazs didn't know this, but he nodded as if he did, and grinned at the thought of Cherry besting the old witch. "Glenroy got put in charge of her, and now she won't eat or drink, and she's clawin' her own legs somethin' terrible. Glenroy tried a few things and it didn't help. We thought you'd—"

"Chrisakes!" Balazs shouted. "Can't anybody do anything around here?" Damned nuisance when Mick was away.

He stood up, tossing the photo envelope aside. The pictures spilled across the desk. He reached to pick them up, then changed his mind and charged out.

They'd put Cherry in the wine cellar. Since Emile only drank liquor, it had never been used until now. There was a cot and a chair, a lamp and a chemical toilet, all in one corner of the big concrete room. Emile's first thought on entering was how cool the place was. It raised goose bumps on his arms. Glenroy was sitting on the cot. He was much smaller than Edmund, and no smarter. Beside him, in the chair, was Cherry. Her ankles and wrists were tied, and she had a sock in her mouth as a gag. Glenroy rose, and a funnel clattered to the floor from his lap, along with a two-foot length of garden hose and a bottle of water.

"Won't drink," he mumbled.

Emile snatched the hose and walloped him. "So you take this damn thing and shove it in her mouth and pour in some water. What do you think, she's a cow?" He hit him again. Glenroy only grunted.

Emile pulled the sock out of Cherry's mouth. Immediately, she began to scream. She was hoarse from all the yelling she'd done already. "Cherry, you have to drink. You'll get sick and nobody wants that, especially your mother."

"You're all jerks," she snarled. She looked up at him, then away, across the room. "All of you!"

"Cherry—"

"Pigs!"

Emile scrubbed his hand over his face. What was he doing here, wasting his fucking time? Walk away, leave her. No. He couldn't let his men see him retreat from a little girl.

Cherry had a new hat, a red beret that was Mick Laraby's. Emile pulled it off. "Mmm. Cute haircut."

That stung her. She tucked her chin down, blinking back tears. "Where's my mom?"

"We'd all like to know that," Emile replied. He squatted next to her. "You have to drink and eat. And your legs, look at those scratches. Why do that?"

"Get away from me. *Get away.*"

Emile's face remained placid. He held her bandaged hand and nodded at the knife on his belt. "We could try another little cut. . . ."

Cherry started shaking, she was so angry. "You don't scare me! *I* go to Catholic school! You can't *imagine* what goes on there."

Her eyes again. She was screaming at him but looking somewhere else.

Emile turned, and smiled. "No, I don't scare you." He stood up. "Edmund, come here."

Edmund shambled closer. Cherry's eyes widened and she shrank back.

"You stay with her. Make her behave."

"No!" Cherry wrestled with the ropes. "*I don't want him!*" Edmund shrugged. Stupid, clumsy, timid—but still her vision of Frankenstein's monster. He took another step.

Cherry wailed so loudly her voice broke and almost disappeared. "Please. I'll drink. Let Glenroy stay! *Please!*"

"All right, as long as you're good," Emile said mildly. He tossed her the hat and motioned Edmund out of the room. As he closed the door, he felt the best he had all day. See? *Everybody* has a weak spot.

TWENTY-EIGHT

Ben and Patrice caught a ride back to Basseterre with an American tourist couple. While he drove, the man made eyes at Patrice in the mirror. His wife kept hers on the road. "Get over, Roger. *Left!* Jesus, you'll get us all killed!"

They stopped on Cayon Street, and Ben and Patrice walked up the hill to Isabel's house on Flambouyant Drive. No one answered when Ben knocked, so they sat on the porch steps to wait.

A few minutes later a car turned onto the street. "That's her," Ben said. "Maybe you should wait somewhere, let me break the ice."

"No. I'm staying. It's time she and I talked."

Mary was in the car, too, but she went inside through the garage, while Isabel came around to the front. She stopped halfway through the gate, when she saw Patrice. Her mouth tightened, as if she'd tasted something bitter. "Vance Audain told me he'd seen a woman at OTI. Pretty, blond hair. I wondered if it was you." She clicked the gate shut. "Well, the garden, I think. We might as well enjoy the evening." She led them to the rear yard.

A table and chairs were set up under a huge mango tree. Behind the tree an oleander hedge blocked the view of the neighbor's house. The plants were in full bloom, bending under a curtain of pure-white flowers. Isabel lit a citronella candle to keep the mosquitoes away. Her dark hair snaked behind her on the breeze. In the dim light under the mango there was something almost witch-like in the way she moved.

Ben and Patrice sat down, but Isabel remained standing. "I want to know who you really are."

Ben told her their names, and where they were from—Washington D.C. and New Mexico. He could fill in the rest of the biographies later.

Isabel hesitated, unsure what to say next. Then she fumbled her purse open and dropped the second safety-deposit key on the table. She watched, wondering what they would do.

Patrice started to pick it up, but Ben warned her off with his eyes. "Does Emile know about that?" he asked.

Mary was coming out of the back door with a tray of food. Isabel let her serve them before she answered. It was an odd assortment: fancy tea biscuits, store-bought white bread with chutney, Oreo cookies, and three icy bottles of Ting, a puckery grapefruit drink made on St. Kitts.

Isabel sat down and pushed the key to the middle of the table. "I never said a thing to Emile. When my husband—" She spoke to Patrice but didn't look at her. "You remember Finney, don't you?"

"Sure," Patrice said.

Isabel said, "When Finney gave it to me, he said to keep it secret. I never told a soul, except Father Saar." She looked down at her lap. "His name wasn't Father Saar, was it?"

"No. It was Peter Kiefer," Patrice said. He seemed to deserve more than that, so she went on, "But he always used the name Saar. Said it sounded to him like a name for a jewel. He was a priest, a long time ago."

"Is he really dead?" Isabel said.

"Yes," Ben said. He didn't tell her how he knew, and Isabel didn't ask. For a moment she seemed far away. Peter Saar had lied to her, yes, but he'd been kind to her, too. She didn't know how to sort out her feelings.

She noticed Mary then, standing by the sunporch. "Why don't you go inside. I'll call if we need anything." Turning back, she caught the look on Ben's face. "Don't worry. I trust Mary with my life. It's just . . . maybe the less she knows, the better."

She passed around the plate of food. "I suppose I've always known about Emile, his business. Just refused to admit it to myself. When Finney died—him lost off a fishing boat, that's a laugher—I thought of asking Inspector Audain if Emby was involved, but I never got up the courage. Even when we were kids, Emby had a violent streak. My dad said he'd come to trouble." She gave a sigh and raised her bottle in a toast. "Here's to me finally growing up."

Patrice and Ben only touched their bottles in reply. Isabel's emotions were as raw as an open cut. There wasn't any magic salve they could apply.

Ben glanced around. Anyone driving by could see them. They should finish their business and get away from here. "Emile thinks Patrice has something of his, that Peter Saar sent her. Do you know what he's after?"

"Well, yes." Isabel was surprised that she knew something they didn't. "Emby said Peter had taken something. He showed me some blueprints, big sheets." She held her hands apart, the way someone would telling a fish story. "It was electronics of some kind. There was a part missing. He pointed to it on the chart—a block with wires and buttons. He called it a keypad."

"Did he say where the keypad came from?" Ben asked.

"Yes." She was surprised with herself again. "From Russia. The writing on the blueprints was Russian, too."

Ben looked at Patrice. She gave a shrug. Blueprints and electronics didn't tie in with anything she knew.

Isabel said, "Emile found out Peter had been to see me and wanted to know what we had talked about. I didn't tell him much, nothing specific. He was so angry he was half crazy. Hurt Mary, almost hurt me. I didn't understand a lot of what he was saying, but Peter had sent him a letter, along with the blueprints. He said he had the keypad. Peter wanted to be paid—what did he call it—a finder's fee."

With that added in, a few pieces of the puzzle fell into place for Ben, but he waited for Patrice to do the explaining. The two women were going to have to deal with each other sooner or later.

Patrice said, "My guess is, the keypad and blueprints were in the safety-deposit box. Peter figured out Emile was after them. Perfect setup for a scam. The blueprints were a come-on. Like an old hooker. Here's a quick pet for free, Emile, but if you want the rest you'll have to pay."

Ben winced. Talk of hookers was awkward here. Still, Patrice knew what she was doing. She watched Isabel, waiting for the storm to begin.

Isabel turned slowly to her. "You sent Peter here?"

"I knew about the safety-deposit box. Takes two keys to open. I had one. Peter came to get your key."

"Play me for the lonely widow," Isabel said, her voice rising. "And how did you come to have a key to Finney's safety-deposit box?" Before Patrice could speak, Isabel gave a cold laugh. "Let me tell you something, sweetie. Finney always had a problem with shiny little pennies like you. I can't count the number of times he came dragging home, three in the morning, weepy and sorry, promising never to do it again. As soon as Vance told me there was a pretty blonde sniffing around, it started to come clear. Old hookers, you said. That's the nail on the head, isn't it?"

Patrice couldn't hold her gaze any longer. She looked down at the table.

"But you're the first one to come slithering to me," Isabel said. She turned away, her eyes full of tears. "That miserable goat. The things he put me through." She wiped her cheeks harshly and glared at Patrice. "And you. *Our* keys were they? *Our* safety-deposit box? Now just why the hell would this keypad of Emile's be in there?"

"Last fall," Patrice said, "Emile had a big deal going. Finney was scared about it, really worried. He told me when I left the island that he'd put a stop to it. He must have taken the keypad and blueprints, hidden them in the deposit box."

Isabel couldn't speak for a moment. When she did, her voice cracked. "Finney . . . told you?" It wasn't just sex then. Her husband had taken his problems to Patrice, too.

Ben had never met Finney, but he was willing to make excuses for him if it would help Isabel feel better about it all. "He couldn't come to you. That would just put you in the middle between him and Emile."

Isabel was so upset, she'd almost forgotten he was there. She looked at him as tears came back to her eyes. "That's why he's dead?" She couldn't lay it out straight, couldn't say, "That's why Emile killed him."

"I think so, yes," Patrice said.

Isabel wasn't going to cry in front of them. She tilted her head up to let the tears dry. "What is it you want?"

Patrice picked an Oreo off the tray. "Let us have the key. Tell us where the deposit box is. Ben and I can take it from there." She twisted the cookie apart and licked off some of the frosting. It was a childlike gesture, immensely appealing. "You won't have to worry about it anymore."

Isabel's expression hardened. "I've heard that before— don't worry, I'll take care of everything. Peter said it when he talked me into giving *him* the key."

"I'm sorry." Patrice set down the cookie. "I learned a lot from Peter. Some things too well."

"I'd say so." Isabel stood up. "I've been played for a fool enough in this. If you've got a problem with Emile, you'll have to work it out with him." She grabbed the key and started away from the table.

Patrice jumped up, but Ben motioned for her to wait. "Isabel," he called, "why did you want to see us?"

She stopped with her hand on the sunporch door. "What do you mean?"

"You told Inspector Audain to find us, send us here. Why?"

"I was just curious—who you were, what you wanted."

He rose and crossed the yard, pulling her hand from the door. "I don't think so. You're after something, just like we are." He stroked the bruise on her wrist. "Must be important for you to stand up to your brother the way you did." He felt her trembling. He knew how confused she was, all the emotions running inside her. "Isabel, help us. Maybe we can help you."

He left her and went back to the table. A moment later she followed.

Ben said, "So you gave Peter Saar your key?"

She looked around. Only the trees would hear, but still she dropped her voice. "One day, about a month ago, Peter showed up here. Said he'd known Finney years ago, in Miami, and had heard he was dead. Wanted to pay his respects. Of course I believed him. Why would a priest lie to me? We went for a drive, ended up at the bar out at the Lemon Inn. I still can't figure out how we started talking about it." She set the key back on the table. "Peter was a slick one. The key didn't mean much to me anyway. Finney had given it to me, but I didn't have any idea what to do with it."

"You didn't know where the safety-deposit box was?" Ben said.

"No," Isabel said. "Last fall, Finney gave me a big envelope of things. Old snapshots and letters, things like that. He told me to keep it hidden—especially from Emile. The key was in that envelope, wrapped in a note that said 'safety-deposit box,' but no other explanation.

"I told Peter about it, and he thought we should go through the envelope. Maybe there was a clue to where the deposit box was. I figured that was bunk, but what did I have to lose? So we came back here, and Peter took the envelope out in the garden. I was inside making dinner. About an hour later, I heard him laugh. He came running in, said he'd found something." She smiled and shook her head, remembering. "I was so damn excited. We both were. But he wouldn't tell me what he'd found. Wanted it to be a surprise. How could I argue? With a priest? He took my key and said he'd be back as soon as he could. That's the last I saw of him."

"But here it is," Ben said, pointing at the key on the table.

"He turned up two days later, when I wasn't around. He gave the key to Mary."

Ben noticed her eyes. She was staring at him, too hard. Trying to slip something past. "What else did he give Mary? Money maybe?"

Isabel blushed. Even in the dusky light he could see it. "Yes. Thirty thousand dollars. Said that was what he found in the safety-deposit box. How did you know?"

He smiled. "It doesn't matter." It had been an easy bet. Saar had split the money down the middle, thirty thousand each for Patrice and Isabel. A true gentleman. But then he'd tried to get his score from Emile. The finder's fee for the Russian keypad.

"Can we see the envelope?" Ben said. She didn't answer, so he pushed the safety-deposit key back in front of her. "We can go through it together, decide what to do."

Isabel took her time thinking it over before she rose and went inside.

Ben and Patrice sat in silence. Up in the mango tree, a pair of mourning doves landed, cooing their melancholy love song. Patrice's face was as sad as their calls. "There wasn't any easy way to tell her," he said.

"No, there wasn't," Patrice sighed. After a moment, she put on a smile.

Isabel was returning. She'd wrapped a shawl around her shoulders, a long train of black silk. There was a purposefulness to her walk that hadn't been there before. She handed the envelope to Ben. "Good luck, but I couldn't find anything in there." She then turned her chair toward Patrice. "So, tell me about you and Finney."

Patrice was caught off guard, but only for a fraction of a second. She stretched, lithe as a cat. It might have been an affront to Isabel, a much larger woman and less elegant, but Patrice finished with a giggle. "Every time I think of him I remember that pet monkey he had, CC. I went in Emile's office once. There was music playing, loud—*thump-thump-thump*. Finney was there with CC. Dancing."

Isabel's mouth made an O.

Patrice went on, " 'Damn beastie,' he said. That Irish accent of his, right? 'No sense of rhythm. Imagine how hard it is t' teach a monkey t' disco.' "

Isabel couldn't contain her smile. "He wanted to put on shows, at the schools and such. Was going to call it 'Monkey Shines.' "

A bit of the tension between them drained away. Patrice started with another story. As she did, she gave Ben a quick nod. They'd be all right.

Twilight was fading. It was too dark at the table to work, so Ben took the envelope and his chair over by the sunporch where light was streaming in from the windows. Isabel didn't mind. She just waved backhanded at him as he stood up.

He emptied the envelope onto his lap—pictures, old receipts and tickets, cheap paper menus, oddball certificates. Isabel hadn't spotted anything out of the ordinary. On the other hand, Peter Saar, in only an hour's time, had found a tip that led him straight to the safety-deposit box.

Something Saar would notice and Isabel wouldn't. . . . Ben began picking his way through.

The women continued to talk. Once they laughed to-gether, but mostly their voices were hushed. There was an array of candles on the table, and Isabel lit them from the one already burning.

After the first pass, Ben was sure there were no marks or handwritten clues. It was something in the photographs themselves, or the paper records. He stacked up the photos and started through again.

He'd almost reached the bottom of the pile when some-thing made him stop. Holding the picture up, he yelped—it was such a surprise—then laughed.

Scowling, the two women turned. Patrice had been de-scribing how brave Finney was when she saw him last, at the Basseterre airport. Definitely not the time for joking.

Ben scooped everything back in the envelope except the one photograph, which he brought over to the table. "Look."

The women bent over it, then had to rearrange them-selves to let in more candlelight. It was a picture of Isabel, standing across a busy street from the camera. From the buildings, it was obviously a Caribbean setting. She was wearing a straw hat and sunglasses, waving at the camera.

Patrice looked up at Ben, shaking her head.

He smiled. "You don't see it, but a man would. Finney, Saar, me." He tapped a spot in the background of the pic-ture, behind Isabel's shoulder. A woman in a short skirt was disappearing down a side street. There was just a bit of her face visible, not enough to identify her. Her legs were in plain view, though. Patrice's legs. "That's you."

Patrice squinted at it, and her face took on a startled look. "Yes, maybe you're right. That's St. John's, I think. Antigua."

"I remember," Isabel said. "Finney and I went over there two weeks before he died. Supposed to be a weekend hol-iday. We took the LIAT flight instead of one of Emby's planes. We'd only been there a couple of hours when he made a call and said there was business trouble. He had to go to New York. Sent me back here on the next flight." She looked at Patrice. "But when he got home, he had a sunburn on top of his head, his bald spot. I wondered, how did he get that in New York in November?"

Patrice's eyes shifted away. "He didn't go to New York. He and I stayed in Antigua that night and the next day."

"That bloody slyboots, and you with him!" Isabel snorted.

Ben put his hand between them, calling a truce. "How did you end up here, in the picture?" he asked Patrice.

"Finney told me to meet him there at eleven o'clock that morning. He didn't show up, but we had another meeting place set for later."

"So Finney staged this to get a picture of the two of you together," Ben said. "But there's no bank—"

"There is!" Isabel said. She drew her fingernail down the edge of the photo. "This building, just showing. Anybody from Antigua would know it. Hot pink stucco, big as a ship. That's the St. John's branch, Royal Bank of Scotland."

Patrice reached for her arm. "You're sure?"

Isabel gave her a frigid stare, making her draw back. "Absolutely. That must be the bank."

Three sets of eyes went to the key. Isabel was first to reach for it. "Finney's dead. Peter's dead. Whatever's in that deposit box has to be worth a lot, and you want to just waltz in there and take it."

"No," Ben said. It was time to let her know the rest of it. "Emile has Patrice's daughter up at Canada House. He's threatened to hurt her if we don't bring him what he wants."

"Daughter . . . Cherry?" Isabel said. "I remember her from last fall. We played Parcheesi." She stared into the candle flame while sadness came over her face. "So much I didn't know." She touched the photo, the pink sliver on the edge, then rapped it on the table. "We'll all go."

"Isabel, no—" Patrice began.

Isabel said, "I've got a stake in whatever's in that safety-deposit box. Besides, Emile's more than a brother. I practically raised him after our mother died. Whatever he's doing, I can't ignore it anymore."

Ben could certainly understand feeling responsible. And Isabel might be a good ally, despite her flighty exterior. She'd proven how much backbone she had dealing with Emile's men at the Jumbi Cafe.

Before he could speak his mind, something caught his attention. The after-work traffic had cleared out, leaving only a trickle of cars on Cayon Street. Now coming from that direction was the throaty snarl of a high-performance engine running at good speed. Maybe more than one engine. Patrice and Isabel had noticed it too.

Lights flashed in the top of the mango tree. A car was turning up the hill, then another, and a third. From inside Mary had heard them, and she came flying out the back door. "Is'bel. Your brother. These two gotta get outta here."

It was already too late to run. The first car was pulling up in front. Ben dropped the Antigua photo in the envelope and grabbed Patrice's arm. He pushed her through the hedge and dove after her, ending up on his stomach in the grassy space beyond. He could see back through the gaps between the oleander trunks.

Isabel and Mary stood in the center of the yard, backlit by the candles. A small man carrying a machine pistol stepped around the corner of the house. He circled to the right, keeping them in sight.

Emile strode into view. His expression was stony, but that soon changed to a smile. He marched to the table and picked up one of the three bottles of Ting. With his palm he tested how cold it was. "So, Iz, havin' a séance were ya?"

TWENTY-NINE

Emile banged the Ting bottle down on the table. "You had lunch with Ben Tennant at the Jumbi today. I saw pictures. Now three bottles here, nice and cozy. Where are they, Iz?"

In the neighbor's yard, Ben and Patrice stretched out in the grass, trying to be invisible.

Isabel hadn't moved since Emile appeared. All through the house, lights were being snapped on. "Get your men out of there," she said in a low voice.

"Can't do that, Iz. It's business."

The man with the machine pistol was circling the garden perimeter. Ben snaked away from the hedge, half on top of Patrice. It was tarry black where they lay. The gunman slipped past, so close they could hear the squeaking of his shoes.

Four large men trooped out of Isabel's house, hulking figures in the faint light. "Nob'dy in dere, sir," one of them reported.

Balazs strutted around in front of Isabel. "All right, now you understand a few things. I'll—"

"*Understand?*" Isabel cut in. Her voice was pitched up, furious.

That's it, Ben thought. *Go after him.*

"I'll tell you what I understand." Isabel took a step forward. She was every bit as tall as Emile. "You murdered Finney, you worthless little shit." With the word "little" she seemed to swell up over him.

Emile's confidence faltered. He looked furtive, as if he were about to invent a quick lie to smooth everything over.

Isabel didn't give him a chance. "I'll have nothing to do with you now, Emby. *Nothing.*"

She turned away, and her advantage played out.

"Oh? Who's going to pay for you then, Iz? Some horny Jack off the ships?" He laughed roughly. "You gonna take two-a-days when you need your roof fixed or your garden weeded?"

"Just go!"

"No, I—" Emile broke off as the lights blazed on in the neighbor's house. The man with the machine pistol pushed through the oleanders to investigate. Ben shifted up, ready to lunge at him. Ten feet, maybe more—too far, but he could try.

A woman's face appeared in one of the windows of the house. She'd heard voices, a commotion. She wanted to know what was the matter. Then she saw the man, and, an instant later, his gun. She tumbled out of sight as quickly as if she'd been punched. Even before the man started to turn away, the lights clicked off, and the yard was again plunged into darkness.

Ben eased back, his muscles quivering. Patrice had risen to her knees beside him, in the line of fire if the gunman swung around. He crashed back through the hedge, and Ben pulled her down beside him.

Emile had used the interruption to unbuckle his belt. He slipped it off. The men by the house started to grin. "Something I've always thought," he said. "You find the right spot, the worst nightmare spot—" He looped the belt around

Mary's throat. "You can control anybody. So what are you afraid of, Iz? Being alone maybe? Really alone."

In his mind, Ben pleaded with her. *Go after him again. Tell him he's a coward.*

But the best Isabel could do was hold still. She didn't dare speak.

Emile tightened the belt. At the first pinch, Mary struggled, but that only made the choking worse. He tightened another inch, and she gave a cry.

He said, "Isabel, I need Tennant and Callan. They've got something that's mine, and there are people I have to answer to. They've set deadlines now." He twisted the belt until the leather creaked. Mary gagged.

Emile said, "Where did they go?"

Ben was straining forward, watching every small thing. If Isabel so much as glanced toward the hedge, he and Patrice were finished. Isabel seemed in a trance.

Mary's nostril's flared; her chest heaved. It was obvious no air was getting in. Emile gave the belt another twist. Then something happened to Isabel. Her head snapped up and she leaned toward him. *"You pathetic fool!"* she screeched.

The men by the house stirred. Their grins were gone. This wasn't normal, someone yelling at Emile.

Isabel leaned closer. "You and your damn messes. Since we were kids, I've been cleaning up after you. Remember London, Emby?" She said his name with a trill, as if she were talking to a baby. "Thirteen years old, you were. Go out in the back alley and climb the fire escapes, watch the neighborhood women take baths."

"Isabel, shut up," Emile said irritably.

She rolled right on. "So one of them caught you. And who took care of it? Not you. Not Dad. *I* was the one who scrubbed that cow's dishes and cleaned her bloody toilets for a year so she wouldn't tell the cops. You and your damn messes."

Emile rattled the belt. "Tennant, Callan—where are they?"

"We've got to go out there," Patrice whispered. "He'll kill her."

"Wait," Ben said. When Emile shook the belt, it loosened. Mary could breathe again. Emile was too focused on Isabel to notice.

Isabel was dead calm. Ben knew she could stand up for herself, but this was far beyond what he'd expected. The wind came up, lifting her hair like a flag. She raised her hand, playing to the men in the shadows. "You want to know what we called Emby after that? Me and Dad?"

She left the question hanging in the air like a threat, and turned on Emile. "I *won't* dirty my hands with your foul troubles again. If you want something from those two who were here, *you* find them. Not me."

She reached and yanked the belt right out of his hand. Mary slumped to the ground, gasping. Isabel pointed a long finger straight into Emile's face. She was a witch, her hair writhing behind her, the light from the guttering candles throwing shadows across her face. "Go away from here. Don't ever come back."

For a moment, Emile seemed turned to stone by her words. He was still the little brother. Then he tried to laugh. It was a bad attempt, like a bark from a nervous dog. He bent and retrieved his belt. "Okay, my mess to clean up. But know this. You've got no more capital with me. None. And if you see your two friends again, tell them things are dead serious now. Got a schedule to keep. If they don't deliver my property by Friday noon, Patrice won't see her little prize again, ever. Got that?" She nodded her head a fraction of an inch. "Good."

Slapping the belt against his thigh, he stalked off. His men followed, well behind.

When they were out of sight, Isabel dropped to her knees to help Mary. The cars started and gunned away up the street. Ben checked to make sure they all were gone, and then he and Patrice came back into the yard. By then Mary was sitting up, rubbing her neck. "Hey Is'bel, get off'a me. I can't breathe, you huggin' like that."

Isabel backed away, but she kept touching her, patting and stroking her hair. They were all stunned, moving at half speed. Ben broke the spell. "We've got to get away from here. If he changes his mind and comes back, you'll be in worse trouble than ever."

Helping Mary up, he said, "There's a boat and a pilot waiting for us at Dieppe. Can we get to Antigua that way?"

Mary nodded. "Sure. Good boat run you over there in five, six hours easy."

"Is there a place you can go?" Ben asked. "Somewhere safe?"

"Nicola Town," Mary answered, "on the way to Dieppe. Got some friends there. I be all right. Is'bel, you can come with me. Your brother won't—"

"No!" Then Isabel shrugged and apologized. "No, Mary. I'm going with them to Antigua."

Ben and Patrice looked at each other. They'd had this argument once already. No use going through it again. He said, "Isabel, you'll need your passport and some extra clothes."

"We always got a bag ready," Mary reported. "Never know when we might get a shoppin' trip somewhere." She grinned. The belt had left a bright welt on her neck, but she was still alive. She was drunk from the experience.

Five minutes later they were in Isabel's car, rolling through the sleepy streets of Basseterre, on their way to the hotel so Ben and Patrice could pick up their things. Mary, in the front seat with Isabel, broke the silence. "What was that name?" She was still feeling light-headed and chuckled as she spoke.

"Name?" Isabel said. Her mind had been far away.

"Your brother's. The one you and your dad called him."

Isabel squirmed uneasily. "Dad did it mostly. Li'l Wee Wanker. Emile would get up on these fire escapes and find some woman in the bathroom, and then he'd take his pants down. Right there outside her window, he'd . . . you know."

Mary laughed. "That's some picture. I' think that boy grew up to what he is now."

What she said sobered them all. Isabel made a turn off Cayon Street. She looked up in the mirror. Her gaze was steady and calm. Standing up to Emile had settled some things for her. No more hiding. "Patrice, what you said before—I can see Finney wanting a fling with you, but that wouldn't be why he'd give you money. He wasn't that much of a fool. Why did he do it, really?"

Ben knew that sooner or later they'd get to the truth, and he knew how desperately Patrice wanted to keep it secret. She'd changed so much, let her strengths come out, learned to deal with her fears. Twice already today she'd put herself between him and a gun. But her past was always there, pulling her back.

They drove a block before she answered. "I wish he was still around so I could say I was sorry. I was trapped. There wasn't anybody else I could turn to, but it wasn't right." She tilted her head back on the seat, her eyes on the ceiling. "I told Finney he was Cherry's father."

"What?" Isabel stared in the mirror and rolled right past a stop sign. "Finney and you . . . that long ago?"

Patrice didn't look down, but she nodded.

Ben was too surprised to speak. They all were. Then Isabel turned halfway around in her seat. "You told Finney that. Is it true?"

Patrice started crying. "No. Emile . . . Emile is Cherry's father."

Several seconds passed, and Mary murmured, "Ain't that somethin'."

Through her tears, Patrice was looking at Ben. She was

worried about what he would think. He gave her hair a gentle stroke. For some reason, the touch made her shiver. She closed her eyes and nestled her face against his hand.

Isabel had slowed the car to a crawl. Ahead a teenage boy and girl were crossing the street. Their arms were looped around each other's waists. They seemed so natural and carefree. Isabel touched the gas. "I know Emby. He won't hurt her. Not his own daughter."

Ben was watching Patrice. He knew what she was thinking: their hotel in Miami, the bathroom counter and all that blood. It was a terrible image, and his mind clicked away, turning a new corner as the car did. They had a deadline now, Friday noon. He glanced at his wristwatch. Patrice was doing the same thing.

Forty hours.

THIRTY

At 7:30 A.M. it was already sweltering in Miami. A blanket of mist, tinged orange by the rising sun, hung over Hialeah Park racetrack. Emile sat in the grandstand, nervously cracking his knuckles. Mick Laraby was on the other end of the bench, putting some space between them because he didn't like the mood Emile was in.

This early the place was pretty much empty except for trainers and jocks and a few owners who came to watch the workouts. There was one spectator, a man leading a small dog through the grandstand. Balazs waited for him to pass, then said to Mick. "Can you believe that bastard Herrera? Dismissing us like a couple of snot-nosed kids."

"Yeah, he's a pisser. He was sure happy t' see Roque though."

It almost hadn't worked out that way. Colonel Roque was supposed to take a Cubana Airlines flight yesterday from Havana to Santo Domingo to meet Mick. It was cancelled at the last minute because of equipment problems. Thinking fast, he caught the only other flight out, to Mexico City.

Mick picked him up there, and they made Miami just in time to get to Hialeah for the meeting with the Herreras.

Balazs looked down the grandstand. With all the fog, he could barely make them out, sitting on the terrace in front of the Turf Club—Morena and Manuel, Colonel Roque, and another man Emile didn't know. A dozen of Manuel's security people were fanned out around them. "That new guy at the table, what's his deal here?" Balazs said.

Mick didn't know any more than Balazs. "Odd duck, isn't he?" he replied.

The man was in his mid-thirties and fat as a butterball. His head was too small for his body, making him look like a dullard. But his eyes were sharp and curious, emerald-colored points behind wire spectacles.

"Hold on," Balazs said. "Fat boy's got something." He was rolling out a large sheet of paper in front of Colonel Roque. "Our blueprints, dammit. I knew I shouldn't have let Herrera take a copy of those."

Behind them the dog yapped, and Laraby glanced around. Balazs didn't take his eyes off Herrera and the others. "What's going on over there, Mickey?"

Mick stretched out. Might as well get comfortable. "Dunno, Boss. Find out soon enough, I reckon."

Manuel Herrera chuckled as he threw the last of his breakfast toast to the pigeons. Things felt *right* for a change. He liked Colonel Roque the moment he set his eyes on him. He was proud and self-possessed, a Cuban from the old school. He'd flown all night to get there, yet, except for a stubble of beard, he didn't show it at all. His black hair was combed back to reveal a high, intelligent forehead. He didn't smile much, but he answered every question quickly and completely. The colonel was at ease, trusting his life to strangers. His calm was almost saintly.

Manuel's expression darkened when he looked at the

other man, the big one. Eric Selano was Manuel's godson. His father had been manager of the largest division of Herrera Construction, until he died five years ago. Since he was a boy, Eric had been the same—fat, worried, anxious to please. Once he started talking, he couldn't stop. That's what he was doing now, yammering to Morena and Colonel Roque.

"My postdoc work was when it got interesting. My professor at Columbia pulled some strings so I could go to Russia, the old archives. It was creepy, y'know? All those KGB-types around. But with glasnost and everything, I was, like, cool. And the Russians had no idea what was in their own files. *No idea!* They figure, here's this American history-of-science dude—what's he gonna find? Original plans for *Sputnik*? So I learned a lot. Nothing specific, basic Soviet nuclear protocol, chain of command, things like that. But it was enough to get me my job at Los Alamos. Say, Luis, you gonna eat that cruller?"

The colonel's English was stiff but functional. "I am not." Eric pulled the plate over and downed the pastry in two bites.

Tapping the plans, Manuel said, "Let's talk about our project, okay?"

Eric nodded, licking his fingers. "Background first. Long version or short, Mr. Herrera?"

Manuel didn't answer, knowing this would bring the long version. He wanted everything laid out for Roque. The colonel might know something they didn't, correct some misunderstanding.

"Okay, start with the summer of 1962," Eric said. "Trouble brewing in the Kremlin. Khrushchev decides to send nukes secretly to Cuba, Operation Anadyr. Only he didn't count on the U-2 flights and other intelligence assets the CIA had."

Eric's face had taken on a glow. He loved to talk about this stuff.

"By mid-October of '62, the CIA had clear photos of the Soviet missile sites in Cuba. John Kennedy gave his speech from the White House, showing Khrushchev the grim face, scaring the hell out of most Americans. He ordered the U.S. naval quarantine of the island.

"At the time, everybody focused on the big Russian missiles, SS-4s, capable of knocking off Washington or Atlanta or New Orleans with a single blow. There was a subtext few people knew about until years later. The same ships that brought in the SS-4s carried other weapons: tactical battlefield missiles with nuclear tips, and a flight of light bombers with six nuclear bombs.

Colonel Roque shook his head. "Eight bombs for the Il-28 bombers."

"Nope." Eric was picking pastry from his teeth with his fingernail. "I've seen the manifests. The *Indigirka* carried six bombs."

"The ship, yes, only six," Roque said. "But two other bombs have been sent by cargo plane. Came late, October thirtieth, after Khrushchev announced the big missiles would be pulled out. These two bombs, a gift you would say. Nikita to Fidel."

Eric's eyes sparkled. This was fascinating. "Or a way of appeasing Castro. Get him to cool the rhetoric, be a good comrade while the Russians tucked their tails and ran."

Colonel Roque made a waffling motion with his hand. Maybe so, maybe not.

Eric smoothed the blueprints out on the table. His touch was gentle. He was an historian; old documents like this were his lifeblood. "That's what these are, wiring diagrams for those bombs. Explosive force of twelve kilotons, the same size as Hiroshima, and just as dirty. When did the two extras go back to Russia?"

The Herreras and Colonel Roque glanced at one another. "They were never sent back, Eric," Morena answered.

"The Politburo wouldn't have approved—" Eric blinked.

His eyes made bright flashes, like Morse code. "You said Khrushchev ordered them to Cuba personally?"

Roque replied, "Few people in Russia knew. Khrushchev made the decision, or a military aide. The directives were vague."

Eric bolted forward in his seat. "You've seen these bombs? Actually *seen* them?"

"I have flown with them," the colonel said.

"They're operational?" Eric blinked again, and answered himself. "After so long, they can't be."

Roque took a sip of orange juice. "In the early times, there was a Russian technician who serviced the bombs. He was recalled after Gorbachev and the, ah, change of climate in Moscow. Now it is a Cuban technician. Three years ago one of the weapons became, how would you say, unsafe—"

"Unstable," Eric tried.

"Yes. We flew out and dropped it into the Atlantic." He smiled. "Perhaps there are fish somewhere that have grown legs and feet and glow in the dark."

Eric didn't seem to get the joke. He was too excited. A new angle on the Cuban Missile Crisis; one with teeth. This could mean a major research grant, a faculty appointment somewhere. "The other one, where is it? What kind of shape?"

"Excellent shape," Roque said. "Every year, we take it for a training run. But I think—" He looked at Manuel. "You have not explained the problem?"

Herrera nodded for the colonel to go ahead. He wanted to study Eric's reaction.

"Khrushchev wasn't as generous as he seemed. The bombs had electronic triggers. You call them—"

"PALs. Permissive action links," Eric butted in. "Fail-safe devices so only the political authorities can initiate a nuclear strike, not military commanders in the field. The old ones looked like simple keypads, but the circuitry was top-end, very sophisticated."

"Correct," said the colonel. "The triggering keypad on the remaining bomb does not work. A fake. We did not know until the Russian technician left and the Cuban man took over."

Eric nodded eagerly. "Khrushchev wouldn't put a working nuke in Castro's hands. That could be suicide for the whole human race. This way, if Castro tried to use it—" He put on a phony Spanish accent. "So sorry *Líder Máximo*, no boom-boom." He grinned while the others stared flatly at him. "After they found out the keypad was a fake, did they try to build a replacement?"

Manuel and Morena glanced at each other. This was why they'd brought Eric here, to talk about the possibility of engineering around the false triggering mechanism.

Roque said, "We do not have the wiring diagrams, so there would have been much guessing. Still, Raúl, Fidel's brother, our Defense Minister, wanted us to build our own keypad. After the first bomb became unstable, Fidel decided no. He was afraid the bombs were booby-trapped. He is complicated, our *Comandante*, superstitious. He told of a dream he had. Someone worked on the bomb. Holguín, where it is kept, ended up a stinking hole in the ground. So he ordered us to leave it alone. The technician makes sure the circuits are in order and there are no radiation leaks. But it might be a museum piece for all the good it could do."

Morena spoke next. "Could the bomb be made operational?" She dipped her head, swishing her auburn hair about her shoulders. "What would it take, Eric?"

Eric enjoyed being the center of attention. He frowned to show he was thinking. "They could try to get the real PAL—the original keypad—from Russia, but that would take some doing. I'm not sure anybody there would know where it is, their security is so lame. Or it's possible something could be put together on site, there in Cuba. These plans give a full schematic to start with."

A fly had landed on Morena's breakfast plate. She watched it scurry around, collecting bits of sugar. "You have a master's degree in electrical engineering, don't you Eric? From before your history work. Could you build a replacement trigger?"

He broke out laughing. "Piece of cake. Whip it up in a weekend." He noticed they weren't laughing with him. "You're kidding, right?"

Manuel stirred. "Hypothetically, Eric. Could someone like you do this?"

Eric's eyes darted from face to face. "Why?"

Manuel shrugged irritably, indicating he shouldn't have to explain such a simple thing. "Show the world that bastard Castro's been hiding a nuclear bomb. Do that and he's not just a cute buffoon in Halloween fatigues anymore. He's dangerous. The government in America keeps the embargo on. Maybe countries like Canada and Spain decide he's not such a good business partner. It's politics, Eric."

Eric was a quick thinker once he was on the right track. "If you're going to use the bomb to embarrass Castro, you'll have to get it out of Cuba."

Morena said, "That's for Colonel Roque to take care of." The officer nodded. "He's squadron commander at Holguín and can get the bomb on a plane and out. To Florida or Guantánamo. Other Cuban pilots have escaped that way. But it will only work if the bomb is operational. Otherwise, Castro can say it was just a relic from the missile crisis." She leaned close enough so he could smell the tiny dab of perfume she'd put on the base of her throat that morning. "Could it be done, Eric? A new keypad?"

It seemed terribly hot all of a sudden. He tugged at the belly of his shirt, slick with perspiration. "It's possible." He bent over the wiring diagram. "I think. . . . Here's . . . oh, yeah. I guess so. It could be done." He looked around the table again. "But understand, if that thing is booby-trapped, Holguín *could* end up a stinking hole in the ground when they try to rig it up."

"A risk, we know," Manuel said. "How long to do the work?"

Eric studied the diagram once more, his lips pursed. Manuel remembered that expression. Eric had come to the office with his father for a few weeks the summer he was seven. He fixed the· broken air conditioner, using only a plastic knife from the coffee room and wire he scrounged from the trash. It was easy to underestimate him because he was so absurd looking, but he had an extraordinary mind, and stubbornness to go with it.

Eric mumbled, "Have to check the power system and the connection architecture. Then there'd be materials to worry about. Have to come up with a coding device, too. But . . . my guess, it could be done in two weeks."

Manuel was disappointed. A cloud came over his face. But he said, "Very good, Eric. If your father was alive, he'd be proud of how much you've learned." Eric blushed while Manuel stared at him. "Yes, this is all very interesting." He motioned to one of the guards. "Arturo, Eric is ready to leave. Take him on a tour, the way we talked about, yes?"

Arturo approached the table. He had a blunt, muscular body, and he carried a gun, a thick bulge in a shoulder holster. He put his hand on Eric's chair. "Mr. Herrera, thanks, but I'll have to pass on the tour," Eric said. "My plane leaves in an hour. I've got to be at work tomorrow."

Manuel looked steadily at him. "No, Eric. I need you. Arturo will drive you to my house in the Keys. A little vacation."

Eric didn't have to be a genius to see where this was leading. His voice rose, edged with fear. "Please, Mr. Herrera. What we talked about—building a new keypad. That's out of my league. And I can't go to Cuba. I don't even speak Spanish. You know that."

Manuel said, "You'll do very well, Eric, whatever happens."

Arturo pulled him to his feet and toward the Turf Club door. Eric made one last plea. "Morena, tell him—" She turned away, hiding behind her shimmery curtain of hair.

When they were gone, Manuel said, "Could you get him to the bomb? Give him time to work?"

Colonel Roque considered it. "Perhaps. It used to be guarded around the clock, but not now. Still, he's the kind of man who would be noticed."

Morena tapped the blueprints. "We could let the colonel take these. He could find someone in Cuba to do the work, someone who'd stand out less."

Manuel didn't like that idea. He rolled up the plans. "We'll keep it in the family, with Eric, if it comes to that. Maybe it won't. We may still convince Mr. Balazs to find the original keypad."

Manuel stood and took up his cane. To Morena he said, "Bring me Emile and his friend." She nodded and left the table. Then Manuel touched Roque's shoulder. "I need to stretch my legs. Walk with me, yes?" They ambled to the corner of the terrace, by the rail that bounded the track.

The sun was well up, a featureless tangerine floating in the watery sky. A big roan horse cantered by. The jockey, dressed in gray, was all but lost in the mist. "That one's mine," Manuel said. "A four-year-old. Past Master." He called to the jock, "*¡Hola, Hector!*"

"*¡Hola, señor!*" came the disembodied reply.

"It is the same for them all, no?" the colonel said. "You name your horses for the past." He glanced at Manuel's hip. "You were shot down at Playa Girón?"

Manuel smiled. So the colonel had checked him out. That was good, two sides of the same coin. In Cuba, Manuel still had many friends. He'd had one of them investigate Luis Roque. He came from a good family, three generations of military men. His record was spotless, until two years ago. Roque's daughter had died. A few months later his wife took her own life with Roque's service pistol. At her funeral, Roque got into a brawl with several other officers. He almost killed one of them. The Cuban Air Force didn't have enough qualified people as it was. They couldn't stand to lose one of their best. The fight at the funeral was hushed up, but a crack had been exposed. Someone decided to exploit it. American military intelligence? The CIA? It didn't matter to Manuel—how Colonel Roque found his way to Emile Balazs, or how Balazs found his way to the doorstep of Herrera Construction. Manuel cared only about results, and the tools needed to achieve them: the bomb, the keypad, the plane, the pilot.

Balazs had arranged for Manuel and the colonel to speak several times by radio phone. They were cryptic conversations, half in code, for they could never be completely sure someone wasn't listening in. Those talks told Manuel little about Luis Roque, the man. For that they needed to meet face to face.

"Do you have a picture of your daughter, Colonel?"

It was a prying question, but Roque was unfazed. From his pocket he took out a cheap plastic wallet, and from the wallet a photo. "It was a year before she died, only a school picture." He made it sound like an apology.

Manuel had to hold it away because he didn't have his reading glasses. The girl had a stoic, level gaze, something sad in one so young. Her hair was tied severely back in a ponytail. "She was pretty," Herrera lied.

Colonel Roque mumbled a thank-you. "It was an appendectomy. Simple, we thought. The operation was fine, but later she developed an infection. There were no antibiotics. None. Try the black market, the doctors said, but we had no money. In thirty-six hours she was dead."

261

Manuel took a last look at the photo and passed it back. The colonel stuffed it away, then turned to face him. "Cuba is dying, bit by bit. We wait, but Castro stays, the embargo stays. Something must break the deadlock. So I offer you the bomb, and I offer myself."

Herrera might have hugged him, a manly *abrazo*, but instead he was gentle, touching the colonel's arm, looking him in the eye. "It is a good thing."

They settled against the railing, watching another horse pass, this one at full gallop. The fog was thinning and they could see the grimace of concentration on the jockey's face. "When we last spoke, you asked about the target," Herrera said. He pulled a photograph from his own pocket. "This was taken last week by our contact in the U.S. Navy." The picture was an aerial shot. It was poorly focused, and the field of view was curved at the edges, but Roque could make out the main features. There was a wide swath of a bay leading out to deep blue ocean waters. Low buildings and an airfield flanked the edges of the bay. Anchored in the center was an aircraft carrier. Three more large ships floated further out to sea.

Manuel's eyes took on a hard glint. "Is the bomb big enough?"

"Yes, yes." The colonel said eagerly. "The entire battle group will be destroyed, and more, everything within miles. But only if I can get to them. My plane will not have much range."

Manuel didn't like negative thinking. "The ships will be where we've planned," he said coldly. Then he relented, chuckling. "Like your *Comandante*, I am superstitious. There are signs we will be successful. Friday is the seventeenth, an anniversary for me—the Bay of Pigs. And then, the target." He tapped the photo. "A Kennedy to kill. What could be more fitting?"

Colonel Roque was staring out over the track and had lost the train of the conversation. A breeze had separated the fog, leaving a band of crystal clear air between layers of gray. From the pond in the infield a hundred flamingos took flight. For a moment their pink-and-black wings flashed in brilliant sunshine. Like a vast conga line they wove upward, fading into the mist.

The colonel made no comment, simply enjoying the sight. Herrera placed his hand on top of Roque's. "Angels, my friend, like your daughter, your wife." He tightened his grip. "Like you."

They turned as the last bird disappeared. Morena was coming back onto the terrace, leading Balazs and Laraby. Manuel felt buoyant. Everything had gone so well.

"Emile, come, I have news." He put his arm around Balazs' shoulder. "Eric, my godson, was here earlier. I didn't introduce you. Maybe I should have." He smiled. "Eric believes he can build a new keypad for the bomb. If he does, that makes you irrelevant."

Emile's shock registered only a moment before his face went stiff with anger. He wasn't going to ask for an explanation. He didn't want to give Manuel the satisfaction. He shoved the old man's arm away. "I'll get you your keypad, and I'll enjoy wiping that fucking grin off your face with it."

Manuel kept smiling. "If the target moves, Emile, you're through. I'll finish it without you."

"Our deal still stands. Don't cross me, Manuel. That wouldn't be healthy." Balazs spun on his heel and strode back through the Turf Club door.

"Come on, Emile," Manuel called. "*No te preocupes.* No worries, huh?" His laughter echoed across the track, sending another flight of flamingos spiraling toward the heavens.

THIRTY-ONE

The priest's words murmured off the dark walls of the Cathedral of St. John the Divine. The church, the largest in Antigua, was a cool, gloomy place. Ben and Patrice sat in the back pew. The service here was Anglican. Isabel, despite being Catholic, had joined the handful of congregants in front of the altar.

They'd come to the cathedral to wait for the Royal Bank of Scotland to open at nine o'clock. The trip from St. Kitts had come off without a hitch. They hadn't had to "assakeeds" where to find Alex, the boat pilot. The moon was up, and they'd spotted him anchored in a cove down the coast from Dieppe. They signalled him to the beach, then filled him in on what they had planned. He seemed happy to be on the move, but he was worried about the coast guard. The RSS he called it, Regional Security System. They ran boat and airplane patrols, looking for smugglers. With the moon, there was a real risk of being spotted. On the plus side, though, the sea was mirror smooth. They made the crossing with the throttle wide open, taking under three hours, never sighting another craft. Ben and Patrice and Isabel even got some sleep in the tiny cabin in the bow of the boat.

Alex dropped them at Fort Bay, an hour's walk from St. John's. They reached town at sunup, and Isabel suggested they go to the cathedral. A caretaker was unlocking the place when they arrived, and he ushered them straight to the donations box. Isabel dropped in a U.S. twenty, the last money in her wallet. Then she went to one of the chapel areas by the high altar and lit two candles—one for Roddy Finney, one for Peter Saar. She was praying over them when people started arriving for the morning service.

The service was over now, and she was coming up the aisle with a balding man in pants buckled high over his belly. "I certainly will," she said to him. He moved off to speak to others on their way out. "That's Reverend Foyle," she whispered. "Wants me to contribute to the children's camp fund." She sounded distracted. Since they left St. Kitts, she'd been lost to the world, thinking about Finney and Patrice and Emile; how she'd turned a blind eye to everything. On top of all that, she had herself to worry about. For the first time in her life, she was on her own.

She checked her watch and pulled her shawl up around her shoulders. "That bank should be open."

Ben led the way downhill toward the harbor. St. John's was more cosmopolitan than Basseterre. The shops were more varied, the sidewalks crowded with people of every hue. In one block, they heard English spoken in accents from Central America, East India, the Caribbean, and Asia.

Ben suggested they take a minute to get their stories straight, what to say if anyone at the bank got curious about them. Patrice and Isabel still weren't comfortable talking to each other. They stared blankly at him. Ben sighed. "Attract as little attention as possible. Get in, get whatever's in the deposit box, and get out again." The two women nodded. That was the plan.

But that wasn't the way it turned out.

The Royal Bank of Scotland was even pinker than it looked in the photo. It was neatly maintained, taking up most of a block in the heart of town. People milled around outside, some heading for work, some chatting with friends. Patrice had to jostle a large woman out of the way just to get through the door.

At the counter in the lobby, ten tellers were at work handling the early crush of customers. Ben asked a security guard where they should go for safety-deposit boxes, and the man pointed across the way to a sign for "Special Transactions." The clerk there wore a trim gray uniform with an RBS emblem on the lapel. She smiled brightly. "One of the vice presidents handles the safety-deposits. I'll get him." She was gone nearly five minutes. When she reappeared, Ben could tell by her expression something was wrong. "Sorry, you'll have to wait. He's not come in yet."

"When is he supposed to get here?" Patrice demanded.

The clerk lowered her eyes. "Twenty minutes ago, ma'am."

For over an hour they cooled their heels in the corner of the lobby. Patrice badgered the clerk so many times the woman refused to talk to her anymore. Ben looked out the window, studying the people who passed by. At CocoWalk he'd made the mistake of thinking no one knew where he and Patrice were. He wasn't going to let his guard down again.

At a quarter to eleven, a man appeared in the back of the tellers' area. The clerk rose to speak with him. He had a face so red he looked as though he'd been slapped on both cheeks, and his red hair had gone gray at the temples. He listened impatiently to her, then waved Ben and the others over. "This way," he said in an officious Highland brogue. No explanation. No apology for keeping them waiting.

He was a short man who walked with brisk steps, his arms chopping the air at his sides. He led them back to a windowless office with his name on the door: James

Harold McGinty. "Identification," he said, holding his hand up as if they should have their passports out and waiting.

Ben hadn't expected this in a bank so far off the beaten path. "Is that normal? Checking IDs for deposit boxes?"

McGinty twitched the corners of his mouth. He made Ben think of a fox who'd just gotten a snoutful of skunk. "Sir, this is my department. Whatever I *say* is normal."

Ben felt his face grow hot and the muscles in his shoulders go tight. He didn't like this martinet one bit, especially now that he knew the reason they'd been kept waiting. The twerp had been playing golf. Ben could tell by the mismatched sunburn on his hands (who wore only one glove? golfers) and the dent that went all the way around in his hair (one of those silly visor caps). But it wouldn't help things if Ben made a scene. He gave an acid smile. "Okay ladies, IDs."

Patrice handed over an old driver's license, under her real name. McGinty studied it, showing little expression. He turned next to Isabel's passport. He hadn't recognized her face, but he knew her name. "Mrs. Finney, welcome to Antigua. How is your brother? Still banking with Barclays? We'd do a better job here, I daresay." Even when he was trying to suck up, he was a snipe.

"I'll tell him," Isabel murmured, not sure what else to say.

Patrice had her deposit box key out. "We're in a bit of a hurry. It's a special box—"

"Set up by Mrs. Finney's husband," McGinty cut in. "Took care of it myself. A strange thing, the extra key. Lot of trouble to arrange."

Isabel shuffled her hands in her lap. "I'm sorry."

That brought a smirk of satisfaction to McGinty's face. He did nothing to move things along, though, just sat staring at them with his foxy eyes. Ben suspected they were being shaken down, that McGinty wouldn't let them see the box until they gave him some cash. But then McGinty stood up. "Vault's down the hall. We'll sign the file cards on the way."

The files were maintained by McGinty's assistant, a gorgeous twenty-year-old with cocoa-butter skin and Asian eyes. The room where she worked was as messy as a trash heap. What bought her the right to be such a slob, Ben wondered, working for a tidy pip like her boss? He got his answer when she moved over to the filing cabinets. She flashed a sly smile as her bottom passed a millimeter from McGinty's hand. Her hips were wagging so sensuously, Ben could almost hear the rhumba music playing.

It took the assistant several minutes to find the log-in card. Ben took it and handed it to Patrice. No one else had signed it in months. But Peter Saar had been here a few weeks ago. Ben saw a twitch of nervousness on McGinty's face. No doubt he remembered that visit. He probably had charged Saar a toll before letting him into the box, and made sure no records were kept.

Moments later they were in the vault. The keys worked; McGinty pulled the box from its slot. It was larger than most of the others, a foot square and two feet long. There was a row of desks along the wall. Instead of taking the nearest, he lugged the box to the far end. At that point he left them, nodding to a button by the door. "Ring when you're through."

None of the three wanted to take the chair at the desk, crowding the others out. Patrice lifted the lid off the box. "What's this?" she said. "A bunch of old newspapers?"

Ben took them out, four copies of the *Miami Herald*, with dates ranging from last September to over two years ago. There seemed to be nothing special about them. He set them on the adjoining desk, and he and Patrice scanned the front pages. They were so absorbed that they didn't notice Isabel. She dropped into the chair and tossed her big handbag on the desk. Her face had an absolutely shattered look. She reached into the box. "Finney's," she said in a husky voice. She held up a gold wedding band. Beneath it was a scrawled note. *Sorry, luv. Just, well, sorry.* Below that was a wedding photo of the two of them.

Patrice picked up the photo. "He had quite a smile, didn't he?" She set it in front of Isabel. "Let's see what else he left."

More photos, layers of them, some with frames, many without. Finney and Isabel. Finney as a child. Finney's family in Ireland. One picture of Finney and Patrice. She sorted them rapidly, not wanting to cause Isabel any extra grief. Under the photos were two large cotton sacks, folded up. Beneath those was another sack, holding something that looked like a double-thick brick. Patrice peeled the cloth back to show four neat stacks of American money, bound with rubber bands. "Ten thousand," she said. She didn't seem surprised by it.

"The other bags?" Isabel asked.

"Those are the ones Peter emptied. Money for you and me. He always figured it was best to leave something behind." She set the money on the desk.

Isabel and Patrice next started looking through a stack of letters Finney had saved. Ben turned back to the newspapers. As he did, something caught his eye.

A security camera was mounted over the door. When they entered, it had been rotating. Now it was stopped dead, aimed over Isabel's shoulder. That's why McGinty had chosen that desk. It was the only one with an unobstructed view from the camera.

"That scum," Ben whispered. He strode from the vault, keeping out of camera range so he wouldn't be seen. Voices came from McGinty's assistant's office. Ben shoved the door open without knocking.

McGinty and the young woman had their backs to him, sitting hip to hip on her desk, watching a TV monitor that had been hidden behind a stack of books. She giggled. "Bet he's boffing the both of 'em."

McGinty giggled, too. "Just watch what's in the box, Peachy."

Ben slipped around the desk, and the woman squeaked and jumped up, tripping over her chair. She landed in the corner, spread-eagled. High heels, hose, black garters. No underwear. Instead, a tattoo of fig leaves over a shaved pubic area. Ben was so angry, it didn't enter his mind that this was odd. He stuck his finger in her face. "You stay down and stay quiet. Got it?"

She nodded so fast her teeth clacked together.

McGinty, meanwhile, was trying to sneak out the door. Ben snatched him by the back of his shirt collar and frogmarched him down the hall. McGinty's feet wheeled in the air, toes tapping the carpet. "*You put me down. . . . Hey! I said, put me down!*"

Ben pushed him into the vault. "This piece of shit was watching us on the security camera."

Isabel turned, startled, but didn't get up. Patrice came straight over. "What do you want?"

McGinty flailed in Ben's hand like a fish on a hook. He refused to answer.

"It doesn't matter," Ben said. "Mr. McGinty's had a change of heart about what he had planned. Right?" He shook the man hard enough to make his hair fly.

"Management policy. I have to watch," he croaked.

"Nonsense," Ben shot back. "The bank would never permit that. More like you were looking for an angle, a blackmail squeeze."

"Absolutely not. Now you will put me down, or—"

Ben lifted him higher and brought him around so their faces were only inches apart. "Listen McGinty, these ladies are *not* going to pay you to get their own property. Not one penny."

Patrice was thinking about something else. What if McGinty decided to phone Emile, report that Isabel had been here with a couple of strangers from America? He might do that just to make a contact, ring up a favor due.

She got on her tiptoes and talked straight into his ear. "Mrs. Finney is a forgiving person. *I* am not. And my privacy means a lot to me."

Ben was thinking the same thing she was about Balazs. He picked up from there. "You're a golfer aren't you? I could show you some nifty new uses for a sand wedge. Like dental work. Now like she said, privacy is important to us."

"I didn't see anything," McGinty said. "Just some newspapers and pictures and money, I guess."

Ben shook him again.

"No," McGinty sputtered. "I didn't see a thing. Really."

Ben glared at him, ready to slap him for good measure, but Isabel spoke. "We should leave. I've got everything." While they had been arguing, she had finished emptying the box. Her handbag was bulging.

Ben opened his hand and McGinty crashed to the floor.

They marched past his office, through the tellers' area, and into the busy lobby. Ben noticed then something was wrong with Isabel. She was hunched forward, hurrying, bumping into people. By the time Ben and Patrice reached the door, she was well ahead of them. "Isabel?" he called. She was still wearing the tight wrap skirt, and she hoisted it to her knees and began to run. In her other hand she was clutching something, hiding it. "Isabel!"

She cast a decidedly frightened glance back at him and vanished into the crowd.

THIRTY-TWO

Ben raced to the corner. He couldn't see Isabel anywhere. Patrice had started the other way, shoving through the crowd, calling Isabel's name. "Wait," he yelled. "She looked up when she came out the door, getting her bearings." He pointed over the buildings, at the saltshaker towers of the cathedral on the hill. "She's going back there."

"I hope you're right!" Patrice said as she trotted up High Street. Ben went left, ducking through an alley. They'd keep her between them, closing the pincers like a military maneuver.

Ben was the one to spot her, pelting up the steps to the main entrance to the cathedral. Isabel glanced over her shoulder but didn't see him.

Ben motioned to Patrice, who was entering the churchyard from the other direction. Together they slipped inside, to a shadowed corner. Isabel stood in front of the altar, talking to the same priest with high-water pants she'd been with at the end of the morning service. He'd been giving instructions to the caretaker, but now he sent the man away. With a comforting hand on Isabel's shoulder, the priest drew her to the front pew. Soon they were deep in conversation.

Ben whispered, "It won't be good if she sees us here. Let's wait outside."

"We can't leave her!" Patrice said.

"Not leave her—wait for her to come to us. It'll be better that way, whatever's going on."

Patrice complained some more, but in the end she went with him. It was scorching hot now in the sun, but bearable in the shade of the lone pride-of-India tree in the churchyard. From there they had a view of all three doors to the cathedral.

In bygone days, the churchyard had been the cemetery for the island's upper-crust families, and scattered gravestones remained. Ben leaned against one, an aboveground box of weathered limestone as big as a dining table. "She didn't plan this," he said. "It's too complicated for her. She must have found something in the safety-deposit box. It scared her and she panicked."

"What could scare her that much?" Patrice said, pacing in front of him.

"We'll find out if we're patient enough."

Ben relaxed and let his mind coast along. A half hour passed. Patrice had quit pacing. She was next to him, leaning on the gravestone, tapping her fingers. He knew what was on her mind: nightmare thoughts of Cherry. She kept glancing at her watch, counting the minutes until Friday noon.

He looked around the churchyard. He was always uneasy in cemeteries, but not today. Not with Patrice. He edged closer, hoping that being together would calm her, too.

Finally, about the time Ben's stomach was beginning to rumble for lunch, Isabel came out of the church with the reverend. They were laughing, and he gave her a hug before she started down the steps. When she saw Ben and Patrice, she slowed, then called, "There you are!" So that explained it. *They* were the ones who'd been gone all this time.

Coming up to them, she continued, "Reverend Foyle's the dean here." She hopped up backward onto the gravestone, sitting with her legs swinging like shapely pendulums. "Old church, so many problems." Her handbag was stuffed with all the things from the safety-deposit box. She set it beside her. Ben noticed how jerky her movements were, uncertain. "I needed to talk to somebody, get some advice." She glanced at Patrice. "I gave him a thousand dollars out of the cash we got at the bank, for the kids' camp fund. Made him cry, he was so happy."

Patrice didn't miss a beat. "It's your money Isabel. Do what you want with it."

Isabel gave a cautious smile. "That's what he said. Trust the generosity of people. Even when . . ." She took a deep breath and leaned forward, as if she were about to plunge headfirst into something. "Here, take a look."

She placed a small black book on the gravestone. At first Ben thought it was a passport, but then he saw the worn embossing on the cover. *Helder-Antilles Bank, NV, Curaçao*. It was a savings book, an old-fashioned passbook account. Patrice picked it up, and the rumpled pages fell open to the middle. She gave an audible gasp and turned it so Ben could see. The last entry showed a balance of 1,908,020, in U.S. dollars. Interest hadn't been posted in over a year.

Isabel allowed them only a moment before she took the book back. "Reverend Foyle let me use the phone to call Curaçao. The man at the bank said last fall Finney made it into a joint account, Patrice and me, like the safety-deposit box."

Ben had known all along that Isabel was after something. "You knew this was here?"

"I knew there was an account somewhere. I never expected this kind of money in it, though."

Patrice said, "Finney hinted around to me that he'd been saving up. Pinching every penny. He and Isabel lived like dogs, he said."

"That's not true," Isabel shot back. "We were happy."

"He only meant the money," Patrice answered gently.

No one spoke after that, and Ben watched Isabel stare at the passbook. "So what do you want to do?" he asked.

Isabel looked at him. Her jaw was set. "I want to get away from Emile. I can't live under his thumb anymore. I just *can't*."

That's what Ben had been thinking since the Jumbi Cafe, how happy she might be on her own. Maybe he could help her on her way. They had a lot to get settled before that, though.

Isabel's other hand was in her purse. Ben had noticed a while ago. Now Patrice did. "So what's the deal, Isabel?" she said.

"Deal, yes." Isabel pulled herself up straight. "The reverend figured it out for me, the investment return and taxes and all. I want to go back to England. Start over."

"So what's the deal?" Patrice repeated.

Isabel took her hand from the purse, holding a cotton bag, the same type they'd found in the safety-deposit box, only smaller. "This was in the bottom of the deposit box. It's what Emile's after. The keypad he showed me on the blueprints."

Patrice reached out, and Isabel jerked the bag back. For a second, Ben wondered if they were going to have a wrestling match right there among the tombstones. But Patrice said, "It's your money, Isabel, all of it. Finney was a fool, in some ways, but he knew what a good thing he had with you. In the end he only wanted you to be happy. *You.*" She pulled the bag from Isabel's fingers and gave it to Ben. "I think he'd like it if you went to England."

All of Isabel's nervousness, all her suspicions, seemed to evaporate. With a sprightly brogue, she said, "But sure now, Ireland'd be better, girl." The two women laughed together.

Ben opened the bag and lifted out the flat metal box inside. It fit neatly in his hand. There were at least twenty wire leads attached, pure gold from the looks of them. On the face of the box was a strangely organized keypad, with ten small buttons in a diamond shape, and three larger ones. The small buttons were numbered. The large ones had characters, Cyrillic, he thought, Russian.

"What is it?" Patrice asked.

"I have no idea." Ben turned it over so he could inspect the back. There was something about it that made it seem ominous. The perfect workmanship. The solid, compact weight. What did those twenty wires connect to?

Isabel hopped down from the gravestone. Her mood was the complete opposite from Ben's. She was the world's newest millionaire. Her feet moved so lightly she seemed to be dancing. "Alex can't pick us up until dark. Let's go to the casino." She hurried down the churchyard path, swinging her purse at her side. "Come on!"

The casino she had in mind was on a quay in the harbor. It was a waste of a great waterfront spot. Like casinos everywhere, it was dim and quiet inside, like a cocoon. Management didn't want the patrons distracted by fair skies and warm seas.

Isabel was a terrible gambler, and she knew it. To keep her losses down, she never bet more than the minimum. As the afternoon wore on, she picked up a few suitors, men with cruise-ship tans who hung over her shoulder, whispering in her ear while sneaking glances down her tube top. None of them stayed long. Isabel chatted and tried to be happy, but there seemed to be a shadow over her. She'd put Roddy Finney's wedding band on her finger. Every once in a while she brushed it across her lips. Then, realizing what she'd done, she snatched up her chips and moved to another table, trying to lose herself in a new game.

Ben and Patrice sat in the bar, watching her. Patrice was calmer now that they had the keypad, but not Ben. He kept trying to sort out the story behind it. "Why did Saar leave it behind? Why not take it with him?"

Patrice said, "Since you showed me the photo of him, the way he died, I figured we'd find something important in that safety-deposit box. It's a perfect cold drop. Peter was hoping for a finder's fee from Emile. Once he had the money he could tell Emile where the deposit box was and let him get the keypad himself. He didn't need to move it. Cons want things simple. Simple is safe."

"But what about the bank deposit book? Saar should have taken that."

Patrice spun her glass of ginger ale on the table, staring at it with somber eyes. "Peter was a gentleman, I told you. He probably figured Isabel deserved the money, but he didn't want to cheat me, either. So he left the bank book where it was. The future could take care of itself."

Ben thought that over, watching Isabel move to a new rank of slot machines. "I wish she'd let us look at those things in her purse. There might be something to explain what Balazs is up to."

Patrice stared down into her drink again. Keep it simple, that was the best way. Swap the keypad for Cherry and be done with it. She didn't want to start complicating things. "It's a long ride back to St. Kitts," she said. "Maybe she'll show you then."

As evening came on, Ben got Isabel to sit with them for a quick dinner. Then she was off for another turn at the blackjack tables. He left to find Alex. They'd agreed to rendezvous at a tourist spot called Hemingway's Cafe. Alex was a half hour late. He had what looked like a bite mark on his ear and reeked of bad perfume. Ben didn't ask where he'd been. After collecting Patrice and Isabel, they took a fifteen-minute taxi ride to a place called Galley Bay. They waded out to where the *Sinkin' Feelin'* was anchored and in short order were under way.

The ocean was glassy again, and Alex let the outboards

purr along until they were clear of the reef. Then he kicked the throttle forward and the twin Mercs roared like a pride of lions. A million stars shimmered overhead. Isabel stretched out on the bench seat in the rear of the cockpit. Freedom is a strong drink. She'd had a taste today and was dreamily looking forward to tomorrow. Before long though, her smile faded. She stared at her hand and toyed with Finney's ring.

Ben's curiosity was getting the better of him. The old copies of the *Miami Herald* were there in her handbag. He was about to ask if he could look through them when Isabel yawned and said she was going to get some sleep. She ducked through the hatch into the bow cabin. Ben followed, and Patrice right after him.

The cabin was barely high enough for them to sit upright on the floor. A stingy twenty-watt bulb provided all the light. Isabel pulled a couple of blankets from the pile in the corner and stretched out in them.

Ben said, "We never got a chance to look at those things in your purse."

"Oh!" She sat up, nearly cracking her head on the ceiling beams. "I forgot all about that." She shoved the bag to him. "Let me know what you find—" She yawned again. "In the morning."

Patrice sat next to him, putting the bulb between them for maximum light. They sorted out everything: newspapers, photos, letters, cash. While Patrice started to read the letters, Ben turned to the photos. Some had paper frames and he took them apart, looking for notes, hidden clues, anything. He found nothing.

"Isabel?" he said. The water churning past the bow filled the cabin with a noisy vibrato. He spoke louder. "Isabel, you there?"

"Mmm, still here," she replied.

"Your brother's only a middleman. He can't want the keypad for himself."

Isabel nodded.

Ben asked, "Who's he been doing business with lately?"

"Cubans," she said without pause.

"What Cubans?" Ben already knew the answer—the Herreras—but he didn't want to lead Isabel in any particular direction, only keep her talking. It was a good thing, too, because her reply surprised him.

"Miami Cubans, Cuban Cubans."

"Did you get their names?"

"Manuel and Morena Herrera, from Miami. Manuel's her father. And there was a Colonel Roque from Cuba. He never showed up, but they talked about him."

"*Colonel* Roque? Cuban Army?"

"Air Force." She was beginning to sound groggy. She rolled over, facing away.

"Anybody else?" Ben prodded. "Anybody from the U.S.?" He was thinking of Aaron Joquand.

"No," she murmured. " 'Cept Herrera's guards. Always had some men with him."

Ben said, "Do you know what his business was with Emile?"

This interested her enough that she turned back to him. "They didn't say much in front of me, but little things slipped out. It was a soap opera really. Emile's got something going with Morena Herrera, but Manuel doesn't know. And that Manuel, he just hates Emile." Isabel was nodding. In the dim light Ben couldn't see her eyes, only the dark hollows of the sockets. "It wasn't all bad, though. There was one time when Emile really scored with Manuel. We were up late, playing cards, drinking."

She yawned a third time and didn't speak for so long that Ben had to prompt her. "What happened?"

"Drinkin' mojitos," she said. "Cuban rum. Emile made a toast. 'Member the—what was it—Kennedy. Manuel loved it. Kept saying it and grinning. He even hugged Emile. 'Course, we were all snootered." She chuckled. " 'Member the Kennedy. What a night." A moment later she snored once, and then her breathing leveled out.

Patrice was still paging through Finney's letters. She tossed them aside and rubbed her eyes. "This is a waste of time."

"We shouldn't give up," Ben said. "We haven't looked at half this stuff."

Patrice glanced at Isabel and dropped her voice. "Ben, don't forget—we came here for Cherry. That's all. Emile can do whatever he wants with this junk."

Before Ben could reply, the boat slowed. He stuck his head out the cabin door. From behind came the sound of an airplane. Alex, standing over him at the wheel, said, "RSS patrol. Dey come round the west, dey see us easy. Then we'll all be in jail."

Seconds ticked by. The plane banked on a new heading, and Alex let out a whistle. "Goin' Montserrat. Be okay now." He kicked the engines over and jacked up the throttle, and the boat once again knifed the water.

Ben closed the hatch as he sank back into the cabin. It was pitch black. Patrice had heard Alex's report on the plane and switched off the light so it wouldn't attract attention. Ben clicked it back on, only to find her huddled in the farthest angle of the bow. She had Isabel's purse, and all the things from the safety-deposit box were back in it. Isabel was tucked comfortably against the hull.

Ben crawled as far forward as he could. "What's up?"

Patrice touched the purse. "I don't want you fooling with this, Ben. We're giving everything to Emile."

Ben motioned toward Isabel. "Her money, too?"

Patrice stared stubbornly at him. "Isabel's great Magical Mystery Tour of England. Yes, if Emile wants that deposit book, we're going to give that to him, too."

"All right, but we can still try to figure out what—"

"No. We trade for Cherry and that's it."

He reached out, intending to take her hand, but she thought he was after the purse. She jerked it away. "Don't." She turned her face into the darkness. "I've made a lot of mistakes with Cherry, but not this time. No heroics now. That made a mess of things in Miami." Then she heaved a sigh. She hadn't meant to go that far. "I'm sorry. I know you only want to help us. And I'm grateful. Really I am. But I'm not taking any more chances." She rolled into her pile of blankets.

"Patrice . . . Patrice?" She didn't move. She was through talking.

After a few minutes, he crawled back to the other end of the cabin and switched off the light. His mind wouldn't stop working, turning over what she'd said. He understood why she didn't want to talk it through. They were both tired, on edge. They might say something they'd regret. Still, the keypad—since he'd first laid eyes on it, he'd had a dark feeling. Just as Inspector Audain had said; something bad was coming. Ben wished he could explain that to Patrice.

He looked over at where she lay. He still felt close to her, even after arguing. And despite the way she'd acted, she trusted him now, and more. He wasn't going to kid himself, though. Whatever they had going was fragile as a snowflake. With the least bit of heat, it would be gone. Ben knew he didn't want that to happen. And that surprised him. Patrice was as beautiful as any woman he'd known. And there was a strength about her, a fierceness that he admired. But that didn't explain the way he felt. The attraction went deeper, something he didn't understand yet. He hoped they'd have enough time together for him to figure it out—and figure her out.

Just enough light from the moon crept in for him to make out the curve of her cheek and the swirl of her hair. He liked it better before she dyed it. Soft, certain brown to go with those starlit green eyes. Maybe tomorrow he'd tell her. Tomorrow.

All in an instant, he was overwhelmed with exhaustion. He pulled his knees up and rested his head on his arms. In his mind he played a game: how much sleep lately? Monday he'd met up with Patrice in Truchas. Today was Thursday, no, past midnight already, so Friday. Two hours on the plane on Tuesday, and three . . . A second later he dropped off the edge of the earth, no dreams, just a vague feeling that he was flying, brought on by the forward motion of the boat.

Ben woke to eerie silence. He crawled onto the deck. Waves lapped at the gunwales, and a breeze lifted and parted his hair. They were back in St. Kitts, anchored in the same cove they had departed from. Alex lay on the transom bench, asleep. Next to him was Isabel's purse, still full, and on top of it was a flashlight.

Alex shifted, and a square of paper slipped from under his shoulder, drifting to the deck. It was covered with handwriting. Squinting in the faint moonlight, Ben picked it up and read it. He looked at the dirt pull-off on the bluff above the cove. Isabel's car was gone.

"Patrice!" He scrambled into the cabin and snapped on the light. "Wake up."

She blinked at him. Yawning, rubbing her face, she took the note.

Patrice and Ben:
I can't turn my back this time. I've got to stop him. I'll get Cherry out first. You've been good friends. Thanks for that.

Your Magical Mystery Girl

Patrice wasn't fully awake yet. "She's . . . what's this about?"

"She heard us talking. While we were asleep she went through the things in the purse. Maybe she found something there or remembered something that made her decide. She's gone up to Canada House after Emile."

Patrice threw the blankets aside. "Dammit. If she goes waltzing in there, she'll screw up everything."

"Alex?" Ben called.

"Right here." He'd gotten up and was standing by the wheel, listening.

"Run us up to Dieppe. Fast." Ben turned back to Patrice. "We'll go to St. Clair Saddler, get him to phone Inspector Audain. He might be able to stop her."

THIRTY-THREE

Colonel Roque walked quickly from the main gate at Holguín Air Base toward his quarters. The exercise felt good, stretching the tired muscles in his legs and back. It had taken four plane rides, seventeen hours, to get home from Miami. Now it was past midnight. The air was steamy, and there was a flash of lightning in the south, but no sound of thunder followed. Except for a radio playing far down the dusty street, the Cuban night was quiet.

He passed the main barracks, then the first of the officers' quarters. His home was at the end of the row. At each intersection a small street lamp glowed. The light was so dim, Roque didn't seem to throw a shadow. If he hadn't been so tired, he might have smiled at that. Manuel Herrera had called him an angel, but Roque felt more like a ghost slipping through the night.

He was halfway down the street when the lights went out. The moon was hidden behind a wall of clouds. The blackness was complete, as if a giant hand had come down over the base. Then his eyes picked up another flash, and again there was no thunder. So it wasn't a storm. The flashes were bombs, detonated at the main power substation on the Bayamo highway, he guessed. The noise couldn't carry in the heavy air.

While his eyes adjusted to the dark, he thought about the terrorists. They were branching out. Havana, then the seaports, now the center of the country. Did that mean something big was planned? A coup? What good would the bombings do if there were a coup?

He took out a cigarette. As he lit it, he noticed the music was still playing. That was strange. Batteries were too expensive in Cuba to waste on late-night radio. He walked on. Soon there were only a few houses left in the row, one-story frame structures with narrow front porches. The two across the street from his were vacant. Captain Cruz, next door, was away on leave. Whose radio then?

On his porch, he saw a spark move—up, stop, back down. Roque looked at his own hand, the cigarette. Someone was sitting on his front steps, smoking, listening to salsa music.

The radio clicked off. A man called softly, "Colonel, come please." At the same time Roque heard footsteps behind him. Three, maybe four men. They weren't out in the open, but in the dark spaces by the houses. No one from the base would sneak around like that, but he knew who would—the Secret Police, the thugs of the Interior Ministry.

"Welcome, all of you," Roque said. He was completely calm. He should have expected this.

"Thank you," the man on the porch replied. He shooed the others away—"Go,"—then came down the steps. "You enjoyed Miami."

It wasn't a question the way he said it, but Roque answered anyway. "It was interesting." He recognized the man, an undersecretary in the Ministry, from Havana. He didn't know his name, but that didn't matter. Roque had enough experience with the Secret Police to know they were as interchangeable as the leaves on the trees. Any one of a thousand men could have been sent to see him. They could deliver a message or a bullet, and wouldn't notice the difference.

"We reviewed the video and audio tapes. You did well. Fidel is pleased."

This annoyed Roque, the way he so casually used Castro's first name. "How is *el Presidente?*"

The jab of sarcasm didn't escape the man. He chuckled. "*El Presidente* is fine. He sends his regards and his thanks." He lifted his cigarette to his mouth. In the glow, Roque could make out his languid smile and lizard eyes. "So, you have met Manuel Herrera. An old lion. Or maybe just an old fool."

"He is no fool," Roque said.

"We will see. But the important thing—did he believe you? We can look at the tape, but we cannot see into his mind."

"Herrera asked for the photograph of my daughter. His hand shook, holding it, while I told him how she died. He believed me."

The man nodded. "Your daughter. We knew that would come in handy."

Another flash came from the south, and both men turned. This time the sound echoed faintly. *Crum-mmp.* "More bombs, every day it seems," Roque said. "Do your people have any idea who is behind it?"

The man from Havana chuckled again. He held his hand out in a cup and closed it up. "We know exactly who set those bombs. Names. Addresses. Jobs. Families. They'll all pay, someday."

Roque couldn't hide his astonishment. "You could stop it?"

"We aren't isolated anymore. The world watches. Satellite news, twenty-four hours a day. What is Cuba—snake or rabbit? The bombings play into that. We seem defenseless, our backs against the wall, as we always are."

Roque looked at his feet. He felt embarrassed for his stupidity. So much he didn't know. Who was in charge of this plan—the Interior Ministry? Castro? Did Castro even know about it? And what about the nuclear bomb? What kind of shape was it really in? They only allowed him to talk to underlings, like this man. From them, he never learned anything important. But Roque was first and foremost a military man. He had his orders. That was all he needed.

The man dropped his cigarette and crushed it out. His tone became serious. "Herrera's target left the U.S. base at Guantánamo this morning."

"The aircraft carrier?" Roque said.

"Yes, the entire battle group. Heading for the Florida Straits for flight training."

"A week early. What will he do?" Roque asked.

"Just what he always planned," the man replied. "Herrera will try every way possible to get the keypad. When he has it, he will send it to you."

Roque said, "He has the wiring diagrams. They talked of building their own keypad, a replacement."

The man huffed with irritation. "The best engineers in Cuba have worked on this. It is not possible. The original keypad from Moscow, that is the only way."

He called his guards back to the car, parked at the end of the street. As they slipped by, he said, "The plan will succeed. Fidel believes it. We all do." He put his hand on Roque's shoulder. "Your part is coming, Colonel, very soon."

He followed his men, then paused, holding the car door open. The dome light cast his shadow past Roque, far down the street. "Enjoy the radio. The batteries are fresh. I doubt you'll have to worry about getting new ones."

They cruised away, leaving their headlamps off. Roque turned to watch, wondering for a moment how they could navigate in the dark. Then he picked up the radio and went inside.

He felt his way to the kitchen, where he lit the small oil lantern on the table. Blown substations weren't the only reason for power blackouts in Cuba. Often the generators were broken or just shut down to conserve. He left the radio and took the lantern into his bedroom.

This was always the hottest room in the house. Stripping off his shirt, he sat on the bed. In front of him was an old bureau topped by a mirror with a carved frame.

The bureau had been his wife's. They had no daughter. That was a lie, to add juice to Roque's story. The rest was true. His wife had committed suicide with his service revolver. That day, they had learned from a doctor at a clinic in Holguín that they couldn't have children. In Cuba it was a shame to have no heir, and that shame fell on the wife. She left no note, just the receipt from the clinic clutched in her hand.

On the plane to Miami the day before, the colonel had tried to remember where he met his wife. A party somewhere. New Year's perhaps. The more he thought about it, the dimmer the recollection became. The past was leaving him. He looked at his reflection in the bureau mirror and saw a ghost staring back.

Roque's eyes drifted to a photograph on the wall. For the past month, everyone had been ordered to keep away from the nuclear bomb. He wasn't even sure where it was stored, probably in the old munitions bunker on the far side of the main base runway. He did have this picture of it, a stubby dark lump in a lead-lined crate. It was an odd photo to have in a bedroom, but the sight of it made him smile faintly.

At the start, Roque had been stunned by their plan. How could they ask him to do this? How dare they? With time the shock wore off. For centuries, soldiers had faced the same thing. Charging the trenches at Gallipoli. The kamikaze pilots of World War II. How did they prepare for death? Not by dreaming of glory and heaven. That was just a sop for the ones who gave the orders. The ones at the front knew the way. The trick was, little by little, to leave your life behind, to empty yourself out. Nothing left but the next minute, the next second, the next breath.

Roque could feel his breathing now, quiet and steady in his chest. He thought of the man from Havana, his sneering laughter. Yes, there was much Roque didn't know. But of one thing he was sure: when he was finally in the air with the bomb, when it was time to charge the circuits and key in the arming code, he would be fine. He would take the next breath and the next. He would do what was expected of him. He would do his duty.

THIRTY-FOUR

St. Clair punched the horn on his truck. "Move you mutton-heads!" The goats plummeted off the side of the road like fish down a waterfall, and St. Clair gunned around the bend. Ahead, lights sparkled through the sugarcane. It was Monkey Hill settlement. "Vance tol' me to meet him where the blacktop turns to gravel." He'd said that three times since leaving Dieppe.

"Right," Ben said, just as he had every other time. Then: "Watch it!" They hit a bump the size of a tree trunk. Next to him, Patrice bounced high off the seat.

St. Clair laughed nervously as he propped his machete back up. "Sorry. Di'n see that one."

A pair of reflective lights loomed in the turnout at the edge of the jungle. St. Clair hit the brakes and the truck slid to a stop behind Inspector Audain's Mazda. The policeman materialized out of the inky spaces between the trees. He had a nasty frown on his face. "Off with those headlamps, Uncle. Wha'chu tryin' do, raise the dead? I hear you all the way down b'low the airport."

"You tol' me come fast; I come fast."

Ben climbed out. Patrice followed. "Have you seen Isabel?" he said.

Audain could see how worried they were, and his look softened. "Her car's up the hill. Engine's still hot. She hasn't been around but a few minutes. What's she doing here?" On the phone, St. Clair hadn't told him much.

"Long story," Patrice said, starting up the road. "Let's just see if we can stop her."

Audain blocked her way. "No use a whole herd going in there."

Patrice spoke to him in a cutting whisper. Ben only heard the word "daughter."

The inspector pulled back. "Your daughter? How's that?"

"Like I said, long story," Patrice replied. "How do we get up there?"

Audain looked at them, one after the other. "Uncle, I suppose you want to come, too?" St. Clair nodded, and the policeman picked up a rock and hurled it into the bushes. "A whole fool herd. All right. We take this way."

They made slow progress on the overgrown path. Ben stayed with the inspector, while Patrice and St. Clair lagged back. Audain deserved more of an explanation than Patrice had given, so Ben told him their real names and said, "Balazs has been holding her daughter for three days. Just a kid; name's Cherry. Isabel's gone in to get her."

Audain grunted as his foot caught in a vine. "Holding her daughter for what?"

"A piece of electronics. He thought Patrice had it, and she does now. We only got our hands on it a few hours ago."

They broke out into a flat space filled with hundreds of tall, feathery plants. Audain plunged through them, clearly furious. Ben grabbed him. "Listen, we didn't want Isabel to get involved. We certainly didn't want her to come up here."

Clouds were rolling in, covering the moon. The inspector watched them while he kicked his toe in the dirt. "This a sacred spot, Rastafarian ground. These plants, marijuana." He smiled at Ben's surprised expression. The fury drained out of him like water out of a punctured cup. "Mr. Tennant, I don't run things here in these hills. There's no tellin' what's going to happen up at that house. So we get Isabel, and we get out. Don't press our luck past that."

"Fair enough," Ben said.

The inspector strode off, with Ben right behind him. At the edge of the field, they leaped a ditch. Audain landed awkwardly, and sat down with a thump. His foot was in a hole. His knee jutted up, the angle all wrong. "Lord no," he hissed. The bones in his leg crackled as Ben eased his foot free. "Damn Rasta trap," the inspector moaned.

St. Clair had arrived with Patrice. "Rasta growers set these little traps," St. Clair said, helping Audain sit up. "Don' mean to hurt no one, just keep folks away."

Audain tried to get to his feet, but fell back again.

"It's broken, Vance," St. Clair said. "Better be still."

"I get a chance, I'll burn this whole fuckin' hill," Audain seethed.

Ben cut him off. "Look! The balcony." It was Isabel. They could make out a hint of green from her skirt, slipping through the dim silvers and grays.

"That's Balazs' office up there," the inspector said.

St. Clair's eyes weren't so good. He had to squint to see her. "Miz Finney always stays out of her brother's business. Why's she messin' with him now?"

"Penance," Ben said. "Making up for all her mistakes with him."

The green shadow disappeared from the balcony. "Damn, and in she goes," Audain muttered. He tried again to lurch to his feet.

Ben held him down. "It's no good. Go with St. Clair. Get your leg taken care of. If we aren't out by daybreak, send somebody after us."

The inspector slumped back. "I got nobody to send," he admitted. It was bleak news, but Ben had expected as much. This was his fight, and Patrice's. He looked at St. Clair, who nodded. He could take care of Audain.

Ben helped Patrice across the ditch and pointed to the spot where the path reentered the jungle. St. Clair held out his machete. "Nephew, you might need t' cut a little cane up there. Mind it now. Lot sharper 'n it looks."

As Ben took it, Audain said, "Remember, don't press your luck." Ben nodded. Audain kept talking. He didn't like being left behind. "Isabel's reckless. Got that streak like her brother. Careful 'round her!" Ben hurried to catch up with Patrice, while the inspector's voice faded and was lost.

Though she knew the inside of Canada House well, Patrice hadn't spent much time on the estate grounds. They made a couple of false starts before they found the steps to the patio. At the top, Ben peered around. He could hear only the hum of the swimming pool pump. Nothing moved. He gave Patrice's hand a squeeze to let her know he was ready, and then he took off, past a row of palms in concrete planters, up the second set of stairs to the balcony. Patrice was only a pace behind.

At night, with the dark cane fields so far below, it was dizzying to be up there. They stayed close to the wall, moving down the balcony until they came to a set of French doors. One was open a crack. Ben ducked inside.

It took time for his eyes to begin to penetrate the new level of darkness. He heard a noise, something scratching on the carpet, and he caught a hint of movement and color. Green color. Isabel. She was crawling along the floor and disappeared into an opening in the wall, a doorway or hall.

Patrice had seen her too. She motioned to Ben, and they hurried across the room. The opening was a hall with two doors on the side wall and one at the end. All were closed. "Isabel?" Ben whispered. She didn't come out.

He moved to the end door and felt for the handle. Patrice said, louder, "Isabel, it's Patrice. Where are you?"

The door to their right opened, and Isabel's startled face appeared. "Shhh. Don't!" She grabbed Ben's hand. "Security alarm. In here. I turned this one off."

She pulled the two of them into the room with her and shut the door. It was black as a cave. "I heard something and went out to check. I thought Emby—"

Patrice cut in, "You think Cherry's up here somewhere?"

"No," Isabel said. "They'll have her on the lower level. I had to get these to get in down there." She jingled a key ring. "This is Emby's records room."

She clicked on the lights, and they huddled together, listening. Everything remained quiet. The room was large, almost as big as the outer office, with lines of filing cabinets and shelves of ledgers.

Ben said, "Let's get out of here. We'll give Emile what he wants, a safe trade for Cherry."

"Wait," Isabel said. "I want to show you something." She indicated the table behind her, where a newspaper was spread out. "This is one of the papers from the safety-deposit box. This article is marked, but the light on the boat wasn't bright enough for you to see. I had the flashlight. This 'ROF'—Finney made that. His initials."

She only gave them time to read the headline, "Nukes Never Fully Accounted for in Cuba, CIA Admits." She pointed around at the shelves. "Finney kept records of everything. He was a fanatic about it." She pulled over an open ledger on the table. "Finney said something to me about this ledger book before he died. I didn't understand what he meant until I saw that newspaper article."

She had a look that Ben hadn't seen before, a gleam of concentration in her eyes. For years, she'd let people do her thinking for her. That didn't mean she was stupid, just out of practice. She was working at it now, trying to piece things together.

Patrice said, "Isabel, we don't have time—"

"Listen to me!" Suddenly she was on the verge of tears. She didn't want to argue. "The manifest sheets are coded, but I can read them. Finney made me learn. God, that took so long. These entries from last November sixth. A package, three kilograms, shipped to St. Kitts from Miami. Before that it came from Moscow by commercial carrier."

Isabel drew her finger down the page. "Now, see this line? Four things—'Wiring schematic,' 'Field Manual,' 'Initiation Code,' and this last one, 'Sequencing keypad and trigger circuit.' They all came together from Moscow."

"You think that's what we've got?" Ben said. "That sequencing keypad?"

Isabel gave a helpless shrug. "Maybe. I don't know." She flipped a few pages further into the ledger, to a sheet filled edge to edge with code. "These are his diary notes, to go with the manifest entries. Like I said, he wanted everything written down. I can't make all this out, but it says the shipment from Russia was for a man named Joquand. He didn't have the money to pay when it arrived. Emile was left with the keypad and other things, and he still needed to pay the people in Moscow. He arranged to resell it to Manuel Herrera. The entry ends there. Finney never finished it."

"Joquand works for the CIA," Ben said. "He helped take Cherry from us in Miami." He paused, thinking. "Finney was worried about the deal Emile was working on with Herrera. He stole the keypad and left it in the safety-deposit box. Maybe he intended to go back for it some day but never got the chance."

"But why?" Patrice said. "What's so important about the keypad?"

Ben grabbed the newspaper. "This article Finney marked— it says some of the bombs and missiles in Cuba during the crisis in '62 were small, not like the big ones. The CIA and Navy had no way of knowing whether they were taken out."

Ben slumped on the edge of the table and looked at Patrice. "An old bomb. Nuclear. When they came to my house looking for you, Mosby said they were after something big enough to get armies moving. Emile and Herrera must know where it is and how to get it. The keypad is the trigger. That's what the manifest says."

It was too much, too fast. Patrice turned away, avoiding him, avoiding what he'd said. "We can sort this out later. We've got to go."

"Okay," Ben said. "Did Finney keep a code book, a way to translate what's here?"

"It was all in his head," Isabel answered. "Mine, too."

Ben said, "We'll have to talk to somebody from Washington, convince them about all this. We'll take this ledger, but that's it. Put everything else back."

Isabel went to the shelves and started rearranging the remaining ledger books. "Good God, a bomb like that," Ben said to Patrice. "What do you think they want to do with it?"

"What was that?" Isabel whispered, twisting around. They'd all heard the thump outside.

Ben grabbed the machete and clicked out the lights. Someone coughed in the outer office. Feet scuffed across the carpet. Ben ducked behind the door as it swung open. He held the knife high, ready to bring it down in a chop. It was so dark he couldn't see his hands in front of him.

The footsteps edged across the threshold. Ben's grip tightened on the machete, but he hesitated. There was something familiar here. A scent. A form. The sound of the breathing. It was too vague for him to say what, but he knew it.

"Rand?"

As she spun around, he caught a faint glint. She had a gun, pointing at his midsection. "Rand, it's Ben."

Mosby didn't move for what felt like ages. "Ben?" She took a step forward, awkward, half stumbling. The gun swayed. Ben smelled the blood then, lots of it. She started to fall. He grabbed for her, meaning to catch her elbow, but in the dark his hand hit hers. He jerked away as the gun went off.

THIRTY-FIVE

The bullet thudded harmlessly into the wall, but the noise of the gun seemed enormous. Ben slammed the door, and turned back to Mosby as she slid to the floor. He sensed the silence returning around them, no shouts, no running feet.

"It's okay," Mosby said. "Nobody else here." She laughed. "Just us chickens." She reached for him, and he felt the stickiness on her fingers.

Patrice found the light switch and clicked it on. Ben dropped to his knees. Mosby was on her back. Blood tinged the collar of her white blouse. He lifted her coat, and she read the shock on his face. "Real mess, huh?"

Her voice was strong. He felt a wave of hope. "Isabel, can you call for an ambulance?" he said.

"I'll try." She hurried into the outer office.

Ben leaned over Mosby. "Who did this?"

"Van Allen, the prick. We came here with Joquand, to see Balazs, but he was gone. No guards, nothing. I decided to finally tell somebody with half a brain up in Washington what we were into. Van Allen heard me on the phone—"

298

She gave a tight cough. "He's not like you, Ben. Doesn't give as good as he gets. I shot the pretty fucker in the face."

"Good for you," he said. He smoothed her hair, and that made her smile.

"Joquand ran," she said. "Probably headed back to the States. I had to do what he wanted. He knew about the drugs. Had pictures, sworn statements. I gave the coke up years ago, but what good did it do? All I've got is my job. I couldn't lose that." She shook her head, getting past that thought. "You know about the bomb?"

"Some of it."

"Joquand had big plans. Have himself quite a stick if somebody got out of line. Use it in the Sudan maybe. North Korea. Syria. Who'd complain? It's a Russian bomb. The radiation signature. Nobody would suspect the CIA. Joquand had a problem, though. Nobody inside the Agency would back his play. He needed six and a half million to finish the deal, and he couldn't come up with it." She bit her lip, stifling another cough.

"So Manuel Herrera's next on the auction list," Ben said.

"Yeah. You're on top of things." She put her hand on his shoulder. The pain spiked and she lost focus, then came back again. "Herrera used to be CIA. Not inside, but on contract. Did some nasty work in Cuba, a few other places. Had a falling-out with the big boys at Langley. He's on his own now."

"What's he want the bomb for?" Ben asked.

"He's got a target. Florida Straits." The coughing hit her hard, as if she were being punched. Blood trickled from her nose. "Complicated. I left some things in the basement that explain. Ask the girl."

"Cherry?" Patrice said, moving forward.

Mosby stared, seeing her for the first time, and then her eyes slipped shut. "Castro . . . he's watching. Tell Herrera he's got to call the damn thing off."

Ben felt her body stiffen. Her fingers dug into his shoulder. Her words were little more than a sigh. "Five years, Ben. I missed you."

She was gone before he could speak. He leaned back, looking at her. Everything was blurry because of his tears.

Isabel stepped through the door. "There was no answer at the ambulance—" She saw his face and finished in a mumble. "I called a cab."

Ben rearranged Mosby's jacket and smoothed her hair again.

Patrice touched his arm. "She said there's a girl in the basement." She turned to Isabel. "You've got the keys?" They were on the table, and Isabel passed them over.

"Ben, come on." Patrice had to pull him to his feet. She shut off the lights, so they could go without seeing what they were leaving behind.

Now that they knew the guards were gone, they were able to hurry, down to the patio, and inside and down another flight. They tried the wine cellar first, but, except for a few pieces of camp furniture, it was empty. The kitchen storeroom was next. No one there either. The same for the servants' rooms.

That left only the kitchen. Ben snapped on the lights. By then, Patrice was frantic, yelling, "Cherry! Cherry, where are you?" They heard a thud. Ben grabbed at the door to the walk-in cooler. It was locked, but a faint cry came from inside. Patrice fumbled with the keys, found one that fit, and flung the door open.

There was only a small bulb for light. Under it, a huge man stood. His arms hung to his knees, ape-like, and he had short, wild dreadlocks. *"Cherry!"* Patrice looked past him into the dark.

"It's me. Mary." Isabel's housekeeper stepped into the light. Her nose was broken, lumpy and red as a smashed strawberry. Her arms were pocked with cigarette burns. "Cherry's gone."

Patrice reacted before anyone else, snatching Mosby's gun from Ben. *"Where is she?"* She jammed the gun under the big man's jaw. *"Did you hurt her?"*

"Edmun' didn't hurt anyone," Mary said. Her lips were blue and her hands were fluttering, she was so cold. She pushed the gun aside. "He's just hidin' in there with me. Emile and that Mr. Herrera, they're the ones you want."

Mary's eyes rolled up and she started to collapse. Ben grabbed her. "Let's get her outside where it's warmer. Bring some water for her to drink."

They carried her up to the patio and laid her on a chaise. Ben found a towel to cover her with and used a corner of it to clean some of the blood off her face. She didn't want the water, but he made her take a few sips. "How did you get here?" he said.

"Emile had people out lookin' for Isabel and you two. Somebody up Nicola Town must have seen me, told where I was. Mick Laraby showed up with a truckload of men. Was him who did this." She touched one of the burns on her arm and winced. Ben covered it with the towel. "Laraby said you went to Antigua. Wanted to know how you got there and when you were comin' back."

"McGinty, from the bank," Ben said, looking at Patrice. "He must have called Emile."

She didn't respond. Her eyes were full of tears. She was a tangle of raw nerves.

"Did you see Cherry?" Ben asked Mary.

"She's okay, I think. I didn't get to talk to her."

Patrice grabbed her shoulder. "Where is she? Why isn't she here?"

Mary edged away, and Ben tucked the towel closer around her. "It's all right. Just tell us what happened."

"Mr. Herrera took her, about two hours ago."

Patrice's head fell forward, and she gave a broken cry. Ben reached across to stroke her hand. He beckoned for Mary to go on.

"Herrera had somebody here workin' for him, tellin' him everything goin' on about Cherry and you two. Edmun' maybe, I think."

Edmund was slipping toward the corner of the patio. At the mention of his name he hesitated, then plunged down the steps. Isabel moved to follow, but Ben said, "Let him go. You don't want to be out there with him in the dark."

Mary pushed herself up on the chaise. "Herrera had twenty, thirty men with him. Came in all of a sudden. Nobody even tried to fight, but Laraby. They shot him down like a dog, right there." She pointed to a spot by the house, and they could see the blood. Laraby was gone, though. "Runt must have crawled off somewhere to die," Mary said. "Then they brought Emile down from his bedroom, still in his pajamas. He was angry enough to spit, but Mr. Herrera was even madder. They were screamin' about Cherry and about you two off in Antigua lookin' for something.

"Finally Mr. Herrera had enough. He told Emile to get dressed. They all goin' to his house in Funnel Bay, he said. They brought Cherry up and got her ready to go, too."

Mary tilted Patrice's head up so their eyes met. "I got a good look at her. She's tired, but I think she was happy to be leavin' this place. She be all right." Patrice nodded slowly.

Mary continued, "I didn't know what they were gon' do with me. I was right out here with them. Mr. Herrera come up before they left and said, 'When you see them, you tell them to bring it straight to me. Today. Their last chance.'"

"Where?" Patrice said.

Isabel spoke up. "Funnel Bay, Manuel's place near Key West."

Patrice stood and went to the edge of the patio. Thumping her fists on the railing, she stared at the cane fields below. She stifled a sob.

Ben turned back to Mary. "What about the woman with red hair?"

"She's the one locked me and Edmun' in that freezer. She's crazy."

"She wasn't thinking straight, that's all," Ben said quietly.

"Drunk then. Somethin' wrong with her. She showed up about an hour after Herrera and Emile left. I was still here, too scared to leave. I heard a car drive up and went to hide downstairs. Edmun' was there, too. There were some gun-shots outside, and after a while that woman came to the basement and found us. Asked me who I was and what was I doin' here. I told her the truth—why not? She asked if I knew you and Patrice. I said I did, and then she made us get in that freezer. Said we'd be safer in there."

"She gave you something."

"She did. Little briefcase thing. Said to give it to you, or the police if you didn't show up. How'd you know about that?"

"She told us."

"She's still here? I like to see how *she* likes bein' shut up in that damn freezer."

"No," Ben said. "She's not here anymore."

He told Mary to drink the rest of the water, and he went to Patrice. Isabel was already with her. He said, "We can probably get a flight out later to San Juan or the Bahamas, then Florida. If there's a problem, we can phone Herrera, ask for more time."

"I can get us there," Isabel said, pointing down at the air-port. "That's Emile's private jet next to the terminal. There's always a pilot on board. I still rate high enough to give him orders."

Patrice was too worn out to thank her. She only nodded. For a while the three were quiet, and Ben went back to check on Mary.

As he knelt beside her, someone called, "Anybody here?"

Ben whipped Mosby's pistol off the deck. A man stepped out of the darkness on the other side of the pool. Seeing the gun, he lifted his hands. "Slow up, you," he said. He was old and bent and had an unruffled expression, as if nothing in the world could surprise him. "Somebody here call a taxi?"

Ben lowered the gun. "Right."

The man noticed the others. " 'Lo, Miz Finney. Maybe none of my business, but you been out front? Man lyin' by the driveway. I didn't get too close, but looked like his whole face was missin'."

Ben stood up. "It's okay. He's not coming with us."

THIRTY-SIX

Balazs had spared no luxury in outfitting his private jet. Only four seats had been installed, which left room for a bar, a television and computer workstation, a bathroom, and even a shower in the rear of the passenger compartment. In the one-hour hop from Basseterre to San Juan, first Isabel, then Patrice, then Ben, had used the shower. They found spare clothes in a cupboard. There were several outfits for the women, but only one shirt that fit Ben, a silk Henley with an "EB" monogram on the pocket. Ben frowned as he looked at himself in the mirror. With his slick wet hair and that shirt, he looked like the perfect image of an island drug runner.

Maybe that's how the U.S. Customs officers in Puerto Rico pegged him, or maybe they were bored in the slow hour before dawn. They gave the three of them and the pilot a real shakedown, picking through everything in their pockets and bags, even sending sniffer dogs onto the plane. There was nothing interesting to find except the keypad, which Ben carried. One of the Customs men dumped it out of its cotton bag, turned it over, and handed it back. Soon after that the officers sent them on their way. Now they were in the air again, on the long over-water leg to Key West.

Patrice and Isabel had fallen asleep as soon as they took off. Ben dozed, too, but when the plane leveled off at cruising altitude he woke. He'd been dreaming, some vague and violent scene about Mary.

After they left Emile's in the taxi, Mary had refused to let them take her to the hospital. She wanted to go home to Isabel's, to rest and phone her mother in Nevis. Her mum would know what to do about all those burns. At the curb she had a tearful parting with Isabel, begging her not to go. After giving Mary a peck on the cheek, Isabel pushed her out on the sidewalk. "Take care of yourself. We'll have lots to do getting this place in shape when I come home." Then Isabel pulled the door closed and ordered the cabdriver to the airport.

Ben's eyes were half shut as he tried to remember the dream. Mary had been frightened, screaming, while Mick Laraby waved a glowing cigarette in front of her eyes. Then a flash. An explosion. Something. He couldn't bring it back.

He looked at the seat beside him. There was a faux alligator-skin case there, the one Rand Mosby had brought to St. Kitts. It reminded him too much of Rand, so Ben had put off going through it. He lifted it onto his knees and clicked it open.

The waxy smell of crayons hit him. He'd already noticed how battered the case was at the corners. He imagined Rand pulling it out of her closet at home to bring on the trip to St. Kitts, a case she'd had since she was a girl, maybe a good luck talisman. There were no crayons in it now. Instead it contained a videotape, a packet of about a dozen five-by-seven photographs, and a slim folder.

Inside the folder was a computer printout. Most of what it said was too complicated for him to understand, but he got the gist, from phrases like "2,450k gross weight," and "lead shielding," and "enriched uranium core material," and "12kT equivalent." A list of technical specifications for the bomb. Interesting reading for a scientist, but not much help to Ben.

Across the cabin was the television console. Several wires ran from it to a small cabinet. Ben knelt and opened the doors. Once again, Emile's airplane outfitter had included all the comforts. There was a VCR and a DVD player and on the bottom shelf quite a library of tapes and disks. Emile's taste ran to tough-guy Westerns. All the Clint Eastwood films were there.

Ben found the remote and got Mosby's tape started. The first section was a real surprise. Someone had been at the Biltmore Hotel in Miami at the same time Ben was, watching the Herreras and Balazs have breakfast. The film had been shot from a balcony, looking down into the courtyard. The pictures were excellent; the sound was truly amazing. Every bit of noise from the fountain next to the table had been filtered out. Even the smacking of Balazs' lips could be heard as he ate. Ben had seen surveillance tapes before, from the FBI and Marshals Service, and they weren't anything like this. Only the CIA had equipment this good. The video must be Joquand's.

The tape took forty minutes to run. In it were scenes of Balazs and Manuel Herrera, a different setting each time, but always the same topic of conversation, the bomb and the keypad. Ben sat as if in a trance, watching the facial expressions, the twitching hands and shrugging shoulders, hanging on every word and the undercurrent of tone.

The last scene had been shot at a horse track. There was a lot of fog so the pictures were dim and watery. Balazs wasn't there, but Manuel and Morena Herrera were, and two other men. Morena called one of them "Colonel" and

"Luis." He had to be the Colonel Roque from Cuba that Isabel had mentioned.

Ben played the scene to the end, stepping back in his mind, looking past the details. He went through it again like that, and then a third time, in slow motion. He couldn't see as well as he wanted, so he knelt on the floor in front of the television.

"What did you find?" Patrice had woken up and was standing behind him.

Ben held up his hand for her to wait while he concentrated on the screen. When the tape was almost through, he froze the picture. "That man with the dog, there in the back of the grandstand—do you know him?"

She bent closer. "I don't think so."

Ben reached for one of the photos from Mosby's case. "Here's a better shot. He's pretty recognizable with that white streak in his beard."

"I've never seen him before," Patrice said. "Why?"

"Herrera met with Roque, the air force colonel from Cuba that Isabel told us about. This man with the beard showed up and filmed the meeting, using a small video camera he hid partly with his coat."

"He's with Joquand," Patrice suggested.

"I don't think so," Ben said. "The video we're watching was made by Joquand's people. They wouldn't film one of their own men. Something about him must be important, though, for him to be on this tape."

Patrice inspected the still photograph again. On the back was some writing, a name and address. It didn't mean anything to her.

Ben had gone back to the video, playing the end of the scene. Again he hit the pause button. Colonel Roque was in the frame; his wallet was in his hand. Ben studied the picture for a full minute before he sat back, shaking his head.

He pulled the tape out but left the television on, staring at the blue screen. "They talked about the target."

Patrice dropped into one of the seats. "What is it?" Her voice was low and shaky. She was afraid of what he was going to tell her.

Isabel shifted in her chair. She came half awake, mumbled and drifted off again.

Ben pointed at the rear of the cabin. "Let's go back there. Let her rest."

They had to wedge themselves into the tight space. He leaned against the bulkhead while Patrice propped herself on the tiny sink cabinet. "The U.S.S. *Kennedy*, an aircraft carrier," he said. "And there are ships that travel with it, a battle group. Herrera had a picture. They were anchored somewhere, and he expects them to move within range soon. All they need to do is to get the keypad to Cuba so the bomb can be armed, then fly it out. That's Colonel Roque's part in it."

"Bomb Americans? That doesn't make any sense."

"To Manuel Herrera it does," Ben said. "Since the Bay of Pigs he's had it in for the U.S. Navy. But that's not the real reason. Those ships are just tools. Remember what Isabel told us? ''Member the Kennedy,' she said. Manuel was laughing about that one night at Emile's, making toasts. He was drunk, slurring. It was really '*Re*member the *Kennedy*.' Like the war in Cuba, 1898. An American ship blew up in Havana harbor. Hundreds aboard were killed. The U.S. sent armies down there to set things straight. 'Remember the *Maine*!' "

Patrice closed her eyes, shook her head. "He's going to start a war."

Ben said, "If a Cuban plane with a Cuban pilot drops a nuclear bomb on a U.S. aircraft carrier, imagine what will happen. They won't debate it in Washington, they'll just let loose. Retaliatory air strikes, infantry headed for the beaches. Nobody will pay attention to the denials from Cuba. A war, straight out. Castro won't have anywhere to run, no one to turn to for help."

"But Mosby said Herrera can't go through with it."

Ben had been thinking about that, too. "Can't. Shouldn't. I'm not sure what she was trying to say."

"On the ships—" She had trouble finishing. "How many people?"

"I'd guess seven or eight thousand. Maybe more."

Her fists were knotted so tight her fingers turned white. "I told you Peter Saar used to give me advice. He thought I was too sure of myself for scamming. Never knew enough to be afraid until it was too late." The plane pitched, jostling them together. "Since I saw Mosby at Emile's house . . . I'm afraid now. Afraid I'll make the wrong decision. Afraid I won't decide at all when it comes to it. I'll just give up."

He took her hands in his. "You're not going to give up. Not you."

That didn't give her much comfort. She let her head fall forward. "All those people on the ships—" She began to cry. "God, I only want Cherry back. She must be so scared. I can't believe I got her into this."

"She loves you. Just think about that. That's why she wants to draw so much, to do something with you. That's why her haircut is like yours, to be like you." He bumped her shoulder. "Like you, Muzzy."

She gave a faint smile and rubbed away her tears.

He said, "And when it's over, remember what I told you. I'll find a place, perfect for the two of you. You can make up for everything with her."

She nodded. She wanted to believe it. Then she reached behind her into her pocket. "Isabel gave me this." It was the savings account book from the bank in Curaçao. "Told me she thought it'd be safer with me. I didn't know what to say to her."

She handed it to him, but he slipped it back into her pocket. "Isabel's right. Of all of us, you're the real survivor. I guess Peter Saar never saw that."

Another tear streaked down her face, and Ben pulled her head over on his shoulder. "Right now, we concentrate on getting Cherry out. We've got a good chance of doing that, I think, and of stopping the bomb. They'll need time to get the keypad to Cuba, get the bomb ready, fly it out. After we've traded for Cherry, when she's safe, we use that time. There are people I can call in Washington. If that doesn't work, we'll go to the television stations, radio, whatever it takes. Somebody will listen and warn the *Kennedy*."

She stared vaguely at the floor, as if none of what he said was getting through to her. "Hey, you," he murmured. He pulled her off the cabinet and held her.

Patrice looked up at him. Despite her tears, despite how tired she was, her eyes were suddenly so clear and deep he felt he could tumble right into them. "You make it all go away," she said. "The scary things just disappear." She smiled and stroked his arms. "This place you're going to find for Cherry and me—I want you with us, Ben. With me."

It was the last thing he'd expected her to say, that directly. No games. Nothing coy. He wanted to kiss her; he did. And finally, in that moment, he knew why she had such a pull on him. She had a new surprise for him around every corner, twists he couldn't predict. That was a luxury he'd never had with any woman, life played out moment by moment, not according to a script that ran in his head.

He flashed back to her house in New Mexico, falling down the mountainside after her. He did that now, letting go of all the suspicions and worries he had about her. Just falling. "If that's what you want, I'll be there."

She buried her head in his chest and her arms came up, squeezing him tighter and tighter. They fit together like pieces of a puzzle.

Then the plane banked and the momentum pulled them apart. Through the cabin window he could see a long stretch of ocean. There were no ships in sight, but he thought about the *Kennedy*. It was somewhere out there. They rolled a bit more. The horizon came into view. The sun was up over scattered pink-custard clouds. The sea was an endless, blank sapphire. It was going to be a lovely day.

THIRTY-SEVEN

The plane continued west while Ben and Patrice tried to get some sleep. The whole time, they held hands. Ben woke as the jets changed pitch, and the plane slowed to turn. Key West swung into view, first the big Navy installations and the town docks, and then they were over land. It was midmorning now and the sunlight was harsh. He was struck by how busy it was. People and cars thronged the streets. Then he spotted a cluster of satellite trucks from the TV networks. Nearby was a gaping black hole in the ground. The Cuban-American Freedom Foundation. He'd forgotten about the fire and demonstrations. Jesus, what timing.

A moment before touchdown, he tugged on Patrice's hand. Her eyes opened, staring straight ahead, waking to worry. Across the way, Isabel stirred. "Criminy, what crawled in my mouth and died?" Ben laughed. Even Patrice couldn't hold back a smile.

The airport terminal wasn't as crowded as it had been their last time through. Ben thought of checking the Flying

Conch to see if Larry was still there, deep in his poker game, but they needed to keep moving. He led the two women to the auto rental counters. Only one had a "Cars Available" sign. He told the clerk they wanted two. Midsize would do.

"Two?" Patrice asked.

"I'll explain outside," he said. He looked at his Dale Blodgett driver's license and credit card before handing them over. This would be the last time he'd use them, no matter how things turned out.

The weather was breezy and very warm. The Atlantic was just across the road from the parking lot. Windsurfers ripped along the coast. A mother was helping her young son hold a kite that was threatening to drag them both down the beach into the water.

Reaching the cars, Ben took out the map he'd gotten from the rental clerk. The clerk had told him how to get to Funnel Bay. That part was easy. In the Keys there was only one main road, with a few side spurs. But Ben wanted to know exactly where Manuel Herrera's place was. Isabel had been there once. She studied the roads and looked dubious. She wasn't good with maps, she admitted. Then she got her bearings. "It's this end of the bay. Down this lane. Last house for a mile or so. If you get lost, look for the dolphins on the gate, a sculpture, huge thing."

"Dolphins. All right." He set the map on the hood of the car. "Now, we can't all show up there." He held out his hand, cutting off their protest. "If we all go, we lose what leverage we've got. They'll just take the keypad, and we won't get out until they say so, *if* they say so."

"What do you want to do?" Patrice said.

"I'll go to Herrera. You keep this." He took out the bag with the keypad. "Herrera can bring Cherry and me back into town, someplace public. We trade: he gets what he wants; Cherry and I walk away. Then I start making calls to Washington, light a fire under the Navy about the bomb."

"Why should Herrera believe you?" Patrice countered. "Just because you say we've got the keypad doesn't mean we do."

"He'll believe me." Ben pulled a slip of paper from the bag. "I didn't know this was in there until the Customs man checked it in Puerto Rico."

"What is it?" Isabel said. It had a row of blue numbers, like an everyday cash register receipt, except there was Russian script at the top.

"There were four things shipped from Moscow last November," Ben said. "One was an 'Initiation Code,' and that must mean the sequence to arm the bomb. That's what this has to be. I'll show it to Herrera. He'll go along, figure we must have the keypad with us, too."

Patrice started shaking her head, and Ben said, "It'll work, well enough to get Cherry and me out of there, to a place where we can make a safe trade."

He smoothed out the map. "Here's how we'll play it. You two drive to this place by the wharf—Mallory Square. Bound to be crowded there. Park as close as you can to the square, on this street. Leave the keypad on the seat and lock the car. I'll take Herrera there with Cherry. When we find the car, I'll point it out to him, but I'll make sure Cherry and I can get away first. He gets what he wants; we walk."

Patrice said, "What if Herrera doesn't go along? What if he threatens to hurt Cherry? Or just says 'screw you' and throws you in a hole somewhere?"

"It's your call then," he said. "When Cherry and I get out, we'll go to this church." He tapped a spot on the map. "If we don't show up in a few hours, you'll know something went wrong. Go back and get the keypad. Do whatever you think is best."

Before she could argue any more, he pressed the keypad into her hand and hopped in one of the cars. He reached through the window for her, while Isabel turned away to give them some privacy.

"Ben, I don't want you to do this," she said.

"Shhh." He pulled her down and gave her a kiss. "Just wait at the church, okay?" He had to speak up because a helicopter was coming in to land at the airfield. He started the engine. "Good luck."

She nodded, still uncertain, and said something, but the noise was too great for him to hear. He stroked her hand and drove off.

Ben had figured the trip to Herrera's would take twenty minutes. He hadn't counted on the demonstrators. They had gathered at the turnoff for U.S. 1, the main road in the Keys, thousands of people filling the intersection and the sidewalks, all the way back to the surrounding buildings. This was the only route out of the city. If the plan was to cause maximum disruption, it was working. Everyone else on the road was giving up, turning around.

In the crowd, someone was shouting a speech over tinny loudspeakers. The people were restless, milling around, their anger barely under control. This would take finesse. If Ben tried to force his way through, they'd turn that anger on him.

He left the car in the street and slipped into the crowd. Someone had left a placard on the ground. ¡Cuba Libre! it said over a picture of Castro with devil horns. Ben hustled back with it and slipped it under the windshield wiper. Then he inched the car forward, tapping the horn. Wave. Smile. He was one of them. The sea parted.

Progress was painfully slow. There were captains, men with blue armbands, roving around, seeing that everyone stayed calm. There were litter cans and portable toilets. All carefully organized, too organized for a spontaneous demonstration.

He'd made it to the back of the crowd when he had to stop again. Everyone was looking up, shading their eyes. The helicopter from the airport buzzed by. It was so free and easy, above the tangle on the ground, that it gave him a pang of irritation. Then the people realized he was there and got out of the way. He hit the gas.

The road took him past the big naval air station on Boca Chica Key and over the next set of bridges. The traffic was thick, moving at fifteen miles per hour. Despite the slow pace, the turnoff for Funnel Bay came before he expected it. Everything here was smaller than it seemed on the map, a world in miniature. He passed through a development of modest houses laid out on a grid of canals. The houses ended at the edge of a mangrove swamp, and the road ran on, straight and level. Heat shimmered off the blacktop. It was amazing how lonely it was out here, only a few minutes' drive from the highway. No cars, no people. Nothing moved except a pair of turkey vultures wheeling high in the sky.

He turned on the lane Isabel had indicated on the map. Through the trees he caught sight of houses every hundred yards or so. These were huge, gaudy places with gated entrances, padlocked and guarded by "Keep Out" and "Beware of Dog" signs. They were vacation hideaways used only a few weeks a year by the high-roller crowd.

The road was getting narrower and rougher. A military transport plane floated down through the sky, lining up for a landing at the naval air station. Ben was heading back to the west now. The air base was only a few miles away over the sea.

He hadn't seen a house for quite some time. Then, in the distance, he spotted a high gray wall on the beach side, a security barrier around a large compound.

The sculpture on the gate was smaller than Isabel had described, but it was still splendid, three bronze dolphins leaping from the top of the steel frame. Unlike the others he'd passed, this gate was open. The Herreras were expecting visitors. Ben turned in.

Lines of stubby date palms with four-foot-thick trunks stretched away from the driveway. A workman was trudging between the trees, pushing a wooden wheelbarrow. At the sound of the car he glanced over his shoulder, but kept moving.

Ben rounded a curve in the drive and saw the house, a white frame structure set on coral rock piers, with wide porches and a red-tiled roof. It wasn't as grand as the other houses he'd seen on the way in, but it was special in its own way, a stately throwback, like a country hacienda for some 1950s banana baron.

Ben parked and walked slowly up the front steps. How different this was, this Caribbean Shangri-la, from the New Mexico home where he'd found Patrice. Just five days ago—they'd come through so much, it almost didn't seem possible.

On the porch, he got a full view of the compound. There were a couple of cottages in remote corners away from the main house. A canal had been dug in from the beach, and a speedboat hung on davits over the green water. Across the road he could see an airstrip, a long stretch of concrete cut into the mangroves.

The entry gate swung closed on a silent motor. He was locked in, all very slick and quiet. Fair enough. He didn't intend to leave until they let him—with Cherry.

The door opened behind him, and an old woman wearing a blue maid's smock appeared. "Good morning, sir. Come in, please."

She led him through a sparely furnished living room to the rear porch, overlooking the ocean. Morena and Manuel Herrera were there, and Emile Balazs. The Herreras both eyed him keenly, while Balazs hulked near the railing. From his expression, he was in a boiling rage—at the Herreras, at Ben, at everything.

Ben felt his own anger rise, but that was quickly replaced by a tingling sense of anticipation. He had unfinished business with Balazs. Today they'd see the end of it.

Ben turned to the Herreras. "So the gang's all here."

Manuel chuckled. "Absolutely. Now, you have something for me?"

Ben wanted to get the lay of the land before he worked into the deal. "I hear you had a whole army at Emile's place. That must have taken some planning."

Manuel tipped his head modestly. "Morena—she is good at organization."

"And your army just vanishes into the night?"

"Ah," Manuel said. "We're not alone here, Mr. Tennant. My men are discreet, that's all."

That was part of what Ben wanted to know, how much backup Herrera had. Plenty, apparently. He was wondering about the rally in Key West, too, if that was connected somehow. He said to Morena, "You arranged the demonstrations? Organized all those people?"

She said, "The Freedom Foundation was burned. People come. What would you expect?"

"No," Ben said. "That's too much of a coincidence. You want those people here, don't you?"

Morena started to speak, then decided it would be better to keep quiet.

Ben took a stab at something. "It was an old building—famous, but empty. Burning it would be a great way to stir up trouble without anybody getting hurt." He looked at Manuel. "Is that about right?"

Manuel dipped his head in a bow. "Very astute, Mr. Tennant. Yes, the fire was my idea. Later, maybe you'll see why."

"How lucky for me," Ben said.

Manuel scowled. "Enough wasting time. You have the keypad?"

"Not with me, but I know where to get it. We'll have to go to Key West, just the three of us—you, me, and Cherry."

"I'll need proof you have it," Manuel said. "Do that and yes, we can go to Key West."

He'd agreed so easily, it made Ben pause. But all he could do was move ahead. "I have this. It was in the bag with the keypad." He took out the slip with blue numbers.

Immediately, he knew something was wrong. Morena hurried toward him, reaching for the paper. Then a short, heavily built man emerged from the doorway, pointing a gun at him. Morena grabbed the slip and passed it to Manuel.

"Take it," Ben said. "But the deal—"

"Quiet," Manuel said. He moved back and called upstairs. "Eric, come down here!" Eric Selano. Ben knew him from the video taken at the horse track. The science expert.

Selano soon appeared, moving carefully across the porch, giving the gun a wide berth.

"Is this it?" Herrera asked, shoving the slip at him.

Selano's hand trembled as he reached out. He read the list of numbers. "I . . . I think so. The serial number is right. But Mr. Herrera, we really shouldn't be messing with this, you know?"

"Is this it?" Herrera snapped.

Selano stepped back. He didn't want a fight. "Yes. That's the right code."

Ben was struggling to follow this. Why was everyone so wound up all of a sudden? "All right, let's get back to the trade."

"Arturo," Manuel said to the man with the gun, "take him."

"I told you," Ben said, "I want to see Cherry. Now."

Morena and Manuel were smiling. Arturo grabbed Ben and shoved him, almost threw him, inside.

Ben called back, "Herrera, dammit—"

"Shut your mouth," Arturo snarled in his ear. *"You're an idiot, Herrera!"*

Ben heard a noise like a hammer on concrete. Arturo had cracked him on the base of his skull with the gun. There was no pain, just a flash of light, and then black.

Later, Ben remembered the feeling of being unconscious, as if he were swimming through dark water. Once, he came near the surface. His eyes quivered open. Isabel was there, and Patrice and Cherry. They were bending over him, concerned. Nice to see them all together. Ben wanted to smile, but his mouth wouldn't move. What was this place? Little room. Funny smell. Dates. Date palms. Funny. Maybe he should laugh. Then he smelled something else. Cologne. Balazs. But he shouldn't be here. *Out. Patrice, get out! Go!* He tried to call to her, but couldn't. No use anyway. The gang's all here.

Ben dove, unconscious again, hiding in the comfort of the dark, dark water.

THIRTY-EIGHT

Ben came to with a shattering pain in his head. He'd had concussions twice before and knew that any movement, even opening his eyes, would make it worse. He could hear Patrice and Cherry talking. Checking the bandage on Cherry's hand. Joking a little. Not fighting. Good.

Beneath him he felt rough floor planks. That smell was still in the air—dates. Strange.

He lifted his hand, and there was a whirlwind of noise as Isabel dropped beside him. "Ben? Wake up!" He tried to say he was awake, but all he could do was groan. She shook him and pried open his eyelid. That felt like a needle going into his brain. Using her shoulder as a handhold, he sat up. Bad move. If she hadn't caught him he would have fallen straight over. "We were so worried," she said. "Never seen anybody out like that."

"How long?" he croaked.

"Too long. Hours." She was squeezing him and patting him and inspecting the lump where he'd been hit.

"Is'bel, get off'a me," he said, imitating Mary, two nights ago in her garden. She giggled, moving away, and he immediately started to topple back. Patrice grabbed him and sat so that he could loll against her. Sweet, sweet Patrice. He rested, letting his head droop.

Within moments the headache intruded, and he looked around. Cherry was sitting on a box nearby, looking anxiously at him. He was able to smile. "Is that water?" Cherry pushed the bottle into his hand. After a sip, he said, "How did you get here?"

"That damn helicopter," Isabel huffed. "Had four of Manuel's men on it. We didn't even get out of the airport parking lot before they had us."

"How did they know we were there?" he asked.

Isabel said, "The pilot who flew us in from St. Kitts. Wasn't his fault. As soon as we landed, he radioed back to report where he was. Emile and Manuel were monitoring the calls. They figured we had to be on board, so Manuel sent the helicopter to pick us up."

Ben felt well enough to get up, with Patrice's help. They went to the door where he peeked through the screened opening in the top. The light made his eyes burn. She pulled his arm around her shoulder and stroked the small of his back. The touch seemed to soothe her as much as it did him.

"Did they get the keypad?" he asked, trying to sound casual about it. She nodded. He cursed, then quickly said, "Sorry." He didn't mean to blame her. She hadn't taken it that way anyway. She was watching him, her face full of concern. He gave her a squeeze. "I'll be okay."

Ben took a look around. It was an odd little building. The walls were curved and there were two small, round windows, one on each side. The doors at either end were low and narrow. On a post in the middle of the floor there was a wooden wheel with spokes, like the ones used on old-time sailboats. That's what this was. A kid's pirate playhouse. With no children around, it had been downgraded to a storage shed for a few boxes of stale dates.

Cherry was still staring at him, her eyes round and riveted. He imagined she'd thought he was dead, out for so long on the floor. He winked at her. "How's your bowling?"

She broke into a grin. "I could beat you."

"We'll see about that," he laughed. He looked out one of the windows. "Have they been back since they brought me in?"

Patrice said, "There's a guard on the other side. He brought food and water about an hour ago."

Ben crossed to the opposite window. A man was sitting on a lawn chair in the shade of one of the palms. He had a long gun across his lap, a rifle or shotgun, and was bobbing his head to music coming from a small radio. From the angle of the sun, Ben guessed it was midafternoon or later.

He sat next to Cherry and drank more of the water. "They took your hat," he said. She gave a glum nod. "It's all right." He touched her hair. "It's growing back already."

The water had a sharp mineral taste. He remembered that from his other concussions. Afterward, he slipped in and out of focus. He was on an uptick now, the headache fading. His senses were in overdrive—the taste of the water, the smell of the dates. The muted colors inside the playhouse seemed to glow. His hearing was magnified, too. That was why he picked up the voices before the others did. Two men were approaching from the main house. He recognized them before Isabel and Patrice even looked around. It was Emile and Arturo. Emile sounded keyed up. He was laughing. Arturo grunted a few words.

The padlock rattled and the door bounced open. Arturo moved cautiously to the corner, holding his pistol in front of him. Emile strutted across the floor and said, "Sleepyhead, welcome back!" He looked the place over, stem to stern. "It's turned out to be a special day. Colonel Roque got our shipment already. A fast plane to Haiti, then another to Cuba. Nobody following. Installing the keypad was a cinch. A few screws and wires, test the circuit, and he was done. He loaded up and got clearance from his own traffic control ten minutes ago. By now he's in the air with the bomb."

Emile spun the pirate-ship wheel, enjoying the squeak it made. "I should have believed Manuel, that everything would work out. His plan, my payday. He's smarter than I gave him credit for. The target's right out there." He pointed toward the ocean. "We'll be able to hear the explosion, maybe even see the flash and the cloud, but it'll be safe here on land. That crowd in Key West—the demonstrators, all those news people—will get quite a show." He looked at Cherry. "A story to tell the grandkids."

He spun the wheel again. This time the squeak didn't make him happy. His good spirits were souring. "Right. Isabel, up. Come with me."

For a moment the room was pin-drop quiet, and then Isabel gave a sharp laugh. "Got something bad planned for my friends, do you? But not me. Blood's thicker than water, now that you're going to get your money and save your skin."

"Iz, don't make a bloody scene."

"I'll say what I want. You're through ordering me around."

He took a step toward her, but Ben moved in the way. Patrice joined him. Isabel grew bold behind their barricade. "Remember what you said in my garden, Emby? How afraid I was of being alone? Look at yourself. Finney's dead, and Mick. The rest of your men have run off. You're the one who's alone. Nobody will have anything to do with you."

Arturo was laughing quietly. He enjoyed seeing someone stand up to Emile. Emile's face reddened with anger and embarrassment. His eyes slipped sideways. With one quick movement, he grabbed Cherry and jerked her beside him. Ben jumped after her but not fast enough. Arturo leveled the gun, motioning for him to back up.

"Don't hurt her," Patrice pleaded.

Emile smiled calmly. Nobody was going to taunt him now. He gave Cherry a pat. "It's a great thing, what Manuel has with Morena. A helper, somebody he can trust. Father and daughter. And me, alone all of a sudden. Come on, Cherry." He nudged her.

Ben moved to cut him off. "Damn you, you won't take her again."

Emile gave Cherry another shove. It was as if he had pulled the pin on a grenade. Fists, feet, teeth—she exploded. *"I'm not going with you. I hate you."* She bit him twice before he even started to fight back. He slapped her, and that sent her into a complete frenzy. Clawing, biting, screaming. *"I hate you! I hate you!"* There wasn't much strength behind her blows, but there were so many she was forcing him back.

Arturo, like the rest of them, was stunned at first, but then he laughed. "Leave her." He took Cherry by the arm and slung her across the room to Patrice, while he wagged the gun at Emile. For a moment Emile leaned forward, ready to walk right into the bullet, he was so angry. "Go on! Out!" Arturo shouted. With a last murderous look, Emile wheeled away. As he left, Arturo glanced at Cherry and gave a nod of congratulations. He slammed the door and snapped the padlock in place.

Cherry was sobbing, her body quaking as if jolts of electricity were running through it. Patrice clutched her tight, whispering in her ear. They stayed like that until she stopped crying. She gave her mother a shy, lopsided smile. "I got this." She held up a knife with a turquoise handle. She'd taken it from Balazs during the fight, right off his belt, and none of them had noticed.

Ben grinned down at her. "Like mother, like daughter."

"What's that supposed to mean?" Patrice said, sounding offended.

Ben laughed and took the knife.

They spent a few minutes discussing their options. They could try to get the guard to open the door, then jump him.

Ben was against this. If the gun went off inside the small playhouse, there was too much of a chance that someone would get hurt.

Then Ben hit on another idea. The knife had two blades; he opened the shorter one. There were cracks between the floor planks, and he wedged the blade into one and heaved sideways. The metal snapped halfway down the shaft.

"So much for digging our way out," Patrice said dryly.

He held up his hand to tell her he wasn't through. It was the doors that had caught his attention. They were a simple design, cross-nailed planking attached to the frames on the inside by T-hinges. If he could remove the hinge screws, he should be able to open one. He went to the door in the back, away from the guard. Three hinges, three screws each. He told himself not to hurry. A stripped screwhead would ruin everything.

As he worked he thought about Colonel Roque, homing in with his plane. The American military kept Cuba under constant watch. Any airplane leaving there would be intercepted before it got close to the *Kennedy*, especially a fighter plane or bomber. Herrera must have realized that and come up with a plan to get Roque past the surveillance, near enough to detonate the bomb. But how?

Termites had been busy in the lower part of the frame. The last screw came loose with barely any effort. He pushed on the door, twisting against the opposite jamb to get it to clear. It popped open and he almost fell outside.

Patrice started to follow, but he waved for her to stay put. One person alone had the best chance of sneaking up on the guard.

As it turned out, there wasn't much sneaking to it. The man was playing with his radio, not paying attention to anything else. Ben stepped up, set himself, and hammered the guard behind the ear so hard he pitched four feet out of the chair, out cold.

Ben suddenly felt his own knees start to buckle. The concussion had caught up with him. The weakness lasted only moments, but left him sick and trembling. He picked up the shotgun and took the pistol from the guard's belt. Patrice and the others were at the corner of the playhouse. He motioned them over and gave her the handgun.

They were out; now what? Ben checked the compound wall. Three strands of wire ran along the top. It was smooth, not barbed, which meant it was electrified. Even if they did make it over that, they'd be in the middle of nowhere with no transportation. He needed to get to a phone. In his head, he had a list of people he'd call, beginning with Lena Greer at WITSEC. Lena knew everybody in Washington, from the Attorney General on down. If anybody could get the word out about Roque and the bomb, she could.

Patrice had spotted the electric fence, too, and she was looking back toward the house. "What about one of the cars?" she said. Ben didn't want to go deeper into the compound, but he couldn't see any other choice. He made sure Isabel and Cherry were ready, and the four of them dashed from one line of trees to the next. No one else was in sight, just the palms and, down by the beach, one of the guest cottages. Ben went ahead to get a look along the driveway. Damn. There was his car. Four of Herrera's men were standing around it, talking.

Ben clicked off the safety on the shotgun. If he opened up, he'd get in two, maybe three shots before they returned fire. He could smell the oil on the gun and imagined the kick it would give when he squeezed the trigger. Patrice had moved beside him. She had the pistol up. She nodded. She was ready. The moment stretched out.

No. He didn't like the odds, not with Isabel and Cherry back there in the line of fire.

He swallowed the cold lump in his throat and lowered the gun. Patrice didn't complain. She was already moving on in her mind, looking for something else. "The boat," she whispered. She pointed at the canal off the beach, and the powerboat.

Ben surveyed the compound down that way. It was so close to the house and Herrera's guards. Every step would be dangerous. But—the boat, the ocean, a few miles to the Navy air base. Straight to the people who could stop Roque.

"I'll go first," he said. He passed her the shotgun. He didn't want to carry the extra weight. "Follow to the edge of the trees. Wait until I wave, then come as fast as you can."

She grabbed his hand. They looked at each other. Nothing had to be said, just that look. *Be careful.* He gave her shoulder a squeeze. *Don't worry.*

He darted from row to row of the date palms, past a wading pool and a rusted jungle gym, past the crushed coral walkway leading to the guesthouse. From the beach came the soft hiss of surf on sand, and overhead the palm fronds hummed in the breeze. At the last row of trees, he paused to look around. He only saw the other three, far behind, crouched low to the ground. Patrice was handing the pistol to Isabel, now taking it back to show her how to use it.

The boat lift was electric, with a control panel attached to a post on the dock. He'd seen these operated before and figured it would take three or four minutes to get the boat in the water. All that time, he'd be completely exposed. Quiet was more important now than speed. He padded to the foot of the canal and onto the dock.

The controls couldn't have been simpler: Up, Down, Lock. He swung the lever to the down position and the wire began to feed out. The boat inched lower, the only sound a soft whir. It wasn't a big boat—eighteen feet with an inboard motor—but it looked fast. Ben checked behind him, the near side of the house and down the beach. All clear.

The boat had just reached the level of the dock when luck deserted him. He heard voices, and slid forward to take a look. Emile and Morena were leaving the guest cottage, crossing the open patch of sand to the side stairs of the main house. Ben jammed the control lever back to "Lock," and grabbed the boat to keep it from swinging.

Emile was in the lead, walking fast and talking over his shoulder. They would pass twenty yards from the dock, and there was no place for Ben to hide, unless he dropped over into the water, and it was already too late for that. He lay on his stomach beside the boat. Morena was falling further back, but even she was past him now. He thought it was going to be all right. Then she stopped and called up at the house. A man was on the upper porch, one of the guards. He saw Ben.

So much happened in the next seconds that Ben's mind seemed to stop working. He just reacted. The man on the porch snapped up his shotgun and fired. The blast hit the rear of the boat, and stuffing from a seat cushion geysered into the air. Balazs was running, up the house steps and out of sight. Ben had scrambled down the dock, past the boat so he could get into the water. As he went over the edge, the gunman fired again. Ben cried out. He'd been hit in the left side; he couldn't tell where.

He never lost consciousness. Pulling himself under the dock for cover, he got a look at his arm. A pellet had gone through his hand, in the webbing between his thumb and forefinger. Two more pellets had hit his elbow. He could see raw bone, but the arm was working so it probably wasn't broken.

There was an eerie lull on shore. Morena stood half-crouched, her head cocked and twitching like a bird's as she tried to figure out what was happening. The gunman was looking for Ben but couldn't spot him. He yelled for Morena to get out of there, and she pelted toward the line of trees.

Patrice jumped out from the shadows, the shotgun leveled at Morena's face. She looked angry enough to shoot her where she stood. They both started screaming, and the man on the porch did, too. Patrice grabbed Morena, swung her around, and jammed the gun against the base of her skull. They came toward the dock, shuffling sideways. The man upstairs aimed, then lowered his gun. Any shot was bound to hit both women.

"Ben!" Patrice screamed. *"Where are you?"* He moved so she could see him. His mind was beginning to clear. Get back on the dock. Get the boat down. They could still get out of there if the engine wasn't damaged.

It might have worked, too, if Isabel had been a few seconds faster. She was just starting toward the canal with Cherry, both of them fumbling in the heavy sand. Half a dozen men were farther back in the trees, coming fast. Then Emile thundered across the lower porch to the stairs. He'd gotten another shotgun from somewhere.

Isabel stepped straight in front of him, shoving Cherry behind her toward Patrice. Inspector Audain had said Isabel could be reckless. This wasn't the time for it. "Get back!" Ben yelled.

Isabel paid no attention. She still had the pistol, but seemed not to know it was there. She held up her arms. "Wait, Emby."

"Move," he snarled. He looked past her at the others, calculating what to do next.

Isabel shook her head, sidling around to shield Cherry, who was down in the sand and trying to get up.

The guards had reached the beach. Behind him Ben heard a door slap shut. Manuel Herrera had come out of the guesthouse. He'd seen what was going on from inside. "Stop, all of you!"

His men pulled up, but Balazs was moving, along the bottom step to where he'd have a clear line of fire. "Give it up, Patrice, *now.*" His expression was cool and determined.

Isabel moved in his way again. "Emby, come on. Don't." She'd pleaded with him like that a thousand times when they were children. But they weren't children anymore. He swung the gun up. It fit his hands so naturally it seemed to have grown there.

"Here," she coaxed. "Give me that."

"Shut up." He swatted her, trying to get her to move back. Isabel staggered and grabbed at him to catch her balance. "Iz, don't!" he screamed.

The gun went off with a deep *thump*. She flew away, spinning in a slow pirouette. Her eyes and mouth were wide in an expression of complete surprise. She landed on her back, her arms thrown over her head. The blast had torn her nearly in half.

There was total silence after that. Even the waves seemed to stop lapping at the shore. Cherry was first to move, scuttling over to Patrice.

Balazs dropped in the sand next to Isabel. Slowly he reached to touch her, then stopped. He moved his head, trying to look away, but her blank eyes pulled him back, mesmerized.

Ben waded to the shore. His mind was slipping gears, between white-hot anger and trudging sadness. Isabel's hair fluttered in the breeze, just as it had when she was alive. Her pistol lay tangled in it, and Ben bent and picked it up. Several of the men by the trees stirred, raising their guns. That didn't register with Ben.

He looked at Isabel. The surprise was gone from her face. Her mouth was resolute. She really did look like Cher. Ben wished he could tell her that again, and tell her how brave he thought she'd been.

Emile's eyes came up, staring into the barrel of the pistol. Ben tightened his grip, fingered the trigger. He whipped the gun in a crushing backhand, smashing skin and nose and teeth. Balazs flipped backward and landed flat in the sand. Ben stood over him a moment, and threw the gun aside.

It felt like an ending: they should all be able to go home now. But it wasn't over.

Ben gave a last glance at Isabel before moving to Patrice.

He separated her from Morena and reached to take the shotgun. Patrice held on, but he shook his head. *Too many guns here. We can't win that way.*

Ben pushed Morena ahead of him, toward Manuel. He could feel all the eyes on his back. Halfway there, he stopped and let Morena go on by herself. He dropped the shotgun over the bank into the canal. "We need to talk. There's not much time."

THIRTY-NINE

"How long before Roque reaches the *Kennedy*?" Ben said. Manuel didn't reply. He was distracted, staring at Isabel's body. She and Morena were about the same age. One alive, one dead. It could have been the other way around.

Ben moved closer. To hell with the guards. "How long?"

"One hour," Morena snapped. She was still furious from having had the shotgun to her head.

Ben stepped past them to the cottage and opened the door. He'd seen the antenna wire stretching from the roof. There was a long-range radio in there. They might need to use it. "Come on, Manuel."

Manuel seemed willing to hear him out, or maybe he just wanted to get away from the beach and Isabel's body. He came without argument, bringing Morena. Ben beckoned for Patrice and Cherry to come, too. Arturo followed, taking up a post inside the door, where he could cover everything with his gun.

Ben looked around at the equipment in the cottage: two radio sets and two computers; a bank of televisions, muted and tuned to different news stations; something in the cor-

334

ner that looked like a radar screen. The Herreras had prepared well for this day.

"So talk," Manuel said, making his way to the French doors on the ocean side.

Ben studied his face. There was worry in the shadows around the eyes, and even a little fear. It wasn't only Isabel's death that was weighing on him. The bomb was a reality now. An hour to go. The power was awesome. Manuel wasn't so sure of himself anymore. Then he stood up straight, crimping his ruined hip. The pain brought him back to focus. "Well?"

Ben said, "Last night on St. Kitts we met a woman from Washington, the Justice Department. She knew what you were planning. She had files and pictures—"

"What woman?" Herrera asked.

The back door opened, and a guard came in with Balazs. Someone had doused him with water to bring him around. His nose was snapped at the bridge and the right side of his face was torn and puffy. He lurched to a chair, glaring at Ben with his one good eye. "You fuckin' piece of shit. Your fault, bringin' Isabel here—" Arturo cuffed him on the head to make him shut up.

Herrera ran his tongue over his lips, as if he'd just gotten a foul taste in his mouth. He turned back to Ben. "What woman?"

"Rand Mosby. She's with the Marshals Service."

"Never heard of her," Herrera said.

"She was with Aaron Joquand." A look of concern crossed Herrera's face. Ben said, "Mosby told me you used to work with Joquand."

"We had common interests then," Herrera said. "Not anymore."

"I'm not so sure," Ben said. "Joquand had people following you, videotaping your meetings with Emile. They were there at the meeting with Colonel Roque, too, when you were at the horse track in Miami."

Startled, Manuel glanced at Morena. She seemed just as surprised.

Ben said, "I watched that video from the track. How much do you really know about Roque?"

Herrera gave him an acid look. "I know enough."

Patrice spoke up. "You can't trust Roque any more than you trust Emile. He put the deal together, didn't he?"

Herrera wasn't used to getting advice, especially from women. He chopped the air with his arm, telling her to be quiet.

Ben said, "She's right, Manuel. Dirty hands deliver dirty goods."

"*Damn you!*" Balazs bolted across the room. He seemed quicker, stronger than ever, completely recovered. Arturo and the other guard grabbed him. It took both of them to wrestle him back to the chair.

Ben had wheeled around to meet the charge. His muscles were so tight they hurt, and his heart was hammering. But he needed to keep his attention on the Herreras. He took a breath, waited for his voice to be steady. "There was something in that videotape Mosby wanted you to see. Do you know a man named Oscar Alarcon?"

Manuel was still watching Balazs, the way someone would watch a dog for signs of sudden viciousness. "Alarcon?" he muttered. He seemed ready to say no, then changed his mind. "An insurance salesman. Coral Gables. Why?"

"He was at the track that day. He was taking pictures, too, with a video camera hidden under his coat. But he wasn't with Joquand's men."

"So?" Morena said. "A lot of people come to the track."

"Not CIA people. Not that crowd." Ben paused, letting them think about that. "Who is Orchid?" he said.

The question jarred Manuel. His eyes grew wide behind his glasses, and he glanced again at Morena. "Why do you ask this?"

"He was the one at the racetrack, with the camera under his coat." Manuel shook his head, not following him. Ben said, "Maybe you saw him. A tall man, white streak in his beard. He had a little dog with him. Joquand's men took a still photo. On the back was a Coral Gables address and the name: 'Oscar Alarcon—Orchid.' "

Something clicked, for Manuel at the same time as it did for Morena. She moved close to him and spoke rapidly in Spanish. Ben only caught the word, *"traidor."* Who was a traitor?

"Orchid—what does it mean?" Ben said.

Manuel stared at him with angry eyes. "It means you think we're fools to give us a story like this."

There was a clock on the wall over the radar screen. Eleven minutes gone already. Ben said, "Alarcon, Orchid—he was at the racetrack, in the grandstand. He was filming you. Pictures of Roque and the blueprints and the photograph you had of the *Kennedy*. He had sound equipment, too, a parabolic mike. He got it all, just like Joquand's people did."

Manuel glared over at Arturo, as if ready to give an order. *Get them all the hell out of here.* Then that idea passed and he looked thoughtfully at the television screens, the row of silent newscasters. He said, "We have spies in Cuba; Cuba has spies in America. In Miami, we've heard of Orchid for years. Never known who he was, just the name—Orchid. The best of all the Havana spies, too good really. Maybe, we thought, only a myth planted by Castro to scare us. Who is the traitor? Who can we trust?"

Ben's mind was racing, trying to put it together. Orchid, Castro's spy. He'd seen and taped everything at the racetrack. That's what Mosby meant: *Castro . . . he's watching.* So Castro must know. Colonel Roque. The bomb. The keypad. The plane. The *Kennedy.* But if they knew in Cuba—

He grabbed Manuel. "Why did they let Roque take off? What are they doing?"

"Get your hand off of me," Manuel barked. He turned back to the ocean.

Morena hissed in his ear, *"Ese cabrón es tremendo ficho."* That bastard's too sneaky.

Manuel thumped his cane on the floor. *"Sí.* Mr. Tennant, enough of your lies." He pointed at the horizon. "Sit down. Watch. Cuba is about to earn her freedom."

FORTY

Luis Roque checked the time on his wristwatch. He didn't trust the cockpit clock or the other gauges. The airplane was decades old. It had a fat beaver-tail fuselage and flew like a bus. That made it perfect for the job. Who would suspect that a wreck of a transport plane would carry a nuclear bomb?

He was flying one hundred feet off the water, dodging the tiny islands of the Camagüey Archipelago off Cuba's north coast. Two chase planes, MiG-29s, had come after him from Holguín when he headed out to sea, breaking from his flight plan. They turned back ten minutes ago, reporting mechanical trouble. *Adiós mis hermanos.* The MiGs were only for show. Uncle Sam kept an eye on everything that moved down here, using the E-2 radar planes and the electronics blimp, Fat Albert, they had up in the Keys. He was sure they were tracking him, wondering what he was up to, trying to pick up any radio transmissions.

The only radio call he'd taken was from Manuel Herrera. It was brief and coded, just a list of numbers, the arming sequence for the bomb. Roque had written it on a pad taped to his seat. Taped next to it was the keypad. Wires ran from it back to the bomb, spliced with tape. That's how they fixed everything in Cuba these days—with tape.

He checked his map against the three larger islands off his port wing, then turned north. As he banked, he spotted something in the water. For a moment he thought it was a submarine, but that was only his eyes playing tricks. It was a manatee, a pale greenish bubble ghosting through a weed bed. He watched it for as long as he could, entranced by how gracefully it moved.

Far to the west he saw glinting spikes of light, the sun playing off the windows of one of the tourist resorts. Varadero was down that way, and Havana. The land stretched into the mist, grass-colored fields and darker folds where the streams ran. The view here always struck him as extraordinarily beautiful. Today it didn't strike any chord at all. He gave a final look and turned away. He would never see Cuba again.

It took only minutes to reach the territorial limit and leave Cuban airspace. The water was a stunning peacock blue, speckled with shadows of hundreds of small cumulus clouds. He checked his watch again. Time to make his move.

He eased the throttles forward and pulled back on the yoke. The climb was sluggish. He didn't want it to seem easy. At three thousand feet he leveled off, then took it up to five thousand. He put his headset on and dialed in the correct frequency. He listened to the static, imagining what he was going to say.

"Key West Naval Base. Key West Naval Base. This is Colonel Luis Roque, Cuban Air Force. Do you read?"

Half a minute passed. He was about to try again, when a voice crackled in his ears. "Unidentified Cuban aircraft, repeat message, please."

"This is Colonel Luis Roque, with the Cuban Air Force at Holguín. I am flying an unarmed An-26. I am requesting political asylum."

"You're requesting what?" came the surprised voice.

"Permission to land. I am requesting political asylum."

"Oh, Jesus. Just, um, what are your coordinates?" said the Navy radioman. Roque read them off. The man said, "Okay, right. Asylum." He seemed to be leafing through a book. "Hold on a minute, will you, Colonel?"

Roque found himself humming. An old Beatles song, "Octopus's Garden." He was thinking about that manatee. Peaceful thing.

"Colonel, I'd like you to come right to a heading of zero-four-zero. We've got some space on your twelve-o'clock we need to keep clear. All right with you?"

That would be the *Kennedy* and her battle group. Still a long way off. The Navy man was just being careful, keeping him away. "Understood," Roque said. He cranked into the turn, dropping a thousand feet in altitude. As he brought it up again, he drifted off line. "Key West Base, this is Colonel Roque. I have some lateral control problem here. Rudder line, could be. Maybe I took the wrong plane out for a spin today."

The radioman laughed. "Hang in there Colonel. My captain is on the way down to talk to you."

Roque waited. No Beatles song now. He was as calm as a monk in prayer. The sound of the engines was earsplitting in these old Antonovs, but the earphones were thickly padded and made a quiet cocoon against the noise. His mind was so attuned he could hear the muffled thud of his heart. He counted the beats.

The radio clicked. "Colonel Roque, sir," said a very young-sounding voice, "this is Captain Chafee, Key West Air Station. How are you today?"

"I am fine, Captain. Though, I think not so my plane."

"Yes, my men explained that to me. We've got an escort on the way out to you. Tomcats—F-14s. Sit tight, do what they say. We'll have you on the ground in no time."

Roque knew about the Tomcats. Tough old birds. There weren't many of them left around. This squadron was down from Virginia, practicing air-to-air combat. Cuban intelligence kept track of these things. "Sorry," Roque said. "I did not have time to do a preflight before I took off. I'll try to still be here when they arrive." He let his plane slip sideways again, toward the *Kennedy* and the Florida coast.

"Not a problem, Colonel. I'll tell my guys to giddyup."

Over the next few minutes, Roque continued to move in small jogs to the northwest. He had to be patient so it would look convincing to those following on radar. He was being pushed off course. He wasn't making it happen.

He had gone far enough now that the weather was changing, the clouds thickening. In the distance, peeking over the horizon, he could see the anvil crest of a lone thunderhead. The column flickered with lightning, like a faraway matchstick.

"Colonel Roque, Captain Chafee here again. Our boys are airborne. E.T.A. to you in fourteen minutes."

"Very well," Roque said.

"And Colonel, before anybody else steals the honor—let me be the first to welcome you to America."

Roque didn't smile. He touched the keypad and the paper where he'd written the arming code. "Thank you, Captain. That is most kind."

FORTY-ONE

A muted *boom* rolled up over Funnel Bay. Everyone in the cottage whirled to look, but it wasn't the bomb. A squall line loomed on the southern horizon, with one billowing thunderhead, twinkling with lightning.

They had been listening to the radio, the back and forth between Colonel Roque and Key West Air Station. Manuel Herrera nodded. "This is what we planned. Political asylum—a Trojan horse. Roque gets close enough to destroy the ships this way."

Ben was thinking about the radio. Roque was supposed to be defecting. He should be ecstatic, on his way to a new life. He should be damn nervous about his plane, too. But his voice sounded worn-out and empty, a man with both feet already in the grave. How could the Navy men miss that? How could they buy that nonsense about the rudder control? Because all they could think of was reeling him in, their prize catch.

He turned away from the ocean. He wasn't going to just stand there and watch. On the wall was a map of the Keys, and underneath it a framed photograph. Manuel Herrera was shaking hands with Dick Nixon. Manuel had been young and fit then, though he still had his cane. They were dressed in casual clothes, easygoing, like pals about to head for the golf links. The photo had been clipped from a newspaper, and there were others like it all along the wall. Manuel with politicos and generals. One man Ben recognized as a former CIA head.

Ben stared at the picture, and he finally understood it all, to the bottom. Colonel Roque, Havana—the real game.

"They're using you, Manuel."

He touched the lower edge of the map, a sliver of Cuba. "You had the story line all worked out. An old nuclear bomb Castro kept around for decades. He wanted to use it before he died, blow up the *Kennedy*, one last stick in Uncle Sam's eye. So send in the troops. Take the Commie bastard down. That's what you expected everyone to believe. But what if there's a different story out there, with proof?"

He waved at the pictures. "Your whole life is here. It's no secret you hate Castro, that you'd do anything to get rid of him. Then there's Orchid's video from the racetrack, you and Colonel Roque setting up your plan with the bomb. By now, the people in Havana have got that film in perfect order, cleaned up, a hundred copies made, ready to go to newspapers and networks all over the world. If the bomb goes off, it's not Castro's fault, but Manuel Herrera's and his CIA buddies. Bumbling fools desperate to start a war with Cuba. Meanwhile Castro gets—"

"That's bullshit!" Manuel growled. "They couldn't do anything without Roque's help. You never met him, never looked in his eyes. *I know* what kind of man he is."

"No. You know what you *want* Roque to be, like that Navy captain on the radio. You were willing to overlook things. At the racetrack, remember the picture Roque showed you of his daughter? The way he wadded it back in his wallet? He wouldn't do that with a picture of someone he cared about."

Patrice said, "He's right. It was on the videotape. I saw it."

"That wasn't Roque's daughter," Ben said. "He made that up to give you a reason to believe in him."

For a moment, Manuel wavered. He remembered that incident with the photo. It was a small thing, but it was about family. To a Cuban, that made it important. Just as quickly he shrugged it off. "*No*, dammit." He stared stubbornly at the sea.

"Listen," Ben pleaded, "call Roque on the radio. See what—"

"Hey!" This came from Cherry. She was in the back of the room. Balazs had shoved her aside and was hurrying out the door.

Morena rushed after him. "Emile, wait." Arturo followed them.

Ben had seen it out of the corner of his eye. Just before he ran, Balazs had been staring at the map, and his face changed—startled, panic-struck.

"God Almighty," Ben said. "Castro gets . . . a free shot." He spun back to Manuel. "Whatever happens today, Castro comes out clean as an angel, just another victim. They've got Orchid's tape from the racetrack, and whatever other evidence they need. *You* got the keypad from Moscow, Manuel. *You* gave it to Roque with the arming code and told him to go after those ships. But Roque's unpredictable, a turncoat, a crackpot. Whatever he does with that bomb, you get the blame. You put the whole thing in motion."

Ben looked back at the map. "He's not going for the *Kennedy*. They won't waste the bomb on that. Maximum damage—that's what they'll be after. The demonstrations. All the people they hate in one spot."

He looked at Patrice and saw the shock of understanding on her face. Herrera was rigidly watching the sea, shutting him out.

Ben glanced around, looking for something more, anything. He scrambled to the radar console and began flipping switches. He wasn't sure it worked, but figured

Herrera wouldn't have it here unless it did. He probably stole the data feed from the Navy. "Does anybody know how to run this?"

The other guard edged closer. When Manuel didn't object, he snapped on a switch in the rear of the set. The console hummed. It was old and would take a while to warm up. Patrice brought Cherry forward, and they leaned over the screen, all of them except Manuel, who still stared at the ocean. Outside, Morena and Balazs were arguing. Another *boom* of thunder echoed up the bay.

Neon-green images began to form on the panel. A range scale. The island coastlines. A large object, away to the south. That would be the *Kennedy*. Then four small objects in a diamond pattern. The F-14s. Headed for a lone dot at the edge of the display. Roque. He was twenty miles from the aircraft carrier. The dot moved.

Roque was flying away from the *Kennedy*, on a line for Key West.

The guard had listened to enough today to know what cargo Roque carried. "*Coño*," he whispered. Ashen-faced, he backed away and fled out the door.

Manuel had heard the guard's reaction. It was enough. His head was bowed. His eyes were wide and stunned.

Ben pulled him to the radar. Before he could speak, the radio whined. "Cuban An-26, this is Commander Shieffer out of Key West N.A.S., here to escort you in. How do you read?"

"I have you fine, Commander," Roque replied.

"Good, Colonel. I want you to come to a heading of zero-eight-zero. We'll keep formation around that weather ahead, and then tower will call your descent."

"Zero-eight-zero," Roque replied. "I will try."

The five dots were together now on the radar screen, moving in a tight wedge. "When will he detonate?" Ben said to Herrera. "You keep planes down here. You know the flight patterns." Ben pushed him closer to the screen. "When?"

Herrera shrugged, having trouble getting his thoughts together. Still, it was an interesting problem in logistics. "For maximum damage—to the air base, Key West, the demonstrators—" He closed his eyes, thinking of the thousands of people listening to the speeches. His people. "He'll have to pull the fighters off course." He pointed at the screen. "He'll detonate here."

Even Cherry knew what was happening. "How far is that from us?" she asked.

Nobody answered. It was less than two miles.

"Coming on this track," Manuel said. He swept his finger over the screen and glanced at the clock. "Thirty-five minutes, maybe a little less." His eyes were vacant. His hand floated on the same arc, back and forth.

Ben eased him into a chair. "The F-14s can force him away from land, shoot him down if they have to. That's better than letting the bomb go off. I don't know anybody who can get through fast enough. You'll have to call someone, get word to the Navy."

Manuel's face had the cold wooden look of a mannequin. Ben shook him. "Come on. You've got to do it."

Outside Morena was yelling. She sounded frantic. Manuel looked slowly around, drawn by her voice.

Ben hauled him to the window. Down the beach, Morena stood with Balazs, holding him by the wrists. Arturo was crumpled beside them in the sand, and Balazs had his gun. "Don't Emile, please," Morena whimpered.

Ben said, "She's pregnant, did you know that?" Manuel looked at him, his face still blank. "No you didn't, or you wouldn't have her here. You'd have her home with a nurse. Think about it. The new clothes she's been wearing. She's not sleeping well or eating the way she usually does. You've been worried, thinking maybe she's sick."

A spark kindled in Manuel's eyes. He nodded. "I think . . . ," he began, but he couldn't finish.

Ben said, "She's pregnant. Something you always dreamed about. A grandson." He didn't know the baby was a boy, but he was sure that was what Manuel wanted, an heir. And there were all the things in the compound, monuments to Manuel's hopes, the pirate playhouse, the jungle gym, the wading pool. "She should have told you, but she didn't. Now she's here. You have to protect them, Manuel. You still have time."

Herrera was thinking, trying to contemplate this new world that had opened up for him. He was willing to give up his life to bring down Castro. Morena felt the same way. But a baby, a grandson. The radio crackled. The Navy commander was calling out a course correction. In the background they could hear the drone of Roque's engines as he answered.

"No one to call," Manuel said, his voice shaking. "I burned those bridges long ago."

On the beach, Balazs was trying to back away from Morena. She wouldn't let go. He jerked free and clubbed her in the head. She flopped in the sand, then scrambled after him on her hands and knees.

Manuel stiffened. "Pig," he whispered. He shouted it. "*Gutless pig!*" His eyes were alive again, narrow and furious. He thought for a moment, and put his hand on Ben's shoulder. "There is no one I can call. We'll have to try a different way. We need Balazs. You can stop him, yes?"

It was too late for Ben to ask questions. He spun, right into Patrice and Cherry. He touched their faces, then rushed past.

A few seconds later, as he flew down the cottage path, he heard Herrera yell, "He'll head for the airfield!" Ben glanced back to show he'd heard. Manuel stood in the

348

doorway with Patrice. She had a smear of blood on her cheek. Ben had forgotten about his wounded arm. It was completely numb. Everything was numb. He turned a bend and was alone in the date palms, running flat out.

FORTY-TWO

The guard from the cottage had warned the rest of Herrera's men about the bomb, and they'd taken off in two of the cars. They wouldn't get far, not with all the traffic on the highway. The compound seemed unearthly quiet. With the coming squall, even the breeze had stopped. On the steps of the main house Eric Selano sat with his head propped in his hands, like a mopey little boy.

"Did you see Balazs?" Ben yelled as he rounded into view.

Selano pointed. "Over there." Herrera was right: the airfield. "What's going on?" Selano said. "Hey!"

Ben pelted across the road to the service lane that led to the landing strip. It was hot over there, away from the ocean. Through the mangroves he could see a wooden shack and the helicopter. Beyond that was an open-air hangar with a tin roof.

There was an airplane in the hangar, a six-seater with twin engines. It was old but looked airworthy. Balazs had just come out of the shack. He had the gun in one hand and a big key ring in the other. He scrambled around the nose of the plane, under the far wing to the door. In a few minutes' flying time he could be safely out of the area, but first he needed to get one of those keys to work.

Ben cut straight to the plane and dove under the fuselage for Balazs' ankles. Too late, Balazs heard him and tried to jump back. He went down hard but held on to the gun.

Ben scrambled on top of him, and they flailed at each other. The wound in his arm still didn't hurt, but Ben had no strength there. He was on the defensive, using his good arm to keep Balazs from turning the gun into him, which left nothing to strike out with.

Balazs was first to hear the car approaching. When he looked up, Ben grabbed for the gun, but Balazs whipped it away.

The car was an old Cadillac, the same vintage as the airplane. It slid to a halt beside the hangar. Manuel threw open the door and climbed out. He'd lost his cane but was able to lurch toward them, dragging his leg.

Balazs angled the gun around, snapping off a shot. Manuel grunted and crashed against the car. Before Balazs could move again, Ben punched him hard in the side of the head. In the next moment, it was over. Ben was up and had the gun; Balazs was kneeling in front of him. He wasn't badly hurt and might have continued the fight, but he knew if it went on much longer, time would run out for all of them.

Ben backed away, next to the car. Herrera touched his side above his hip, and his fingers came away dripping blood. Seeing Ben's expression, he mumbled, "I'll make it." He motioned at the key ring on the ground. "The smallest key. Open the door. Get him in. The pilot's seat."

Balazs was so desperate to get on the plane that he cursed when Ben dropped the keys, trying to juggle them and the gun. Once the door was open, Ben told him to wait. He helped Herrera on first.

Balazs watched every move. Ben's whole left side was seizing up. He was still panting from the fight. Herrera's shirt was bloody, all across his stomach. His face was creased with pain. Balazs smiled faintly. One strong man with the drive to live against two wounded and fading. Even if one of them had a gun, he'd take those odds.

Herrera told Ben to help him to the copilot's seat. Balazs then came forward and took the seat beside him. "So what's the plan, Manuel?" he said, barely hiding a sneer.

Herrera tapped the control panel and pointed out the windshield. "Roque."

It took a moment for Balazs to understand. "You think you can bring him down? With this old boat and those Navy fighters all around? You're bloody crazy."

"God willing," Herrera wheezed. "We fly straight, on target. You just get us in the air."

Herrera took the pistol from Ben. "Thanks," he said. "You'll have a good view from the beach." The gun dipped. He needed both hands to hold it up.

Ben hesitated.

"Come on," Herrera barked. There was still some steel left in him. "In or out." Balazs was openly leering, figuring his odds were about to get much better.

But Ben wasn't seeing Balazs. He was seeing his own father walk away in the moonlight across a lonely Pennsylvania graveyard. A burden of bravery Ben had carried since that day. A burden that was about to be lifted.

Ben swung the door shut, grabbed the gun back and jammed it against Balazs' jaw. "Fly."

Balazs glanced around the cockpit and started hitting switches. He primed the starboard engine and cranked it, then the port. Once they were lit, the plane bolted forward, so fast Ben was almost knocked off his feet. The passenger compartment had four seats facing together in a club arrangement. He dropped into the rear right, where he could keep the gun on Balazs.

The hangar was located in the middle of the length of runway. Normally they would have taxied to one end so they could use the full distance for takeoff. Balazs didn't even consider that. He hit the flaps switch and goosed the throttles. The plane surged forward. The dense mangroves at the end of the runway hurtled closer. Balazs jerked the nose up. They cleared the trees by a half-dozen feet.

"There," Manuel said, pointing where he wanted Balazs to go, east to the Atlantic. He looked around at Ben. "I remember how to steer one of these, but it would have taken me an hour to figure out how to get it in the air. Damn electronics they've got now." He glanced at the floor and up again. His face was grave, and for the first time his voice had a touch of softness. "Maybe you chose too quick, coming with us."

Ben didn't answer except to try to smile. The vibration from takeoff had shaken something loose in his arm. It was hurting like it was on fire. His head was hammering again, too. He had to struggle to keep his eyes focused. He'd been in shock, running on adrenaline since he was shot. Now that was wearing off, leaving sharp agony in its wake.

Propping his elbow on the armrest, he looked out the window. Below he could see Herrera's compound, the lines of trees and the red-tiled roofs. He caught a glimpse of the beach and canal. Patrice was there with Cherry. They had the speedboat in the water and were getting on board. Good. Smart. With fifteen minutes' head start, they might get away. That gave Ben something to work for. Fifteen minutes. With Herrera's help, he'd see Patrice at least got that much. But first they had to find Roque, and now that they were in the air there seemed to be an immense amount of sky around them. The sun was going down and the clouds were thick in the west. Everything was getting dusky—or were Ben's eyes going out of focus again?

Manuel was looking, too, straight off the nose. The planes weren't there. Then Ben spotted them, way to the northeast, five midge-sized dots. The storm had pushed them up the Keys. They hadn't made the approach turn to the Navy airfield yet. "There," he said.

Herrera turned and squinted. "Good. That gives us a few more minutes." To Balazs he said, "Stay on this heading. Keep your airspeed down."

"They won't let us anywhere near him," Balazs snorted.

Manuel ignored him, looking around at Ben instead. "The Trojan horse worked once, maybe it will again." He clicked on the radio and put on his headset. "Key West Air Station, this is a civilian aircraft outbound from Funnel Bay. Come in please." He chuckled as he listened to the reply. "Yes, I know. Restricted frequency. Don't pee your pants. And this is all the ID you need. We're from Operation Freedom, here to welcome our brother, Colonel Roque, to Florida. We'll join in formation." As he listened to the reply, he began to scowl.

Ben had heard of Operation Freedom, pilots from South Florida who helped people escape from Cuba. They were aggressive, always looking for a fight. Castro called them terrorists. In Washington, they gave them medals.

Manuel hit the button on his mike. "We all have problems, Captain. We are Americans in American airspace. We are going to join the formation, take photos of our jets and our newest citizen. If you don't like it, shoot us down, and see how it plays in the newspapers." He clicked off the radio.

Manuel had been sitting forward, talking fast, his voice hard and unyielding. It had taken a terrible toll. His head lolled back. "That should get us closer. Close enough, maybe." He slumped against the window.

Ben jumped out of his seat and knelt next to him. The bleeding from his side was horrendous. The carpet under him was saturated. "Manuel? Here, sit up." Ben lifted the headset out of the way.

Balazs timed his move perfectly. Just when Ben was leaning over, he kicked the rudder pedals. The plane bucked sideways, and Ben flew across the cabin.

Balazs dove for Ben's hand. Ben was off balance, swinging wildly. He couldn't save the gun, so he pitched it forward, out of reach under the control panel. Then he grabbed Balazs by the shoulder and wrenched back. They flopped into the passenger compartment. Balazs came up on top.

The plane was still pivoting, its right wing beginning to dip. Manuel struggled to get his feet on the copilot's pedals and his hands on the controls.

Ben hit his head when he fell back. His vision began to close in, a black cloud spinning tighter and tighter.

Balazs hated Ben, and he was terrified for his life. He attacked with shattering ferocity, throwing huge windmilling punches. All Ben could do was wave some of them off. Numbness came over him again. He welcomed it. He could endure. That's all he had to do, while Herrera got control of the plane and brought it around toward Roque's. His mind scurried, flashing on one thing and another. He remembered Patrice, beside him in bed at the Ocean Terrace Inn. He imagined her in her boat, racing away from here.

Balazs was winded from all the punching. He thought Ben was through. He tried to lurch away, but Ben grabbed him. Screaming, Balazs hit him one more time, then locked his hands around his neck.

Instantly Ben felt the loss of oxygen. In seconds, his strength was all but gone. The black cloud came back, closer, closer. It was comforting, like a blanket. Nestle up. Go to sleep. But Ben wouldn't quit. He managed to get a bit of air. With it came a whiff of Balazs' cologne. In the back of his mind, like a voice whispering, Ben remembered something.

He reached for his pocket. He had to use his wounded arm, and his hand fumbled clumsily. Balazs was on his knees, using his weight to try to crush his throat.

Click.

Balazs looked down. There, in Ben's hand, was his own turquoise-handled knife. Astonishment came into his eyes. *How?*

"Cherry," Ben gurgled.

He drove the blade up, under his ribs, straight to his heart. Balazs gave a soft gasp and collapsed. He died so quickly the look of shock never left his face.

Ben rolled out from under Balazs' body. He barely had the strength to claw his way to the cockpit. The plane was wobbling badly as Manuel fought the controls. "Power," he said. He pointed a shaky finger at the levers in the center quadrant. Ben eased them forward, as he had seen Balazs do. The engines hummed at a higher pitch, and the plane leveled out.

Manuel pulled into a climbing turn. Ben could see the other aircraft, close enough that he could tell Roque's bigger plane from the smaller fighters. He looked down at the Keys, five or six miles off. He didn't recognize the islands. They were well away from Key West. He couldn't guess which direction Patrice had gone. He hoped it was away from here. Ground zero.

"Balazs?" Manuel asked.

Ben was still gasping for air. "Finished."

Manuel nodded. He turned to Ben. His face was drained and ancient looking, but his eyes were bright. "There's only one way to stop him, you understand?"

"Like you said, fly straight, on target."

Manuel said, "There's something you should see in back, behind the seats." When Ben didn't move immediately, he said, "Go!"

Ben was too played out to walk, so he crawled over Balazs' body, past the two rear seats. There was a box, like an oversized picnic cooler. He fumbled with the latch.

Manuel was coming around to a new heading. He was flying well now. He touched the St. Christopher medal on the bracelet he wore. "Superstition can be a good thing. Morena figured if we had those we'd never need them. Like carrying an umbrella to keep away the rain."

Ben finally cracked the latch. Inside were six square packages made of tough poly fabric. He pulled one out and sat on the nearest seat, staring dumbly at it.

"You ever jump before?" Manuel called.

"What?"

"For God's sake, open it up."

Ben tugged on the Velcro seal. Inside was a grid of straps and snaps, another fabric bag. He didn't understand until he had it out on his knees. A parachute.

"Did it twice before," he muttered. "I hated it."

"That's better than never," Manuel replied. "Put it on."

Ben looked up. The other planes were very close now. He felt too tired to move. "You could miss, Manuel. And if you do hit him . . ." He gazed around at the sky, imagining the fireball.

Manuel rattled the St. Christopher. "Superstition—it does wonders for your attitude. Now hurry. I've got enough to feel guilty about today without adding you to the list."

Ben picked through the straps. This one around the waist. No, the legs through here. And over the shoulders.

"Hurry, damn you!" Manuel croaked. Two of the Navy jets were peeling off to take up attack positions. The others were covering directly in front of Roque's plane.

Ben cinched the shoulder straps. Best he could do. Maybe it was on right. He stood by the door, wanting to say something to Manuel, but having no idea what. He turned the handle and shoved. Nothing happened. Exhausted as he was, the wind pressure was too much. The second time he got it open a crack, but no more.

Manuel was watching. "Try again!" Ben pawed at the handle and leaned. Manuel shouted, "Someday, you go see my grandson. Tell him what happened here." He snapped the controls. The plane slowed and heeled over hard to the left. Ben was slammed sideways. His momentum carried him out the door as easily as if he'd been poured from a bottle.

He slipped under the stabilizer and began tumbling. He'd forgotten to check where the rip cord was. The wind was battering him. His eyes were streaming tears. He felt up and down his chest. There. The handle. *Ziippp.* The chute popped, and he was jerked upright, swinging wildly, disoriented.

As he came around, he saw Herrera's plane, continuing to roll. The two Navy jets that had peeled off were maneuvering in on him. Then Ben lost sight of them, wheeling under the parachute. He heard the jets' guns firing.

When Ben came around again, Herrera's plane was standing up on the left wing. Smoke billowed from underneath. He drove straight between the other two jets. He'd come in high and had to nose over suddenly, his wing slicing at Roque's canopy.

The chute swung Ben around again. He didn't see the impact. He was surrounded by a flash brighter than any he'd ever witnessed. The *BOOM* was so enormous it knocked the wind out of him.

The parachute luffed; the lines creaked. Ben twisted to look. No mushroom cloud or even any smoke. The fuel had exploded, that's all. Wreckage from both planes was spiraling down a mile away. It was a terrible, beautiful sight. Ben felt light-headed, as if he were drunk. He wanted to laugh or cry out, make some noise, but he still hadn't caught his breath. The water below seemed as far away as China. Then the pain screamed back into his arm and head. He closed his eyes and drifted.

The water, when he hit, revived him enough to climb out of the parachute harness. The harness had a flotation device, so he detached the chute and held on, letting it keep him afloat. Dusk was lingering. Miles off, he could see the low blue coast of the Keys. It was raining hard over there, and there were occasional flashes of lightning. Feebly, he tried swimming in that direction, but the current was running the other way. Once, he heard the sound of a helicopter, and he shouted and waved. It kept a straight course, passing to the east.

Where were the rescue ships? The military choppers? Didn't they want the bomb? No—they didn't know about the bomb. The Navy pilots had been so busy they probably never saw his parachute. So this was just an oddball air crash with no survivors. With night falling and the bad weather, they'd wait until morning to sort it out. The salvage crew would be in for a hell of a surprise.

He ground his teeth and kept swimming. The current was getting stronger.

Sometime later, when it was dark enough that he could see lights winking on the shoreline, he caught the sound of another engine. And maybe—yes—a voice. Summoning all he had left, he yelled, "Here!"

"Ben?"

"Here!"

A silhouette formed in the gloom. A boat. Cherry standing on the bow. "He's over there!"

"Ben!" Patrice screamed.

He waved and shouted and laughed. Surprised by her again and again.

It took all the strength they had to get him out of the water. He lay back, letting Patrice kiss him and hug him. Cherry was babbling, "I knew he was here. I told you." She pushed Patrice away so she could see him. "We followed your plane." She grabbed a pair of field glasses from a rack on the seat. "I saw you jump and figured out where you came down."

Ben ran his fingers through her hair, that wretched haircut. She grinned. "I was scared. All the lightning. But Mom wouldn't give up. She said we were going to stay out here a month if we had to."

Patrice was inspecting his arm. "We've got to get you to a hospital."

"No hospital. Just a doctor, somebody who won't ask questions."

"Why?"

He closed his eyes. "Because there's still a snake left in the garden." He was shivering, getting cold. "We'll take care of that later," he mumbled.

For a moment he drifted on the edge of consciousness, and then he smiled. "After the doctor, you know where I want to go?"

"Where's that?"

He kissed her and whispered, "To bed."

FORTY-THREE

Ben tossed the football high in the air. The sky was so bright his eyes watered as he watched it. "I got it!" Cherry yelled. It bounced off her hands and down the powdered-sugar beach to the surf. "¡Hijo de puta!" she grumbled.

They'd been in Mexico for five months. Cherry had a string of local friends, good kids mostly. Her Spanish was much improved, but some of it was a little too colorful. "Cher, what would your mother say?" Ben chided.

Cherry held her nose and quacked, "Sewer mouth, young lady. You'll get nowhere in this world acting like that!" She did a pretty good Donald Duck imitation.

Ben laughed and pointed behind her. "Be careful. Here she comes."

Patrice was picking her way down the narrow path from the limestone bluff at the edge of the beach. They waved; she did, too.

This was their favorite spot to swim, a wide sweep of bay backed by low jungle, always gorgeous, always deserted. There were a hundred places like it along this stretch of coast. On maps it was the Yucatan Peninsula, the state of

Quintana Roo. Travel agents in the U.S. and Europe called it the Mayan Riviera.

They'd come out early, expecting to leave by midmorning when the heat started to build. The breeze was pleasant, though, and the sun not as strong as usual. They decided to stay on. That meant someone had to drive back to Punta Allen to buy lunch. Patrice drew the short straw.

She was still a hundred yards away, scrambling over the rocks on the steepest part of the path. Cherry tossed the ball back to Ben. Until a few minutes ago, she'd been drawing. She chose her own subjects now, and didn't need Patrice's help with the outlines. When she finished working on it, he offered to play catch. He lobbed her an easy one. "So, where'd you two go yesterday?" he asked.

Cherry caught the ball and froze. "I'm not supposed to say." Ben arched an eyebrow. "Cancún," she blurted. "But I can't tell you any more."

He grinned. "Under orders, huh?"

Instead of answering, she tore off toward Patrice. "Mom! We saw dolphins! What'd you bring? I hope it's not fish. I'm *so* sick of fish."

They'd come to Mexico the day after Ben got his arm patched up in the Keys. Cancún had been their first stop, but it was too busy, crowded with tourists, too expensive. Not that money was a problem. They had the nearly two million dollars Roddy Finney had left Patrice and Isabel. Still, Cancún wasn't for them. So they moved south along the coast. Playa del Carmen. Akumal. Tulum. Finally they reached Punta Allen, pretty much the end of the road. It suited them fine. And if it was so perfect, what was Patrice doing back in Cancún? Ben didn't have a clue, but that was all right. She'd tell him when she was ready. Until then, well, she liked her little secrets, and he was happy to let her have them. It seemed to keep them balanced.

She dropped her purse and the bag with lunch on the blanket, and he kissed her. Her hair, grown in brown again, swirled around her face. "Got to get this cut," she muttered.

She pulled a newspaper from the handbag. "I just saw this." She had a bad habit of reading while she drove. "Look at it. There's no justice in the world."

It was *The New York Times*, four days old. She must have picked it up yesterday in Cancún. The article was titled, "New Man to Lead Spy Agency." Ben read the first paragraph: "Aaron Joquand, who figured prominently in the recovery of a Cuban nuclear weapon from the Florida Straits last spring, has been named by the President as the new director of the Central Intelligence Agency. Joquand, a career Agency official, was considered the leading contender for the job. 'He'll bring badly needed credibility to the CIA,' said a congressional source. 'He's got real name recognition after what happened with Cuba. He's as close to a hero as we get in this town nowadays.' "

Patrice was setting out the food, a peanut-butter sandwich for Cherry, the inevitable snapper with red sauce and tortillas for her and Ben. "Do you believe that? A skunk like Joquand? No justice." She looked up. "What are you smiling about?"

"Timing, that's all." He knelt to help her. "You remember the money I borrowed from you?"

"Twenty thousand? You bet I remember." She handed a bottle of water to Cherry.

"I want Coke," the girl whined.

"Water or go thirsty, kiddo," her mother threatened.

"I gave the money away," Ben said.

Patrice sat back, shielding her eyes from the glare off the water. "You *what?*"

"It was a good cause. Joquand—a little justice. I called Larry Jong in D.C. and had him go around to Joquand's house, sift through the mail in the mailbox. Came up with a bank statement. Then I talked to Inspector Audain in Basseterre. He sends his regards, by the way. Audain arranged the transfer, the twenty thousand into one of Balazs' old Golden Pyramid accounts in St. Kitts, then straight into Joquand's account in Virginia."

Cherry was already halfway through her sandwich. Patrice told her to slow down; maybe dolphins eat without chewing, but not people. "How's this justice?" she fumed. "Joquand gets Christmas in September, and I get the bill?"

Ben started to eat. The red sauce was hot today; he cooled his mouth with a swig of water. "Did you ever wonder why the Cubans didn't go public with the videotape they had from the racetrack in Miami? It was all there— Herrera and Roque planning to steal the bomb, take out the *Kennedy*. That tape would have saved Castro a lot of grief."

It had taken two days for the Navy to find and identify the bomb in the wreckage of Colonel Roque's plane. It was intact, not even leaking radiation. Castro used the time to step up his rhetoric, claiming the U.S. had infiltrated his air force and was stealing Cuban military secrets. When news that the bomb had been discovered hit the TV and newspapers, Castro held a press conference, blaming the *yanqui* spies. The U.S. administration blamed Castro. Nobody knew who to believe. Still, the suspicion that the Cubans might have ordered a nuclear strike on Key West was enough to turn off a lot of foreign governments. Canada stopped all direct investment in the island. Sweden and New Zealand went further, severing diplomatic relations.

"Sure, I wondered what happened to that tape," Patrice said.

"Mick Laraby is what happened." Patrice started to interrupt, but Ben went on, "No, Mick isn't dead. He managed to slither away from Balazs' place that night he got shot. He showed up again in St. Kitts a month later. Audain told me.

Flew in from Havana—on his own plane, with his own platoon of Cuban thugs. Stayed just long enough to clean his things out of the house, and then he took off for France. Cannes."

"Mick?" Patrice said. "Where would he get that kind of money?"

"Havana. I wasn't sure until now, but that *New York Times* article makes it all click. Joquand was taping Balazs, every step he and Herrera took. What if Balazs turned the tables, made tapes of Joquand negotiating for the bomb, talking about how *he* planned to use it?"

Patrice made a mound in the sand and smacked it flat. "Joquand was freelancing. Going after North Korea or the Sudan, Mosby said. If that got in the newspapers—"

Ben said, "Joquand would be out of a job, maybe land in jail. He'd be radioactive for life."

Patrice rolled her eyes at the pun, but she was nodding. "Blackmail, that's what Balazs had in mind. And Mick picked up the string. He sold the tapes of Joquand to Castro. And with those tapes under wraps, Castro's got permanent leverage over Joquand." She grinned. "He's the last snake in the garden. That's what you meant."

"You never asked, but that's why I wanted to come here. It's a good place to lie low for a while. Joquand's been looking for us, I'm sure. We're loose ends he'd love to tie up. Now he's up for a promotion, and that changes the picture. Think how happy it must make Castro and all the little ministers in Havana. The director of the CIA right in their pocket."

"So why the twenty thousand?" she asked.

"After Audain made the transfer, I called a friend of mine—somebody I know anyway—in the IRS. An auditor from Richmond. I hinted around that Aaron Joquand had some unexplained income. That'll get my friend started, and before Joquand knows it, the Revenue Service will be inside him like a tapeworm. Every penny in his bank account, every travel expense and business lunch. That kind of man, there's no end to what they'll find. And all just when he's about to hit his confirmation hearings in Congress. Arne, the IRS guy, is one of those dog-after-a-bone types, and he's got a grudge against Joquand, big-time. Insulted him at my house one day, even ruined his suit. I'd say Joquand's in for a career change all right, but he's not going to be heading up the CIA."

Patrice thought it over and began to chuckle. "Then it's worth every dime." She laughed harder, so hard she choked on a bit of food and started to cough. "Let's go . . . into town tonight . . . Lario's, with the TV. CNN. I want to watch that prig squirm."

"Uh-oh, Mom said a bad word," Cherry commented.

"I did not. P-r-i-g. Prig. Are you done already? Sheesh. Go play. Go on! Ben and I need to talk."

Cherry made a sulky face as she got to her feet and dusted the sand off her legs. She waded in the shallows, then went skipping cheerfully down the beach, hunting for seashells. She really was a happy kid, almost always smiling. Recently she'd lost a couple of baby teeth and the new ones were growing in. It made quite a change. Ben had seen dozens of pictures of Roddy Finney from Isabel's manilla envelope. Finney was slightly bucktoothed, but he had a perfect Cupid's-bow smile. To Ben's eye, there was no denying the resemblance. Cherry had the same teeth, same smile. She was Finney's daughter, not Emile Balazs'. Ben had dropped a few hints to Patrice. Sooner or later, she'd see it, too.

"What are you thinking about?" she asked.

He smiled and wagged his head. "Nothing important."

"I talked to Rosa today."

"Rosa of the Ruins?" He meant the Mayan ruins in Tulum. Rosa had a stand there selling trinkets to the tourists.

"You know who I mean. Rosa Chumil, at the market. She

still wants to go to Chicago." Ben slouched sideways and drew a stick figure in the sand with his finger. "You can help her," she said.

He sighed and drew another figure, this one running.

Patrice picked at her fish, took a bite, and made a face. She never seemed to eat anything these days. Dieting, Ben thought, though heaven only knew why. "Rosa told me the real reason she has to go. Her husband got mixed up in a Mayan relics deal, selling to a collector in Germany. The stuff wasn't authentic. There was a lot of money involved, and now her husband's gone, disappeared."

"That's why you two are such buddies," he said. "It was a con, this relics deal, wasn't it? Do you people have a secret handshake? Like the Masons? A little pinkie flutter?"

Patrice pouted, but only for a moment. "Some men have been around to talk to her. Muscle from Mexico City. She's scared, Ben. You should have seen her crying."

"So she wants to go to Chicago. And how much will she enjoy that? It'll be winter up there soon."

"Her sister lives there. Rosa speaks some English. And she's a huge Cubs fan. She'll be all right." Patrice poked at her food again and pushed the plate aside. "Help her. You're the only one who can. Besides, it'll be fun."

"*Fun?*" Then Ben broke out laughing. He reached into the pocket of the coat he'd brought along and tossed a passport to Patrice. "United States of America" it said on the front.

She opened it up to look at the picture. "Rosa?"

"I said I'd talked to Larry. That came in from him yesterday."

She punched him in the shoulder. "You creep. Why didn't you tell me?"

"I wanted to make sure everything was set. She'll fly out the day after tomorrow."

Patrice smiled. "Thanks." She ran her fingers through his hair. "You can't turn down a lady in distress, can you?"

Ben wasn't sure how to answer, so he just shrugged.

Since he'd come to Mexico he'd been drifting, healing. But over the past month he'd begun to feel itchy, on edge. Talking to Larry the other day had brought it home to him. He missed Larry; he missed his work. He'd always figured that once he dealt with Aaron Joquand, he and Patrice and Cherry would go back to the States, and he'd pick up where he left off with WITSEC, a Laundry Man client now and then. But maybe that wasn't the right direction. It was a big world, filled with Rosas who needed help.

"Thanks," she said again. From the tone of her voice, he thought she was going to kiss him, but she didn't. She rubbed the scar on her palm, something she did when she was distracted. She didn't try to hide it from him anymore, but she wouldn't tell him how she got it. Another little secret.

They both stared down the beach at Cherry. She was walking a pattern in the sand, scuffing a picture with her feet. A heart, no doubt. Cherry loved hearts these days. Patrice said, "We went to Cancún yesterday."

"She told me." He didn't want to get Cherry in trouble, so he added, "She wouldn't say what you did."

"Appointments . . . doctors."

"Oh, that's it. She needs glasses."

Patrice looked at him, surprised.

He explained about Cherry. "She squints when we go out to look at the stars at night. She doesn't catch the ball as well as she used to." He smiled. "I'll bet she wanted heart-shaped lenses."

"Wanted, but didn't get them. No daughter of mine is going to go around looking like a circus clown."

She reached into her purse suddenly and handed him a package, wrapped in last year's Christmas paper, with pictures of red and green chile peppers. "Here," was all she said.

As he tore it open he watched her from the corner of his eye. She stared at the ocean with that dreamy Mona Lisa smile of hers.

It was a cheap tape player with a single tape rubber-banded to the front. "Start it up," she said. He fumbled with the latches and buttons until she grew frustrated at the delay and took it back. In a few seconds she had it going. The music was familiar, but he couldn't say from where. "Djavan," she told him. "Brazilian. Last fall, remember? Georgetown?"

Now he did recall. It was the music that had been playing in Club Monde, when she'd slipped away and he found her dancing with the gangly lawyer. An odd choice for a memento, but he liked it. It was cheery music, sunny as the beach. He propped the player on a fold in the blanket. "So what was the other doctor for?" he asked.

"What?"

"You said doctors' appointments. More than one."

"Did I?" She stretched from head to toe, leaning back on her hands.

Ben was watching her closely. "I saw the drawing Cherry was working on today. It was you, except here. Too big here." He touched her abdomen.

Patrice stared right at him. He couldn't read a thing in her face. Then a hint of that dreamy smile came back.

Ben felt a shiver go up his spine. He laughed and gave a whoop that sent the sea gulls flapping into the air for a quarter mile in each direction. Cherry came running. "What's wrong? What's the matter?"

Patrice never took her eyes off him. She turned up the music. "You asked me to dance once, and I said no. Is the offer still open?"

He answered by pulling her to her feet. Their first steps together were awkward. Ben's arm had healed, but it still was stiff, throwing him off balance. Soon he loosened up, and they spun down across the hardpack, right into the surf.

"Hey, Cher," he called over the music. "How would you like a little brother or sister someday?"

She was tossing shells at the waves. "I'd rather have a Barbie."

Ben laughed again. "We can probably work that out, too."

Cherry turned to watch. They swirled in perfect sync, every twist and spin, every arch of the back and twitch of the hip. There were no mysteries now, no puzzles. Ben sensed every movement in her before she made it.

Cherry's mouth hung open in amazement. "Wow . . . you guys are good."

They didn't reply. They just kept dancing, dancing.

Scot McCauley
REVENGE IN EXILE

With crime lords openly challenging the Mexican government for control of the country, and an exiled former Mexican president plotting his return to power, Mexico City is a ticking time bomb—and one that an ambitious US National Security Adviser can use to his own ends. He has sent CIA officer Elizabeth Cramer and old Navy friend Cole Palmer down to Mexico, but as the situation deteriorates and the country threatens to explode into revolution, a deadly plot could take the lives of both the US President and his Mexican counterpart. Palmer and a small, clandestine group of Navy SEALs might be the country's only hope.

DAVID LAWRENCE

CIRCLE
OF THE DEAD

The man died of a broken heart. Literally. But what broke his heart was a sharp object shoved hard between his ribs. When they found him he was sitting in a circle with three other corpses in a London apartment. That's when Detective Stella Mooney got the case. Suffering from brutal nightmares and a fondness for too much vodka, Stella's trying to hold it together long enough to find the answers to this bizarre puzzle. But the closer she comes to cracking the case, the more her personal life seems to fall apart. From the glamorous homes of the wealthy to the decidedly tougher parts of town, Stella has to follow the evidence—even when it seems to be leading her in circles.

Dorchester Publishing Co., Inc.
P.O. Box 6640
Wayne, PA 19087-8640

_____5613-5
$6.99 US/$8.99 CAN

LETHAL
DOSE
JEFF BUICK

Veritas Pharmaceuticals is a corporate powerhouse. But many of the drugs Veritas puts on the market are extremely dangerous, even potentially fatal—and Bruce Andrews, CEO of the company, is well aware of it. Andrews isn't about to let that or *anything* get in the way of Veritas's profits.

Gordon Buchanan is devastated when his brother dies. And very suspicious. Could the drug his brother was taking have caused his death? The more Gordon investigates, the more evidence points to Veritas. His lawyer warns him that a lawsuit against the huge corporation would only ruin him, but if the law won't help him bring down this deadly Goliath, he'll have to do it on his own.

ALAN RUSSELL
MULTIPLE WOUNDS

Holly Troy is a beautiful and talented sculptor whose only sanctuary is her art. She also lives with dissociative identity disorder, her personality split into many different and completely separate selves—including a frightened five-year-old girl. But now Holly's gallery owner has been found murdered, surrounded by Holly's sculptures. Holly doesn't know if she was a witness to the crime, or if she committed it. She doesn't know where she was that night. She doesn't even know *who* she was.

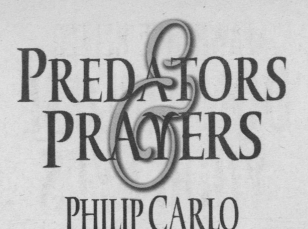

PREDATORS & PRAYERS

PHILIP CARLO

Someone is brutally murdering priests in New York City. The killer seems to be everywhere at once, striking almost at will. With pressure mounting, the mayor, the governor and the police commissioner all want this madman stopped before one more body is found. But they're not the only ones. The Church and the Vatican need to have the killer silenced, for he is their worst nightmare come true—the living embodiment of a terrible, dark secret.

LAWRENCE KELTER
DON'T CLOSE YOUR EYES

Stephanie Chalice is a cop's cop. She's bold, smart, independent and beautiful—a powerhouse working in NYPD's homicide unit. She's seen a lot in her years on the force, but she's never come across anything like the case she's up against now. A murdering psychopath is stalking Manhattan, on the prowl for a very special type of woman. Part of his twisted game is intentionally leaving clues for the police, clues designed not only to taunt, but to do something much worse. Will Chalice be able to discover his real purpose before another woman dies?
